TERMINAL CITY

DEN & HUGO
BOOK TWO

C.R. EATON

Line Edits by Shavonne with Motif Edits

ISBN: 979-8-89316-489-3 - eBook
ISBN: 979-8-89316-470-1 - Paperback

To Grams
For being the most nurturing, caring grandmother a man could ever ask for
And showing me that family is far more than blood and documents.

PROLOGUE

The moonlit night casted a shadow on those who gazed upon its splendor. Illuminating the creatures who sought to hide from its light.

It was a sight Gilligan Hodgson was not used to seeing. So many of his nights were spent in his office cubicle, working diligently long after everyone else had gone home. Where their wives, children, pets, and mortgages awaited them. Where their stomachs were filled by hot meals and their bodies rested in warm beds.

Hodgson had no such frills. Just a condo he had inherited from his late parents, cluttered by junk he rarely even touched. His floor-bound cot was nestled in frizzled sheets and his refrigerator was filled with whatever leftovers he could not finish from the previous night's delivery. Nothing to appreciate. Nothing to go home to. So he just kept typing away at his desk. Because in those quiet hours, there was only work. No melancholic thoughts nor visions of grandeur. Just work and nothing more. A respite from the void.

It was only now, as he stood looking at the moon, that Hodgson felt some semblance of purpose. Even if that purpose was not exactly what he had planned for. He stood in an alleyway, graffiti littering the walls and the pungent smell of garbage filling his nostrils. His hands were shaking and he had no idea whether it was from the night chill or the task he was about to perform. This wasn't like him, he thought. He wasn't this kind of man. But standing here, there was no denying it. Gilligan Hodgson was now and, in some ways, would forever be a drug dealer.

Hodgson's existential crisis was soon interrupted by the sound of approaching footsteps. Their stride quick and with purpose. From the shadows, two figures appeared. One in a hoodie and jeans. The other in a tank top and sweats. Hodgson didn't have to wonder if these were his clients.

"You got the stuff?" the hooded man asked.

"Yes," Hodgson replied, his tone as low as he could realistically make it sound, his stance up straight. This was a new world to him, but he could at least act the part of someone more seasoned. Less chance of getting screwed over. More chance of getting his cut. "You got the money?"

From out of his pocket, the tank top man took out a plastic bag. Inside was what Hodgson desired most: Rias. Sweet, sweet Rias.

Established at the dawn of Adalia's founding, Rias had been the country's currency for generations on end. And as the free nation grew in power and influence, not just on the Western Continent, but the world over, so too did Rias become one of the dominant currencies across the Four Continents. Many lives had been both saved and lost on the turn of these blue paper bills and silver coins. And Hodgson was looking to finally cash in.

Hodgson examined the bag closer. The bills had been wrapped together in a roll—a common method of exchange for these sorts of extra-legal deals. And it was a thick roll at that. More than enough, he figured.

From his own pocket, Hodgson took out a clear plastic bottle, its dimensions small enough to be cupped in his hands. Inside the bottle was a light-blue powder with texture akin to sugar. He held it up, showing the contents to his new clientele.

Slowly, Hodgson stepped closer to the two men. Without another word uttered, both parties exchanged their wares. Hodgson began counting the bills as soon he got them. Making sure the spoils of his criminal trade had borne fruit.

The hooded man opened the bottle and took out what looked to be a thermometer. He sank its tip into the powder. For several seconds, the machine whizzed and clicked before making a final ringing noise. "It's good," the hooded man told his companion. He removed the device slowly, tapping it on the side to release as much of the powder back into the bottle as possible.

Hodgson was still counting his earnings as the man closed the bottle back up and put in it in his pocket. The two gave Hodgson one final look before they began their walk back into the darkness.

"Excuse me," Hodgson said, stalling the men's departure, "I believe this is only half."

"You get the rest later... if we're satisfied with the results," the hooded man replied.

"And when might that be?"

"*Later*," the hooded man insisted. "Be happy we even gave you that much!"

Hodgson gulped without realizing it. He was getting conned and he knew it. His instincts yelled at him, pleaded with him, to accept what he got and walk away. Yet his body start moving on its own. Heading towards the two men. His stance widened, shoulders broadening.

"I'm afraid that's not going to work," Hodgson replied, his legs shaking, heart palpitating, and breath quickening.

The two men did not spare Hodgson another word, instead meeting the businessman's movements with their own. Their footsteps widened. Their expressions became more abrasive. Fists clenched. The hooded man now stood right next to Hodgson, staring him straight in the eyes. So close he could feel the man's breath touch his skin.

Hodgson's mind went utterly blank. Yet he continued to stare into the hooded man's eyes, unsure if his expression was one of confidence, intensity, or utter fear. A clicking, metal sound came from the tank top man's pants pocket. Hodgson knew the cocking of a gun when he heard it. Perhaps this was it, he thought. A single instance of asserting his dominance was about to reduce him to nothing more than another report at the local morgue. Hodgson finally broke his staring, closed his eyes, and awaited the inevitable.

Except... it did not come. As soon as Hodgson closed his eyes, another tapping of footsteps came from nearby. But these were not the quickened pace of Hodgson's potential killers. Each step was calm and equally timed. The stride of a man knowing he'd arrive at his destination regardless. No need to hurry.

"Well if it isn't Rizzo," came a voice from just outside the darkness. Clearly the very owner of those steps. "And Ozzy too! Gotta say though, I didn't think you guys had the guts to pull off something this brazen!" With each word, Hodgson could hear the voice move closer. A slight echo came through the alley. "Breaks my heart, really. Thought you respected me more than that!"

The man had now fully stepped out of the shadows, his tanned skin beaming in the moonlight. He was an attractive man with high cheekbones and a smooth nose bridge. He sported a lean build, in contrast with the bulky men whom Hodgson had been in conversation with. Yet the outline of his shirt made it clear that the man had more than enough muscle underneath. But it was the eyes that caught Hodgson's attention. They were slightly strained. As if he needed just a few extra minutes of sleep or a nice, hot cup of coffee to wash away the midnight stress. Both eyes focused on Rizzo, the hooded man, and Ozzy, the tank top man. It was a piercing gaze. As if no one else in the world existed in this moment. No one who deserved his attention, at least.

"You got a problem with that, Matches?" Rizzo yelled.

"Rizzo, please, we've known each other long enough. Call me Noland! All my friends and colleagues do." There was not a hint of fear in the man's voice. Each word exuded an air of confidence the likes of which Hodgson had rarely seen. Every word was smooth and concise. Noland cracked a smile towards Rizzo, as if towing the line between deescalating the situation and making things even worse.

Rizzo and Ozzy moved away from Hodgson, pulling out guns from their pants pockets and aiming them straight at Noland. They were some model of pistol Hodgson did not recognize. While he was not exactly well-versed in guns to begin with, the sight of such weapons made Hodgson's stomach sink. Yet still, he could not move. Whatever was about to happen, either Hodgson was going to walk away from this or he was not. It was entirely out of his control.

Noland lifted his hands in the air. "Oh come on, fellas! No need to get violent. Tell ya what? Let's all calm down a little bit and work this out like gentlemen! We can even grab a bite and—"

A bullet went straight into Noland's forehead, cocking his head up towards the sky. The deafening sound of the shot pierced Hodgson's ears. Tinnitus briefly took over his auditory system. Then another bullet came. And another after that. The two men kept blasting until the sound of gunshots had been replaced by the clicking of triggers, the rain of bullets already brought to an end.

Yet in spite of the maelstrom that had just occurred, Noland's body had not fallen down. It hadn't even moved. It just stood there. Head still gazing up at the sky. Arms still raised. The bullets creating holes in the man's shirt and pants. "Not bad," came a voice. "Though next time, I'd recommend you shoot for the eyes." It was Noland. "That way, if I survive, you can at least *try* to blind me!"

The talkative man moved his head back down. A piece of metal fell from his forehead. Hodgson took a glance. It was the bullet. The very same one that had just hit him. Pressed and crunched. Now lying on the ground. A light red mark on Noland's face was the only evidence that the bullet had ever even hit its mark.

Noland tugged at his shirt. The other bullets that had hit him scattered to the ground. "You know, all I wanted to do was wear something nice tonight," Noland explained. "Even as Tillman kept nagging me to come in my cheapest clothes. Silly me, I didn't listen! I wanted to look good. Maybe even go out on the town after this and pick up some nice ladies. But now you've gone and made a mess! You'll pay me back, right?"

The two shooters stood in silence, their hands trembling. Their sights were still focused on Noland, even with all parties fully aware that they had just run out of bullets.

Noland just stood there, eyes far more piercing than they were just a moment ago. Strained and sunken. Yet his smile hadn't ceased. On the contrary, it had grown wider. His teeth were fully exposed. Eyes dilated. A single drop of sweat rolling down his neck. Hodgson couldn't believe what he was seeing. This man, who had just been shot up, was not only standing perfectly unscathed... he was enjoying every second of it.

Ozzy moved his hand towards his pants, trying to grab a new magazine. But his shaking had become a tremble, causing him to lower his pistol ever so slightly.

Noland rushed Ozzy, each step so fast it looked as if he was gliding on ice. Noland rolled his fist back and slammed it straight into Ozzy's stomach. The sheer force of the strike was enough to cause the man to collapse in front of him, convulsing as he did so.

Rizzo tried to use these precious few seconds to reload his pistol. But Noland was already upon him before Rizzo could do so. With a single backhanded slap, Noland flung Rizzo's gun away. The hooded man tried to run, only for Noland to grab Rizzo by the neck.

His grip was inhuman. Rizzo could feel his windpipe already starting to crush under the weight. "And to think I trusted you," Noland chided. "Well, not that much, really. You've never come across as a nice guy. Still, I thought we were cool with one another... Can I ask you a question?" Noland eased his grip, allowing Rizzo enough air to breathe, each inhale more painful than the last. "Why did you try to steal my client?" Noland asked in a calm manner. Like a supervisor criticizing his employee's mistakes. "I was the one who found out about him. I was the one who set this meeting up. I was the one who even made the phone call. This was my operation..."

Noland's voice faded out. He moved his head even closer to Rizzo, making sure the hooded man was staring him squarely in the eyes. "So why *the hell* did you steal my client?" The smile was gone. In its place a snarl. Nostrils flared. Eyebrows lowered. Teeth bared. And those eyes. Stained in red. Flooded in a haze of crimson. Pupils shrunk and beady. There was no man in this moment. Only a beast.

Rizzo tried to speak, in spite of the pain. Yet all that came out were guttural screeches. Screams of fear. Noland clenched his fingers further into Rizzo's windpipe, tilting him upwards until a single cracking sound could be heard. And all at once, Rizzo was silenced. His windpipe destroyed. His neck snapped. The hooded man would get no chance to explain himself.

Ozzy was still convulsing on the ground, spasming from Noland's attack. His single punch had ruptured the tank top man's internal organs. But soon enough, the spasms stopped and the man lay silent forevermore.

Noland laid Rizzo's body beside his companion, picking through his pockets and grabbing the powder bottle and thermometer-looking device. He measured the blue powder in the same manner as Rizzo had only a moment ago. The same whiz, click, and ring noises came from the device.

In the chaos, Hodgson had remained frozen. He hadn't moved a single inch since the newly-deceased Rizzo had threatened his life. He wasn't sure if he would ever move again.

"Sorry about that," Noland said as he placed the bottle into his pocket. "I hope that didn't bother you too much. You good?"

Hodgson couldn't believe what he was seeing. The very person who had just murdered two men right in front of him was now asking about his well-being. Hodgson couldn't help but look at Noland again. That animalistic scowl was already gone. Not a hint of bloodlust or even a look of agitation. Instead, what greeted Hodgson was a genuine look of concern.

"I'm... I'm okay," Hodgson replied, his bass voice now returned to his usual baritone. Any confidence he had tried to exude towards the late gunmen was now all but shattered.

"First time, I take it? It's all good! Happens to the best of us."

Hodgson simply nodded.

"Oh, that's right," Noland continued, tapping his forehead. "How could I be so rude!" From out of his pockets came another bag of Rias. "This should cover the rest of your payment. I must apologize for my coworkers' *very* selfish behavior. But I can assure you, they have been dutifully punished for their actions."

Hodgson slowly grabbed the bag, hands trembling with every inch of movement. Noland still looked at him with a cheery smile and calm disposition.

"Go ahead," Noland said. "Count the bills. I certainly won't get offended. Make sure it's all there!" Hodgson nodded and started counting the bills. "If there's any extra, keep it, by all means. Think of it as an apology for what just transpired."

Hodgson finished counting the bills as quickly as he could. "It's... It's all here."

"Excellent!" Noland replied. "I gotta say, I'm really looking forward to seeing how this mixes. Heard it's the purest stuff on the market."

"Ye... Yes. I'm... happy to be of service..."

"Same here, same here! And hey, I can count on you for another dose, right? Shouldn't be a problem?"

"No... I can... I can get it..."

"Very good! Well, again, I'm so sorry about all this. I promise it won't happen again. In fact, from now on, make sure to only deal with me. No one else, okay? Even if they say they're connected with me. Because, well..."—Noland moved his hands towards the bodies—"I think you can guess why."

"I will," Hodgson replied. "Thank you."

"My pleasure! Well, I guess I'll see you again soon. You have a good day, Mr. Hodgson! Or should I say night? Morning, even? Point being, have a good something, Mr. Hodgson!"

"Thank you, umm... Mr. Noland?"

"That's right. It's Noland. Noland Macchianado." With a final smile, Noland turned away and walked back into the darkness.

Hodgson stood in place for a few minutes longer. The flies had already started to move around the freshly-made corpses. He gulped several times and wondered if he was going to throw up. Yet nothing came. Not even a dry heave or a moment of queasiness.

He stared at the contents of his hands. More Rias than he ever thought he'd see in a single sitting. And it was all his. His and no one else's. It wouldn't even take much effort to launder it. Perhaps, after enough of these nights, he could even become a millionaire. The thought alone was enough to make him finally start his walk back home. His legs were still wobbly.

There would be no sleeping for Gilligan Hodgson this night. His mind rattled. His body was tense. He took one final look at the moon, its milky glaze lighting the night skies. "I hate this city," he said under his breath. Yet he had no intention of going anywhere. Wayport was his home and, if fate willed it, Wayport would be his grave.

In a place like Wayport, there's a sucker born every minute. And with every sucker, there's three guys ready to pounce. One who tries and fails because he's too obvious in his schemes. A second who is only half-successful because he can't identify the naive from the knowing. And a third with a spotless track record, who graces everyone one of his victims with a white wine voice, a smooth complexion, and words that not only reel them in, but keep them coming back for more. And if the sucker ever finds out he's been had? The man is already in another state, starting his business all over again.

—Mortimer Eterno, *The Con and the Con Artist*,
769 AU (*Anno Unificationis*)

CHAPTER 1

TERMINAL CITY

I

"I'm bored, Hugo," a certain scarred boy said.

"I know, Den," a certain Historian replied. "You've made your current mindset very clear to me over the past three hours. Suffice it to say, repeating such words ad nauseam does nothing but make time flow even slower and cause untold amounts of annoyance to all those who hear it. Tell me, if I had the ability to contain or distract your boredom, would I have not already done something to end your continuous statements of pure catatonia?"

"...I'm bored."

The young Historian, already worn down by his own efforts at linguistic wisecracks, simply sighed. It had been a slow ride since they had left Harten earlier that day. A series of stops at other stations, combined with a slower haul due to weak train tracks, had already eaten up much of the first day of their Journey.

Hugo Statferd knew early on that not every day would be as exciting and whirlwind as the epics his teachers, namely Nash and Rasmus, had told him. He was not so spellbound by their yarns to believe he would duel a dragon or meet a wizard. Not that such beings existed anymore. But to summarize his first day as sitting his caboose down on a locomotive for most of it? It was not exactly the stuff of legends. Hugo hated to admit it, but he was finding himself agreeing with Den. The malaise of travel had already seeped in.

"I might be able to help," a certain bounty hunter said to the scarred boy.

Next to Den and Hugo sat Grill, his attention focused on a book neither of the brothers recognized. Though given the contents of the cover, a man and woman wrapping their arms around one another, Hugo assumed it to be a romance novel. Certainly not the type of entertainment either of them expected Grill to be reading. Though what Hugo found even odder was his expression as he read. There was no bemusement at whatever antics the characters were getting involved in. Nor a slight nod of enjoyment or wince of embarrassment at the potentially raunchy scenes that lay within. Instead, Grill merely read the paperback with his usual deadpan, focused stare. Just a man in the moment. Living the way he was supposed to.

"You got something, Grill?" Den's bemoaned voice had perked up at Grill's mere words.

The bounty hunter closed his book and placed it in his bag. From the same pocket he had just placed his book, Grill took out a deck of playing cards. They were a standard deck of fifty-two, plus two jokers. Their backs were adorned with a forest theme—a generic design that happened to sell well at local Harten shops. "Anyone up for a few rounds?"

"Yes!" Den replied before Grill could even finish his question.

"I'm game," Hugo replied. "So, what are we playing? Poker? Blackjack?"

"I'm open to anything," Grill said as he started shuffling the deck.

"Old Maid!" Den proudly announced.

Hugo nodded in agreement. "Can't say I've played that in a while."

"Old Maid it is," Grill confirmed.

The game was basic enough. No strange house rules to muddy up the play. The order went from Den, then to Hugo, and finally to Grill. Cards were swiped and discarded. A simple guessing game which only grew more difficult the fewer cards there were. Each player never truly knew when the joker, the dreaded Old Maid itself, would come to curse their hand.

Soon enough, however, a pattern started to form. As the cards dwindled in number, it was Hugo and Grill who managed to get down to smaller and smaller hands. Den was burdened with a much heavier load. Each time the scarred boy found himself stuck with the joker, it was nigh impossible for him to get rid of it. And each time he managed to avoid it, that silly clown would invariably come back to him. By the end of each round, Den had to say the same thing over and over again.

"Guess I'm the Old Maid," the scarred boy announced. For the first couple of rounds, there had been an enthusiasm in his voice. A proclamation of loss that he took in stride and with pride. Yet now, after seven rounds, the words had lost their luster. "Seriously, guys, what the hell am I doing wrong?"

"Poker face," Grill responded.

"Yeah, Den," Hugo confirmed. "Sorry to say, but you're not exactly an enigmatic player. You tend to put too much focus on the cards you want in and out. It gets pretty obvious."

"Seriously? I had no idea! Either of you have sunglasses?"

"Wouldn't work either," Grill said. "You move your fingers the same way you do your eyes. We'd guess just as quickly."

"We can play a different game," Hugo suggested. "Go Fish is nice and simple."

"No way," Den growled, a fire in his eyes. "I ain't stopping until one of you is the Old Maid instead!"

"So be it," Grill conceded as he passed out the cards.

For as much he wanted to see Den improve, Hugo was already becoming less enthused by the game. It had never been one of his favorites, but he would happily continue playing if it meant Den was happy. Besides, the structure of the game allowed room for conversation to be had. Especially in the early game when more focus was placed on thinning out the hand. And there were questions Hugo had been meaning to ask.

"By the way, Grill," Hugo began, "if I may ask, what exactly were you doing the past two weeks?"

"Errands," the bounty hunter replied. "Just getting ready for the Journey." The day after their victory party, Grill had informed Den and Hugo that he was leaving Harten in order to get some affairs in order. It made sense, given the abrupt creation of their brotherhood. Grill had been traveling solo for some time, making it easy for the bounty hunter to travel about however he pleased. But now as part of a group, such spontaneous action could not be as easily accomplished.

Den and Hugo were well aware of this and were more than happy to give Grill the time he needed. Even offering to start their Journey a little later, if necessary. Grill declined the offer, not wanting to eat up any time from their travels. Sure enough, the bounty hunter made it back to Harten just in time to set off with them.

"I'm aware of that. But you were out of town, right? That was the reason you didn't come to the Spring Festival with us."

"Correct. But I'm not big on festivals anyway. Probably for the best you all went without me."

Hugo could see what Grill was doing: avoiding the conversation altogether. But for as much as Hugo honored his friend's privacy, it seemed a little suspicious that he wasn't giving even a basic idea of what he was doing, apart from a word as generic as "errands." Still, to pry any further would be rude. For everything they had already gone through, there was still so much about Grill that Hugo didn't know. Perhaps one day, as they got to know one another better, the young Historian would finally get his answers.

"And where did you go?" Den asked, his primary attention still focused on the game at hand. It was not a question asked in a prying tone. Just a simple response to what he had heard. Hugo sometimes wished he had his brother's lack of tact.

“A few places,” Grill replied as nonchalantly as Den had asked. “Melkiora, Rocky Way, the Terragen Steppes. Met up with a couple of colleagues. Simple stuff.”

“You went to all those places in two weeks?” Hugo asked. “Isn’t that all kind of far?”

“They’re all in the same general vicinity, so it was fairly easy to travel between them.”

“Seriously, Grill, how many places have you been?” Den asked. It was the first time his concentration had broken entirely from the game.

“A lot. I’d have to think about it, but I’m fairly certain I’ve been to all twenty-seven states.”

By this point, the cards had trickled down into only a few per hand. Den had managed to get on more even ground this time. Though the scarred boy wondered if that was from his newly concentrated wit or because his friends were going easy on him. But sure enough, only a few rounds later, Den lost once again. Without much thought, they began another game.

“You said you went to the Spring Festival. How was it?” Grill asked, trying to keep the conversation going.

“Very nice,” Hugo replied. “Nash had us all go right after my last day of work.”

“Yeah, it was great!” Den added. “Carnival games! Fireworks! Delicious food! Granted, I was in a wheelchair at the time, but you gotta make do with what ya got. At least I could move my hands well enough!”

“It was nice getting some quality time with everyone before heading out,” Hugo said. “The victory party was fantastic, but the sheer amount of people made one-on-one chats pretty difficult.”

“Not that you did much of that at the festival either, buddy,” Den added, a shrewd smiling forming on his face. “You were too busy making smoochy-smoochy with Rindi, after all!”

“Hey! That’s... I mean...” Hugo tried coming up with a retort, yet nothing came to mind. His blushing face was the only proper response he could give.

Den couldn't help but giggle like a schoolgirl. Even Grill smirked at Hugo's reaction.

"Sounds like smooth sailing," Grill concluded.

"I'm gonna miss everyone," Hugo added, a touch of melancholia peppering his voice. "But we'll be back. No doubt about that."

"Absolutely," Den concurred. "You're gonna get smooch withdrawals at some point, and I am *not* gonna be your substitute."

"Yeah right. Like I'd lower my standards that much!" Hugo uttered in as theatrical of a tone as he could muster.

"You say that only because you know you can't afford me!" Den said.

The two couldn't help but crack up at their own theatrics. The sound of their laughter caught the silent, perturbed stares of other passengers. Night had already fallen on the Righton Train. Many of its patrons were getting ready to move to their cabins for bed. Hugo noticed the glares first. He piped down and tapped Den on the shoulder to inform him to quiet down as well.

Outside, mountains greeted them in the distance. The moonlit night illuminated the far-flung snow caps. An ocean of grassy fields covered every inch of their surroundings. This was the side of Corridia Den and Hugo had rarely seen. The openness of it all. Plains that stretched for miles on end. Trees only planted at particular spots. For as beautiful as Kelvin Forest was, the new scenery was a welcomed change of pace.

"Think I'll head to bed after this round," Hugo said.

"Aw come on, buddy!" Den gasped. "Three more rounds! Two?"

"I'm afraid Hugo's right, Den," Grill agreed. "Probably best to hit the sack soon. We've got plenty to do in Wayport tomorrow."

"Really?" Den sighed. "Fine... All the more reason to win this last game!"

As Grill shuffled and dealt the cards, a thought crossed Den's mind. "So this whole Terminal Cities thing," Den said. "Mr. Rasmus said they're cities which all the surrounding states equally own, right? So why call them Terminal Cities in the first place? Seems like a pretty random name."

"Think of it like Harten's train station," Hugo explained. "How all four trains converge together, even though they all come to and from different places. The Beckstone Train goes exclusively through Castella, but the Righton Train, as we're currently experiencing, goes a much greater distance. And yet they all meet back at Harten. It's the same with Terminal Cities. People and places from the surrounding states all converged into one territory."

"And that's really where the trouble comes in," Grill added. "Because it means having to deal with the problems of all four states as well. Corridia, Astier, Dorado, and Kamir."

By this point, Den was having trouble following the game while also trying to understand what Grill was saying. His face made strange contours in response.

"Permission to pause the game?" Grill asked. "Just for a moment."

Den and Hugo nodded in agreement. Den in particular felt relieved at not having to multitask.

Grill took out five bars of Rosette Chocolate from his bag, each of them a unique chocolate flavor: milk, dark, white, strawberry, and blueberry. The latter two were exclusives only found in select locations, flavors Grill happily grabbed while he was running his errands.

"Geez, Grill!" Den exclaimed. "I think you brought enough Rosette for the whole city!"

"And they will be savored slowly over the coming weeks," Grill said. "But I have my reasons for bringing all of these out at once. Let's say each of these bars represents a good or service. Whatever you can think of. The center of this table represents Wayport, while the four corners represent the surrounding states. Now let's pretend that Corridia outlawed strawberry chocolate." Grill grabbed the strawberry bar and placed it at one of the corners. "Then Dorado outlawed white chocolate." He placed the white bar at a different corner. "Astier outlawed blueberry and Kamir outlawed dark." The bounty hunter placed the blueberry and dark bars on the other two corners. A single bar of milk chocolate was now all that stood at the center, sitting atop the discard pile. "Since none of the four states ever outlawed milk chocolate, it gets to be sold in Wayport without any problem."

"It seems so counterintuitive," Hugo said. "By trying to appease every state, they're left with basically nothing."

"It gives me a headache," Den said, rubbing his temples in an exaggerated manner. "This is why I don't follow politics."

"But what if we were back in Harten and all of sudden I wanted to grab strawberry chocolate? I would be out of luck. I'd have to go all the way to Dorado, Kamir, or Astier. But what if Dorado or Astier followed suit? I'd have to go to Kamir every time I wanted to buy strawberry chocolate... However, what if there was another option? What if one of the local places happens to sell them under the table? I'd certainly be happy about it. But then how did they get all these sweet bars of strawberry without causing any problems? Going against those kinds of sales laws could result in major fines. Perhaps even jail time, depending on the items in question. It's possible they managed to go around to the other states, collecting each of the banned foods, and stashing them without much notice. Sacrificing a lot of time doing so... Or they just went to Wayport." Grill grabbed the other four bars and placed them back in the center.

"Mr. Rasmus said it best back at the party," Grill continued. "You can't regulate this kind of stuff to oblivion. Black markets are an inevitability. And since Wayport intersects with all four states, it makes it even easier to get as much of the other state's banned items as possible. Less travel. Less hassle. Easier to cross state lines. It's the biggest irony of all. A place where all of these items are banned instead becomes the center point for more black market trade than any other place in Central Adalia."

"I never went that far into thinking about it," Hugo stated. "But it seems to make sense."

"And of course with the black market comes gangs. They go hand in hand, really. Plenty of people live in Wayport. Which means a lot of cronies to control or suckers to take advantage of."

By this time, it was as if Den's brain had short-circuited. The scarred boy simply listened in a daze. The use of chocolate had confused him more than helped. "I shouldn't have asked," he finally said. "Can we get back to the game?"

"Of course," Grill replied, placing the chocolate bars back in his bag. He left out the bar of white chocolate to munch on for the rest of the game.

Den managed to be far more proficient this time around. The scarred boy finally seemed to maintain the poker face Grill and Hugo had told him about. Grill managed to discard his cards once more, leaving him entirely free of the Old Maid. He watched on as Den and Hugo played back and forth. Perhaps Den's momentary lapse of thought had instead acted as soft rebooting of his skills.

"Terminal Cities have another meaning as well," Grill said as he watched the final plays of the round. Once more, Hugo paused his playing. For as confusing as Grill's explanations had been to Den, the young Historian had grown fascinated by them. The scarred boy had no choice but to pause his play as well. "Going back to the train metaphor, terminal stations can also refer to the endpoint. Where there's no track left. The final stop. Nowhere else to go, at least not without going backwards...

"That criminal element? It's not just a bunch of bigwigs and high-swinging mob bosses, like you see in the movies. So many of them are down on their luck. Broken apart, whether by their own choices or by circumstances beyond their control... Those with no future.

"In a place where people are constantly vying for power, it goes without saying that a lot more of them are gonna get hurt. Or worse. Hence the other meaning: Terminal City. City of the End. Where their lives mean so very little. Where they could end at any time..."

The manner in which Grill spoke was chilling. As both a bounty hunter and a soldier, it was clear he had seen that side of humanity before. And in more ways than one. He'd seen the depths a person would go to and witnessed the destruction such ambition left behind. What Grill spoke of was not simply interesting trivia—it was a warning to anyone hoping to find glory in a city devoid of it.

"What a barrel of laughs right before bedtime," Den commented as he started playing again. "Can't wait to dream about that!"

"I think it's important," Hugo said. "Thank you, Grill. As much as I hope we don't have to deal with it, it's good to know regardless."

"Like I said, I'll make sure you two are safe," Grill stated. "I promised Karina. I refuse to let her down."

"I'd like to see her in these parts," Den joked. "I can only imagine the kind of damage she would cause!"

"She's probably been to at least one Terminal City," Hugo noted. "But she doesn't tend to talk too much about all that." He grabbed one of Den's cards, managing to discard a pair in the process. By this point, Hugo had two cards and Den only had one. The game would soon be over by a simple 50% chance.

"Be that as it may, I'll make sure we stay in safe areas," Grill said. "Thankfully, both the bank and the WHS are close enough to each other. So we shouldn't have to deal with too much trouble."

"Ah, it'll be fine!" Den assured. "After killing a giant plant monster and bashing zombie animals in the skull, I'm ready for absolutely anything!"

With his proclamation, Den took his last chance and grabbed at Hugo's right card. The scarred boy hesitated for a moment to see if his fortune had finally turned. He looked at it.

"Whaddya know?" Hugo stated. "Guess I'm the Old Maid!"

The smugness on Den's face was exacerbated only by the shout of victory he made right afterwards. Causing many of their fellow passengers to give Den the dirtiest, angriest looks the scarred boy had ever seen in polite society. Hugo and Grill couldn't help but chuckle.

Hugo took another look outside. How different things already seemed. They hadn't even stepped outside Corridia yet and it already felt like they were entering a whole new world. Black markets? Criminal underworld? It was like a story he had seen in a movie a hundred times before. But it was real. And as much as the young Historian hoped things would run smoothly, he couldn't help but wonder what else was out there. What had he missed in all his days studying the past? What would he find?

Hugo moved into the cabin portion of the Righton Train, resting his tired body onto the thin pillows of his one-man bed. He waited for sleep to take him. One more sleep and they'd be in Wayport. The first stop on their Journey. The beginning of a new life.

II

Again. Once again, Hugo Statferd stood in the heart of Kelvin Forest. The very music he had once fought to protect now rang in his ears. Birds chirped, snakes hissed, squirrels rustled, and, somewhere in the distance, a bear roared and growled at whatever poor soul was now its next victim. There was a serenity in the noise. All things were once more in a living balance. All was right within this little world.

Hugo took a few steps forward, his shoes crushing fallen leaves. Adding to the chorus that made up the music of the forest. It wasn't long before his steps turned into strides and his strides turned into a proper walk. The young Historian did not know where he was going or what he was doing. Yet he walked with the belief that the forest would guide him to where he needed to be.

So he kept walking along. Seconds became minutes and minutes became hours. The sun circled through its regular rotation and dusk was soon upon him. And still he walked. Even as the burgeoning night made his walkabout harder to see. Until there was only darkness ahead. A black void greeting him on all sides. Hugo stared into the night sky. And still, only pitch black greeted him. No stars twinkled about. No moon waxed and waned. Just pure black and nothing more.

Hugo took a few more steps. Yet he heard nothing below. Neither the familiar crunch of dead leaves nor the sound of his foot stomping onto the dirt below. There wasn't even an impact in his steps anymore, as if he was walking on air. It was only at this moment that Hugo realized just how quiet his surroundings had become. The chirping, rustling, hissing, and roaring had all gone silent.

And once again, Hugo stood there. Waiting to see if the sun would rise. For hours he waited. Even counting the seconds. No other thoughts crossed his mind. Only the seconds. Only the darkness. The nothing at the end of the trail.

Until finally the allure of sleep crept towards him. His body gave out. Whether by exhaustion or hunger, he slumped down, lying on what he assumed was the ground below. His limbs felt sore and his eyes grew heavy. With what little strength he could still muster, Hugo moved his right hand to his chest. He felt nothing but skin. Not the grooves and nicks of his scars. Not the sweat from his walk. He placed his hand under his left pectoral and let the seconds pass. Hoping for at least one familiar beat to still flow through him. And once again, all he was met with was silence. Hugo Statferd's heart had stopped beating. Or perhaps it had never beaten at all.

Hugo wanted nothing more than to get up and run. Scream for help. Try to find some semblance of life. But the mists of slumber finally took their toll. Whatever came next would not be for the young Historian to decide. He had no choice. He had no freedom. He was a man without a heart, in a land of void. Enraptured by the unknown and a slave to the dark.

"Hugo..." came a familiar voice. "Hugo." It spoke again. "Hugo!" it yelled. "Wake up, buddy!"

With a single burst of air, Hugo snapped back awake. A cold sweat dripping from his brow. He glanced at his surroundings. Still in the Righton Train sleeping quarters. Still in the one-person bed with its flat pillows.

And right in front of him was Den. His sunken eyes still managed to beam in excitement. His pale skin and many scars made him stand out even more amongst the other passengers.

"Must have been one hell of dream!" Den said. "Been trying to wake you up for minutes."

"Yeah," Hugo replied, "you could say that." The Historian continued his glances around the cart. "Where's Grill?"

"Getting his things ready."

"Ready?"

"Wow, you must have been in deep. The engineer made the announcement an hour ago. We're about to arrive!"

"Arrive? Why didn't you wake me sooner?"

"Thought you heard it, but decided to go back to bed. Plus, you looked so peaceful it seemed like a sin to wake you up!"

"Peaceful," Hugo repeated. He touched his chest for just a second. Enough to feel the grooves of his scars and the beating of his heart. A sense of relief washed over him. He was indeed alive. "Yeah, I guess I was."

III

One of the things that distinguished Wayport's train station from Harten's was its design. Whereas Harten's was meant to evoke a forest environment from the get-go, Wayport's was more utilitarian in nature—a simple brick and mortar setting, with signs and other directions plastered in their appropriate spots. But there was no decorum or atmosphere. Just a simple train station. With one exception: a large welcome sign plastered at the center. Its multicolored layout stood in stark contrast to the grays and browns that decorated everywhere else.

The sign featured a map of all four states surrounding Wayport: Astier, Dorado, Kamir, and, of course, Corridia. They were simple representations, only meant to show the basic shapes of each state and lacking any other finer details. At the center of the map, clearly meant to represent Wayport's location, was a giant cartoon heart. The symbolism was as clear as it was obnoxious. Perhaps intentionally so. Just another case of marketing being out of sync with its actual environment. Not that most passersby gave it much mind. It was meant to be seen once and promptly ignored. Given the sign's relatively low standards, it had clearly done its job.

As the trio made their way out of the station, their eyes became transfixed, not on what was near them, but on what they could see beyond. At the exact center of Wayport, surrounded by its most renowned shops, stood the one true skyscraper in all the city: the Lang-Meyer Courthouse. The place by which all forms of commerce and politics were sorted and settled. Where the eyes of the public could watch as their representatives and fellow residents debated on the matters at hand. At least, in the "legal" sense. Many were unaware that, for every new agreement or deed made within those hallowed halls, a thousand smaller trades and treaties were fashioned within its underbelly, whether in the alleys, the bars, or the local shops of ill repute. And from all streets of the city, no matter where one was, the tower could always be seen. A behemoth watching over its peasants.

"It used to be an outpost," Grill explained. "A neutral territory during the states' land disputes. The federal government had to send in agents, completely unaffiliated with all states involved, to make sure nothing crazy happened. But ultimately, it was here that the Terminal City concept came to be."

Den and Hugo stood in awe at the towering sight. Grill couldn't help but be amused at their surprise. For too long the bounty hunter had traveled alone. Always focused on the task at hand. Rarely taking in the sights all around him, apart from his occasional off-day. To watch these two engrossed by their new surroundings made him feel young again.

"Alright, you two," Grill said after giving them a moment. "Let's make haste, not waste. We have places to be."

"Think we can go up there?" Den asked.

"They give guided tours at certain times," Grill said. "If things match up, I don't see why we couldn't."

"Think I'll pass," Hugo said. "Me and heights don't mix."

"I wonder what it looks like from all the way up there?" Den wondered.

"They say at night you can see the soul of the city," Grill said.

Den's imagination burst at the seams.

The trio continued their walk, bags in hand. Den and Grill had prepared lightly, Den's backpack only carrying a few key essentials and a single change of clothes. Given Den's comments on getting new shoes, Hugo assumed he was simply going to buy some new clothes in Wayport. Grill was still using his rifle bag as his all-purpose carry-on. Without all the bombs and other explosives to pack in, it could easily be used to store whatever else the bounty hunter needed.

Hugo was another story. His single backpack was stuffed tight with clothing and a few other essentials. Pants folded into thin squares. Shirts, socks, and underwear rolled into little balls. It was a technique he had learned from his mother years ago when his family would visit his grandmother in Kamir or on the rare occasions when they ventured further out west. His journal was tucked away neatly between the soft fabrics of his shirts. The method proved useful, as the young Historian had managed to pack several weeks' worth of clothes into a single, albeit hefty, backpack.

One which gave Hugo's lanky shoulders a bit of a workout. Only a few minutes out of the train and he could already feel the burn. But the fact of the matter was that they were going to be traveling a lot. If this was the inconvenience he was going to have to deal with, then so be it.

Den and Hugo followed Grill through the streets of Wayport. They copied his steps to avoid getting lost in a city they knew almost nothing of. The further the trio walked into the Terminal City, the more crowded it became. People of all kinds surrounded them. The rich and the broke. The tall and the small. Young and old. Strong and weak. All walks of life walking together, having no qualms with butting and shoving someone getting in their way.

The trio of travelers would simply move around the crowds, trying not to start any unnecessary altercations. Grill had been in such environments long enough to know this instinctually. Den and Hugo did not have such natural reactions, but they had dealt with enough crowds during Harten's busiest times of the year to know when to bob and weave.

"Friendly folks," Den commented as he moved around a family of three.

"You get used to it," Grill replied.

"I guess I got spoiled by Castella," Hugo said. "The streets were rarely this packed and... cluttered."

"It's the reality of Main Street," Grill explained. "Lots of businesses and tourists about. Plus the regulars who couldn't care less about basic manners."

"Sounds kinda harsh," Den noted.

"When you live in a place like this, it's becomes second nature," Grill said.

"So how far till we get to the bank?" Den asked.

"Not much longer," Grill answered. "The First National Bank of Wayport was specifically designed to be near the station. They get a lot of business from the surrounding states, so they wanted it to be as convenient for incoming travelers as possible."

"Must be pretty good for Madame Lake to put her trust in it," Hugo noted.

"Must be," Den agreed. "She's never been subtle about the things she loathes. Though I guess you could argue it only makes her praises all the more meaningful."

"Hey, mister," came a voice near Hugo.

Instinctively, the young Historian turned around. The voice came from a young boy, no older than eight or nine, standing on the side of the crowded sidewalk. "Excuse me?" Hugo said.

"Could you please help me?" the boy asked, puffing his cheeks out. Doing his best to appear innocent.

"Don't fall for it, Hugo," Grill interrupted. "Just another street urchin looking for some cash."

"Please, mister, I just need some money for food." Hugo turned back around, trying to ignore the child's begging. "My mama's outta town and

I gotta take care of my brother!" The boy's words grew louder. Tears started forming in his eyes. "Please, sir! I'm so scared!"

Hugo stopped and let the words sink in. Odds were, this was just another ruse. Possibly by the kid. Possibly by some other force. But it was still a child in need. And Hugo couldn't let that stand. "Alright," he said. From out of his pocket, Hugo took out several small Rias bills.

"*Hugo*," Grill said again, emphasizing the Historian's name.

"It's alright." Hugo walked back towards the boy and showed him the cash. The boy stared at Hugo's bills, eyeing the amount. "You can have this on one condition. You go get some food right away. Okay? Get whatever you can afford with this."

The youngster nodded and grabbed the money. Spirits high, he began a quick dash towards a nearby deli. Hugo watched the boy, seeing if he kept his end of the bargain. About halfway down, the boy slowed his pacing and turned around. Sure enough, as soon as he saw Hugo watching him, the boy accelerated his pacing once again until he finally reached the deli.

"Okay, we can go," Hugo said.

"Not gonna stay to see if the kid actually followed through?" Den asked. He had said nothing during Hugo's exchange and simply watched the moment pass by, curious to see how Hugo would handle the situation. All the while, the crowds still bumped and moved.

"No. It's fine. He already has the cash now anyways."

As the young Historian started walking back towards his friends, he could feel someone slam into his side. It was another boy, older than the one Hugo had just aided, though still clearly a child. Their collision was brief, but impactful. Hugo nearly fell over before just barely catching his footing again. "Sorry!" the boy yelled as he jogged away. Not even giving Hugo a glance.

"You get used to it," Grill said. "People in such a hurry they become blind to everything else."

"At least he apologized," Hugo noted. The kid had already disappeared into the crowd. "Still, it's a good thing he landed on me and not Den. Kid may have broken a bone." Hugo chuckled.

"What can I say?" Den replied as he approached Hugo. "I guess I don't know my own..." Den's voice trailed off as he looked at Hugo. All at once, his laid-back demeanor morphed into a stern stance. His eyes focused on the crowd ahead.

"Den?" Hugo asked, a tick of concern in his voice. "What's wrong?"

The scarred boy took off his backpack and gave it to Hugo. "Be back in a minute." Without a single word of explanation, Den darted into the crowds. If Hugo or Grill were yelling something at him, he didn't hear it. He bobbed and weaved among the people, avoiding every possible collision, which caused him to slow down considerably. Though at the very least he was able to maintain a consistent speed.

But his movements were not just some spontaneous burst. There was a target and a purpose in his stride. And in seconds he managed to find it: the older boy Hugo had just bumped into. He was in Den's sights and was moving surprisingly fast for a child of his age. But he was still a kid all the same. The boy turned to a nearby alleyway. Den followed suit mere seconds later.

"Alright, kid!" Den yelled. "Hand it over!"

The boy stopped in his tracks and turned around to see who was talking to him. "What?" the boy asked. His only response.

"The wallet, kid. You took my friend's wallet. Now give it back." Upon closer inspection, Den was surprised to see that the boy was about his same height. A cruel reminder of Den's below-average stature.

"I don't got nothing!" the boy said. "If I scream, the police will come and arrest you!"

"Yeah, not gonna happen. A quick search of that wallet will confirm it's my friend's. You haven't had the time to throw away the I.D."

The boy clenched at his pocket.

"Look, you can have the cash," Den suggested, his voice calmer. "I just need to get that wallet and the rest of its contents back to my buddy." He cringed ever so slightly at the thought of handing Hugo's money over, but knew he could quickly pay his brother back. "Please."

The boy started shaking. "No!" he screamed. The boy rushed his hand down to his other pocket and pulled out a pistol. "Stay away from me!"

Den raised his hands in the air, trying to maintain his composure. Shocked at what he was seeing. A child no older than twelve wielding a weapon he may or may not even know how to use. Ignorant of its sheer power and the dangers that came with it. A thousand thoughts raced through Den's mind, trying to come up with some way to deescalate the situation as calmly and quickly as possible. "It's okay," Den spoke, his voice even calmer. "There's no need for that."

"Move back!" the boy commanded.

Den did so, slowly inching backwards. He had never been shot before. He hadn't even been shot at. Even with all the strange happenings he had encountered during the Crimson Maple incident, Den wasn't sure if his body could withstand a bullet. And he had no intention of finding out today.

As Den continued moving backwards, the boy did not stay in place or move away. Instead, he approached Den. One forward step for every time Den stepped back. Den glanced behind him. It wouldn't be long before the scarred boy would be out of the alleyway and into the streets. Perhaps that was the boy's intention. Getting in public again would mean being able to mask himself into the crowds once more. Still, Den continued moving.

That's when Den looked into the boy's eyes. Strained, red, and beady. His breathing was tense and his arms were shaking. Whether this was the first time the boy had ever wielded a gun or not, it was clear he had not been trained. Never taught proper trigger discipline. His movements were not planned. Moving on instinct alone. Instinct and fear. Fear of being caught. Fear of being disciplined. Fear of facing consequences he may not even understand. A true loose cannon in every sense of the word.

All it would take was a small slip-up. A single tinge of fear. And then boom—a bullet to the head. Possibly for Den. Possibly for any innocent soul who happened to be passing by just outside the alley. And if Hugo and Grill had managed to follow Den here… The scarred boy knew what he had to do. He just needed that single second of courage.

Den stopped his movements. He waited to see if the armed boy would as well, but he just kept advancing. He hadn't even noticed Den had stopped. Den stood in place, waiting for the boy to get just close enough to him. And when he did, Den started his sprint.

In a single glide, Den managed to close the gap between himself and the boy. Only now did the boy realize Den's true speed. Den used his left hand to grab the bottom of the boy's trigger hand and lifted it up to the sky. With his right hand, he firmly grabbed the boy's shoulder and pushed him down to the ground, careful to keep his trigger hand up in case a shot rang out. Though thankfully, no shot came.

The boy was already on the ground before he could comprehend what had just happened. Den managed to grab the gun away and immediately unloaded the bullets, dropping them to the ground. Den had no real knowledge of guns, but he had seen Grill and his fellow Hartenians disassemble them before. He simply followed what he remembered. He could not break the weapon down into every individual component. There was no need for such meticulous action. Instead the scarred boy simply dismantled the firearm into several large pieces. Just enough to remove the danger that had filled the air.

The boy stayed down for a few seconds before Den helped him back up. "I'm sorry it got to that point," Den said. "But please know I am not here to hurt you."

The boy was still shocked, yet Den could already see tears start to form. But the boy held them back, trying to maintain a stoic demeanor.

"It's alright," Den said. "I'm not gonna lecture you. I'm not gonna rat you out." Den showed him the pieces of his gun. "But please, don't use stuff like this until you've been trained. Okay?"

The boy said nothing, but nodded.

"My name's Den. What's yours?"

"Vi… Vito," the boy said in a timid tone.

"Vito... can I please have the wallet back?"

"O... okay..." From his pocket, Vito took out the wallet and handed it to Den.

The scarred boy inspected its contents to make sure nothing had been stolen. Sure enough, the interior had remained untouched. Still, Den knew he couldn't just let the situation end like this. He took out all of the cash from his own wallet and handed it over to Vito. "Use this wisely, okay? Do something better with your life. Can you do that for me?"

The boy simply stared at him. Only now did Den remember how strange he looked. Gray skin, white hair, scars all over. It was no wonder the youngster freaked out like he did. Vito put the money in his pocket and slowly got up and walked away, deeper into the alley. Never giving Den a final response.

Den looked at the gun pieces in his hands. Gold and red in color. Designed for flash rather than substance. These chunks of metal were meant for killing. Used in both assault and protection. Neither good nor evil. Only a means to an end. He took the pieces and placed them in several different trash cans that littered the alley, taking care to place them underneath other filth. Hoping no one would find them. That they would simply be hauled off with the rest of the trash. Until he was left with the trigger itself.

That singular half circle which acted as the final line between life and death. That same gold-and-red finish mocked Den as he held it. He clutched it in his hand.

"Den?" came Hugo's voice. He and Grill had just managed to catch up to him. "What the hell is going on?"

"Nothing," he responded, putting the trigger in his pocket. "Not anymore, at least. Pickpocket. Thought he could get away with taking your wallet. But not with these legs of mine! Caught him quick and sent him on his way."

"That younger boy could have been a distraction," Grill suggested. "I've seen that tactic used before. One kid manages to get the victim to open their wallet. The other kid, from close by, bumps into the person and takes the wallet before they have the chance to put it back up."

"Guess I'll need to travel lighter," Hugo noted. "Thanks, Den. You have no idea how much that means to me."

"It's no biggie, buddy." Den smiled, handing back the wallet to his brother. "You'd have done the same for me... if you weren't so slow!"

"Fair enough," Hugo chuckled. "I am honored to be in the presence of the Speed King."

"Fastest legs in all of Corridia!"

The two laughed together, any tension from the situation now utterly drained.

Grill took a quick glance at the alleyway and saw the bullets on the ground. "Den," he began. "Did anything else happen?"

"No," Den answered quickly. "Well, I did give him some of my own money. Felt bad for the kid."

"And that's it?"

"That's it."

In a place like Wayport, it was not uncommon to see bullets lying on the ground. Gun owners of all kinds frequented the area. Still, Den's reaction did not sit well with Grill. But there was nothing else he could do. Over the years, both as soldier and a civilian, the bounty hunter had learned when to pursue a situation further and when not to. The situation had cleared and they had places to be. "Alright. Let's head to the bank."

Together, the trio made their way towards their next destination. And for just a moment, Den glanced back at the alleyway and the bullets. The boy's face had been so afraid. What type of life had led that poor, young soul to such a result? What awaited him in his future? Den wanted so desperately to know and do more. But even he knew that, in a place like Wayport, there was nothing else to be done. Den gave a quick prayer for the child and moved on.

And they called it Terminal City. Some believed it was because of all the states coming together. A crossroads of cultures uniting in harmony. But I always knew what its true meaning was. The end of the line. Where dreams came to die. Where the last vestiges of sanity slipped through the cracks. Whether it be Wayport or any of the other God-forsaken land masses that dare amalgamate into such a form, anyone who remains here is bound to their end. Leaving nothing but an empty shell and a broken corpse.

—Jeremiah Deodato, *Streets of the Blighted City*, 774 AU

Chapter 2

Kulver Street

I

What the First National Bank of Wayport lacked in outer extremities it made up for with its lavish interior. Golden streaks lined the marble floors. Each bank teller station was made from granite countertops, smoothed and pristine. And a crystal chandelier hung above the heads of all those coming in and going out. What seemed like any other concrete structure on the outside housed one of the finest banking establishments Central Adalia had to offer.

"Welcome, sirs," said one of the bank tellers with a smile. He was adorned in a dark-blue suit that was as comfortable as it was fashionable, each crease pressed and intentional. The name "Lance Decker" was embroidered just above his left breast pocket. Even his glasses had a tint of gold. Whether real or fake, the design was immaculate. "How may we help you on this fine day?"

Den approached the man with a nervous sway, feeling underdressed and overwhelmed. "I think someone left a message for me here."

"Of course, sir. May I see a form of identification, please?"

Den pulled out his I.D. card. It was a simple design, not meant for anything other than official identification purposes. Madame Lake had given it to him some years ago, in case he ever needed it for official business.

Contrary to what some people in Harten believed, Den's full name was not "Den Lake." Den had no family name to speak of. Neither did Madame Lake nor Fairchild, for that matter. It was an uncommon occurrence within certain regions of Adalia, such as Faradin. A relic from generations long before Adalia's founding. When certain ancient cultures bestowed only one name upon a person at the time of their birth. A result of many early tribes rarely interacting with other groups. In the modern era, those with only a single name would be identified by their hometown. As such, the scarred boy's name was officially registered as "Den of Faradin."

The teller eyed the card. "Thank you, Mr. Den. Are you aware of the name of the messenger?"

"Madame Lake. Although she might be using the alias Louie Chateau." Den handed over the letter, the Old World seal Dr. Voltaire had described still on it.

Decker examined the seal with an amused grin. "Very interesting, sir. Seals like these are very rarely used in this day and age. A fascinating find. I'll go see what we have in our facilities. This may take a few moments." The teller moved away from his post and towards the gated vaults behind him. Even his steps were smooth—calculated movements meant to evoke the perfect fusion of efficiency and professionalism.

"I feel like I should have worn a suit or something," Den said.

"You're fine," Grill replied. "I've seen people in pajamas come into places like this before and the staff don't say a thing. If you're money's good, they'll take it."

"I didn't know Madame Lake very well," Hugo said, "but this is definitely a place I could see her going. You know, the high-end kind of stuff and whatnot."

"I guess I just never paid attention," Den said. "She does love dressing herself up, though. So I guess it makes sense."

"This is one of the most secure banks in the region," Grill added. "If she had something to keep safe, this is certainly the place to leave it."

"*Has*," Den replied.

"Pardon?" asked Grill.

"She *has* something to keep safe."

"*Has*..." Grill repeated, taking a moment to interpret Den's correction.

Hugo patted Den on the back. "She's out there, Den. Don't worry."

"Yes," Grill noted, finally realizing what he had unintentionally implied. "And we'll find her. No question about it."

As if on cue, Decker arrived back to his post, a new envelope in hand. "Thank you for your patience, Mr. Den." Decker handed the envelope to him. "Though there is something that I must bring to your attention... There were actually two envelopes addressed to you. However, the second envelope in question is under strict orders not to be given to you until you have read this first one and followed the instructions inside."

Den, Hugo, and Grill crowded together to see the Madame Lake's next message. There was nothing fancy about the envelope. There didn't need to be, given it was meant to simply sit in the bank's vaults. Carefully, Den took out the letter and read aloud.

Den,

For a time I pondered if I should even make this. If maybe it was best to just let you live the life you had chosen. But if you're reading this, then you have chosen this of your own volition. And I must respect that decision.

You may be thinking that this letter will reveal some grand secret. A map leading to where I am. But the truth of the matter is that even I don't know. I've gone too many places and met too many people to know how everything might pan out. All I can give you are clues to where I might end up. And there's no guarantee of that either.

But before I can divulge such secrets, I have a task for you. The one thing I fear the most is that this hunt becomes your one obsession. In all my years, I have seen too many people go down very dark paths. Paths only taken because they had nothing else. Paths which dictated their entire lives. As such, this is the task I present to you: Get a job.

As blunt as that may sound, please don't take offense. You're a very hard worker. One who can and will excel at whatever you do. And by that, I don't mean a string of part-time jobs you take as you travel. I want you to set a career for yourself. One that you are actively pursuing while on this quest. I have no qualms about what it might be. Successes can come from anywhere. I just want to make sure, regardless of where this all ends up, that you will still have something to live for, and especially to strive for.

When you have done that, present your official qualifications to the bank teller and he will hand you the next letter. I believe in you. Never give up.

—Till our lines entwine again,
Madame Lake

"So I guess we know what our next step is," Hugo said.

"Her logic is sound," Grill added. "I was already going to make Den my apprentice. All the more reason to start it up as soon as possible. Any thoughts, Den?"

Den stood in silence as he held the letter, looking through the words again. He could feel a smile melt over him. His heart beat just a little faster. A warm glow encapsulated him. Tears bottled up to the surface. "No," he finally responded, still smiling.

"If you have any qualifications on you, I'd be happy to give you the second letter," Decker added.

"Afraid I'm unemployed," Den responded in a chuckle. "But I'll be back."

"Of course, Mr. Den." Decker nodded. "And if I am here the day you make your return, I would be most happy to hand you the second letter myself. Good luck. I look forward to seeing you again."

"Thank you, Mr. Decker." Den shook Decker's hand. It was a small gesture, but appreciated nonetheless. Whether it was for appearances or out of genuine care, Den would always accept kind words from strangers.

The trio made their way out of the bank and back into the busy streets of Wayport.

"That about does it for Main Street," Grill said. "At least until we come back."

"Are our other stops close by?" Hugo asked, still lugging his backpack.

"Fortunately for us, our remaining destinations all rest on the same street," Grill said. "It's called Kulver Street. An area primarily used for business centers and the like. Hence why the Wayport branches of both the World Historical Society and the Bounty Hunter Association of Adalia reside there. Albeit several miles apart. Not exactly a tourist spot, so we won't have to deal with all the crowds much."

"And our hotel?"

"Also on Kulver. Merryville Suites. Nice place. Perfect for travelers."

"And let me guess," Den interjected. "You've got hotel points too?"

"Yes," Grill admitted, bluntly. "Anyway, it's still gonna be a while before our rooms are available. So we might as well make our way to one of our other stops."

"If it's alright with you guys, I think now would be the time to split up," Hugo said. "Figured I could head to the WHS while you go do your bounty hunting stuff."

"Oh no, no, no!" Den said, intentionally wagging his finger. "After what just happened, I don't feel safe leaving you alone like that."

"It's fine," Hugo replied. "Nash knows the guy who runs this branch."

"Not what he means, Hugo," Grill added. "The WHS shouldn't be a problem. It's getting there that leaves us a little concerned."

"Oh, come on, guys! I'm not an invalid. Besides, I don't want to slow you down."

"You won't, buddy. Tell you what? We drop you off at the WHS and then head straight for the BHA. Then after that's done, we swing back around to pick you up."

"Take it from me, Hugo, Wayport is not a place you want to walk alone at night. Not without proper protection at least."

"So consider us proper protection!" Den exclaimed.

Hugo couldn't help but chuckle. "Alright," he conceded. "I understand. And hey, I've got the Iron Sniper and the Speed King by my side. What's to fear?"

"That's the spirit, buddy!" Den patted Hugo on the back. "Now let's go out there and make our futures come true!"

"You know, Den, you'd make a great a speechwriter." Hugo smirked.

"Nah," Den replied. "Too much paperwork."

"You say that," Grill added, "but wait till you see all the forms you're about to fill."

"What?" Den said. Then the sudden realization kicked in. "Ah, crap."

II

In the past, Hugo had called Harten's branch of the WHS "rustic"—a strange mixture of bookstore, library, and office space. But the setting was calm and his coworkers were helpful, allowing everything to remain in a semi-organized state, at the very least. There was a quaint charm to it all. Just like Harten itself.

Upon first glance, it was difficult for Hugo to describe Wayport's branch as something so complimentary. "Archaic" was the word which sprang to his mind.

Stale air filled his lungs. Towers of books were stacked atop one another in no discernable order and for no discernable reason. Other books were clumped together on shelves, crammed in. Looking as if they were about to burst. And there were even more books splayed across the floor. Though at the very least, enough books had been separated to form a clear walking path from the door to the front desk. An absolute jungle of disorganization. Though some eccentric minds may have seen it as a perfect example of controlled chaos. Perhaps even archaic was too nice a word.

"Hello!" Hugo called out as he moved towards the front desk.

"Just a moment," came a deep voice from behind the desk, echoing from one of the back doors. "I'll be right with you, sir!"

Hugo took another look at the huddled masses of literature around him. The very sight of it all gave him a tinge of homesickness. Not because he was far from home. On the contrary, it was because the WHS was the most familiar thing he'd seen all day. If anything, the place felt a little too close to home, even with the mess.

The young Historian gave a closer look to the books near his feet, which acted as a border to the walking path. There were books on hiking, cooking, martial arts, and horse riding. Each from different writers and, going off the covers, from different eras as well. In fact, there was no discernable order at all. Not a tinge of structure or reason. They simply lay there, waiting for the next reader to pick them up. Hugo couldn't help his own curiosity. He slowly picked up the book on martial arts, tucked just under the cook book. Yet just as soon as he took the book out of its spot, so too could he hear a rumble and a clap.

An avalanche of paperbacks came down on him all at once. Hugo had only a second to cover his head with his arms before the wave of books came in full force. Enough to knock the young Historian down to the floor.

The result was almost comical. Hugo was now covered in a menagerie of treatises and tomes, a look of bewilderment in his eyes. He couldn't help but laugh at himself. His laughter was cut short as soon as he saw a man coming from the doorway.

"Had an accident, I see," the man commented, a wry smile skirting across his face. He was an older man with a mane of long white hair flowing down his back and a beard just as long running down his face. He chuckled upon seeing Hugo, his portly belly bouncing as he did so. In ancient times, this man's appearance would have been mistaken for a wizard. And while such beings had dispersed into legend, a man of his demeanor was still a wondrous sight.

"I'm so sorry, sir," Hugo apologized as he crept back up, trying to find his footing in the sea of prose.

"Not a problem, laddie! Happens to me all the time," the man replied as he grabbed Hugo's arms, helping him back up. "Now, might you be the young fellow that Nash was telling me about?"

"Yes, sir," Hugo replied. "Hugo Statferd. I just started my Journey yesterday."

"Ah, yes!" The older Historian vibrantly shook Hugo's hand in greetings. "Good to meet you, Mr. Statferd! Nash has told me all about you. I am Gino Andolini, proud manager and owner of this fine branch."

"Good to meet you, Mr. Andolini." Hugo had not expected such a kind yet bombastic greeting. A far cry from Nash's calm demeanor. Though certainly more in line with Master Rasmus's theatrical zeal. "Happy to be here. This place is... very nice."

Andolini's chuckle evolved into a guttural guffaw. "No need for pleasantries, boyo! I know it's a dump. I'm just glad to have some company for once! So now that you're here, how's about a tour?"

"Tour?" Hugo took another look around. "Is this not everything, sir?"

"Oh no, my boy. You haven't seen the backroom yet!"

Hugo walked slowly around the huddles of books into the backroom where Andolini had just been. It was shrouded in darkness, concealed to the side of the building. Andolini flicked the light switch.

The room was the exact opposite of the front desk. Wide and clean, with enough floor space to put several beds. Its walls were a warm gray, broken only by the red emergency switch near one of the corners. But it was what surrounded the walls that caught Hugo by surprise: antiques of all kinds contained in glass cases. Just separate enough from the outside world. Yet close enough to be within inches of rich history.

Each case housed its own unique artifact. A dagger from an ancient war. Runes from a dead civilization, long before Adalia's founding.

Ancient documents on brittle paper, preserved only by delicate care and restoration. A room full of wonders.

"Each one represents a part of Wayport's history," Andolini explained. "Whether it be a hundred or a thousand years ago. Even further back than that. When Adalia was not even a concept and only a few scattered peoples migrated along its paths."

"Mr. Andolini... this is incredible! Would you be open to some questions?"

"Of course, Mr. Statferd. Ask me anything about these beautiful pieces. It's bound to be stored somewhere in this noggin of mine!"

"That's great! And please, Mr. Andolini, call me Hugo. Mr. Statferd is my father."

"Absolutely, Mr. Hugo."

It was at this moment Hugo knew he had made a new friend.

The next several hours consisted of long discussions on each and every piece in Andolini's private exhibit. The dagger had come from Adalia's expansionist period which eventually saw Wayport's founding and the creation of the first Terminal City. The documents were pieces from that very founding, though these were only secondary papers. The primary documents being kept safe and secure within the First National Bank of Wayport.

Each and every artifact had a long and defined history. Hugo absorbed as much of the information as he could, noting in his head which pieces to study more in the future. And they were all preserved thanks to Andolini's delicate procedures.

The weaker antiques were given specific instructions on how to preserve them. The right kind of light. How much moisture they needed or didn't. The temperature that best kept them from rusting or breaking apart, at least more than they already were. While Andolini could not help how they were when he found them, he could at least make sure that they would be maintained for future generations to come.

"How long have you had this collection?" Hugo asked after a time.

"A while, I suppose," Andolini responded. "Just a slow build over many years. I love each and every one of these beauties. After all, what value does something hold if there is no one to remember it?"

"*The future is unknown*," Hugo began, chanting a phrase he had heard so many times.

"*So let the past be our guide*," Andolini continued.

"*And perspective be our key*."

"*Until the day arrives, when we discover the greatest secrets*—"

"*And unlock the True History!*" The two clapped their right hands together as they spoke in unison. This was the oath of the World Historical Society. The phrase they lived by. What gave them purpose to forever chronicle the past and build the future.

Hugo and Andolini needn't say another word. Two men of different ages and different lives—one just beginning his Journey, another decades past from it. Yet still they came together as Brothers of History. The Salt of the Ancient World.

Hugo looked back at the front desk. The contrast between the two areas was palpable. "You love those books too, don't you?"

"Aye, lad," Andolini responded. "It may not seem like it, but I do." He moved back to the front desk and picked up one of the books, thumbing through its pages. His movements were delicate and precise. "I spent a lot of years doing work I hated for people I didn't like. But the money was good, so I barely even questioned it. Then one day, something in me just snapped and I realized I couldn't handle it any more. So I spent the money I saved up to attend the Academy… and open up this lovely place." He turned his attention back to Hugo. "I'm no Victor Rasmus or Lockheed Burrelles and that's perfectly fine with me. If I can't make my own mark, I can at least preserve all those who have."

Hugo couldn't helped but be moved by Andolini's words. These books were not just a pile of forgotten texts. They were his life just as much as the antiques. They were all his purpose. His only problem, Hugo deduced, was that he had spent so much time preserving the antiques that he hadn't had given the books their proper attention. So much ambition, but so little time.

Hugo picked up one of the books and began sifting through it. Trying to imitate Andolini's same delicate touch. "This one's about local trade and commerce. How many other books do you have on this?"

"Hm... I hadn't thought about it in quite a while. I've got records of everything in the storage room."

"Then let's start from there."

"And what might that be?"

"I wanna help you clean this place up."

"Oh, Hugo, it's fine. You don't have to do that. Yes, it's a dump out here, but that's on me."

"This place is amazing, Mr. Andolini! These books deserve to be organized and maintained. Honored to the fullest. Please, sir. Let me help you. Together, we'll make the Wayport branch an honor to the WHS. Because your legacy deserves to be preserved too!"

Andolini saw the fire in Hugo's eyes. That youthful determination that reminded him of his own early days. It brought a smile to his face. "Alright, then. Summer may be here, but I'd say it's about time we do some spring cleaning. Take the lead, Mr. Hugo!"

III

Visions of grandeur had filled Den's head as he and Grill made their way to the Wayport branch of the Bounty Hunter Association of Adalia. He thought of deadly assassins crowding around a large guild entrance and looking through wanted posters to catch their next mark. All the while old legends would tell stories of their greatest hunts as cigar smoke filled dimly lit hallways; a sense of nostalgia wafting through their voices. A haven for the greatest of private warriors.

Grill had not prepared him for the disappointment that awaited. No need—the location spoke for itself. "Dive bar" may have been the most optimal word, but "hole in the wall" was all Den could think about.

The basic facets of Den's vision had indeed been true, though only by the most simplistic definition. A few men eyed available wanted posters, but each of them showed little real interest. One man was even using a folded-up poster as a coaster for his drink. The bar itself was nothing to look at. A simplistic design built with 2x4 blocks of wood, appearing as if it had been built simply by stacking the blocks together until they had formed something that looked close enough to a bar.

Den tried brushing off these lacking features as quickly as possible, though he found it harder than expected. He made a mental note for himself to temper his expectations in the future.

"If it makes you feel any better," Grill said, noticing Den's underwhelm, "not all of them are like this. Some have air conditioning."

"Gee, Grill... thanks," Den replied.

"Any time." Den's unenthused response was not lost on Grill, but he paid it no mind.

Near the back of the main hall sat a burly woman at a desk. Her arms were covered in tattoos of spikes, flames, and roses, the kind Den had seen bikers adorn in movies. Her hair was cropped and she sported a leather jacket. She had a face that, at one time, could have been considered pretty, but had been weathered with age. Still, there was a sense of authority in her upright stance. Even if her frowning expression came across more threatening than welcome.

"Well, if it isn't the Silent Death himself!" the woman shouted.

"With all due respect, Hilda, just call me Grill."

"Nope. You're not cooking steaks or putting weird things on your teeth. So you ain't no Grill to me, Jack."

Grill sighed. "Fine. Jack, then. Look, I didn't come here just to chat." He pointed at Den. "This kid here is looking to be my apprentice. I need the proper paperwork to get it started."

Hilda gave Den a once-over. Eyeing him left to right, up and down. The scarred boy's unorthodox appearance didn't faze the female bounty hunter in the slightest. "He looks pretty young, Jack. No minors."

"He's eighteen. Den, show her your I.D."

Den did so.

"Fine, then. He's perfectly within his rights to register." Hilda turned her attention entirely to Den. "I am required by law to directly inform you that registration alone does not grant you entry into the Association. You will be required to pass a written exam and a basic physical. Only by passing these tests will you be granted the title of apprentice to Mr. Jack Trent."

Grill had heard this explanation enough times in his eight years in the business. Primarily through his fellow bounty hunters taking on apprentices for themselves. But he knew Den needed to hear it. These words were his first steps on a long road ahead.

"I understand, ma'am." Den straightened his spine and placed his arms at his back, trying to imitate the pose of a soldier at full attention. Grill quickly saw the mistakes in his posture, but knew the scarred boy was merely imitating what he had seen in movies and meant no offense by it.

Grill couldn't help but feel a sense of nostalgia. He had had no need for an apprenticeship. His years in the military had automatically qualified him to be a bounty hunter. Yet seeing Den at this moment, ready and willing to be his apprentice, would have brought a tear to his eye, if Grill expressed his emotions in such a manner.

"Alright, then," Hilda said as she took out several pieces of paper from inside her desk. "Fill these out. I've got more I need to print."

"And by that, she means a *lot* more," Grill quipped.

"Since when did you get a sense of humor, Jack?"

"Let's just say an apprentice can teach his master a lot of things too."

"This kid must be something special, then."

Hilda got up from her desk and walked down a nearby hallway. Den and Grill started filling out the papers Hilda had handed them. Basic identification questions, the kind someone was expected to fill at a doctor's office. Given the danger that bounty hunting entailed, even Den quickly understood that having one's health insurance information made enough sense.

"So how much are we expected to sign?" Den asked. His wrist already getting tired.

"This is just the tip of the iceberg. We're free to take what we don't finish and bring it back later, though I'd advise just finishing it here and being done with it."

"What in the hell is all this even supposed to cover?"

"Payment methods, potential tax breaks, insurance coverage. The agreed-upon cut for each bounty, which I will gladly split down the middle, by the way. It's basically a lot of lumber that covers the asses of the Association itself. Puts liability for any potential problems on us."

"I can already feel the migraine coming on... What happens if crap hits the fan and it all gets pointed at us?"

"Simple enough. I have good lawyers. Bounty hunters have to be ready for anything. The last thing you need on your mind is some sleazebag suing you for 'wrongful endangerment' when all you did was ask for directions. Besides, nothing's more powerful than an attorney who can sway a federal judge."

"Wait a minute... That prick Weldon talked about the government investigating the Crimson Maple... I've been wondering why Hugo and I never got a knock at our doors from the men in black. Grill, are you saying—"

"I have *very* good lawyers."

"Yeah, fair enough. Thank you, by the way."

"We made a vow. Your problems are now mine. So with all that said... You mind telling me what you've been hiding inside your pocket?"

"I..." Den paused. "I should've expected this." Den took out the trigger from his pocket. "The pickpocket was a kid... A kid with a gun." He handed the trigger to Grill. For the next minute, the scarred boy explained what had gone down between himself and the boy known as Vito. He expected a disparaging look to come over his master-to-be. Instead, Grill simply listened with his same stoic expression, only moving his eyes away from Den to examine the details of the trigger.

"I'm sorry," Den apologized as he concluded his explanation. "I didn't want to worry you and Hugo. It just... didn't seem right."

"No apology necessary," Grill said. "Though to be clear, it's not how I would have handled the situation. I probably would have phoned the police. However, given Wayport's reputation, especially after everything I had told you and Hugo about last night, it was probably for the best to avoid any potential ripple effects. The boy is not our responsibility. As callous as that may sound. You did nothing wrong."

A sense of relief washed over Den all at once. "Thank you, Grill."

"I'm your master. Or at least I will be soon. I'm honor-bound to tell you the truth. For both of us. And if it's no trouble, I'd like to keep this. Try to examine the trigger a little further to figure out where it came from."

"Sure. To be honest, I'm glad to get rid of it."

A moment later, while Den and Grill once more continued to fill out paperwork, Hilda walked back out with two more stacks as big as a dictionary. At least, as far as Den was concerned. In actuality, the pages were thick and the text larger than any normal dictionary. But they did contain pages and pages of what Grill had described.

"Mr. Den, would you be willing to take the physical today?" Hilda asked. "If not, you're more than welcome to wait until after the written exam is finished."

Den had stared down the barrel of a gun only a few hours earlier. He had fought bears, wolves, and a literal man-eating plant monster. Yet it was this stack of documents most foul that made his spine tingle. "I'd like to take the physical now, please!"

"The pile will still be waiting for you when you're finished," Grill stated.

"Yeah, but at least I don't have to look at it *now*!"

Hilda took Den to a nearby gym setup. The equipment, while not rusty, was aged. Used again and again over the years. Maintained enough to fulfill its duties and nothing more.

"We'll be covering your speed, stamina, and physical strength," Hilda explained. "A simple two-part system. First a treadmill, then weightlifting. In the first scenario, you will start on the treadmill at a moderate pace, which will gradually increase in speed. Similarly, in the second scenario, you will begin lifting small weights and will be consecutively given more until you call off the exam. If you reach a certain point in both scenarios, you pass. Are there any other questions?"

Den had already started limbering up as Hilda gave her explanation. He could feel his blood pumping and heart racing. A test that would have filled some with anxiety instead made the scarred boy's adrenaline pump. Not only could he show off his skills, but he could do it to a brand new audience. "No, ma'am," Den responded. His mouth contorted into a cocky sneer. "No questions at all."

Grill had stayed at Hilda's desk, his face planted in the documents. His calloused fingers barely even registered the amount of signing and check-marking he had already done. There was no need to watch Den's physical; the tests meant absolutely nothing compared to what he had seen the scarred boy accomplish back in Kelvin Forest. He was a shoo-in.

Several moments later, Den came back, his cocky sneer now morphed into a massive grin of absolute self-satisfaction. Barely a bead of sweat traveled down his head. "I passed!" he cheered.

"With flying colors," Hilda added. "Haven't seen a newbie like that in a while. Always a nice surprise when one comes through the door."

"Excellent work, Den," Grill said. "There was no doubt in my mind."

"You know it! If only Hugo could have seen me. He might as well call me Mr. Muscles now, too!" Den flexed his arms, still thin in comparison to his physical strength, but also just as toned as they had been when he had fought the Crimson Maple. The two weeks Den had spent in a semi-invalid state seemed to have caused no lasting repercussions.

“I’m sure he will,” Grill said, giving Den his deserved gloat. “Now I hate to be the buzzkill, but…” He tapped at Den’s pile of papers.Den sighed, his grin wilting into a gloomy frown. “Yeah… Might as well get it over with…”

As the scarred boy continued his own half of the paperwork, Hilda moved in closer to Grill. “Is he an Enhanced?” Hilda inquired, keeping her voice down to avoid Den hearing her.

“Not officially,” Grill answered. “Perhaps undiagnosed. But that’s just speculation on my part. He’s certainly something.”

“I can register him as one. His results today are proof-positive enough for that. I just can’t imagine why he’s never been properly tested before.”

“He’s had a… strange upbringing, to say the least.”

“I just hope you know what you’re getting yourself into with this one.”

“More than you’d know, Hilda. More than you’d know…”

IV

Night had already fallen on Wayport before Hugo noticed how much time had passed. The two Historians’ first order of business had been to start taking out all the books on the shelves. But since there were already too many books lying on the floor, they moved piles of shelf books into the backroom, keeping the books at the center so as to not disturb any of the antiques.

The WHS had a storage room for extra supplies, a few more chairs, a cot, as well as a bathroom. The thought of putting the shelf books in there had certainly crossed their minds. But since the storage room also contained a radiator and pipes for the bathroom, it didn’t seem worth the risk of getting them wet.

Their movements back and forth had taken them the rest of the day to accomplish. The shelves were now wholly empty. The next step would have to wait for another day.

"I have to say, Mr. Hugo, I'm already liking the new results," Andolini admired.

"We're gonna have to come up with a system to sort everything out," Hugo said. "But I agree. It's already looking nicer." The young Historian's focus on the task at hand had distracted him from the calls to Mother Nature. With their day's objective done, the call was ringing louder than it had all day. "Mind if I use your bathroom?"

"When you gotta go, you gotta go! Take your time. No rush."

"Will do!" Hugo sprinted to the bathroom.

Andolini took this quiet moment to admire all the work they had done. The first bit of real improvement the old Historian had seen in quite some time. Nash was right: Hugo was a truly good kid.

His focus quickly broke when a knock came from the front door. Customers were rare as it was, so closing for renovations earlier in the day had made sense. Andolini had been expecting Hugo's friends to show up; he thought it only an odd moment of chance that they happened to arrive when Hugo was preoccupied.

Andolini unlocked the door and opened it. It was not the two men he was expecting, but it was certainly two men he was more than familiar with.

Noland Macchianado stood at the entrance. "Andi!" he cheered. "How's it going, big guy?" His flowing brunette hair was frizzled and unkempt. Perspiration covering his oily skin. His eyes were immediately set on Andolini, as they were every time the two met.

The very sight of the man made Andolini shake. His usual buoyant composure was whittled down to a meek acknowledgment. "Good, Noland," he replied. "How are you tonight?"

"Oh, you know, was in the neighborhood. Seemed like a good time to come and chat with my favorite Historian. Brought along Tillman, too!"

Just behind Noland stood Tommy Tillman. He was an old man with a sharp sense of fashion. Far from the rags Noland preferred to wear, Tillman adorned himself in a cream-white suit, complete with the finest pair of loafers money could buy. His hair was slicked back with as much gel as a man his age could apply. And while his chin remained clean cut, with no beard in sight, he sported a thin black mustache, which appeared as if it had been penciled on. The picture of aristocracy, whether the man had been born into it or not.

"Mr. Andolini," Tillman greeted in a low, hoarse voice. Andolini had wondered if the voice was truly natural or a byproduct of many years of poor lung health.

"Say..." Noland said, "looks like you've finally started cleaning up around here. I like it! Not to be rude or nothing, but it was kind of a pigsty. I mean, I like ham and bacon as much as the next guy, but I can't say I like looking at where it comes from!" Noland laughed, a vain grin already covering his face.

"It seemed like the right time," Andolini replied.

"Right time, huh?" Noland placed his hand on his chin, his movement intentionally exaggerated. Pretending to think about something he had forgotten, when it was clearly the first thing on his mind. "That reminds me. You know, there's something else that seems like the right time to do... Care to ask what that might be, Andi?"

Andolini hesitated on the answer. But knew staying silent would do nothing to help. "The right time to pay."

"Correct!" Noland looked at Andolini like a teacher proud to his student, his tone condescending. "I am so glad we're understanding each other. Now, might I expect this in cash or check? Not like your card is valid here."

"I... Noland, I don't—"

"Shh..." Noland hissed, placing his finger on Andolini's lips. He moved closer to the old Historian as he did so. "I didn't come here for excuses, Andi. I came here for payment. You knew this was coming sooner or later. So I don't know why you think you could get away with a few nice words. And for the love of God, don't tell me you spent it all on books!"

"They're donations," Andolini said, his voice almost in a whisper. "I haven't bought anything recently that wasn't essential. I just need more time to cash flow—"

“And I need your cash to flow to me. *Right. Now.*” Noland’s hiss had become a growl. This was the part Andolini hated the most. The thing that kept him awake at night, wondering which day he’d have to see them again. Wondering if the next time... would be his last.

“Oh well,” Noland continued. “If you don’t have the money I suppose all I’d need to do is look you straight in the eye and—”

“*Bang!*”

Andolini felt his heart stop at that very moment. He couldn’t help but close his eyes and clutch his chest. His entire body tensed in silent shock. Waiting to see what happened next. Yet all that followed was silence. Was he dead? Was this what eternity felt like? Only... there was a sound from just outside his periphery. Clicking and clocking... It was his clock. The clock which adorned the front entrance. Ticking on at the same beat as always. Then he noticed the hum of the radiator and the flushing of the toilet. Gino Andolini was still very much alive.

The old Historian opened his eyes ever so slightly. Noland stared back at him, a ravenous smile adorning his face.

“What’s wrong, Andi?” the man inquired. “Can’t you take a joke? Bahahahaha!” Noland and Tillman burst into laughter. Tears filling their eyes. Cheeks a solid red. The bang sound had clearly come from Tillman. “And you wondered why we keep him around?” Noland lightly grabbed at Andolini’s head and shook it, the same mild antagonism a teenage boy would show his younger brother.

“You’re right, Matches,” Tillman replied, tears still in his eyes. “The man’s a natural!”

Tillman started slapping Andolini on the back, as if they were friends laughing together at the same bit of comedy. “Mr. Andolini, you have no idea how much we needed this. In fact, I think you deserve a little discount. How about just seventy-five this week?”

“You know what, Tillman? I’m feeling generous. Fifty percent! And you won’t even have to pay that other half off later. On the house! And hey, if you can make us laugh like that again, maybe it’ll only take you twenty years to pay us off instead of forty!”

"At least then you'll be able to spend your debt-free days in the dialysis center instead of six feet under. Hahahaha!" Another round of laughs ensued.

Andolini just stood there and took it. Clutching his fist. Wanting so badly to do something about it, but knowing nothing could be done that wouldn't make the situation worse.

"Mr. Andolini?" came Hugo's voice. The young Historian crept in from the back, eyeing the situation.

His appearance caused the two men to stop their laughter almost instantaneously. Noland's ravenous smile morphed into a humble grin. The wolf transforming into a sheep in front of Hugo's very eyes.

"Andi!" Noland said in an enthusiastic tone. "You didn't tell me you had an assistant." Noland moved away from Andolini and walked towards Hugo. "I don't think we've met before. Noland Macchianado. Pleased to meet you." Noland grabbed onto Hugo's right hand, delivering a firm handshake.

"Um, yes, good to meet you," Hugo replied in an uneasy fashion. The young Historian peaked at Andolini and quickly noticed the near catatonia of his expression. "The name's Dominic. Dominic Sullivan. I'm actually not his assistant. Just a fellow Historian trying to help out. Came in today, actually." Hugo's demeanor changed just as quickly as Noland's had. Any nerves that had come up from seeing the stranger's threatening personality instantly fell away. For at least this moment, he was not Hugo Statferd. He was Dominic Sullivan.

"Oh really? Where you from, if I may ask?"

"Castella. Born and raised."

"Castella? *The* Castella? That's a big, romping place. I haven't had the fortune to go myself, but I've heard great things. Not many can say they'd trade a place like that for this old watering hole we call Wayport."

"Well, I was in need of a vacation anyway. Seemed like the best time. Though I suppose you could call this a working vacation."

"Sure, sure. I was just talking with Andi here. Checking to make sure things are shipshape around this place. He and I go way back, you see."

"Of course. Don't mind me." Even Hugo was surprised at his own demeanor. He was not one for small talk, at least not amongst strangers. Yet here he was lying to a man he had just met. A man who immediately came across as far more dangerous than he was willing to let on. The young Historian wasn't confident enough to call himself a wolf, but he could at least convince this Noland Macchianado that he was a sheep. And that was good enough.

"It's fine. We're done anyway." Noland turned to face Andolini. "For tonight, at least." He moved his attention immediately back to Hugo. "Well, nice meeting you, Mr. Sullivan. Can I call you Dominic? You can call me Noland."

"Sure, Noland," Hugo replied, opening his hand for another handshake.

"Good stuff, Dominic," Noland said as he shook Hugo's hand once more. "How long you in town for?"

"Who's to say? A little while, probably."

"Well, if you came here for this little cleanup—great job, by the way—I'd imagine it'll take some time. Still, have a good night."

"Thanks. You too."

Noland moved back towards Andolini, patting the old Historian on the back. "Like I said... for tonight." And with that, Noland and Tillman walked out. Tillman had never even once acknowledged Hugo's presence.

Hugo watched as the two strange men walked away into the night. As did Andolini, who slumped down to the ground as soon as he knew they had truly gone. He did not cry. He did not breathe heavily. There was no panic attack or moment of pure anxiety. Andolini was just tired. A tired old man. The verbosity he had shown Hugo that day had all but extinguished.

"I'm sorry you had to see that, Hugo," Andolini quietly uttered. "I was hoping you wouldn't have to."

Hugo sat down beside Andolini. "What was all that, Mr. Andolini?"

"I owe them money. Simple as that."

"Loan sharks?"

"Essentially. Remember how I said I wasn't just the branch manager, but the owner? This is my place. It's where I live. All that space in the center of the backroom? I sleep there on the cot you saw in storage."

"Mr. Andolini, I'm so sorry. All the books there… I can move them right away."

"Not necessary, Hugo. But appreciated. I was just going to sleep in the storage room tonight anyway…"

Hugo wanted to ask Andolini more questions pertaining to his debt. Its origin, the price, the reason he got involved with these strange men. But he knew it best not to. He didn't want to risk exhausting his colleague and newfound friend even more than he already had. "Is there anything I can do to help, sir?"

Andolini cracked a small smile. "No, lad. You've already done more than enough tonight. Thank you so very much." The old Historian started getting back up, Hugo following suit. "Now, I expect your friends should be arriving soon."

"Yes, sir. Probably any time now."

"I just have one request, Hugo."

"Of course, Mr. Andolini. Anything."

"Please don't tell them about all this. It's enough that you saw it… That you had to talk to *him* like that."

"Yes, sir. Absolutely."

"Thank you, Mr. Hugo."

Hugo took the next few minutes to move a few more books out of the way, trying not to think of what had just happened. Soon enough, another knock came from the door. Only this time, it was indeed Den and Grill.

"Hello, Hugo," Grill said. "How did your day go?"

"Can't complain," Hugo replied. "Though not too shabby. See all these shelves? Filled with books when I first came in!"

"I'm afraid I don't fully understand the context."

"I'll tell you on the way to the hotel. By the way, how'd it go today, Den?"

"No more papers... No more papers ever again..." Den's hands throbbed. His eyes were bloodshot. Hugo wasn't sure how much was theatrics and how much meager paperwork truly caused harm to the boy who'd once killed a bear.

"I still haven't had the heart to tell him that he needs to start studying for the written exam," Grill said.

"Wait, what?" Den shrieked, a truer look of terror in his eyes than Hugo had ever seen in him.

"Consider yourself told," Grill concluded, a smirk coming through.

"Well, hello there!" Andolini greeted Den and Grill with his usual jolly voice. As if the events of the last few minutes had never happened. "You must be Den and Grill. Good to meet you both! I have to say, Hugo has been an absolutely tremendous help today. And he's a great speaker to boot! Say, would you like to see some antiques before you go?"

"He's got a pretty cool collection in the back," Hugo noted. "See for yourself. I just need to get my backpack."

"Sounds good," Grill agreed.

"Oh thank you, God!" Den said. "Something actually interesting!"

The bounty hunter and his would-be apprentice joined Andolini in the backroom. The old Historian gave them shorter and simpler explanations compared what he had told Hugo earlier in the day. The kind he usually reserved for tourists.

As he went into the storage room to get his backpack, Hugo couldn't help but feel a sting of concern. What had happened to Andolini that caused him to get involved with people like them? To bring a man like him down to such a low level? And how much of his real personality was that showboating side of him? Was it his true, optimistic self? Or a mere cover to hide the anxiety that filled his soul?

At least Andolini wouldn't spend the end of his day in pain and fear. For tonight, at least, he could be cheery once more. When he had first arrived in Wayport, Hugo wasn't sure where his path would take him. Now he was more certain than ever.

V

The underbelly of Wayport sported much in the way of dark corners and narrow alleyways. Where the vermin and libertines gathered, itching to escape from the shackles of modern society to indulge in their seedy delights. Delights one would rarely dare speak of in public circles and polite company.

Grill sought no enjoyment in these domiciles of ill intent. The mere stench of them, even from several miles away, could make his stomach churn. Yet they were a necessity in his line of work. Not for their actual services, but rather for the information they provided. Information which effortlessly found its way among the very souls who profited from such businesses. Whether it came from lowly office workers, high-class philanthropists, or mid-level politicians, there was always news to be told and facts to be sold.

And the single greatest mixture of debauchery and information throughout the Terminal City was Brockson's Grotto. Once reveled as the pinnacle of fine dining, poor financial and managerial decisions over several generations saw this once-beloved establishment decay and rot into a bar and social club which now stood as a shell of its former self.

Grill had found himself here with a purpose, the trigger Den had given him once more gripped in his hand. He looked at his watch. Nearly midnight. It had only been about half an hour since he had said goodnight to Den and Hugo at the Merryville Suites, not telling them he had a meeting to attend before he too could go to bed. A meeting the other party was none the wiser of. With a man he cared very little for.

Jerry Baratzi. It was a name that fueled nothing but ire and disgust in those who heard it. An information broker with a gold tooth replacing his left canine and connections that could make a king or president blush. Few could say there was a bigger sleazebag in the east side of Wayport. But his info was always good and at a reasonable price. He had made his mini-fortune by staying low to the ground. Laying with the rats if he had to. His scrawny, bone-dried build fit perfectly within the cracks. It was a position he deserved, as far as his acquaintances were concerned. And it was a life he loved.

Baratzi had purchased Brockson's Grotto some years ago with his earnings. It was a place he had taken great pride in. Thinking himself a true restaurateur, when in reality his menu was mediocre, his drink selection basic, and his services nonexistent. Many of his waiters and waitresses were hired simply to look pretty. What truly kept his customers coming back was information, discussions, and connections. A central hub of sorts that the eastern section of Wayport had desperately needed. Considering how much wealthier Baratzi had become since his purchase of the Grotto, it was an investment that had clearly paid off.

Grill made his way through the Grotto, ignoring any and all hoots and hollers coming from other customers and staff. At the back of the Grotto was a private area meant for special occasions and personal meetings. Acting as Baratzi's office, of sorts. Several guards stood by its entrance. They looked at Grill, clearly aware of who he was. The bounty hunter said nothing, instead taking out several large Rias bills and handing them to the guards. The guards remained silent in their response, grabbing the bills and allowing Grill inside.

"Jackie!" Baratzi greeted the moment he saw Grill enter. The office was decorated in gold and red. Large chairs and couches filled the room. Comfortable to sit in, but gawdy in design. Each piece covered in expensive furs. The corners of his desk were encrusted with diamonds. It was a room of pure excess. Just the way Baratzi liked it.

"Didn't think I'd see you in these parts!" Baratzi continued. His cocksure smile made Grill's stomach turn. "How ya holding up? Heard about that Riviello guy. So sorry for your loss. Oh, and can I interest you in some gold nuggets? Fresh from the gold city of Quensius itself! You wouldn't believe how valuable these things are! And I can give you this hunk of beauty for the low price of—"

Grill slammed Baratzi's head into his desk. The broker nearly screamed in pain... only to realize that his head hadn't actually been slammed at all. Grill had simply grabbed Baratzi's head so fast that it looked as if he was about to smash it down, only to stop mere centimeters from actual impact.

Grill pulled Baratzi's head back up, moving it so that the two were now looking one another eye to eye.

"What are you, some kinda lunatic?!" Baratzi screamed. "You coulda killed m—"

"Do you still have pick pockets on your payroll?" Grill inquired in a low, raspy tone, his hands still positioned on Baratzi's head.

"Ye-yes! But I just take a flat fee. They get to keep the rest!"

"Do any of them happen to be children?"

"I mean, with all these Half-Maines and Quarter-Maines running around, you never know which half-pint is really a child and which one is old enough to be your grand—" Grill started squeezing Baratzi's head. Not enough to hurt him, but more than enough to make his intentions clear. "Yes! Okay? Yes there are! Not all of them, mind you! Just a few. Some orphans no one will miss. They're not even the cute ones that get adopted or—"

Without another word, Grill slammed Baratzi's face down. This time for real. The sleazebag could feel the force of impact on his face, his wooden desk like concrete.

"Be happy the diamonds are only at the corners," Grill growled. "Otherwise whatever you're feeling right now would be a million times worse."

Baratzi let out several whimpers, expecting his guards to come in and save him. Yet no one came.

"Never knew you hired such cheap security," Grill quipped. "Amazing how low their rates are for turning a blind eye. Even for just a few minutes. Now... talk!"

The bounty hunter gave Baratzi a moment to catch his breath. "The kids just do some quick jobs for me," the broker explained. "Just swindling some tourists. Nothing more. I don't control them. They do it by their own choice. If they wanna go, then they go."

Grill took out the red-and-gold trigger and showed it to Baratzi. "Why the hell are they armed?"

"What makes you think those are my gu—"

Grill grabbed at Baratzi's head again. Squeezing his temples. This time, he intended to hurt him. "Your design work, Baratzi! I know you like to have your cronies wave them about to show you mean business!"

"Yes! They're mine. I just thought it made sense to give them protection!"

"No training? No supervision, even? Just sending kids out with guns to cause who knows what kind of trouble to themselves and innocents alike?"

"Please, Jackie! It hurts!"

Grill kept his squeeze going. He knew the strength of his own grip. How far he could take it before it resulted in something permanent. After a few more seconds, he finally released Baratzi. The gangster breathed heavily in relief.

"You will immediately stop using children! Understood?"

Baratzi shook his head wildly in agreement.

Grill moved his lips towards the sleazebag's ear. "And I don't care who you have to tell or what you have to do," he continued, his words a gnarled whisper, "make it clear to everyone you know *not* to mess with me or my associates. Make them know the Iron Sniper has come back to Wayport!"

"Yessir, Jack— I mean, Mr. Trent! Completely understood!"

"It's Grill."

"Yessir, Grill—"

"Mr. Grill!"

"Yessir, Mr. Grill! Please have a good night!"

Grill walked out of the Grotto in silence, a tinge of disgust lingering in his mouth. A backwash of filth. He didn't bother looking back to see how the sleazebag reacted. Probably screaming at his guards or calling up some associates to cause trouble. But the bounty hunter knew nothing would come of it. Grill's reputation was too strong and Baratzi was too despised. The perfect combination to accomplish what he just had.

What had turned Baratzi into the way he was, Grill wondered. Nature? Nurture? A form of both? A bad breed mixed with an even worse environment? Or someone so self-absorbed that they used their personal troubles as an excuse to be as harsh and manipulative as possible? It wasn't his place to think about it, and it certainly wasn't his matter to solve.

Grill thought of Den and Hugo as he walked back to the hotel. Their souls were far more innocent than almost anything this city had to offer. But this was where they were going to be, for a little while, at least. He only hoped that the sins of this lowly place would stay as far away from them as possible. If only for now... If only for now.

After a rocky start, we've reached our first destination: Wayport the Terminal City. I find it funny how quickly my enthusiasm has changed since my first entry.

But I suppose that's just part of the Journey. Smooth sailing is never guaranteed. Even with all the precautions in the world, sometimes all it takes is that one oversight or unpredictable event to bring things to a halt.

I've been told about Wayport's dodgy reputation. The criminal presence that is shrouded about it. And already, I have witnessed it several times today. Pickpocketing on one end. Extortion on the other. No one dead or beaten, at least. I can't help but take that as a cold comfort, even though I know I shouldn't. Yet my mind wanders to what may come into play, should we stay here long enough. What fearsome creatures may lurk just under the surface?

But I know just as well that danger is a given, considering who I'm traveling with. Grill says he'll keep us safe. And as much as I appreciate his care, I wonder how well he truly knows this city and its many hidden depths. Den is unperturbed by all this, of course. I can only dream of having the kind of grounded faith that he does. He's now on his way to becoming Grill's apprentice. Good luck to any criminals that land in his sights.

Still, despite what concerns I may have, I know the only way out is through. Maybe, just maybe, after everything with the Crimson Maple, I'm starting to get used to it all. I suppose only time will tell. Time to take the plunge.

—Hugo Statferd, May 29th, 840 AU

Chapter 3
Alleyway

I

It had been five years since Gilligan Hodgson had started collecting his ill-gotten gains. Five years of extra money without much extra work. Five years to get into a nice house and a warm bed. To spend nights with ladies that caught his fancy, even if they only stayed until the morning. To finally feel some sense of worth in his life, however small his impact actually was.

And it was all thanks to one substance: Paradicium. Taken from the Paradisis tree originated in the Southern Continent, the effects of Paradicium had been used to treat long-term physical injuries. Broken bones, torn muscles, perforated organs. Truly a miracle drug in every sense of the word. But it came with a price. Too much in a single batch had the risk of being fatal, overworking the body at an accelerated rate and triggering cardiac arrest.

It had taken many years for Paradicium to finally come into the legal marketplace, but never in its purest form. It had been watered down again and again until it was finally deemed a treatment for the masses, though at the cost of being nowhere near as effective as it once was.

That's where Hodgson came in. While usually a simple desk worker at Helvetica Pharmaceuticals, once a month Hodgson would also act as one of the heads of inventory. He ensured items within the west wing of Helvetica's Wayport warehouse had been properly cataloged. This included batches of the infamous Paradicium.

But the scales used were never exact. Some of them could only measure to the nearest hundredth of a milligram. Some only a tenth. Hodgson wondered if this was a cost-cutting measure or merely an overuse of antiquated material, but such an answer was far above his pay grade. That's when it had dawned on the lowly office worker: What if he could shave some off the top? Take mere fragments from each batch without it ever registering? Nab a single scrap from the pot of gold?

It had taken Hodgson several test runs to see if he could get away with it. Examining where the warehouse's cameras were located, what spots he could stand in without being spotted, and what methods he could use to take his scraps. Soon enough, he had found the perfect spot. At the west wing's corner, just out of the camera's sights, was where the containers were opened to be sifted through, checking for contaminants. Hodgson would open the lids and a different worker would sift through them with gloved hands. This was done to keep the hands free from any other elements, even the containment lids. All the while, Hodgson would hold onto the container to make sure it didn't fall to the ground.

However, there was a catch to it all. Each worker's movements followed a standard pattern. That pattern resulted in the container becoming tilted as the worker's hand moved through the Paradicium. This tilt was barely noticeable, especially with someone else holding the container. But Hodgson noticed it and knew what to do.

Right after the worker finished his job, it was required that he move to the nearby sanitation area, take off his gloves, and wash his arms. For at least thirty seconds, Hodgson was always—consistently—alone. It was at this moment, without any cameras on him nor a coworker to watch, Hodgson would position himself to a container's corner and lightly tilt the box ever so slightly. This extra tilt on its corner would cause a small trickle of Paradicium to fall down… right into Hodgson's breast pocket.

Hodgson had tried the method many times at home with similar-sized containers and with substances of equal mass and density, such as sugar. He'd counted the seconds and measured the amount he could take, as well as the time that was required. At first he'd started with just one container: soon enough, the office worker managed to take a trickle of Paradicium from each and every container in his care.

Each time he would measure on the scales, he could always feel his heart stop for a few seconds. Yet each and every time, he managed to fool the scales once again. Perhaps he had been blessed by God or taken over by the Devil. Regardless, Hodgson had found his monthly side hustle. One that had made him a rich man.

Laundering had been simple enough. Officially, Hodgson got this extra money by working as a part-time financial advisor to Matches Personal Loans, Noland Macchianado's loan company. A role Hodgson had found ironic, given how little Noland ever actually listened to him. But the situation had worked well. Good money upfront, with even the occasional residual check of sorts on holidays. For all intents and purposes, Hodgson was living the good life… a life he knew he would never escape.

His connection to Noland had opened himself up to other dealings in Wayport's underworld. Though thankfully none as violent as what he had experienced on his first night. And it was through one such client that Hodgson had found himself in one of the most high-end restaurants in Wayport's downtown district.

The Baiser de fée, or Fairy's Kiss, was where the upper-class wined and dined. Discussing business, culture, and politics. Each word stained in bravado. Spouting facts they had only learned the day before and acting as if they themselves had discovered some new phenomenon. Bloated ignorance disguised as intelligence.

Hodgson paid no mind to such verbosity, instead enjoying a fine meal of rare steak and white wine, compliments of the man he was sitting face to face with: Jun Takeda. Like Noland, he was a gangster and unabashed in his role. A thin man of Eastern descent, with hazel eyes, pale skin, and a face that could be described as classically handsome. He maintained a smile during any and all meetings, never once displaying the tinge of anger and malcontent buried just beneath the surface.

By his side was his brother, Miki Takeda. A silent man, thought mute by all his associates, yet never confirmed. He had long curly hair, a horseshoe mustache, and consistently sported sunglasses, regardless of the time of day. He acted as Jun's muscle, always standing or sitting right beside him. Hodgson had never seen Miki's skills in action, nor did he have any intention of witnessing them. He had heard stories of the mute man's ferocity, and that was enough.

Despite these eccentricities, the Takedas had maintained a positive back-and-forth with Hodgson since they had started speaking the year prior. And today was the culmination of something very important.

"Mr. Hodgson," Jun began, "are you aware of the amount we are requesting?"

"Of course!" Hodgson replied, a piece of meat caught in his teeth. "I've talked it over with Noland and Tillman. They got the go-ahead from Santino. We can have the full amount to you by then!"

"And how might these goods be transferred? Even with you and your associates' connections, we still run a large risk of exposure."

"It's all clean and down the middle. Just you guys, us, and Baratzi. No holes."

"Fair enough. Though I hesitate to put my full trust in Baratzi. What is he to gain from all this, apart from some extra funds?"

"Clout, I'd imagine. You know as well as I do how much of a punching bag he is."

"I suppose you're right... Very well. We shall contact your superiors once we have set up a formal time and place. Please enjoy your meal. Order more if you'd like. On the house."

"Oh, thank you, Mr. Takeda! The food is wonderful!"

"Enjoy these delights, Mr. Hodgson. If this goes well, you'll be able to come to places like this far more often."

The two exchanged a formal handshake as they said their goodbyes, Jun's light hands giving the impression that he was far weaker than he truly was, perhaps out of necessity. Yet as Hodgson started pulling away, Jun's grip tightened, pulling Hodgson's hand right back where it was.

"But remember, Mr. Hodgson," Jun whispered with his cold smile. Miki appeared right beside him, and the aura of the brothers encapsulated Hodgson. "*If* this goes well... Should it not... well... let's hope for the best." The Eastern man dropped his hand, releasing Hodgson from his intense grip.

Hodgson gulped. "Of course... for the best."

Jun and Miki bowed to Hodgson, a common farewell within their particular form of business, before leaving the restaurant.

Hodgson felt a cold sweat drip down his back. "Waiter! Another bottle of chardonnay and two more steaks, same cut and so rare they could still moo! Also a full order of tiramisu."

Hodgson had grown portlier in his wealth. Fine food and drink had become more plentiful. Never again would he be stuck with day-old microwave dinners. He would eat in happiness. Eat in success. Or at this moment, eat in anxiety. Stuffing his face. Trying to forget the future.

He was halfway through his tiramisu when he finally stopped and stared at the whipped dessert. He saw nothing in his future. Nothing in his present at all. But Hodgson would still finish the tiramisu and be on his way. Walking into the abyss he had put himself in.

II

When he had first left Harten, Den had no idea what or where this journey was going to take him. New lands to explore and strange people to meet. Wonders beyond his imagination right at his fingertips. And now here he was, in a city of infamy, ready to take on the world as the apprentice of a famed sharpshooter… He had not taken into account the studying such a position would require of him.

Two weeks in and the most the scarred boy had accomplished was memorizing texts that he would inevitably forget after the exam. Stuck inside their hotel room or the WHS day in and day out. Now here he was, miles away from Harten, savior of an entire forest, and what did he have to show for it? Knowledge regarding minutiae related to firearm sales, current tax rates, and a deflated sense of wonder from the supposedly great Bounty Hunter Association of Adalia. All this after having already finished mind-numbing hours of paperwork. One of the things Den had learned early on about Grill was his hatred of flagrant bureaucracy. Den was finally starting to understand why.

"And what's the going rate for serial arsonists?" Grill asked, his head glued to the study book.

"Uhh…" Den rubbed his temples together. "Private residence or business property?"

"Excellent response." Grill wrote the answer down on a notepad. "Now name each of those rates."

"Uhh…" Again, Den rubbed his temples. "Pass!"

"You can't you use that as a valid response for every third question."

"On the contrary! Some places will happily pass you at sixty-six percent!"

"What makes you think all the ones you actually answered were correct?"

"Optimism, Grill. Sheer, unadulterated optimism!"

"This all sounds about right," Hugo said as he walked in on the study session. The WHS had a small room in storage, right next to the bathrooms, originally reserved for quick meetings and break times. It had been sitting vacant for some years, becoming all but obsolete after Andolini took over as its sole proprietor. Too small for any real storage. Yet just right for what Den needed to accomplish.

The elder Historian had been quite happy lending the room to Den and Grill. The bounty hunter had wanted to pay rent for the room's usage, but Andolini declined. Having company around was payment enough, especially now that Hugo was here. "How you holding up, Den?" Hugo asked.

"My butt hurts," Den replied. "My butt never hurts. I don't think it's even supposed to hurt. Grill, can I *please* go outside?"

"Ever the C-plus student," Hugo remarked.

"C is only two letters behind A," Den said back. "And bronze trophies are cooler looking than gold."

"I suppose a break is in order," Grill replied.

"A break sounds wonderful!" Andolini said from the front desk. "I'll make some tea!"

The trio made their way to the front room of the WHS. Its interior was now nearly unrecognizable. The shelves, once crammed and jumbled, were now organized and pristine—books separated first by genre, then by author, and finally by title. A whole section dedicated to Wayport's own history adorned the shelf closest to the backroom.

But it was the ground that Hugo and Andolini were most proud of. Not a single shred of paper nor speck of dust littered below, its polished walnut wood finishing finally showing itself to the rest of the world. And its once stale air was now replaced by a fresh summer breeze. What had been two tedious weeks for Den had been two of the most fulfilling weeks Hugo had experienced in a long time.

"Wonderful sight, isn't it?" Andolini admired as he brought along tea and cookies, placing them at the front desk for everyone to enjoy. "It's like how it was when I first bought the place."

"Speaking of which," Den began, his mouth already stuffed with cookies, "I'm still a little confused about that. I thought the WHS was government-funded."

"It's a mixed model," Hugo replied. "It comes down to state and local laws."

"Indeed," Andolini confirmed. "Some branches are fully financed by their state or local governments. Especially in the big cities. Other places, like small towns, tend to be financed through other means. Donations, fundraising, or, in my humble case, private ownership. Think of it like a franchise. There's a certain model you have to follow, but many of the details are yours to decide."

"I would have assumed this place was given some notable funding, considering the cultural significance," Grill said.

"There was a time when that was true," Andolini admitted. "However, when it came time to cut budgets, sadly our poor WHS was one of the first things on the chopping block. Wayport's local government preferred to keep their most valued historical items within the First National or at the courthouse."

"And yet they still increased the tax rate on just about everything else," Grill added. "Budget cuts, my ass!"

"Of course!" Andolini agreed. "I would understand if it was for security reasons, at least, but they never even said a single thing about that! They just wanted us gone. Probably because they couldn't mooch enough money off the top!"

Den and Hugo didn't say a word as Grill and Andolini talked local politics. Hugo preferred to keep his opinions on such matters to himself, while Den barely paid attention to current goings-on as it was. When an inevitable discussion would pop up, they preferred to remain silent until the moment passed. Even in times such as this, when both parties were in full agreement. Best way to keep things calm, they figured.

"Anyway," Andolini continued after he and Grill blew off some steam, "I knew I couldn't let the WHS come to an end, so I filled out all the necessary documents and managed to open up my own private branch. Most of my current collection comes from donations. And I'm able to make some money by getting involved in local research and development projects. Acting as a Historian for any teams requiring data on Wayport's past events. I can't say I've made much, but I believe there is still a sense of freedom when not having to rely on the government teat."

Hugo grimaced ever so slightly, knowing Andolini had no intention of mentioning his debt. While Hugo didn't know the amount, it must have been large, given the tension that had arisen when Noland Macchianado had appeared. The young Historian was grateful he hadn't seen hide nor hair of the man since. Though it still sent a shiver down his spine knowing he was out there.

Hugo tried breaking out of his thoughts, easing his mind by grabbing a cookie. Only to realize how few were left. Den had stuffed his cheeks with sweets, washing it all down with several big gulps of his tea. He let out a sigh of satisfaction as he drank the last drop. "Fantastic stuff, Mr. Andolini!" the scarred boy said. "Now I think it's time I *really* go on my break."

"Den," Grill cut in, his tone like that of a father calmly disciplining his child. "This *is* your break. You can sit here for a little longer, but you've got to get back to the books."

"Come on, Grill! My nose has been stuffed in books for so long I'm afraid I'm gonna get a sinus infection! And we've barely explored the city. I'm grateful beyond measure for Mr. Andolini's help, but I know there's more to see!"

"To be honest, Den," Hugo said, "from what I've seen, I don't think there's much here you haven't already seen in Castella and Harten."

"Aye," Andolini agreed. "As much I love this place, much of the talk of unity between the states and a melting pot of cultures is just a bunch of publicity. At one time it was true, but now it's all been regulated into the same cityscape you'd find in any state."

"Fine," Den conceded. "But could I at least go and get some new shoes? Since we've basically been focusing nonstop on the license exam, I haven't had the chance to do it."

Grill gave Den's request a moment to breathe. "You'll need some time to break them in. Better to do it while we're here, instead of traveling about. Alright. You can go."

"Yes! Finally get to spend Winslow's money! Okay, I'll be back in a bit, everyone! Later!" Den raced out the door as fast as he could, though still taking care not to scuff the floors.

Hugo, Grill, and Andolini sat for a moment, taking in the quiet, quaint atmosphere... until a thought came to Hugo's mind.

"Does he even know where a shoe store is?" the young Historian asked.

"...Damn," Grill swore.

"I can make you a list," Andolini suggested. "Not too many options around here. Friar Tom's is pretty good. Got some moccasins there once that were quite comfortable."

"I'm indebted to your generosity once again, Mr. Andolini," Grill said.

"You owe me nothing, Mr. Grill. Debts are sins made to weigh you down. The sins of your past come to roost. Your thanks is all I'll ever need." Andolini wrote down the shoe stores, along with their addresses, on a nearby piece of blank paper and handed it to Grill.

"Thank you again, sir," Grill acknowledged. "Don't worry, Hugo, I'll make sure to bring him back in one piece. He's still got chapters to finish tonight." The bounty hunter made his way out.

Andolini waved Grill goodbye with the same smile he always showed.

"Did you mean that?" Hugo asked.

"What, lad?"

"What you just said about debt."

"Oh... that." Andolini's smile lowered, as if caught in a lie. Forgetting for a moment what Hugo had seen merely a fortnight ago. "Yes. Every word."

"May I ask how... or why?"

"How does one get into debt in the first place? Ignorance? Pride? Bad information? Probably all those things and more... The job I mentioned? Well, I used to be an associate of Tillman, the older man you saw with Macchianado."

"And by associate... do you mean gangster?"

"I suppose. Though more of an indirect source. I had helped in some black market dealings in the past. Nearly cost me my life. But I managed to get out of it, all the same. In exchange for not blasting my head open, I had an enormous debt to fill. A debt which took almost everything I had earned, up to that point. I lost my home and my riches all at once.

"I remember those nights after. Sitting in agony in a dingy apartment. Completely afraid of what the future held... That's when I started reading about Wayport's past. Those harrowing, uncertain days. When there was constant fighting and bloodshed. This city in the middle of one of the biggest battles Adalia has ever known. It gave me the courage to press on.

"I was able to attend the Academy's adult program via a scholarship and later joined this very branch. Not knowing I would be its last new member. Once the branch was shut down and my fellow Historians left, I knew I had a choice to make: leave Wayport like them and start anew elsewhere... or keep the spirit of the WHS alive in Wayport by whatever means necessary. As you can tell, I chose the latter... by getting back into debt with the very people I had sworn off."

"Surely you could have gone somewhere else," Hugo suggested. "The First National could have probably helped you."

"My credit has never been very good and other places wouldn't give me a large enough loan, even when combined. Noland had heard about my struggles and offered the loan to me personally. We had never met while I was in the life, but the second I met him, I knew I was getting myself into trouble... Yet I still took it. Even though I knew from day one that I'd be owing him for the rest of my days."

"Mr. Andolini... I'm so sorry."

"Nothing to be sorry for, Hugo. I made my choice. I can certainly take a bit of roughhousing and humiliation."

"It seemed more like a threat."

"Perhaps, but there's nothing to be done."

Hugo sat still, his mind racing. Trying to think of something that could help Andolini from his current strife.

"No need for that, lad," Andolini said. His smile returned. "It's not your battle to fight."

"Yes, sir. I just wish I could do something more."

"Something more? Have you looked around? In two weeks, you've added more to the property value of this place than I have in all my years owning it. Hugo, you have gone above and beyond. And you have my eternal thanks."

Hugo smiled at Andolini's compliment. "Thank you, sir."

A creaking sound at the front door soon caught Hugo and Andolini's attention. From the front entrance came a group of tourists, each one adorned in cameras, sunglasses, and backpacks meant for long walks. "Excuse me," one of them said, "is this the World Historical Society?"

Andolini's smile grew wider than Hugo had ever seen from the man. "Aye, sirs and madams! Welcome to the Wayport branch of the World Historical Society! Feel free to browse our massive collection of books or take a look at our collection of Wayport's finest antiques!"

Hugo felt a sense of pride welling up inside. All from the simple smile of an old, dedicated man. "That's right, everyone!" Hugo greeted. "Come take a tour as we show you the wonders of Wayport's past!"

It was going to be a good day indeed.

III

To call the alleyway Hodgson stood in "shady" was to acknowledge that a cusp of sunlight could even come within its grasp. Rather, the spot where Hodgson was about to make his latest transaction could instead be described as "secluded." An unseen spot within the catacombs of streets, boulevards, and unmarked ghettos. Where the legal and black markets entangled with one another until it was impossible to know if the goods being sold and transported came from a lawful source or were merely fronts for far seedier dealings.

Hodgson had been waiting nearly half an hour for Noland to arrive. But by this point, he was used to it. Perhaps his client had been spotted by the authorities and was making efforts to avoid being followed. It was a perfectly reasonable assumption to make. Though it was far more likely that Macchianado's tardiness was yet another sign of disrespect the gangster was actively showing to his dealer. It certainly wouldn't have been the first time.

Yet there was a feeling of an unease on this occasion. Hodgson had barely slept since his meeting with Jun Takeda. Days passed overthinking every waking moment, never truly clearing his mind, regardless of how much food, booze, and pills he put into his rotund body.

Hodgson checked the number of bullets in his revolver. Six all together. It had been his blanket ever since that first night, when he was nearly robbed and shot. The night he met Noland was the night he knew just how far down into Hell he had already been pulled. But after all these years, he'd never had to fire a single shot. Hodgson took that fact as at least one thing to be grateful for.

Still, his hands shook and his teeth clenched. He was unsure if it was just the meds in his system or the genuine unease of the whole situation. But there was no going back, as the very familiar tips and taps of Noland's footsteps came rattling down the alleyway. Always the same beat and stride. A piece of order in a world of chaos.

"Hoagie!" Noland said with his same cocksure attitude. Naturally, Tillman was just behind him. "How's my big, fat buddy been? Tried any good eats?"

"Hello, Noland," Hodgson greeted, a pit already forming in his stomach. "And yes, I just ate at Baiser de fée a few days ago."

"Ugh. That stuffy place? Gimme a burger and fries any time over all that froufrou junk! And why bother paying someone else to cook you a steak? Any man worth his salt can make his own, even if it's just eye rounds!"

Hodgson gave a fake chuckle. "Yeah, you're right. Guess I've just gotten lazy."

"Becoming a fat cat will do that to ya, Mr. Businessman!"

"Anyway, here's this month's." From out of his pocket, Hodgson removed a stuffed bear. It was nothing special to look at. Round ears, brown fur, button eyes. A simple doll with a simple design. He tossed it to Noland.

"What, you couldn't put it in a pony?" Noland replied as he carefully peeled the bear's back off, its stuffing falling to the ground. Checking, as always, to make sure the contents were inside.

"It was easier to walk around with. There are rumors Inspector Walton's getting stricter in his investigations."

"That drunk? Nah, his underlings probably just said that to spark some fear in the street urchins. Man's got a spirit more broken than a dropped shot glass." Noland eyed the bottle, confirming the same amount. He had been working with Hodgson long enough at this point to trust that he was being given the same, pure Paradicium. And if not, he would know about it as soon as it was sent over to the manufacturers. And should the purity ever prove lacking... Noland would make sure Hodgson would be made aware too. "Still, cute bear. Think I'll keep it." He placed the bottle back in the bear, folding its peeled parts into the stuffing.

Noland tossed the bear to Tillman. "Hold onto this for me, Till. Looks good on ya! Really complements your style!"

"I assume you also came with the information," Tillman said to Hodgson, ignoring Noland's comment.

"Yeah, how goes it with the Takedas?" Noland asked.

"Good. Very good," Hodgson replied. "Said they'll give Nicky a call when the date's been finalized."

"Well look at you, Hoagie!" Noland gave a small clap. "A fat cat who knows how to negotiate! Mr. Businessman is too low a title for you now. Mr. Executive, more like. Mr. CEO, even!"

Again, Hodgson faked a chuckle. "Just doing my part."

"And your part's gonna get you paid very handsomely!"

This was it. This was the moment Hodgson dreaded. But it was a moment he knew he couldn't pass up. If he didn't say it now, he would always regret it. No matter what came next. "About that... I had a question I wanted to ask."

"Oh really? Ask away, Mr. Executive!"

"How much would it cost me to get out?"

"Out? Out where? Outta Wayport? I assume the cost of a train ticket."

"No, I mean *out* out. Outta the business."

Noland stood there a moment; he made no change in his demeanor. Tillman scowled, though such an expression wasn't anything new coming from him. Finally, Noland turned around and looked at Tillman. Neither man's expression changed. They merely locked eyes and turned back to face Hodgson.

"A lot more than you can afford, Hoagie," Noland replied coldly.

"Please, Noland!" Hodgson begged. "Look, whatever money you were gonna give me in the Takeda exchange can go to this. You want me to sell off my house, I'll do it! I'll even make more trades until you're satisfied. Just as long as it means you'll let me go!"

Noland snorted, trying to hold in a laugh. He placed both hands to his mouth, keeping the noise at bay. After a few seconds, he stopped trying to hold it back at all and let out a massive cackle. His booming baritone echoed in the alley. Tears ran down his face and it was hard for him to breathe. But the laughter soon subsided and the man calmed down.

Hodgson stood by, completely confounded by what he was seeing. The pit in his stomach was now a chasm. Then a creeping feeling came over the office worker. That same feeling from his very first night. The only time he had seen Noland's truest side. The side he hoped to never see again.

"You're here for as long we want you here," Noland said. He had grown calm. Calmer than he had ever been around Hodgson. No smarmy remarks nor witty retorts. Only the opposing figure of a man with power at his fingertips. Power that was nothing compared to kings, presidents, CEOs, or even other gang members. But it was power over Hodgson. The only power he needed.

Hodgson silently nodded. Not even looking Noland in the eyes.

Noland and Tillman started walking away, their backs fully turned from Hodgson. Moving on without a care in the world.

Hodgson's shaking hands started pulsating. His teeth clenched so hard he could have almost chipped them. The chasm in his stomach was now an abyss. Hodgson was past the point of anxiety and fear. It had evolved into full-blown anger, his vision tainted in red.

Hodgson drew his pistol with speed he never knew he possessed and fired straight at Noland. By the time Macchianado heard the burst of bullets rushing out of Hodgson's chamber, it was already too late.

The bullets impacted him. Noland had no time to react as they struck his arms, legs, shoulder, and back. The gangster was already on the ground by the time the last shot hit its target. Six shots. Six hits. Hodgson was only sorry he hadn't saved any for Tillman.

"Ahh..." Noland squirmed.

Tillman had turned around to see Noland on the ground. He said nothing, but looked straight at Hodgson, whose gun still smoked.

Yet to Tillman's surprise, Noland managed to rise back up almost as quickly as he had fallen. The only real damage came from the back of his right shoulder, the bullet embedded within. Noland used his fingers to dig it out, his screeches of pain resonating through Hodgson's ears.

Tillman still said nothing and simply stood by to watch what would happen next.

Noland turned around and stared at Hodgson, a look of disbelief in his eyes. He still hadn't fully processed what he had just experienced, nor wanted to believe who had just caused it. He looked at the bullet again. It was larger than the rest. Sharper in design and heavier, too.

That's when Noland got angry. It wasn't the shooting that caused this, nor the realization that it was Hodgson behind it. It was the bullet itself. A bullet which showed this was no mere moment of hate-filled passion. This was planned. And even if the shooting was not meant to occur today, it was still something Hodgson knew he would do someday. It only happened to be today that the chickens had come home to roost.

"A Buster Bullet?" Noland said through his teeth. "A Buster Bullet?!" Already his anger was swelling. "How much debt did you have to go into, Hoagie? How many loans? How many favors? Well, Hoagie? How many? I thought we were friends, Hoagie! I thought we were friends!"

Five bullets to stun him, if only for a moment, and one bullet to finish the job. One far stronger than the rest. The only one that wouldn't bounce back. But something had happened beyond Hodgson's control. Noland had not fallen because of the actual force of the bullets. He simply tripped in surprise. That final bullet, the Buster Bullet, which was supposed to go for his head or heart instead went squarely into his shoulder. A trip which saved Noland's life… and had effectively ended Hodgson's.

Not a single word came from Hodgson's lips. Not a cry of fear, not a plea of forgiveness. Only silence. Eyes widened. Breath stilled. There was only this moment and nothing more. The future was not his to control.

Noland slammed his right fist into Hodgson's face, then used his left to strike into Hodgson's stomach. Right. Left. Right. Left. A continuous motion. Like a machine accomplishing the tasks it was programmed to do. Or an animal attacking on instinct.

Hodgson barely felt the pain of each blow. But these were not the punches of a weak man. So powerful was each attack that the doughy middle-aged man could not even comprehend the pain he was experiencing. Perhaps his brain was cutting off all receptors to save him from the overwhelming agony. A small gift at his most dire moment.

Soon Hodgson fell to the floor. Yet still Noland continued his assault, as if trying to bruise or maim every single piece of his flesh. A butcher tenderizing meat.

"Noland!" Tillman yelled. "That's enough! More than enough!"

Noland slowed down his beatings. Yet he took every bit of care to savor the last of his blows. The spark in Hodgson's eyes was already beginning to fade, his vitals ceasing. Convulsions starting. His skin growing lighter—tanned into sickly pale. Until, at last, his body finally gave out. The spark of life had now truly faded away. Gilligan Hodgson was dead.

Noland stared at Hodgson's body, triumphant in his victory, with an ecstasy he could only truly feel when his life was on the line. A feeling Hodgson would never know again.

"Alright," Noland said to Tillman as he calmed down, "let's head back before someone—"

At the edge of the alley was another figure. A witness to the atrocity that had just occurred. An innocent bystander now caught in the darkness of the underworld. Yet his own appearance was otherworldly. Gray skin, sunken eyes, white hair, and scars all over.

Den had just witnessed a murder.

IV

Den did not know Wayport's layout. He had no idea about the turns and passageways. So suffice it to say, he had no idea where to find a nice pair of shoes.

Naturally, this led him to getting lost. Taking turn after turn. Thinking the next one would be the right choice. But it never was. It would take some time before the scarred boy had to admit to himself that he was rightly, truly lost.

Then Den heard the voices of people nearby. Voices that might have been able to help him find his way back. Yet as he drew closer, the voices grew faint. Until gunshots echoed out. He dashed towards their origin, but the noise died down once more. All noise, except for what sounded like the slapping of meat mixed with the cracking of bones. Was he near some hidden deli?

By the time Den had arrived at the scene of the noise, all he saw was a man bashing the body of another. His face was utterly swollen and his stomach distended. His exposed skin was bruised and gray. And even from the angle he was staring at, Den could see the man had stopped breathing.

There was no need to question the situation. No deduction nor evidence necessary. Den had just witnessed a murder.

And for only a moment, his body was still. Then came the rage. The sorrow. Knowing, in his heart of hearts, that a life had just been extinguished and there was nothing he could do to save it. That maybe, just maybe, had he arrived only a few seconds earlier, the man on the ground would still be alive. Bruised and bloody, but alive. With time to heal. Time to live again. But that fleeting chance was gone. Extinguished by the figure in front of him.

At first fixated on the body of his victim, the man quickly turned around to see Den standing aghast. Now he was fully aware that there was a witness to his dark deed. The man's eyes were bloodshot and pulsating, his pupils shrunk and the corners of his eyes covered in what looked like pure black. The eyes of a killer.

Den did not say a word. He made no utterance or cry. He simply ran. Ran as fast as he could towards the man. His fist clenched. His muscles tightened. His veins pulsated. And all at once, that rage manifested itself into one powerful swing aimed straight at the killer's face.

The man took in every second of the charge. He made no maneuvers to avoid Den's attack. Instead, he greeted the challenge with a smile. His legs stayed in place. All he had to do was move his head a few precious centimeters.

And just like that, Den's choreographed attack missed, the force of the swing met only by air. The attack had titled his body too much to one side, causing the scarred boy to trip on himself, moving his head even closer to the killer.

The man took no time bashing his own skull straight into Den's. The shock of the headbutt knocked Den to the ground. The scarred boy had no time to react to the pain, as the killer used the full force of his leg to kick Den in the stomach. The impact raised his body just enough off the ground for the man to land a downward punch right into Den's face. His head collided with the pavement.

Three strikes. That was all it took. In just three quick strikes, this man had taken Den down. Mere seconds had passed. The savior of an entire forest, reduced to a bleeding mess in the alleyway of a dark city.

Den's head throbbed. He had felt every inch of pavement smashing into the back of his skull. A bitter reminder that, for all his inhuman abilities, he was not an invincible warrior. Merely a young man with a bit more durability than most.

His ribs remained unbroken, but his stomach ached. He lay on the ground for several seconds, anticipating another attack. Yet none came. Den moved his head upward and saw the man staring right back at him. That same smile still decorated his face.

"Now that was fun!" the man exclaimed with the enthusiasm of a child experiencing his first rollercoaster. "Can't say I've dealt with someone like you in a while! My name's Noland. Nolando Macchianado! What's yours?"

Den remained silent.

"Nothing? Ah, it's fine! I'll just call you Weird Boy. I'll try to say it enough times until you get so sick of it you'll have no choice but to tell me your name!"

Den only glared in response. Catching his breath. Seeing how quickly he might be able to get up, in spite of the pain.

"Tough crowd. Still, can't say I was expecting something like this! Were you a friend of Hoagie over there? He some kinda uncle figure to you? I would've said father, but I can't say I see the resemblance."

"Enough, Noland," came another voice. Den had been so focused on attacking Noland that he hadn't even noticed another man had been at the scene this entire time. It was an older man in a fine suit who wore a scowl on his face—a perfect contrast to Noland's grin.

"Just let me have this, Tillman!" Noland responded. "This kid is a rare find! Sure, he didn't land a blow on me, but he's certainly not your ordinary adolescent!"

Tillman merely scoffed at Noland's remark.

"Wh... why?" Den finally spoke.

"He speaks! What a miracle!"

"Why... did you kill him?"

"Hmm... Good question, Weird Boy. Let's just say that there are some times when you just have to make sure a guy *really* gets the message. Otherwise he'll just keep doing it again and again. Hoagie needed some reminding. Simple as that."

Every second of Noland's rambling was another second that Den could recover and get his bearings. If he could just get him to keep talking for a little longer...

"What... are..." Den's voice started growing softer, his body getting woozy. He had no idea how much or how little blood he had lost from those strikes.

"What's that, Weird Boy? Either my hearing's going out or you're speaking awfully quiet!"

"What... are..." Now it had become a whisper.

Amused at the sight, Noland crouched, tilting his head towards Den. "Say that again, Weird Boy. I'm all ears."

Noland sat there, expecting a response. He was not expecting another headbutt.

On all fours, Den pushed his body straight at Noland and struck the killer's forehead with his own. Noland slumped back, allowing Den the precious seconds he needed to jump up and dash a few feet away from the killer. He thought of running away. Running as fast as he could from the situation.

Then he thought of Hugo. What if Noland followed him? What if he intentionally trailed behind until Den had returned to the WHS? Where Hugo, Grill, and Andolini awaited him. What if he went after Hugo in revenge? Den had started this fight because of his uncontrolled anger. He was not about to let his best friend and brother suffer because of him. He knew he had to finish what he'd started.

Den raised his fists to his chest, trying to imitate a combat stance he had seen in martial arts movies. But Den knew nothing of hand-to-hand combat. Up to this point, he'd seen no need for it. In Kelvin Forest, all the scarred boy had ever needed were his wits, speed, and fists. That had always been enough to grapple with the forest's most ferocious beasts. But beasts had patterns, natural contingencies to follow in order to survive the wilderness. Den had never fought a human being. He knew nothing of that innate chaos factor that had transcended humanity from the rest of the mammals. And he had certainly never fought a being like Noland before.

Noland rushed back to his feet, rubbing his temples and squinting in mild pain. Yet still he smiled, cackling as he did so. "I like you, Weird Boy! I like you a lot. Takes me back, really. Like a younger me. Thanks for giving me that sweet jolt of nostalgia!"

Den waited for Noland to make the next move, keeping light on his feet. Remembering the fight with Pork Roast. He took a deep breath in, slowly inhaling and exhaling. Hoping Noland wouldn't notice.

"You know people tend to expect some kind of acknowledgment after a thank you. '*You're welcome*,' for instance. '*It's fine*,' is pretty common. '*No big deal*.' That's my favorite! You get to gloat a little as you do it. Everyone wins!"

"Fine." Den couldn't hold back anymore. "You want a reply? How about this? You turn yourself in to the police, and I won't have to bash your skull into the ground."

"Woah ho ho! Look out, Tillman! We've got a bad boy with us. News flash for you, kid. One hit against three is still a losing score!"

"Yeah, well in some places sixty-six percent is passing. I just need to land one more hit." Den instantly began his next dash towards Noland, abandoning his initial plan of waiting for Noland to strike first. But this was different from his first emotional punch. Den's feet barely touched the ground, gliding along with each thrust of his feet. He may have not fought another person before, but the fights with both Pork Roast and the Crimson Maple had taught him the importance of footwork.

Noland followed suit and dashed at Den as well. Den didn't try to throw a punch as he moved closer, simply keeping his fists up, covering his head like a boxer. Noland's hands stayed to his sides, as if they were floating alongside him.

Macchianado made the first strike. Swiping his right hand straight up, aiming for Den's jaw. The scarred boy angled his right foot, turning his entire body to the right. Just barely missing Noland's attack. The failed strike kept Noland on his tiptoes for only a second. Just long enough for

Den to swerve his entire body around, right fist clenched. Allowing him to strike straight into Noland's back.

And for the first time since their clash began, Den heard Noland scream. It was only a light wail. Possibly brought on by the surprise of the attack, rather than the pain resulting from it. But it was still the first sign of weakness Den had witnessed.

Noland's back bent, the shock of the strike sending his body a few centimeters into the air.

This was it. Den swung his body to give his left fist the strongest strike possible. He would go for Noland's legs, then swerve around one more time and go after his head. Surely this would be enough. Surely he could stop this before any more damage could be done.

His left arm was about to connect with Noland's legs when he felt something strike straight into his shoulder. His arm immediately went limp. Den couldn't even process what exactly was going on. Had his body broken down again, like after his fall against the Crimson Maple? Had Dr. Voltaire's assessment been wrong and Den had actually gotten weaker? Then the pain settled in, and he knew exactly what had just happened.

Den had been shot.

V

Noland had managed to just barely land on his feet after his tiny flight of fancy. His back ached in pain. "Sonuvabitch, that hurts!" He began rubbing the affected spot, treating the newly-bruised area like a knot. "Gonna need to get on the heating blanket after this!" Noland turned back around to face Den. "Nice shot, Weird Bo—"

It was then that Noland saw Den's bleeding shoulder and his limp left arm. The scarred boy stood perfectly in place. Den's body had completely stopped.

Behind Den stood Tillman, gun in hand. The barrel still smoking. A silencer placed on its tip. Silencers were expensive, the kind of add-on

Noland didn't see the need for. But Tillman preferred it. While not truly silent, they were the perfect utility when striking a target that was distracted by the world around him. A target like Den.

"Tillman, what the hell? I was having fun!"

"We don't have any more time for your stupid games, Matches! We need to get this thing to the refrigeration units, stat!" Tillman held out the stuffed bear with his other hand. "Like you said, you've had your fun. Now it's time to get back to work!" Tillman blew out what smoke remained in his barrel, placing the gun back into his holster. "But I'm generous when I want to be." Tillman's face cocked into a smirk. "Bury his head so hard in the ground that not even his mother'll recognize him."

"Aw, shucks! You mean it, Till? Thanks, old man!"

Den was still standing in place. He had no idea why he had completely stopped. Why he wasn't running for his life. Perhaps the shock of the bullet had gone through his whole body, the pain far more intense than what he was expecting. Despite his scarred appearance, Den's skin had rarely ever been cut. Its toughened exterior required stronger needles whenever he needed an injection, like when Dr. Voltaire had given him his specialty concoctions. Yet now his skin had been perforated through means he had never experienced. This was a new weakness he had never explored, his body experiencing a pain he had never truly known.

Now there was nothing he could do but stand there. Waiting to see what Noland would do. How this crazed man would drive his face straight into the ground. Den did not know if he could even react to it, let alone get away from it. He was staring into the abyss, and it was staring right back.

Noland's smile returned to the sneer he'd had when Den first saw him. Those very same killer eyes. He cracked his knuckles and moved his fingers about.

"Well, Weird Boy, it's been fun! And I mean that wholeheartedly. If only we could do this again some time! But I guess that's life." Noland pulled his right arm back. His fist clenched, muscles tightening, preparing a punch headed straight for Den's face. "See ya!"

Noland threw his punch, only for a series of loud bursts to echo across the alleyway. Gun shots, each one louder than the last, blasted into the air. Ringing in Noland's ears and breaking his concentration, stopping his punch. He used his hands to cover his ears.

Noland turned around to see the cause. It was a tall, lanky man with long, flowing hair and guns in both hands. A rifle in his left, and a revolver in his right.

Grill had entered the scene.

"Another one?" Noland yelled as he put his arms back down. "Who might you be? From the looks of things, I'd say you were a bounty hunter. Well, I got news for you, buddy. I don't have a bounty on my—"

A single, powerful burst of air sliced straight by Noland's left ear, the sound so piercing it deafened him for a few seconds. Noland screamed once again.

"That shot was a blank," the bounty hunter declared. His voice was calm, yet threatening. He cocked his revolver once again, shifting its sights squarely on Noland's head. "The next one won't be."

"I'll kill you, you bastard!" Noland screamed. "You don't screw with me and—"

"Noland!" Tillman yelled. "Shut! Up!"

Noland silenced himself immediately. It was rare for Tillman to command him in such a manner. For as much as the old man scowled, he rarely yelled. And especially not like this.

"That's Jack Trent," Tillman informed him. "The Iron Sniper! And here I thought Baratzi was just busting his chain."

"So what?" Noland retorted. "What, is that some kind of wrestling name? Am I supposed to be scared he's got two guns on me? You think this is the first time I've looked straight into a barrel, old man?"

"We don't mess with him and he doesn't mess with us. That's an order! Now shut up."

Noland did as he was commanded. Very few people had the authority to stop his winding soliloquies. But when those few told him to stop, he knew he had no choice in the matter.

"Mr. Trent," Tillman began. "I do not know what your relation to this boy may be, but I would like to extend my sincerest apologizes to—"

"Get away from him... now!" Grill demanded, a sharp hiss in his voice.

Tillman quietly started moving backwards.

"You too!" the bounty hunter told Noland.

Noland turned to Tillman, who nodded his head in confirmation, causing the younger gangster to begin moving backwards as well. He was careful to move around Den when he came up to him.

Noland nearly tripped when he stepped on Hodgson's corpse. Barely a moment since his death and already his body seemed like it was starting to bloat. He couldn't help but quietly chuckle at the sight. To see a man he readily called fat inflate even more seemed like the most apropos comedy he could think of.

"Now get out of here," Grill commanded. "I don't want to see you again."

Noland and Tillman turned their backs, moving further into the alleyway until turning a corner, disappearing from sight.

The bounty hunter slowly lowered his arms, placing his revolver in his holster and the rifle to his side. Grill moved to Den, still standing, his shocked expression unaffected by Grill's appearance.

Grill patted Den's right shoulder. "Den?" he spoke softly. "Den, please say something."

"I... I can't move," Den said. "My arm's bleeding... my head's aching... and I can't move..."

"I heard sirens as I was coming. Police should be here soon. I'll flag them down to our location."

"No, don't go!" Den yelled. "Please, Grill, stay with me!" There was not a single teardrop in Den's eyes. But his expression said everything he couldn't. The shaking of his lips. The widening of his eyes. A boy who didn't want to be left out in the cold.

"Alright," Grill said. "They'll find their way. The shots I fired up should be enough." He examined Den's wound. "We'll need to get it properly checked, but the wound doesn't seem deep. Otherwise you'd be bleeding a lot more."

Den nodded in understanding. He didn't have the heart to say anything else. Nothing that wasn't necessary. Together, the two stood there, waiting on the police to arrive. Avoiding the empty gaze of the corpse right behind them.

"Hey, Grill," Den softly spoke.

"Yes?"

"Could you... Could you give me a hug?"

"A... hug?" It was a request Grill had not expected to hear. He had rarely been hugged. Not since his childhood when his mother held him so close in her arms. But that was long ago. A distance so vast no train or boat could travel there.

"Just a small one... Not on my wounded shoulder, of course... But just a light hug... Please?"

Grill knew he couldn't say no. Couldn't abandon his future apprentice in his time of need. The bounty hunter turned to Den's side and gave him a half hug on his good shoulder. It was stiff and awkward. Grill was unsure of the proper angle to stand in or how long the hug should last.

He had seen the chaos of war. Experienced the darkness of humanity. Seen wonders of the world many would never know. Yet this was a challenge that Grill was unsure he could face. But he stood beside Den anyway. Letting the moment pass by.

Den remained still. Yet even in this awkward embrace, he could feel Grill's care. He wished he could cry, but nothing would come out. He spoke a silent prayer for the dead man. The sirens of the police finally moved towards them. A requiem for the dead.

VI

Inspector Walton did not have time for this. Another murder in a city filled with them. A newly-minted cadaver to add to the list of poor souls who made one too many wrong moves in a place that was not kind to failure. But it was a simple enough case: battery, hemorrhaging. Forensics would come back with the same data they always did. At least there wasn't much to deal with. No big splatter from a gun. No puncture wounds from a knife. No property damage from an explosion. Maybe he could finish in time to get a decent meal and a few hours shut-eye. A mini-vacation, as far as he was concerned.

But there always something to spoil the mood. A fly in his metaphorical soup.

A weird-looking kid covered in scars stood only a few feet away, just beyond the tape keeping the crime scene untouched. Apparently he had witnessed the whole thing and got shot for it, his shoulder wrapped up in bandage. Poor little bastard. The kid probably had a rough life looking the way he did. And now whatever innocence he'd once had was shattered by his soiree into Hell. Walton examined the scarred boy's eyes. Faint and distant. The signs of someone witnessing a true act of evil for the first time.

Just behind the boy was a tall, lanky man, his hand on the boy's good shoulder. Clearly uncertain how to handle the situation, but standing by him nonetheless. A bounty hunter, according to his I.D., with a revolver holstered to his side and rifle on his back. Models the inspector wasn't familiar with, but perfectly legal. And in a city where guns could be sold at whatever price to whatever people, it was at least one less thing Walton had to deal with.

"So, Mr. Den, you're saying you can identify the culprit?" Inspector Walton asked the boy.

"Yes," Den said in a calm, stoic tenor. "He said his name was Noland Macchianado."

"Tanned skin? Lean build?"

"Yes, sir."

"I'm familiar with him. He owns a loan company on Kulver Street."

"What, does he kill his victims if they don't pay up?" Den screamed, his stoicism quickly rupturing into fury.

"Den," Grill spoke out, his voice low and demanding. "Not here. Not now."

It was all he needed to say for Den to once more lower his tone and speak quietly.

"I will admit I'm aware that his methods are not... orthodox," Walton said. "But that's beyond my means. To clarify, are you absolutely sure it was him?"

"Yes," Den replied, his stoicism returning just as swiftly as it had left. "He told me his name directly to my face."

"Would you be willing to take this to court?"

"Yes," Den repeated.

Walton looked at Den's face again. For as muted as his skin was, for as faint as his eyes appeared, there was conviction in his few words. A willingness to go to the end of the line. If only the world could be that simple.

Walton moved in closer to the two and began speaking as quietly as he could so that only Den and Grill could hear him. "Then I would recommend that you both move on from this situation as fast as you can."

"Huh?" Den spoke, voice crackling.

"Is that a threat?" Grill replied, his voice sharper, eyes tightened.

"It's a warning," the inspector replied. "And I don't mean from me or my boys. Macchianado is not to be messed with. He's too connected. You're digging your own graves by going any further."

"I'm a bounty hunter," Grill said in a sharp tone. "Threats to me are nothing more than a coward's words."

"Again, I'm *not* trying to threaten you, Mr. Trent. If anything, I'm trying to make sure I won't have to examine you the same way I've just examined Mr. Hodgson. You're not from here. You don't get it. Please, just leave this whole thing alone."

"Then what's the point of you?" Den asked, his voice still hushed. "This man just died and you're not gonna do anything about it?" Once again, Den's voice shot up. "Then what the hell is the point of having police who don't solve the damn crime?" Den's scream was loud enough to echo in the alley. Passersby hearing the scarred boy's cries of protest.

Grill said not a word, his hands still clutching Den's shoulder to make sure the scarred boy didn't do something he would later regret.

Inspector Walton sighed. "We can cuff him," he said. "There's probably enough evidence here to get him to trial. But someone will pay something or other and he'll be let go regardless. Best for everyone involved not to waste their time and expenses. The taxpayers in this city have enough bills to worry about as is."

Den remained silent, yet his gaze was the stuff of nightmares. A look of sheer hatred had entered his eyes, now focused squarely on the inspector. Walton had seen those eyes before, on the vengeful victims of a system that had utterly failed them. In his rookie days, that look pierced his very soul and made him want to throw up. Yet he had seen it enough times to know that the anger within those eyes was not for him. It was for the criminals responsible for such heinous acts and the so-called laws that let them go.

"Do you have anything else for us, Inspector?" Grill asked, his own voice now more hushed. His expression was still vicious.

"We'll call you if there's any more paperwork that needs filling out on your end," he replied. "Otherwise, you're free to go."

"Thank you," Grill replied halfheartedly. With his hand still firmly on Den's good shoulder, the bounty hunter moved the scarred boy away from the crime scene. The two walked away slowly until they disappeared into the crowd that had formed behind them.

Inspector Walton looked at his watch. Lucky for him, he would indeed have time for that nap. He took out a single cigarette from his coat pocket. One he had been keeping for a special occasion. He bummed a lighter from one of his subordinates and lit it, taking a puff as big as he had done in his rookie days. When chain smoking was his only oasis from this damnable city.

He stood at the crime scene until the paramedics took the body away—a task one of his subordinates could have done. Yet he always wanted to make sure the victim made it to the morgue. Because if nothing else, at least the departed's family and friends could get some kind of closure. However faint it may be.

As he waited for the paramedics to do their job, Walton looked into the crowd. The usual citizens and tourists curious about the crime scene that was at hand. The typical snoopers eyeing into others' business, curious about the details. Yet fickle enough to forget about them once their interest lapsed.

It was from the corner of his eye that Walton thought he saw a strange sight. A man in a full black suit. Eyes covered in sunglasses. A vacant expression as he looked at the scene. Walton rubbed his eyes again and the man was gone. A waking daydream, Walton assumed. A result of seeing too many midnight movies on nights when sleep eluded him. Just a figment of his imagination and nothing more.

Walton had reached the butt of his cigarette by the time the paramedics finished. He dropped it to the ground and stomped on it. In a nicer street, in a better part of town, he would have picked it up and thrown it in the trash. But in a place like this? A cigarette butt was appropriate enough decor.

There were those days when Walton wished he could do more. To be like those detectives he saw in the movies or in the papers. The ones who could solve any mystery and apprehend any criminal. But that was not him. And that was not Wayport. All he could do was hold back even worse evils and hope that one day Wayport's sins would be exposed for all the world to see. Then maybe, just maybe, he could sleep peacefully at night once more.

Wayport started as a town of unity. A communion in troubled times. When bloodshed was so close, yet brotherhood was even closer. A place that, at one point, could have been the flashpoint for civil war, instead became a sanctuary when such an event finally happened several generations later. Yet now, on these hollowed-out streets, where the rats mingle with the bugs, and the bugs mingle with the scum, I wonder if any sense of brotherhood still exists.

Perhaps it's there in the crime families that dominate the alleyways, away from the light that exposes all sins. Each of them making a vow to honor the family and the family alone. To forsake their fellow countrymen, and even God Almighty, for a cause that is selfish in nature, yet masquerades as honor and virtue.

I always wondered if Wayport's decay came because the people distanced themselves from God. Their spirits controlled by the flesh and the flesh controlled by desire. Yet perhaps it was always there. A foundational rot which has grown so large that it can no longer hide itself in ignorance.

But what do I know? I am no priest, nor any kind of parishioner. I cannot speak to the word of God. I'm not sure he even exists.

But one thing I do know: Wayport's sins will come to roost. It may not be now. But some day, and sooner than we might think. When just enough people, at just the right time, finally expose everything to the harsh light of day.

-Vincenzo Mortaddeli, *Dark Eyes: The Underworld of Terminal Cities*, 818 AU

CHAPTER 4
RESOLVE

I

Ten years ago...
February 12, 830 AU

Den had never been in a hospital before. Never walked those long, white hallways. Never breathed in the sanitized air. Never saw the suffering of those ailing from things he did not quite understand. A foreign place to a boy who looked so unearthly.

It was a time he had never comprehended. A time he wish had never come to pass. Fairchild, the one person he loved most in all the world, was dying. And there was nothing the scarred boy could do about it.

Fairchild was an old man. One who had seen over a century and a half's worth of days. The average life expectancy of a male Half-Maine.

In his life, he had seen the Old World make way for the New. A witness to the War for Ragnarok and all the chaos and renewal it had wrought. To see the final days when the age of the Mystics came to its end. When technological innovation manifested from the scars of both the fallen and those left behind.

All those moments in time leading to this. Lying in a hospital bed, barely conscious of the things going on around him. His pain suppressed by drugs flowing through his veins. Tubes sticking into places that could no longer function on their own. Den did not know what illness ailed his father figure. Nor could he make speculations. He had not been educated on such things. Not been told by the doctors. Such information had been shared exclusively with Madame Lake, at her request.

Though perhaps that was for the best. Knowledge would lead to estimations and generalities, taking a single situation and assuming the worst possible outcome. So for now, at least, Den's ignorance could be his safe haven.

In Fairchild's final days, Den sat beside him. Holding his hand. Wiping the sweat from his brow. Sitting with him in silent prayer. Hours upon hours passing by. And still, with the exception of an occasional trip to the bathroom, Den sat by his side. Eating meals by him. Reading him stories. The very same ones Fairchild had once told Den. Even as night approached, he would lay his head on Fairchild's bed and let sleep take hold of him. Each moment was another precious gift Den could still have with him. Not a single second wasted or taken for granted. Even in the sorrow that was, as well as the sorrow that was to come, there was peace.

"Den," came a familiar voice from just behind the scarred boy. It was Madame Lake, her voice eloquent and precise. Yet underneath that shell of refinement lay a voice that was warm. A crackle of fire in the cold. "It's time."

And for just a moment, Den did not realize what she had meant. Until the two words truly sank in and took over his entire being. It was time... Time to let go. Time to move on. Time to say goodbye.

Madame Lake placed her gloved hand on his shoulder. She did not know how to show affection. She had never hugged Den. Never rubbed his head or patted his back. She only did what she knew. Her hand felt so very cold. Like ice on bare flesh. But Den embraced her care nonetheless. Thankful to know that, at least in this moment, he would not be alone.

Den thought back to the last words Fairchild had told him. After he had collapsed in their quaint, little cottage. As the scarred boy, so very afraid, held him in his arms. "Don't... be afraid... of who you are..." Fairchild had whispered. "Embrace... everything... that you are... Because you... are... Den..." The scarred boy had still not grasped the meaning in Fairchild's words, but they were words he'd never forget.

Den peeked at Fairchild's monitors. And while he did not understand what the numbers meant, he knew that seeing them go down meant only one thing. So he gripped his father's hand one last time. He didn't know what to say or how to think. Instead, he simply said what came to mind:

"Good night."

For decades, Fairchild had been a thinker, a hermit, a gardener, and a poet. But in these last eight years, he had finally achieved his greatest accomplishment: fatherhood. And though Den was not his son by birth, Fairchild knew without hesitation that Den was his. A son he would always be proud of. A son that God Almighty had blessed him with. A son he would always love.

With his last ounce of strength, Fairchild smiled at Den and welcomed eternity with open arms.

II

For three days, Den had sat in his hotel room. Slumped in his bed. A sling keeping his shoulder secure. The bullet still lodged in.

His quick recovery had baffled local doctors. Though it was not because his injuries had healed quickly. Such examples were relatively common for people possessing similar abilities. Rather, it was the manner by which the healing process was taking place. The bullet's location had already changed since the initial examination. Tillman had shot him from behind and the force of the blast had pushed the bullet deep into Den's shoulder, just barely missing any vital points. Yet not only was the bullet wound recovering, it appeared as if Den's flesh was both healing around the bullet as well as slowly pushing the bullet out.

One doctor theorized that, given enough time, the bullet would naturally pop out from the front of the shoulder. As if his own flesh had created a natural, healing exit wound. Once again, the anomaly that was Den's existence had saved him.

Another doctor even asked Den if he could participate in a medical study, one which Grill immediately denied, going so far as to cite his lawyers, Benmire & Associates, in order to stop the man from inquiring any further.

It was early afternoon in Merryville Suites and Den had just finished a sandwich Hugo had bought him from their hotel's restaurant.

"Good?" Hugo asked as he took his empty plate.

"Yeah," Den replied with a nonchalant nod. "I guess I'm just spoiled by Karina's cooking."

"Sis certainly set a high standard, that's for sure. Need anything else?"

"Think I'll use the restroom."

"Need any help?"

"Hugo, come on."

"I just want to make sure your shoulder isn't damaged any further."

"I've got a literal bullet slowly popping out of me. I think I'll be fine."

"Fair enough. Enjoy your business."

Hugo sat on his bed. The past couple of days moved through his head. Den's fight and recovery. The state it had left him in. And the fact that same man who caused this, Noland Macchianado, was the very same one to whom Andolini owed so much money. That their paths with this man would cross in this way, at this time—it was enough for the young Historian to ponder Divine Providence. The very concept that had forged their trio back in Kelvin Forest.

Then Hugo thought back to Den. There had been other times when the scarred boy would take full advantage of his ailing days. The recent rests he had taken following both the Mungo-Boar and Crimson Maple incidents being such examples. Days when he could enjoy his time.

Sleeping, eating, reading books, and watching movies. Relaxing days after taxing days. Something Den was more than happy to enjoy.

Yet the scarred boy sought no such frivolities this time around. He would eat what Hugo or Grill would bring him. He would sleep his regular hours. If something was on television, he would mindlessly watch it. But he gained no pleasure in these moments. He felt no self-pity either. He simply seemed empty. Hollowed out.

Hugo stayed by Den's side the first two nights. Making sure he was rested and fed. He probably would have even helped Den to the bathroom, if need be. Though thankfully Den was perfectly capable of handling such necessities.

Hugo knew Den was grateful to be alive. Grateful to have his friends by his side during such a time. Yet that void still persisted. Hugo only hoped it wouldn't last long.

Den came out of the bathroom and moved back to his bed, sitting there as time passed on. He stared at their room's dresser, a bouquet of flowers sitting neatly atop it.

"Didn't expect them to still be so fresh," Hugo noted. "Should probably change the water in them soon."

"They're nice," Den commented. "I should tell Mr. Andolini thank you next time I see him. By the way, shouldn't you be at the WHS?"

"He told me to take as much time as I need. My job is basically just volunteer work anyway, and we already did the main cleanup. So it's fine. Besides, my *real* job right now is to be here with you."

"I'm fine, Hugo. I don't want to hold you up on your other duties."

"Trust me, Den. You're not."

"Fine. Think I'll take a nap, if that's okay with you."

"Sure. I'll just go in the living room." Hugo turned off the lights for Den and shut the bedroom door. He wasn't sure if Den would actually fall asleep or simply use it as an excuse to be alone.

A knock came from the front door not long afterwards. Hugo answered it immediately. It was Grill. While the bounty hunter was staying in a separate room, he had made sure to check up on Den every few hours. Sometimes to Den's knowledge, other times not.

Grill had not been as outwardly caring as Hugo, but he too made sure Den was doing well. He did not hound Den about studying. Nor did he try lecturing the scarred boy about whether or not he had made the right choice going down that alley. He simply tried letting Den be.

"How goes it?" Grill asked.

"Wish I could say there's improvement, but no. He's just... there."

"Shell shock can take a while to work out. Might even be full PTSD."

"From what you told me, it very well might be. And I know that feeling quite well... Should we call Karina? Or Dr. Voltaire?"

"Den was adamant about keeping this quiet."

"Yeah, but is that the best option? How do we know we're not just making it worse?"

"I'd say give it a little longer. After his shoulder's recovered. See if he comes out of his shell naturally. This *is* Den we're talking about."

"Yeah, and it probably won't take long for it to fully heal... Still, I can't help but remember what you told me. Before we faced the Crimson Maple. What determines the victims from the victors."

"Den is a victor, Hugo. You know that better than anyone else."

"You're right... I guess a part of me just wants to see him happy again. But then I remember how he was after seeing little Pennymill. This is him. To a tee."

"Everyone has their breaking point. Den included. How about this? If he's still not good after losing the sling, we'll call everyone. Until then, let's let him process this the way he wants. It's the least we could do."

"Alright." Hugo nodded. "But if Den recovers soon... I have a feeling he's going to try to go after Macchianado."

"I won't let him. In spite of what happened, Macchianado is not wanted. And if someone is not on the posters, they're not in the game. Bounty hunters are not police officers. Those posters are what separates us from the vigilantes."

"What about as an assistant? Finnegan called you about Forrest Packer. At the time, we didn't know that was connected with Bloodless Jack, but he called you anyway."

"Finnegan called me because of what we did during the Mungo-Boar incident. He thought it was connected. He ended up being correct. But from his perspective, the fact that it ultimately led to Jack was merely serendipitous. However, you are right. Assistance and advice is perfectly legal within my purview, wanted poster or not. All that said, I *still* need approval from on high. But with this one, it's clear they're not going to budge."

"That makes sense... I just hope we don't have to do something drastic to stop Den from doing something stupid."

"We'll cross that bridge if we get to it. It's all we can do."

Hugo nodded in agreement.

From the other side of the living room, in the cold, dark bedroom, Den listened in on his friends' conversation. Taking in their words. Appreciating their understanding and respect. Den didn't know what he was going to do next, but took solace in his friends and everything they had done for him.

Another knock came from the living room door. Housekeeping, Hugo thought. Grill, standing closest to the door, opened it.

"Hello, Jack," said the man who knocked.

"Jewels?" Grill replied, taken aback by the man's sudden appearance.

He was a man in an all-black suit. One appropriate enough for social gatherings, yet thin enough to allow for mobility in almost any situation. His cropped hair and stern expression gave him a sense of formality on all occasions. And his immediate familiarity with Grill meant there was far more to his coming here than whatever excuse he was about to give.

"Jewels Romero?" Grill questioned.

"The very same, Jack," Romero answered. "It's good to see you. May I come in?"

"I'm afraid now is not a good time. Maybe later."

"I'm aware of your current situation, Jack. And of Mr. Statferd and Mr. Den."

Grill's exasperated expression turned serious in less than a second. "And what do you know?" Grill maintained his upright stance, making a silent declaration to his colleague that he would not be let in unless otherwise permitted.

"I have my connections. You know this."

"I'm aware you sold your soul to the Feds. That's more than enough for me not to let you in."

Hugo remained silent in this exchange, watching for how Grill dealt with the situation. Den had already gotten up from his bed and slowly cracked open the bedroom door. Peeking out at the goings-on while staying just outside of Romero's field of vision.

"You have every right not to. But I came here for a specific reason. It concerns Noland Macchianado."

"I couldn't care less about that scumbag. He can rot."

"And that's precisely why I'm here. I can't say any details in public... but my people and I have a strategy to bring him down."

Somewhere deep inside Den, without even realizing it, a spark had just ignited.

"What you do with that bastard is none of my concern. I wish you luck in your endeavor, but that's all you'll get out of me. Good day."

"Please, Jack. If you'll just give me a few moments of your time, I think there's information that you and Mr. Den would be very interested in."

"I said good day!" Grill belted, not caring if any other guests heard his yell.

"Grill," Den said in a softened tone, making himself known. "Let him in... please."

Grill wanted to say something back. Try to convince Den not to listen. Yet he saw Den's expression. Blank and void. A boy just trying to find an answer in the mists of his own mind. Seeking closure where none could be found... Someone desperate to go down another path if it meant finding the answers he sought.

The bounty hunter shrugged and said not another word. He opened the door wider and let Jewels Romero inside.

III

Romero planted several candid photographs and mug shots down on the living room coffee table, as well as articles and declassified reports. These were faces and names that Den and Hugo had never heard nor seen before, with one clear and obvious exception: Noland Macchianado.

"What I have here," Romero started, "is Wayport's most wanted. 'Most wanted' in this case being a turn of phrase. None of these men are currently on the wanted posters. Their connections are too good and their culpability factor is negligible."

"Florenza," Hugo read from one of the reports. "Can't say I'm familiar."

"It's the family Macchianado is in," Romero explained. "Though don't be fooled by his air of superiority. He may not be small potatoes, but he's also not at the top of the food chain."

"The Florenzas were one of the crews that found their stride after Ragnarok," Grill stated. "During reconstruction."

"Established by a man named Giuseppe Florenza," Romero elaborated. "An immigrant from the Northern Continent. Not much is known about where he started or what he did during the war. But given his later track record, I'd say the sonuvabitch saw some pretty serious stuff. Murders, armed robbery, torture against any and all enemies. He'd eventually get the name Joey Flowers because he'd leave a single flower at the scene of his victims'... bodies. It cost him, though. He ended up pissing off every other major family. Eventually, someone managed to riddle him with bullets. Huge gang war erupted after that. Messy situation."

"Going by what Macchianado just did," Hugo stated, "it sounds like that particular manner of business is still alive and well. Minus the flower itself."

"Any descendants?" Grill asked.

"No one involved," Romero answered. "At this point, the name itself is an artifact. Joey had some kids, but none of them amounted to much. The ones that went into the family business ended up in the gutter. Just like the man himself. The ones that didn't managed to get away from everything entirely. Some grandchildren and great grandchildren are alive, but they're completely cut off. The only reason the name is still around is because of the fear it instills."And while his descendants may not have amounted to much, his followers sure as hell did. The old man who you saw with Macchianado being one such case: Thomas Tillman. He was a real estate tycoon in his youth. Made a large fortune. When he was middle-aged, he used that fortune to become a sports manager, focused primarily on power lifting. And through it all, he was ably serving the Florenzas. Always keeping himself just under the leadership position. Presumably so he wouldn't have to be burdened by it. There's been debate for years on how much of his fortune came from actual business dealings and what was from his other extra-legal operations."

"And what of Macchianado?" Grill asked.

"Less than you'd think," Romero answered. "He's only been active for about a decade. Official reports show that he lived a fairly normal life in Astier. Just doing odd jobs. No criminal record to speak of. Whatever caused him to join this life is unknown, but he's certainly made a name for himself since. Running an infamous loan company, Matches Personal Loans. One only the most neglected and desperate type of people go to."

Again, Hugo couldn't help but think of Andolini.

Romero talked on about other members of the family. Some deceased, others still very much active. "Which brings me to my main point. There are four families that run Wayport's underworld," Romero explained. "The Florenzas, the Takedas, the Javieros, and the Minchesters. Each of them with their own codes, ethics, disciplines, you name it."

"They basically control separate sections of Wayport," Grill added. "Akin to how the world is divided up into four continents."

"Yes and it's the politics between the families where our mission is concerned," Romero continued. "Specifically, between the Florenzas and the Takedas. Long story short, the Takedas have connections with other families on the Eastern Continent. It's where they descend from. They're looking to make a deal with the Florenzas in order to start a distribution ring in the East. And that's where Noland Macchianado comes in."

Agent Romero took out another series of documents, these ones medical in nature, specifically held back until he got to this point in his explanation.

"Compound ZX-78153," he began, "otherwise known by its street name: Atlas Tear Drop. It's an artificial enhancer meant to... well, enhance an Enhanced. Basically, it increases the strength of an Enhanced individual."

"Sorry," Den interrupted. "Enhanced? I'm confused."

"My apologies," Romero clarified. "It's the most common term within our ranks. I'm referring to people with abilities beyond normal human scope. There's many names for them. I believe around Harten you call them Miracles."

"The superhuman people, yeah," Den replied, finally understanding.

Even in a place like Harten, news had spread far and wide over the years about people who had defied human capabilities. Whether it be in strength, speed, knowledge, or power. These demigods among men had become celebrities and heroes in their own right, emerging from the War for Ragnarok and becoming icons the world over.

"Essentially, yes," Romero confirmed. "Sadly, there are quite a few who have remained in the shadows and use their abilities for lesser deeds. Mr. Macchianado being one such case. His strength and durability have made him a danger to his enemies. And his consistent consumption of Atlas Tear Drop has only made him stronger over time."

"It sounds too good to be true," Hugo stated. "The way you're describing it, I assume Atlas Tear Drop is outlawed. Why?"

"It's highly addicting and makes the user unstable," Romero explained. "Especially when angered or even just annoyed. To put it simply, Macchianado has become quite possibly the most infamous user of Atlas Tear Drop, and we have reason to believe he will be directly involved with this deal."

"And how do you figure that?" Grill asked. "Consumption and business are two very different things." The bounty hunter kept his sights on Romero. Analyzing his responses. Seeing how his former colleague reacted to whatever question was asked. Trying to spot the nonsense, if there was any.

"I cannot get into too much detail at this time, but suffice it to say, we have an insider."

"Florenzas? Takedas? Someone else?" Grill suggested.

"That's classified. Plus, the date of the deal itself hasn't been firmly established yet. Though we can surmise it will be within the next two weeks."

"Alright, Jewels, you've given us the lengthy explanations," Grill said, "but where are you going with all this? How does this involve us?"

"Simple, really," Romero answered. "As your confrontation showed, you and Den have the potential to be formidable foes against Macchianado and his cohorts."

"Really?" Den asked, his attention piqued.

"Yes," Romero confirmed. "It's clear by your abilities that you're an Enhanced yourself. As such, with a little training you might be able to fight Macchianado hand-to-hand. Your support would be a great help to us in this mission."

"Alright, Jewels, you can stop," Grill stated, cutting in before Den could say anything back. "If you're expecting Den and I to act as your pawns, you've got another thing coming. I gave up that life long ago and I'm not about to subject Den to it."

"With all due respect, Jack," Romero replied, "this isn't a draft, by any means. Nor is it a voluntary signup. This would strictly be a collaboration for this particular case only. You would not be bound by our rules, only your usual rules as a bounty hunter. And, of course, we will pay you both a handsome sum once it's done."

"Bounty hunters don't hunt people who aren't wanted. You know that, Jewels."

"Consider the people we're trying to capture preemptively-wanted."

"Typical government talk," Grill chided as he shook his head in disappointment. "And to think I thought you were gonna make something more of yourself."

"With all due respect, Jack, not all of us had the luxury of getting out when *you* did. Not everyone got to take as much from the honeypot."

Grill gripped his fist, but kept it to his side, knowing nothing good would come of it. "I think we're done here, Jewels."

"Very well." Romero picked up his photos and documents, placing them in the same envelopes he had taken them out of. "Thank you for your time. Nice to meet, Mr. Den and Mr. Statferd. The offer is still open, if you change your minds." Jewels promptly walked out without saying another word to Grill.

For several minutes, the trio sat in silence. Still processing all the information Agent Romero had just told them, expectations and realities going through their heads. Until Hugo finally spoke up.

"I met him once," Hugo stated. "Noland Macchianado." Den and Grill's eyes shifted to him, though both remained silent, expecting the young Historian to elaborate. "It was our first night here. Not long before you guys came to pick me up." For the next several minutes, Hugo recalled his sole encounter with the gangster. His loud mouth and strange eyes. The fact that Hugo had given a fake name. And of course, Andolini's debt.

"And why are you only telling us this now?" Grill asked.

"Mr. Andolini told me not to, and I wanted to respect his decision. Not to mention, I didn't want to bring up Macchianado if it was going to traumatize Den."

"Fair enough," Grill admitted.

"Hugo... I can handle it," Den stated.

"Den," Hugo replied, "I didn't mean to assume—"

"I know... And I understand. Thank you."

"This all seems to fit his modus operandi," Grill stated. "The man has a need for control. All while trying to appear friendly on the surface."

"Muscles bigger than his brain and a bad temper to boot," Hugo added.

"I wanna do it," Den stated, his words blunt.

"I refuse," Grill said. "Not without more details first."

Grill expected to hear a strong rebuttal from Den. Yet the scarred boy just sat there, weighing his next words.

"Grill, do you know why I don't read the news very much?" Den asked.

"I assumed you were like Hugo. Simply not having much interest in it."

"It's the opposite. I love this world. There is so much beauty and wonder. New discoveries being made. Lives being saved. Stories of the past coming to life in the present... Then I look at the papers. Famine, murder, war... Injustices behind every corruption... And there's barely a thing I can do about it. I pray to God and move on. Trying to ignore it all as best as I can. It was easy in Harten. Sure, there's corruption even there. But it's limited. Petty. The kind of thing I've made jokes about, usually at Winslow's expense... But this? To witness a murder and not even try to bring the bastard responsible to justice?"

"I understand, Den. But you can't be putting the weight of the world on your shoulders like that."

"I'm not!" Den screamed. His first eruption since the fight. "Just this. Only this. He made it my problem... And I'm gonna solve it... with or without you."

"You're not a bounty hunter," Grill stated. "You haven't even gotten your apprentice license yet."

"Then I'll get back into the books. I'll get my license. And if it means having to find someone else that'll do the job with me, then so be it!"

"Den, you can't be serious," Hugo interrupted.

"Not now, Hugo," Den yelled, only to calm down as soon as he uttered those words. "Please..."

Hugo gave Den his moment and remained silent.

Grill closed his eyes and rubbed his temples, a tension headache setting in. Yet he stayed calm in the moment, remembering all the times his subordinates would act up or use their emotions at a time when logic was the only answer to the puzzle. When someone needed to be the adult in the room. He sighed. "Alright. I'll help you. But I want to make this clear: If I find something that seems too out of place, I'm calling it off. And I would hope that you would join me in doing the same. I know Jewels, but that doesn't mean I trust him."

Den nodded. "I understand. Thank you, Grill."

"But if we're doing this," Grill added, "we're doing it by the book. If you don't have your license by then, it's off. And in between your studying, I'm gonna make sure you get the training you need. There will be no time for frivolities. At all times, you will either be studying, training, eating, sleeping, or resting. Is that understood?"

"Yes, sir!" Den belted. Once more trying to imitate the form of a soldier.

"Alright then. Hugo, do you have anything to add?"

"No," the young Historian said after a beat.

"We start tomorrow," Grill said. "Hugo, will you be good at the WHS? After what you told us, I'd imagine Mr. Andolini will appreciate your company."

"All good, Grill," Hugo replied. "Just don't push yourself too much, Den."

"It'll be fine, Hugo," Den said.

"Right," Hugo nodded.

"I have some materials I need to get ready," Grill stated. "Plus"—he groaned—"an apology to Jewels… I'll see you two in a bit." The bounty hunter took his leave.

"Think I'll actually take that nap now," Den said. "Might as well rest while I can."

"Hey, Den," Hugo said.

"Yeah, Hugo?"

"There's a spot pretty close to here that I heard the concierge say was really nice in the evening. Wanna go in a bit?"

Den smiled at the suggestion. A faint smile, but a smile all the same. "Sure. I'm already looking forward to it." Den closed the bedroom door and promptly took his nap.

Hugo sat in the living room. Again, the events of their meeting played in his head. As well as the danger of Noland Macchianado and the ones he was connected with. Den's mindset in all this and whether Grill's acceptance was out of pity or because he genuinely believed in what he was saying.

For just a single moment, Hugo wished he was back in Harten. Away from all this. His chest started to ache and his breathing grew heavy. His scars felt as if they were pulsating. *You're not a victim*, he told himself. *This is something beyond your control.* He took a single, deep breath, just as Karina had told him, and exhaled slowly and cautiously.

The aching stopped. His yearning for home ceased. Hugo Statferd was back in the present. *And you can do this.* The young Historian looked at the room clock. Waiting for the evening stroll to begin.

IV

Wayport sported much in the way of temporary lodgings. From five-star hotels in the center of downtown to the rat-infested motels at the edges of the city, it was nearly impossible not to find some place to stay, regardless of budget. Quality and safety, on the other hand, were a very different story. The edges were rough places only meant for those who had no other options. Where their own life was cheap, but the cost of living was at least cheaper. Where it wasn't uncommon for a brawl to break out every few days or a gunshot to ring out every few hours.

It was at one of these edges that Noland and Tillman had found themselves in. Normally, a man of Tillman's dress sense would not be caught dead in such a place, lest he risk being mugged and looted for all he was worth. For Noland, however, this was not the case. The reputation he had crafted was not one to be messed with, allowing them to walk the streets without a care in the world.

This would not always be the case, as on occasion new blood would come along, trying to make their first score. Thinking Noland and Tillman were nothing but easy prey. All it took from Noland were a few shots straight to the mugger's stomach or head to make the situation clear. And while no such ignorant fool had approached them on this day, Noland secretly wished someone had.

Breezy Days Motel may not have been rat-infested, but it was not exactly a hot spot for family vacations, either. Located at Dead End Boulevard, a strip consisting of almost exclusively low-quality motels, it sat with rest of its ilk as nothing more than a place to sleep for the night.

Noland and Tillman made their way to Room 206. Noland made three knocks at the door. Which in turn was responded to by four knocks from someone on the inside. Noland waited three seconds before giving an additional two knocks. This little code was enough for the door to be opened, allowing the two gangsters to make their way in. They were greeted by all-too-familiar faces.

The room was nothing special, sporting the most basic essentials any motel would have: a bed, a few chairs, a television, and a bathroom. But they were not here for the actual accommodations. It was a simple but effective meeting place without a discernible pattern. Merely one in a maze of other motels of its same ilk throughout the Terminal City. Always making it difficult for the police or other rival gangs to discover where they would go next. Security in obscurity.

"Let's get this party started!" Noland said as the door closed.

"Matches!" one of Noland's associates said in delight. He was a man known by the name Barrett the Fire. Tall and wide, with shoulders as long as a bench press and muscles thick enough to withstand needles. He had an open smile for all those who treated him well, and a bruised face and shattered ego for anyone who tried otherwise. He knew his orders, knew his targets, and knew what he liked. It had gotten him this far and that was all he cared about.

Barrett gave Noland a large hug, grabbed his head, and started rubbing his fist down in a noogie. Roughhousing was a common method of greeting for the two. "Tillman told me how you got into a shakeup the other day! Glad to see your boyish good looks weren't roughed up... if you had them!" The large man burst into laughter.

"Little bastard didn't stand a chance!" Noland replied, pushing himself off of Barrett. "Kid comes at me again, I'll make what he got last time seem like a day at the spa!"

"Rip him apart! Rip him apart!" came a sniveling voice from beside Barrett. This was Jacob the Smoke, small and lanky in stature with the smile of a horse and arms longer than his legs. A gremlin of a man whose love of all things flammable made him a menace to anyone who dared challenge his dominance or made fun of his small size and strange proportions. "Kill the boar! Roast the meat! Kill the boar! Roast the meat!" His habit of repeating certain phrases was not lost upon his colleagues.

"I'm afraid we're not here to discuss your fighting prowess, Macchianado," came a voice from just behind Barrett. This was Nicky "the Grass" Santino. Cold and calculating, while at the same time sharp-eyed and quick-witted. A man of average build accentuated by his appealing dress sense. Not unlike Tillman, though still more casual in appearance. His classically handsome looks made him popular with the ladies and a friend of the men. Calm and collected, his strong manner of speaking beguiled many a client. While still hiding a far darker persona, willing to cut and cross anyone, as long it met the family's needs. "We have far more pressing business to attend to."

"Yes, sir," Noland spat out, immediately going quiet and straightening his back.

Nicky the Grass, Jacob the Smoke, and Barrett the Fire. Reputations which spoke for themselves. Body counts their competition dared not speak of and minor fortunes that would make even members of the aristocracy jealous. Along with Tillman, these were the four men who dominated the Florenza family. The men Noland looked up to more than anyone else... and the very men whose spots at the top he wanted to usurp.

"Before we begin our main topic, there's something the boss wanted me to inform the rest of you," Nicky said. "There's rumors that Sziliard is in negotiations with Dusk Caravan."

"Dusk Caravan?" Noland questioned. "The mercenary group?"

"The very same. They've been ramping up their activities the past few years. And I can only guess that Sziliard is doing this in order to make a statement."

"They're nothing but kids," Tillman huffed. "Kids with guns and dumb luck. They think because they're Enhanced, they're invincible."

"True enough," Nicky agreed. "Though I'd say Sziliard's doing this to deliver a message: 'Don't screw with me. Or else you'll have to deal with them.'"

"If Sziliard is so ignorant to think some for-hire thugs are enough to maintain his reputation, he'll have a nasty wake-up coming." Tillman spoke to Nicky as a familiar, not intimidated by the man's rank as Noland was. He had no qualms giving his opinion, and Nicky had no say in the old man's judgments. Nicky may have been second-in-command, but in moments like these, they were essentially equals.

"He's got the liquid to keep them employed for some time to come," Nicky added. "Still, the boss isn't worried about it. Just something to keep in the back of our minds."

Nicky snapped his fingers, his usual manner of changing the subject. "With that said, we all really know why we're here. Hodgson is dead..."

There was no warning with what came next. Not an order from Nicky. Not a remark by Tillman. Only the blunt force of Barrett's fists as they slammed straight into Noland's face. The gangster hadn't had time to react as his large colleague began pounding different parts of his body. Each shot was precise and deliberate, not meant to cause lasting damage, but certainly effective enough to get the message across. Barrett felt a sense of delight in his actions. Noland being an Enhanced meant the large man could inflict more pain on Noland without the risk of causing serious harm.

"The boss had us gather to discuss the changes that are being made to amend the situation," Nicky continued, unflinching at the assault on Noland.

"Have the Minchesters or Javieros said anything?" Tillman asked, also unmoved.

"Not a word. Nor would it be in our best interests for them to know. This has, and will remain, strictly between us and the Takedas."

"No third parties either?"

"The Takedas wouldn't accept them even if there was. Fact is this agreement was made on the backs of two men. And with Hodgson dead, we had no choice but to bring Baratzi back into the fold."

"Baratzi?!" Noland exclaimed just as Barrett had finished his beating. His eyes were swollen, outer skin bruised all around. Things he'd be able to recover from quickly, but wounds that hurt nonetheless.

"Hodgson may have been the one to cultivate the deal," Nicky explained. "But it was Baratzi who started it. If anyone can keep us in good graces, it's him."

"And why the Hell should he be trusted? It's Baratzi, for God's sake!"

Calmly, coldly, Nicky walked up to Noland. It didn't matter that he stood several inches shorter or that he did not possess Noland's physical strength—Nicky was the one with power. His stance and composure were all he needed to make the room his. And there was nothing Noland could say or do that would change his mind.

"Baratzi wasn't supposed to come back," Nicky explained. "We paid him his finder's fee and let him be on his way... until someone just happened to kill Hodgson."

"He got me with a Buster Bullet!" Noland screamed, blood spitting out with each word.

With many Enhanced, particularly those with increased strength and durability, it was always a question whether normal bullets could work against them. Some untrained or newly discovered Enhanced could be downed with a single shot. Others bounced the bullets off or withstood the shots with only a scratch on them.

Buster Bullets were the ultimate answer. Far stronger and heavier in design, the power of their shots was one of the only ways to down an Enhanced through normal firearm use. However, the materials to make them were scarce, resulting in individual bullets being sold separately, and at high prices.

Nicky listened to Noland rattle on until, in one smooth motion, he sent his knee straight into Noland's crotch. The pain so unbearable that Noland sank to the ground.

"A broken wrist. A sprained ankle. Hell, even a bullet in his shin. Lotta warnings you coulda given him to make your message clear while still keeping him alive." Nicky hunched down, looking Noland straight in the eyes. "Your reckless decision-making almost compromised this entire deal. If you don't want to end up like Hodgson, then I'd suggest you follow every word I say from here on out. No. Lip."

Noland sucked in his lips, trying his best to keep his mouth shut as he writhed on the floor.

"Now," Nicky began as he straightened, "despite the loss of Hodgson, we're still in good standing with our other suppliers. Losing Hodgson's supply of Paradicium won't affect our bottom line much. He certainly had the purest source, but his methods were far too minimal to get much in the long run.

"Still, he would've been the best person to give a full rundown of Atlas Tear Drop's effects. So instead, the Takedas have asked for a live test subject. They want to see the effects of the compound, how quickly it can change the system, and what that means in the long term. As such, Matches, you are to stop taking Compound ZX-78153. Effective immediately."

"What?" Noland said as he slowly got back up, his legs still wobbly from the kick.

"We need someone whose body is used to it. But at the same time, the presentation will have no impact if you're just taking it like any other day. As such, you'll be going sober until the day of the meeting."

"Sir, with all due respect, that just isn't gonna work. I could actually die!"

"I am quite aware of that. As are the Takedas. You'll be given other stimulants in the meantime. Just enough to keep you going, but not enough to affect the meeting's performance."

"Sir, please. If there's anything else I can do... I could start cutting back, lower the dosages."

"There's not enough time. Meeting's in ten days. You'll live."

Noland wanted to say more. Scream out his refusal to do something so painful and, in fact, degrading. But what would that get him? Another beating? Maybe even a Buster Bullet to the head? Noland had sold his soul to the family long ago. And if it meant becoming their guinea pig, he had no choice but to obey.

"Yes, sir..." Noland finally replied, his tone calm, without any smart comments.

"Very good," Nicky said. "And don't worry, we don't expect anything else out of you until then. Tillman and Barrett can do whatever needs to get done in the meantime. You're lucky, really. Not many people are punished with time off."

"Rat in his maze! Spinning for days!" Jacob finally said, rubbing his hands together and cackling at Noland's misfortune. "Rat in his maze! Spinning for days!"

"Alright, everyone, that's it," Nicky said. "Reminder that only Noland and I will be attending. The three of you stay low that day, in case something happens. You have a week to decide which of your men will be accompanying us. Until then..." Nicky made one final snap. The meeting had officially concluded. Everyone began saying their goodbyes in a mannerly fashion. Noland's blood was already staining the carpet.

"See ya, Matches," Barrett said with the same smile as when he had first greeted him. "No hard feelings, yeah? Just business."

“Yeah...” Noland replied in a daze. “Just business.”

Noland and Tillman’s walk back was just as awkward. Not a single word passed between them. The sinking silence of both men ready to pop off at what the other was about to say.

“I hope you’re proud of yourself,” Tillman finally said.

“I’m getting punished,” Noland replied. “Doesn’t exactly fill me with pride.”

“You were supposed to finish the deal and leave.”

“*Finish the deal*?” Noland moved close to Tillman, his bruised eyes locking with his elder’s. “Do you know how much damage a Buster Bullet can cause? It’s a miracle the idiot had such bad aim as it was! I could have been paralyzed! And you know, for all the hounding and beating I just got, I seem to remember you not saying a single word as I was making Hodgson my new punching bag. In fact, I could have sworn I heard a few giggles and guffaws coming outta your shriveled neck.”

Tillman remained silent as Noland went on his rant. Staring him down. Never breaking eye contact. Knowing it was a move meant to intimidate, and he had no intention of playing the victim.

Tillman had known the addict long enough to know when adding flames to the fire did nothing but burn everyone around him. The only way to combat his anger was through silence. Silence and a stern stare to remind him of the pecking order. An order that no amount of violence would change. At least, not violence alone.

“Are you done?” the old man finally said, a low rumbling in his voice.

Noland broke eye contact first, realizing his own folly. Anger still flowed in his veins. But this was the reality of the pecking order: the flies were caught and the spiders roamed free. And for as lofty as Noland’s ambitions were, at a time like this he knew he was nothing more than a fly.

Their uncomfortable silence was soon broken up by the cocking of a gun. A thug wearing sweats came out of a nearby alley, headed towards them. “Alright, nobody move,” he demanded. “Hands where I can see them!”

Noland and Tillman stopped in their tracks, but had no intention of raising their hands. For as dangerous as the thug tried to act, his hands were shaking and his aim was crooked. Tillman scoffed. He knew fresh blood when he saw it. Some young punk thinking a cheap gun and a few harsh words were enough to make a name for himself.

Noland, on the other hand, was brimming. A smile came over him the very moment he and the thug made eye contact.

"Did you hear me, geezers? Hands where I can—"

Noland bashed the thug in the stomach before he even saw what was coming. The gangster dragged the thug into the alleyway and proceeded to beat him senseless. "Gee, thanks, buddy!" Noland told the hooded man as he continued his beating. "I really, really, *really* needed to blow off some steam just now. Thanks for being a friend!"

Tillman didn't move from his spot. He had seen this same scene a dozen times. Another punk getting what was coming to him in a city that wouldn't have cared either way. Tillman didn't need to imagine the look on Noland's face right now. It had already been embedded into his mind. That same, sick smile every time he got to lash out.

Eventually, the beating stopped. The hooded man lay in a pool of his blood. Beaten, broken, but alive. "I feel like a new man," Noland declared. "Come on, Till, let's go downtown! Let bygones be bygones! Have some fun before I start convulsing!"

"No alcohol," Tillman stated. "Won't mix well with the stimulants."

"Who said anything about alcohol? I'm talking about ladies!"

Tillman chuckled. "Ah, what the Hell!"

The two men laughed as they made their way downtown. Tillman knew the agony his subordinate was about to go through. It seemed appropriate to give him a little slice of Heaven before he went to Hell.

V

Dusk waned on the horizon as the tiring day made way for the burgeoning night. Just outside Merryville Suites, Den sat on a bench which overlooked the setting sun. The Lang-Meyer Courthouse stood in the foreground, its towering presence appearing like the sun's guardian, making sure the night could be ushered in calmly and safely. It was a beautiful spot in a serene part of the city. Unburdened by politics and crime. A calm place where Den could take in the fresh air and cool atmosphere.

Hugo sat beside him, also enjoying the calm surroundings. Grateful to have found a spot where they could relax outside of their room. "I'm not sure about this," Hugo stated. "How do you know Agent Romero isn't trying to manipulate you? Grill clearly thinks so too."

"He probably is," Den admitted. "I can't deny that. But I also can't deny my feelings on the matter. Truth is, there's nothing I want more right now than to bash Macchianado's face in. And if it means I have to work with the Feds? So be it."

"But is it even worth it? These guys probably already have a strategy to catch him. Justice will come to Macchianado regardless. Why bother getting yourself involved?"

"I'm a bounty hunter... Or at least I will be soon. If I can't deal with something like this, then what good does that make me?"

"A bounty hunter stays objective. At least the good ones do. Even when Grill was hunting Bloodless Jack, he maintained his professionalism throughout. He only even told us about his past with the guy because he came to trust us. But this? Den, I know you. You're taking this personal. That's not going to help you."

"I can separate the two. When on the mission, I'll stay focused. It's like Agent Romero said, I've got the strength to beat him. I just need a little training. Please, Hugo, give me this chance."

Hugo let Den's plea set in. He knew his brother didn't need his permission. Yet the scarred boy sought it out anyway. Knowing that he could not follow through unless he knew Hugo was okay with it. Hugo knew he held the strings to Den's involvement. But at the same time, did he have the right to keep Den away from this? To keep him from facing his trauma? The Crimson Maple had changed Hugo's perspective on many things. But those outlooks had yet to cement into a solid foundation, at least not entirely. It was a guessing game. And Hugo only had his own knowledge and faith to go on.

"So why this one?" Hugo finally asked.

"Because I could have stopped it." Den didn't hesitate in his response.

"I understand that. It's what you told Grill. But crimes and other obstructions of justice happen all the time. Especially in a city like this. Fact is, there's a million things we could do to save someone else. So why him? Considering how you found him, getting beaten by Macchianado in an alleyway like that, I doubt he was an upstanding guy. Probably involved with him in some way."

"Not the point. It was still a life. A life cut short."

And all at once, Hugo's mind cleared. The answer was obvious now. He just needed Den to admit it.

"That was the reason you went in... But that's not the reason you want to go back, is it?"

Now Den was the one who sat silent. Trying to articulate the words. "I'm not a victim, Hugo."

"I know you're not. You never have been. But you don't need to risk your life fighting this guy, either. There's safer methods. Better methods. You can move past this—"

"No I won't, Hugo... not unless I face this head-on. This is my Crimson Maple..." Those very words struck a chord, and Hugo couldn't deny what Den was saying. "Please, buddy, let me have this."

Hugo took in a deep breath, composing himself. A debate raged inside him. Questioning whether his next response would give Den the freedom he deserved... or would enable him to go down the path of revenge. But

Den was his own person. A young man trapped in the body of a scarred boy. Those choices were his to make.

"Alright." Hugo nodded. "Whatever happens, you have my support."

"Thank you, Hugo." Den raised his right hand and tapped his temple. Hugo did the same with his left hand. The very sign they would always give one another to ensure that they were on the same page. That they trusted each other's judgment. Their silent vow.

"Everything good?" Grill asked as he came towards them. Unbeknownst to either, Grill had been standing nearby for the past few minutes. Not wanting to intrude on their heart-to-heart. Waiting for the right opportunity to make himself known. This seemed like the most opportune time. "Sorry. Hope I'm not interrupting."

"It's fine," Hugo stated.

"We're good," Den replied. "Is there something you wanted to add, Grill?"

"Not so much add," the bounty hunter replied. "More so something I wanted to do. Den, would you please get up and come towards me?" The scarred boy rose from the bench and walked towards Grill. "Stop right about there." There was a gap between the two roughly the distance of a grown man lying on the floor.

"What is it? I'm a little confused."

"Get yourself into a defensive position. Whatever you think works." Grill followed his own orders, slightly crouching and raising his arms.

Den followed suit, taking a stance akin to what he had used against Noland. "We sparring? Is that safe with my sling?"

"Yes and yes," Grill replied. "I want to get an understanding of your combat capabilities. But don't worry, I won't target your left shoulder. Think of it as training for times you may end up incapacitated."

"You two sure this is okay?" Hugo asked.

"Yeah, I don't want to accidentally break your arm or something, Grill," Den added.

"That won't be a problem," Grill stated. "You're far from the first Enhanced I've dealt with. Both with and without weapons."

Grill closed his eyes and breathed in. All tension in his body ceased. He opened his eyes back up, only for them to appear strained and pulsating. Den had seen this from Grill before. This enhancement of his abilities. "Now, come at me," Grill said.

"Alright, then," Den replied. "You asked for it!" Den charged straight at Grill, swinging his right arm as soon as he got into range.

Grill dodged the strike simply by moving to the left, his reactions appearing almost innate. The bounty hunter made no move to strike back, instead giving Den an opportunity to try again.

Den moved his legs around, getting even closer to Grill. This time going for an uppercut. Yet once again, Grill dodged the attack, shifting straight back without a second's notice. Again, he did not hit back.

With each missed strike, Den grew more annoyed. He even tried kicking and headbutting. Yet without fail, Grill managed to avoid Den's attacks. His movements appeared fluid, as if they were second nature to him.

"Alright, that's enough for now," Grill declared. The bounty hunter's composure had remained steady. Instead it was Den who was huffing and puffing from the bout.

"I don't get it," Den said as he took in a breath. "I'm not supposed to get winded this easily... I guess I'm still recovering."

"That's only partially the reason," Grill explained, his eyes already back to normal. "In reality, it's because you were overexerting yourself harder out of sheer frustration. You're not used to this type of combat, hence you kept pushing your body further with each strike."

"And yet you never fought back. Why?"

"Unnecessary waste of energy. Plus, as you said, I don't have that kind of strength. Not worth spraining or breaking my limbs."

"Your eyes," Hugo stated. "I thought I saw something similar during the Crimson Maple fight, when you threw me the dynamite. Den told me you've gone into a trance or something like that before."

"Yeah," Den said. "Grill even used it to destroy the Maple's main vine. But it wasn't the same. Blood didn't drip from his nose this time. And I think his veins are supposed bulge out too."

"It's a technique I've spent many years honing," Grill explained. "Just as natural a part of me as my arms and legs. At its peak, I can shoot a target from large distances, though at the cost of placing great strain to my system.

"What you just witnessed is a toned down variant. Good for training exercises or when I need to escape an enemy, but not as helpful when I need to strike back or when I'm surrounded. Hence why I never used it against the Crimson Maple's puppets."

"Grill," Hugo asked, "you're an Enhanced, aren't you?"

Grill chuckled. "Yes. That I am."

"And you're just now telling us this?" Den questioned.

"To be honest, I thought you already knew. Given what you've seen."

"I mean, yeah, I saw it," Den replied. "But I thought that was just stuff you learned in the military or while bounty hunting."

"No normal human can do that," Hugo stated. "Though since I haven't seen it in full until now, I thought your shot at the Maple was just lucky. Or that Den was just being hyperbolic."

"We fought a giant plant monster last month and you're putting logic into this?" Den asked.

"The existence of the extraordinary does not mean someone becomes a believer in the unusual. Like how I don't blindly follow everything Al or Heinrich spout out."

"Fair point," Den replied. "Although even you've admitted that they're not necessarily wrong in their assumptions."

"They make great arguments," Hugo admitted. "What can I say?"

"My point being," Grill said, getting back on topic, "the fact is, Den, you're putting too much force into your blows. Getting frustrated too easily when you're not able to hit your target."

Grill walked up to Den, placing his hand on the scarred boy's left arm. He gently moved it around as if it was floating. "You need to refocus your concentration. Flow like water. Let your opponent be the one to lose steam first." In a split second, Grill thrust his fist into Den's face, stopping just shy of actually touching him. There had been no warning. Den's eyes widened now, staring straight at Grill's knuckles. "So that way you can strike without them even knowing." Grill put his fist back down. "Sorry for the surprise. But in the heat of battle, you're not gonna have that luxury."

Den's heart raced. Not from the fear of the punch, but from the exhilaration of the moment. Grill's words soaked into him. Determination flared in his eyes. His figure. He stood taller than a boy of his stature could. For the first time since the alley fight, Den felt alive once more. The emptiness inside gone. His fiery spirit once more lit aflame.

"Alright, then," Den replied. The scarred boy unhooked the sling from its base and plopped it on the ground. His arm was now free from its constraints. "Ready for another round?"

"Alright," Grill agreed. "If you think you're up for it."

"Den, are you sure about to this?" Hugo asked in a concerned tone.

"Oh yeah!" Den exclaimed. "I'll be fine, as long as I keep my shoulder from getting any direct hits."

"I'm not sure if that's how that works," Hugo admitted. "But I guess I can't stop you at this point."

The bounty hunter and his would-be apprentice positioned themselves once more. Grill activated his Enhanced abilities just as Den started his next wave of strikes. This time with both hands ready to go. "Let's go, Grill! You and me. Man-to-man!"

Hugo watched on as they sparred, proud of his brother, yet concerned all the same. Wondering if he had made the right call. If this decision would end in something far worse.

Then the young Historian thought back to Karina and Rindi. Back to Milly's when they were trying the new soups. A convenient excuse to get Rindi to let out her own worries and anxieties. Hugo remembered what his sister told her: that she would not worry. Be concerned, yes, but she knew that what was happening was what had to be done.

And then he remembered those last words she spoke soon after Rindi had left. "*Whatever comes after*," she had told him, "*it'll be yours for the taking*."

It was in that moment, sitting on that bench in Wayport, that Hugo made another silent vow. Not to Den nor Grill, but to himself. To embrace these moments. To learn from them. To be steadfast. To embrace the future.

The burgeoning night had finally settled in.

At a time of great traumatic stress, when the body and mind have been crushed, and the soul becomes hollow, a spark ignites an impossibility. Or rather, an improbability. For a select few, a single physical trait within their bodies is heightened to levels that many would call superhuman. A boxer breaking stones with his bare fists. A runner outracing the newest motor vehicle. A singer who can shatter glass with a single note. Or a sniper who can hit a target further than the human eye can see.

Hidden in plain sight. Manipulated by gangs, governments, and organizations the world over. The few who are known with these abilities are as revered as they are feared. They go by many names: the Gifted, the Blessed, the Privileged, the Enhanced, the Cursed, and the Burdened. But for my part, I prefer to call them what they truly are: the Miracles.

—Lockheed Burrelles, *The Blessed and The Cursed: Being a Miracle in the Modern World*, 797 AU

Chapter 5
Mac

I

Den could almost cry. After weeks of studying, he held in his hands the results of the very exam he had plunged his heart and soul into. 78%. Not perfect by any means… but he passed. Far above his very own 66% curve.

"Yeaaaaaaaaaahhhhhhhh!" Den screamed at the top of his lungs, his belting tenor echoing through the Bounty Hunter Association. Everyone turned their attention to the crazed, scarred boy. Only to just as quickly turn back. Certainly not the first time people of their profession had witnessed howls of victory. "I'm a professional bounty hunter!"

"Apprentice," Grill corrected. Still, he couldn't help but smile at his newly-minted student's achievement. "But a damn good one. Congratulations, Den."

"Thanks, Grill… Or should I say Master Grill? Mister Grill? Grill-sensei?"

"Just Grill is fine, Den. No need to overcomplicate."

"Yes, sir, Just Grill! Where are we off to next, Just Grill? I can't wait to show this to Hugo, Just Grill!"

"See, now you're pushing it."

"Whatever you say, Jack!"

"Too informal."

"Ya did good, kid," Hilda complimented. "Can't say I expected ya to pass so quickly. Takes some people three to six months to get all the material memorized. And you did it in... what?"

"Twenty-five days, ma'am!"

"And a damn fine job at that. So, you boys got anything special planned to celebrate?"

"Grill already bought me a cake after the test yesterday," Den replied.

"Which you immediately scarfed down," Grill retorted.

"A wise man once said to enjoy the moments you're given. He never said anything about how long the moment is meant to last. Five bites was more than enough for me! Besides, think of it as good training. You got to see the ferocity of my molars!"

"So you already had your little celebration," Hilda noted. "Does that mean you're gonna start on Phase Two?"

"Phase Two?" Den questioned. "Was the cake Phase One?"

"Phase Two is an unofficial term that's used for newly-minted bounty hunters," Grill explained. "To put it simply, Phase One is the paperwork and exams. Phase Two... is the capture of your first bounty."

"I already know who my first bounty is gonna be," Den declared.

"And who might that be?" Hilda asked.

"Under construction," Grill replied. It was a common response bounty hunters would give one another when questioned about their next target while still trying to maintain a certain level of secrecy.

"Lock and key," Hilda replied. The usual response when told such a phrase.

"But that's also not what we'll be doing today," Grill said. "I've got another task for my new apprentice. Think of it as Phase One-And-A-Half."

"Okay, now I'm completely lost," Den said.

"I'll explain on the way. Now if you'll excuse us, Hilda, we'll be taking our leave."

"Good luck, you two!" Hilda said. "Whoever your target is, they're gonna need it more than you!"

Den and Grill kept quiet for a time after they left the BHA. Not wanting to accidentally give out information until they had gotten a far-enough distance from prying ears.

"So spill it, what do you have up your sleeve?" Den asked.

"Nothing special," Grill replied with a brazen grin. "You're set on Macchianado being your first target, so we're not going to be bounty hunting on a literal level today. But we are most certainly on the hunt."

"Still not fully getting where you're coming from."

"To put it simply, there's a contest I want you to win. If you do, you'll join me on the mission. Simple as that."

"What kind of contest? If it's cooking, I never really learned Karina's skills. If it's a beauty contest, well, as much as I think myself a handsome devil, I doubt any judges would believe that."

"Contest of strength."

"Seriously? Am I gonna get to beat someone up?"

"That may be the result. Though don't assume it going in."

Den popped his knuckles and made the same brazen grin Grill was sporting. He hopped up and down, his new shoes fully broken in. "My kinda contest!"

II

The only people who could ever call the Birrias district of Wayport "pleasant" were the extremely elderly, whose senses had faded over time, or the unlucky sort of individual whose eyes, ears, and nose had been gouged out and ripped apart. Either through some horrific accident or during a particularly crude interaction. Interactions which were more than commonplace on Birrias's sordid streets.

It was not a spot advertised in the many tourist pamphlets that covered the train station and hotels. Nor did it tend to be featured in many of the cosmopolitan articles focusing on Wayport, unless the article happened to be situated right next to the obituaries. It was a place only for the scum, the bullies, and the brave. And rarely did a person walking these streets only fill one of those criteria.

Den hated places like these. For all his talk, he was an innocent soul, preferring a quiet street on a cool autumn morning over the many schemes and scams Birrias had to offer.

Grill, on the other hand, found himself more at home than he cared to admit. During his years of service, districts like these were not an uncommon place for him and his fellow soldiers to frequent for rough fights and even rougher play. The few times he had been to Wayport before, Grill always found himself walking to Birrias once again. At this point, it had become a habit. So what better way to wet Den's feet than straight into the thick of it? A trial by fire.

There were too many dive bars to count in these parts. The look, feel, and even name of each place all melded together into a single, long hall of anti-sobriety and poor decision-making. But there was one particular place Grill had his eyes on: The Ferret's Nest Egg.

Far from Brockson's Grotto, which at least maintained an outer shell of class in its design and presentation, The Ferret's Nest Egg was far sleazier and a lot more lively. Loud, blistering music wracked the ears of all those who were still blessed with an auditory system. Rough men, bodies covered in tattoos and scars, were the most common type of customers. Women of all sorts hung to their arms. Smoke filled the air. Cigars and cigarettes were lighted and snuffed out all around. And the drinks consisted of only two kinds: the ones that got you drunk and the ones that got you *really* drunk. The customers were gruff and the service was gruffer. It was a place reserved only for those who could stand amongst the rabble of Wayport's criminal underunderworld.

"I'm not even sure I'm supposed to be in here right now," Den said. "Am I even old enough?"

"You're eighteen," Grill replied. "That's old enough in these parts. Though I'd advise not getting anything to drink."

"Fine by me. I can't stand alcohol."

Grill took his time to look around the bar, knowing his target would inevitably be there. And sure enough, he was. "There's our guy," Grill told Den. "I'll do the talking. You'll know what to do when it's time."

"You sure about that?"

"I have faith in you."

The master and apprentice made their way to the man Grill was looking for. "Brisket!" Grill belted out. Sure enough, the man turned around, locking eyes with Grill.

"Trent?" the man replied in a disgusted tone. "What the hell are you doing here?" Chuck "Brisket" Brisken was a large man and a fellow bounty hunter. A behemoth whose was as tall as he was wide, with a torso the shape of a box, long, flowing hair covering his wrinkled head, and a pair of large sunglasses obscuring his constantly swollen eyes. A massive man with a massive appetite and a poor attitude.

"I've got a favor for you, Brisket."

"I ain't doing nothing for you, Trent! I heard what you did to Baratzi. You trying to scare my biggest info source?"

"I'm afraid that's a completely separate incident. Unconnected entirely. In actuality, it's about helping out my apprentice here."

Brisket gave Den a once-over, eyeing him in the same manner as Hilda had. "Kid got a skin condition or something?"

"That's an unrelated matter. To put it simply, I'd like you to arm wrestle him."

"What, you want me to play with him? Want me to babysit the little bastard too? Play Uncie Brisket for a few hours so Papa Jackie can go play? Bahahaha!" The crowd around Brisket erupted in a sea of laughter. All eyes now focused on Grill and Den.

Den maintained his stoic position, back straight and eyes forward. Not showing any weakness to the potential dangers around him. Trusting Grill's process.

Grill kept a keen smile, acting as if he was playing along with Brisket's jabs. "How does a thousand Rias sound?" Grill suggested. The words alone made the crowd gasp.

"That much? For arm wrestling? You must be desperate to see your little apprentice broken and beaten. What, he steal your precious chocolates or something?"

"I'll reiterate: a thousand Rias. Whether you win or lose, money's the same. Deal?"

"Ha! If your pocket's really that fat, why not just skip the formalities and write the check now? Less painful that way!"

"Are you in, Brisket, or not? Last chance."

Brisket cracked his large, intimidating knuckles. Slamming his left elbow on a nearby table. "Your funeral, then. Or should I say, your student's! Bahahahaha!" Once more the crowd laughed.

Grill simply nodded at Den. The scarred boy now had no need to ask for his master's reasoning. It was clear as soon as Brisket slammed his elbow on the table. Brisket was left-handed. Den had been shot in the left shoulder. This was not just a test of strength. It was one of durability and recovery. If Den couldn't handle a single game of arm wrestling, however rough it might be, there was no way he could handle the mission ahead.

Den placed his left elbow on the table as well and clasped it with Brisket's. The difference in size was immediately apparent. Den's small, lean digits versus Brisket's large, meaty fingers. The two looked one another in the eyes. Determination shone brightly in Den's. Condescension showed in Brisket's.

"Ready?" Grill's voice announced. "Go!"

Immediately, Den was met with a strong, forceful push. Brisket was already proving himself to be far more than just a large mouth and a big belly. The strength of his left arm alone would have been enough to tear a regular man's limbs apart.

Den held his own for a time, only to feel a stinging pain shoot to his shoulder. The scarred boy had thought it had already recovered and was strong enough to handle the stress. It was only now that Den realized how wrong he was. Still, he took the pain. This was Grill's test. And a good one at that. Den knew that if his arm couldn't survive this, then he stood no chance going against Noland Macchianado again.

The scarred boy persisted in holding his own, but the force of Brisket's push was proving to be too much, causing Den's arm to slump down further and further.

"I gotta hand it to ya, kid!" Brisket yelled. "You've already held your own better than I thought. But you're still nothing but some scrawny little brat! So tell you what? Give up now and I won't break your arm. Then you can go back to Mommy and Daddy with just a little sprain!"

"No way!" Den replied. "I ain't outta this by a long shot!"

"You got spirit, kid, I'll give you that too! Fine! If this is the best Trent's got, then he must be one crap of a teacher. It figures! I'll make you squeal. Bahahaha!"

The sound of Brisket's cackling... it was enough to make any man mad. But Den wasn't like that, it only gave him more drive. More push. And push was what he did. Den increased his grip, digging into Brisket's hand with his fingers, denting and bleeding them as he did.

"Aaaah! What the hell is wrong with you?" Brisket yelled in pain.

"You want me to squeal, fatso? How about this? You're the one that's closer to a pig... So why don't *you* squeal?" With as much force as he could muster, Den threw his arm up, moving the combatants' hands back to their starting positions. But Den didn't stop there. He continued his triumphant comeback, using the force of his initial push to slam Brisket's hand down on the other side. Not only planting the back of his hand onto the table, but smashing the table itself. Throwing Brisket, hand and body alike, down to the floor below.

Den let go of Brisket's hand. He clenched his own hand in a fist and raised it in the air. "How do you like that, Porkface?"

The crowd erupted in cheer.

"You broke it!" Brisket wailed. "You broke it, you little bastard!"

"Don't make threats you're not willing to take," Den replied.

"He's just being a drama queen," Grill said. "Nothing more than a sprain, I'd imagine. Oh, and before I forget." From his pocket, Grill took out a check already written to Brisket. One thousand Rias, as promised. "A deal's a deal, Brisket." Grill placed the check on Brisket's head. "Try not to spend it all in one place."

The crowd continued their cheers as Den and Grill left the bar. Onlookers offered them drinks and other activities, each one Den and Grill politely declined.

And just near the broken table, not too far away from where the action had taken place, a single bullet rolled around. Free from its imprisonment.

"Gotta say, I can see why you go to places like that," Den said as they went outside. "Hell of a rush. I feel fantastic right now! My shoulder feels lighter and stronger than it was when we went in!"

"I try to stay away from places like that, for the most part," Grill replied. "You stay in there long enough, you start getting accustomed to their rotten mindsets and atrocious mannerisms."

"Yeah, and it smelled bad too. So lay it on me, did I pass Phase Two? Or I guess, Phase One-And-A-Half?"

"With flying colors."

"Hell yeah! So when do we meet up with Romero again?" Den asked.

"Tomorrow," Grill replied. "He's trying to keep things under wraps and its sounds like the meeting will be soon at hand. Keeps the danger of leaks to a minimum."

"Gotcha. Can't say I'm very surprised. He earn any of your trust back?"

"Absolutely not. But we have a deal. And if that's how this is gonna go, it's how it's gonna go. It's our code."

"*Honor the deal. Follow the hunt*," Den quoted. Speaking a truncated version of the Bounty Hunter Association's oath.

"Well, look at you," Grill chuckled. "I knew you were teachable."

The two bounty hunters made their way to pick up Hugo, satisfied by the spectacle they had made. They had entered The Ferret's Nest Egg as laughing stocks and left it the talk of the district. The Iron Sniper and his newfound apprentice. A duo many dared not mess with, lest they risk their arms and their reputation.

III

Even with the day of the bust nearing, Hugo Statferd's work at the WHS had remained consistent. The only string of stability in an otherwise changing situation. And though the clutter of Andolini's collection had been rectified, there was still much to do. In particular, Hugo put it upon himself to start the digitization process of the books. Many of which had yet to be submitted into the WHS's central archival system.

Yet even as monotonous as the work could be, Hugo took great care to appreciate the circumstances; he was happy not to be involved in the mission at hand, at least not directly, and all the dangers that came with it.

Still, the young Historian felt a lingering sense of concern. Not the fear he had previously felt, but rather his contribution to it all. Hugo had become so invested with the Crimson Maple incident that he had created a false impression for himself that he would somehow be continuously involved in Den and Grill's hunts. But he was not a bounty hunter like them. He was a Historian. And for all the adventure and glamour his colleagues, like Helena, or his superiors, like Victor Rasmus, had experienced, Hugo did not possess their kind of adventurous, thrill-seeking spirits. But at least he was still doing his job. And that counted for far more than he was willing to give himself credit for.

"What's ailing ya, lad?" Andolini spoke up.

"Huh? Oh nothing, Mr. Andolini," Hugo replied, still typing away. "Just on the job."

"That stuff can't be too exciting, I'd imagine. Scanning and typing. Typing and scanning. Editing where necessary. Don't get me wrong, I quite enjoy all these new innovations coming out with computers, but the work just seems soul-crushing."

"It's fine. This was my job back in Harten. So I'm used to it."

"Being used to it and being happy with it are two very different things."

"True, but it's not like a job is meant to make you happy. It can just be a positive side effect sometimes."

"Tell ya what, lad, how about we take a walk down to the shops? I've got a new item coming in that's sure to catch your fancy."

"Sounds good, sir. I'll just finish up here and we can go. What shop are we going to?"

"Why, the antique shop, of course!"

Moments later, the two Historians were outside and making the walk to Andolini's destination. Kulver Street was at its most peaceful at this time of day, as the sun rose to its zenith and high noon set in. A cool breeze had come through, creating a spring atmosphere at a time when June was well underway. Hugo breathed in the air. Fresh and tranquil. It was on a day like this in Harten that Hugo would have seen his fellow Hartenians taking day naps on their lawns or soaking in the sun's rays. And while the young Historian spotted no such activities being practiced at the present time, he took heart in the knowledge that there could still be peace in a city of chaos.

The antique shop they entered was quaint and quiet. The kind of store a tourist would find in any rural setting. As such, its existence in a place like Wayport was even more of an anomaly. There were no flashy substances nor loads of advertisements spewed about. Or rather, there were. They were just older, defunct ads or facsimiles of those ads. Fragile pieces sitting atop even more fragile glass. Toy figures and record players placed on shelves in inconsistent order. Carpets and shirts sporting designs Hugo's parents and grandparents had once found fashionable. Time capsules thrown together. A haven for Historians who found beauty in the obscure.

"Hello, my dear Gretchen," Andolini greeted. "Might you have what I have longed for, you sweet angel?"

"Always the flirt you are," Gretchen chuckled. She was an older woman. At least a decade older than Andolini himself, if not more. She wore plain clothing and glasses several times too big for her face. Yet she adorned them with pride, and was happy to talk to Andolini any time he came in. "And I see you've brought that young man you've been telling me about."

"Yes, hello," Hugo greeted. "My name's Hugo. I am also a Historian."

"And a great one at that," Andolini complimented. "He's the whole reason my place isn't so disorganized anymore!"

"I just did what seemed best," Hugo said humbly.

"Well it's good to see the next generation is doing so well," Gretchen admired. "Makes me optimistic for the future, knowing it's in the hands of young ones like you. Now, for the main course..."

From her counter drawer, Gretchen pulled out a wristwatch. Its design was simple: a regular watch which ticked in sync with the other clocks throughout the store. To a regular person, it seemed like nothing special. Yet for someone like Andolini, it meant the world.

"This is one of the watches worn by President Josiah during the War for Ragnarok!" Andolini explained, the excitement in his voice at a fever pitch. "Naturally, the man had many like this. But to see one in person? I can't believe how well preserved it is!"

"The seller had kept it in wonderful condition," Gretchen explained to Hugo. "He didn't want to just throw it out or sell it to someone who wouldn't appreciate it. So I told him about Mr. Andolini here and the seller was more than happy to give it away."

"What an honor," Hugo said. "Seems unreal to know one of our presidents wore it."

"Aye, Hugo, and it's ours now! Oh, Gretchen, I can't begin to tell you how grateful I am!" The spark in Andolini's eyes brightened the room. Those same eyes Hugo had seen the first day they had met. Andolini cared so much for the history he possessed. No item was too small. No event had been forgotten. Everything mattered. It was all part of the same tapestry.

Hugo and Andolini would spend some time at the shop, chatting with Gretchen and looking around at all the wonderful pieces and oddities. Even as stereotypical as a Historian visiting an antique shop was, Hugo still enjoyed himself immensely.

He hadn't been to one in years. It reminded him of the days when his mother would bring him to such places. Taking his first glimpses into the wonders of the past. When those initial sparks were lit. Sparks that would form the very foundation of the rest of his life.

Their walk back to the office was still breezy and calm. A simple day in a city which refused to be so. Yet simple it still was. Hugo wished he could experience more days like this.

"What's been on your mind, lad?" Andolini suddenly asked.

"Mind?" Hugo questioned.

"We didn't go out today just to get this watch, as amazing as it is. Truth be told, for the past week I've seen you in deep thought. I know you've got something deep down you want to get out."

Hugo sighed. "It was that obvious, huh?"

"Maybe not to some, but in my time, I've seen enough young men like you with that face. Tell me what ails you, if you're willing."

"It's just... To put it simply, Den and Grill are about to go on a hunt. Den's first one, mind you. I feel like there's more I should be doing, but I just don't know what. I'm not in their profession, just like they're not in mine. I have this yearning to do more... and yet nothing comes to mind. Nothing that wouldn't just get in their way, at least."

Andolini had not been made aware of Den's clash with Noland. Nor did he know about the scarred boy's Enhanced abilities. The anecdotes Nash had told him in the past merely implied that Den was in good shape. Instead, Andolini had been told a cover story that Den had been mugged. An easy enough pill to swallow.

"That feeling of being left out in the cold," Andolini remarked. "It can make you brittle. Give a man frostbite even on a warm, summer day... But a man doesn't give up like that. He hunts and searches for what he can do. Finds something he knows his friends and allies wouldn't be able to find. And he gives them the information without expecting a single word of gratitude. He just moves on and goes back to work."

"So you mean... find the missing piece?"

"Aye, Hugo. Use the resources at your disposal. And, well"—the two had just made it back to the WHS—"we have plenty at our fingertips."

"Mr. Andolini, I don't know what to say. Thank you!"

"Don't mind me, boyo. I just gave you something I had that you needed: experience and perspective. Two things you'll have in spades in the future. And you'll be amazing with them, too."

The young Historian nearly teared up. He gave Andolini a strong handshake and headed back inside.

The next few hours were rife with looking through archives, both in the digital records and within Andolini's collection. Hugo's focus was unwavering and his determination unsinkable. He had found the public records of Tommy Tillman. What Romero had told him had been true, among other things. Petty theft, sports gambling, murder accusations. Yet there was something about these records that kept aching him. Something racking the back of his mind that was yearning to be discovered. Hugo Statferd had grown curious.

And all at once, it came together. His search was never about looking into Tillman and Macchianado's criminal backgrounds... it was about looking into their careers. Macchianado's was an utter mystery, outside of his loan business. But Tillman's? Sports manager for many a successful athlete. And among those athletes was a certain man. A certain man involved in a moment of history that had lived on in infamy. That's when Hugo found it. That final piece to the puzzle. Still not confirmed by pure facts, but conjecture too consistent to be mere coincidence.

"This changes everything!" Hugo stated, his eyes widening and jaw dropping.

"What does, lad?" Andolini asked, flabbergasted by Hugo's expression.

Hugo grabbed Andolini's phone, dialed a number, and waited to hear it ring. Sure enough the call went through.

"Hello?" came Den's voice on the other line.

"Den, it's me! When are you leaving for Romero's final meeting?"

"In a few minutes. Why?"

"To put it simply, I think I just found the missing piece! Please wait for me. I'll be right over!"

"Hugo, what are you—"

Hugo hung up the phone before Den could finish his question. "Mr. Andolini, I need to go now. It's urgent!" Hugo gathered his things together and signed off from the computer. "I swear it will make sense later."

"I can manage just fine, Hugo. I'm just a little concern by your expediency, is all."

"Oh don't worry, sir. I'm more than okay. I can assure you of that! In fact, something tells me you're going to be more than okay pretty soon, too."

Hugo rushed out of the WHS. Sprinting back to Merryville Suites. Whatever was to come next, he was not about to miss it.

IV

Hum, tick, drip. Hum, tick, drip. Hum, tick, drip. Those same repetitive sounds reverberated through Noland's apartment.

On paper, Noland Macchianado lived in a small condominium in the residential area of Wayport. It was the closest thing the Terminal City had in the way of suburbia and was among its safest spots. A place to raise a family and live in relative comfort. Near enough to downtown to allow for a relatively normal life, sequestered from the decay and melancholy that plagued so many other unfortunate citizens.

The condo was small, yet robust. Enough to comfortably house a childless couple, just starting their new lives. His furnishings were sparse. A simple bed and basic appliances. Simple and clean... And it was a place he rarely spent even a night a week. It was only if he had someone to impress, or a companion to bring home, that his head would even touch the pillows. Yet even on the nights when such affairs took place, he had found it so very difficult to sleep. Whether by himself or with a woman, he would always toss and turn. Watching as the clock went by and the morning sun shone again.

Far more often, the gangster would find himself in his so-called "safe house." One which was anything but, nestled amongst the worst of Wayport's slums. Where rent was cheap, life cheaper, and families utterly broken. Where it wasn't uncommon to see a knife fight in the hallways or the remains of a four-legged animal rotting near a window. His furnishing were even lesser. A single mattress with no frame or sheets to cover it. Two flat pillows and a blanket of cheap material were all that stood atop it. Several holes cracked through the walls and roaches would, on occasion, walk across the ceiling. A place only those in desperate need of shelter would ever choose to stay at... And he slept like a baby each and every night.

Except at times like this. The withdrawals. The spasms. The uncontrollable feeling that he had been deprived of something his body desperately needed. He could feel his entire being shake. Not just his limbs or head. His organs gyrated in movements he had never felt before. Heart palpitating at erratic times. Bones aching from the very marrow that flowed through them. And eyes burnt as if salt and flame combined into one ferocious blast. Tears inching down. Mouth salivating. The stimulants his only salvation from going into an all-out seizure or stroke.

At the height of his abilities, Noland knew strength the likes of which few men had ever grasped. A fraction that only those graced with the right genetics and a honed body could truly understand. He had once seen the top of the world. Yet here he was now, in the slums. Huddled in his damp, broken apartment. Roaches rustled not just on the ceiling, but under the floorboards. Addicts screeched only a few rooms down. And his very soul quivered for another taste of that sweet, sweet medicine. He'd always thought he knew the bottom. But the abyss stretched even further down than he could have possibly imagined.

Noland eyed what little he had kept in his one-room board. Cheap furniture, a few needles, a dirty refrigerator, canned foods to avoid cooking. A man who lived the high life coming back to lowlife surroundings.

That's when he spotted the bear, still barely touched since his last trade with Hodgson. Preserved as it had been since that day. It looked at Noland with its button eyes. Single black drops staring into him. Yet there was a softness to them, an invitation to anyone looking for a companion. Made for children. Accessible to all.

Noland grabbed onto the bear's body, its fluffy texture a relief to his aching hands. The stuffing inside provided a soft comfort. He hugged the doll in his arms, focusing on its materials as he did. Feeling every stitch.

Noland Macchianado did not remember his mother. Not her face. Not her voice. Not her soul. But he remembered her song. A humming lullaby that she'd sing to him on those lonely nights when he could not sleep. Everything else a blur.

The hours would linger on. He had no other tasks to accomplish. Nor was he expected to. Instead he sat in the darkness. Sunrise to sunset. Barely moving. Barely sleeping. Waiting out each and every second. His mind nearly succumbing to the pain. And in all that time, he clung to the bear and hummed his mother's tune. His little slice of Heaven in the pits of Hell.

V

16 years ago…
August 13, 824 AU

Neil McKorkendale was at his peak. Sparkling eyes, buzz-cut hair, a complexion that accentuated his rippling muscles, and a pretty boy face that made him popular amongst his peers, even with his crooked nose. And in a matter of moments, the world would know his name.

It was here in Sutter's Stadium, the greatest sports arena in all of Adalia, that he was about to accomplish his greatest feat: to break the world power lifting record and officially be granted the title of world's strongest man.

The crowds were cheering, and he knew it. Yet inside his locker room, as he sat in quiet meditation, his heart raced. Pumping so loud that not even a single hurrah touched his ears. Just that same beat over and over again. The sole reminder that he was nothing more than a mortal man.

A single knock from the locker room door broke McKorkendale from his meditation. "Mac," came the gruff voice of a man he knew all too well. "You got five minutes. You decent?"

"Yeah," Mac responded, a hint of nerves in his voice. "I'm good."

The locker room door opened, revealing the visage of Tommy Tillman. Middle-aged with auburn, shoulder-length hair, a mustache which curled at the edges, and adorned in a suit made of high-quality fabrics that would not stain so easily from sweat caused by the summer heat. A man whose entire being emphasized high class and high living.

"You don't sound so good," Tillman replied.

"Ah, it's nothing. Just some pre-game jitters. Like that time I had to face that big guy from the Southern Continent. What was his name?"

"Espinoza."

"Yeah. At the time, I thought, '*This guy's like three time's my size! I'm screwed!*' And then what happened? Dude could barely lift half my score. What a load of crap he was!"

Yet for all of Mac's talk, even out of meditation he could still hear his heart beating away. Rattling into his head.

Tillman stared Mac straight in his eyes and grabbed him by the shoulders. Mac could feel his coach's roughed, calloused palms. "I know you're not gonna quit on me, Mac," he stated. "I know you're not gonna let those little noises in the back of your head get to you like that."

"What are you talking about? I'm good!"

"Not what those eyes are saying. You slept enough, right?"

"Yeah, like a baby."

"So what's making you so nervous? You've known about the risks for months!"

"You wanna know? It's because I finally got a look at the stuff yesterday. Ten cubes of Maizonian Ore all just sitting there at once like that! It's kinda, you know, intimidating and such."

Maizonian Ore, the heaviest known substance in the Western Continent. Possibly even the entire world. Mined from the great Maizo Mountains, the ore which presided within had been used for all forms of goods and services. Construction materials, military equipment, even certain heavy machinery. And it was also in the field of power lifting that it had become the standard measurement for all Enhanced wanting to prove to themselves and the world that they were the strongest.

The current record was seven cubes and had been matched by multiple Enhanced men. To go further had been seen as insurmountable. Yet it was during a recent press conference that Neil McKorkendale had made his greatest proclamation: to not only break the record, but exceed it to such a degree that no one else would be able to surpass him. A decree uttered in ignorance now made reality.

"Let me ask you something, Mac," Tillman said. "What do you like more than anything in the world? Fame? Power? Women? Money? You don't have to answer. I already know. It's the applause, isn't it?"

Mac chuckled. "Hell yeah! But you know, it ain't just that... It's knowing I'm right at the top. That not a single soul in this world is above me. And that applause? Don't get me wrong, I love people cheering my name. But what it really means is simple. I'm the greatest of all... and everyone knows it!"

"Then show them that. So no one else has done it? Who cares! Go out there and be that one!"

"Yeah..." Mac spoke. "Yeah!" His voice raised. "Yeah!" He screamed at the top of his lungs. "I'll do it! I'll make them scream my name!" The two men clapped hands and began laughing. Ready to take the world by storm.

"Ladies and gentlemen!" came the announcer's big, booming voice. "We now welcome to the arena, Neil McKorkendale!" Mac readied himself and exited the locker room, Tillman by his side.

They made their way to the center of the stadium. The Maizonian Ore sat there, waiting to be lifted. All eyes were on Mac. All applause for him and him alone. He could hear their cheers, drowning out his heartbeat with each clap and yell.

Mac had partaken in many an illicit substance. Tasted the ambrosia of products known only to those in the know. And had experienced the absolute ecstasy that came from the consumption of things no normal man or woman would have the opportunity to even touch.

Yet there was nothing he loved more than the applause. The finest of ales, sweetest of women, and intoxicating of contraband could hold nary a candle to the prestige and idolization that followed. It was a big world, and he was about to be at the very top.

The challenge was simple. Atop the ore was a single long, wide metal tray. Easy to lift, yet highly durable. Once per round, one cube of ore would be placed on it via a small crane which stood nearby. Mac would then lift the tray from the ground and up to the top of his head. Then place it back down. The next round, another ore cube would be added. Mac would repeat this same action until he could no longer take it. The standard rules for every ore challenge.

The applause died down as the challenge began. The first few rounds were easy, Mac effortlessly lifting again and again. The applause always rising back up as soon as he lifted the tray. Tillman stood by, silently watching his star athlete surpass all expectations.

Even Mac himself could not believe the simplicity of it all. Another cube, another lift, another round of applause. The sweat flowed from his back, glistening in the spotlight. He was in pure ecstasy, his endorphins activating at levels he had not thought possible. The sixth ore was added, and he felt on top of the world. Just two more times. Two more times and he would break the world record... until a single twinge came from his shoulder.

It started as a mild ache. Neither piercing nor heavy. A light strain and nothing more. Mac was about to reach the zenith of his entire career. The apex of what the human body could accomplish. And nothing as negligible as a mild sore was going to halt his ascension into the history books.

He prepared himself for the seventh round, stretching in between, as was the common and preferred practice. Yet the strain grew stronger, if only just a little. Mac ignored it and continued on. He lifted the tray once more. Pushing his muscles to their limits. Only for the pain in his shoulder to increase. That soreness finally evolving into something sharper.

But still, Mac did not stop. He lifted seven cubes of ore, officially matching the record of many who had come before. The audience's applause was massive. All the cheers when he had first entered now seemed like a whisper. They truly knew his name.

One more. Just one more round. That's all it would take. The eighth cube was added. All stood with bated breath. Mac was about to begin his lift... only for an official to come by and stop him.

"That's enough, McKorkendale!" yelled the referee.

"What the hell are you doing, ref?" Tillman screamed from the side.

"I'm afraid we'll have to call it off," the referee responded. "Mr. McKorkendale is in no condition to lift any further."

"He's fit as a fiddle. Let him do it!"

"Mr. Tillman, his movements imply the potential for internal bleeding. On both a legal and ethical basis, we cannot allow him to continue any longer."

"Oh, bull crap! You just don't want to see him break the damn record."

The audience booed out against the referee. Some even tried to throw food and drinks at him.

More officials started making their way towards Mac, a doctor among them, preparing to assess his immediate damage. Mac hadn't spoken a word since his lift was stopped... and he hadn't truly comprehended anything that had happened since.

He was in a daze, a high from the strain of his lifting and the audience's cheers. All he could focus on was the ore and the tray. They were sitting there, just waiting to be lifted. Yet he knew something wasn't right. He knew these people were coming up to him, trying to stop his record-breaking moment. Trying to take him away. To destroy everything he had built.

Mac was not about to have that. He grabbed the bottom of the tray, eight ores deep, and began lifting it upwards. The audience's boos morphed into cheers. Their champion had gone against the officials, proving himself to all who doubted his abilities. His muscles began tearing up. His eyes and nose bled. The pain in his shoulder now ruptured throughout his body. Yet still he lifted. Lifting until he felt no more pain, only the pure adrenaline of the moment. Lifted until... he had reached the top of his head.

Neil McKorkendale had broken the record. In this very second, he stood atop the world. He could not hear the applause any longer. He couldn't hear anything. He couldn't feel anything. Except for his heartbeat, pumping so very loudly.

His body gave out all at once. And it all came plunging down. All eight cubes of ore and the tray that held them. Some fell away and smashed into the ground. Others stayed on the tray for the entire descent. A descent which came to its end on Mac's very body. Bones shattered. Muscles ripped apart. Blood shot out. Everything that was once Neil McKorkendale crushed under its weight.

Mac would not die that day. He would only wish he had. But he had done it. The one thing he'd wanted to accomplish more than anything else. The audience was screaming his name.

VI

"So you mean to imply that Noland Macchianado was once the late powerlifter Neil McKorkendale?" Agent Romero asked.

It had been less than an hour since Hugo Statferd had left Andolini and sprinted towards his companions. Together they made their way to Bronco's Business Rentals, an office and meeting room rental company, and entered one of the building's most inconspicuous rooms. The room which housed Romero's final plans for the Florenza/Takeda bust that was only a day away.

"Not just imply," Hugo replied. "I fully believe it. Let me direct you to McKorkendale's publicity photos versus Macchianado's mugshot." Here the young Historian stood, making an impromptu presentation to a group of government agents he did not know, apart from Agent Romero himself.

Romero, Den, Grill, and the other agents whom Hugo presumed to be under Romero's command each sifted through the freshly-printed pictures. McKorkendale only had a single proper headshot, as was customary for athletes first entering the official weightlifting leagues. But it was in black and white, and not finely detailed. His publicity photos, on the other hand, were in full color and showed many different sides of him. Photos of him lifting weights and other heavy objects, as well as photos of him in his daily life.

"I would like to point you to the ridge of his nose, the mark on his right cheek, and the shape of his eyes," Hugo explained. "On initial viewing, none of these match up. But if you take into account procedures within the field of cosmetic surgery, you'll notice that those discrepancies seem to align. For instance, it's within our current medical abilities to smooth out the cartilage of McKorkendale's nose and form it into Macchianado's pattern. The mole on McKorkendale's face can be taken off, though not without a skin graft to mask the scarring. And the eyelids can be restructured to match the new shape. Plus the constant use of Atlas Tear Drop has only reddened his eyes more over time."

"It's all an interesting theory, Mr. Statferd," Romero commented, "but the amount of physical trauma McKorkendale sustained would have required years of recovery. And that's not including the time it would take to make all the cosmetic changes. By the time the timelines match up, Macchianado was already well on the scene."

"And that's where the X factor comes in," Hugo continued. "I theorize that Atlas Tear Drop itself was able to speed up the healing process at the cost of getting him hyper-addicted. According to your own files, sir, Compound ZX-78153 has never been tested in that way. But even you can confirm it has been shown to heal Enhanced faster than normal."

"It's been used in small surgeries, yes," Romero confirmed. "But nothing to such an extent. Even Enhanced don't usually survive that kind of damage. Some can certainly take far more abuse, but their bodies are more durable to begin with. With the sheer destruction McKorkendale suffered, it was a miracle he didn't die on the spot."

"But is it so outside the realm of reason to think McKorkendale couldn't have survived through his own sheer force of will? We've all heard stories of stuff like that! Impossible situations that people can not only live through, but heal from and become even better than before. And I'm not even talking about Enhanced, soldiers, or athletes. Just normal people. McKorkendale survived, at least the initial trauma. That's a fact. Who's to say he didn't push even further than that?"

"And that's why we call them Miracles," Den stated.

"I think I speak for all of us here, Mr. Statferd," Romero said, "that this has been an eye-opening theory. But a theory nonetheless. We're dealing with a highly-publicized case, however old and out of the current public eye it may be. That Mr. Tillman had the means to finance this recovery without it getting out into the public just seems too conspicuous."

"Is it really though, Jewels?" Grill intervened. "Tillman was an even richer man back then. With connections that you and I will never know about. Is it that strange that he could pay off a few doctors and rig a few tests?"

"A body was buried, Jack, one that matched McKorkendale's file. He hung on for a bit after the accident, but it didn't take much longer for him to flatline."

"'A *body was buried.*' You mean a body whose credentials, like the rest of this case, could be forged? A body that could have easily been some John Doe in the coffin? You and I are perfectly aware of what can be done with the right connections, Jewels. We may not be at liberty to say, but we know enough. You fake a death, the public mourns for a bit, and then they move on, as usual. Now without fear of immediate public scrutiny, you have carte blanche to do whatever it is to your liking. And you know as well as I do what can be accomplished from the shadows."

Another agent came into the room as Grill was finishing his explanation. Accompanying this agent was another man, his face and hands obscured by towels. Appearing like an inmate covering his features from paparazzi. But there was no chain rattling from the man's hands. It was nothing but a cover.

"Seems our guest of honor has finally arrived," Romero said, relieved he did not have to deal with Grill's words any longer. "Gentlemen, I'd imagine this is a face that many of you know. A man that has lived in infamy in these parts. You can take them off."

The man did so, and his appearance was enough to make Grill's blood boil. A gold tooth and weaselly smile. A look reserved for only the lowest scum. The face of Baratzi.

VII

Non-disclosure agreements, pacts to secrecy, and all other forms of silence had to be signed by the gold-toothed man before he'd even had a chance to come to today's meeting.

Baratzi's demeanor was calmer and less bloviating than it had been the last time Grill had seen him. He had no honor, but Baratzi was not a stupid man. No longer surrounded by his guards and wealth, he knew best when to hush up. Keep things calm.

For many years he had dealt with some of the worst scum of the Earth. The types of people that would have happily blown his brains out just for looking at them funny. Maintaining a certain level of calm was ultimately what had kept Baratzi around this long. And he had grown tired of it. Tired of constantly looking around the corner, wondering if his next turn would be his last. Then one day the government came knocking, and it seemed like the right call to make.

For the past few minutes, Baratzi was briefed on Hugo's theories. Cracking a smile at the details. A look of intrigue in his eyes. "And here I thought it was just some whacked-out conspiracy theory," Baratzi quipped.

"You've heard this before?" Romero asked.

"Matches has made enough of a name for himself for the idea to come up on occasion. Usually just some bar-room talk. Like how people may think a guy looks like some celebrity or politician, but he really just shares a few superfluous details. But Noland's an unknown outside of Wayport. And not enough people in these parts care enough to look any further. Plus, like ya said, the timelines don't match..."

Baratzi turned to Hugo. "Though I gotta say, this young man here has certainly got a brain on him. Keep a leash on this one, Grill. You never know who might try to sweep him up!" Baratzi's cackle was as disgusting as it was aggravating. But it didn't last long. One look at Grill's face was enough to silence the rat immediately. Grill was in no place to do what he had done to Baratzi before, but the bounty hunter knew how much a single glare could accomplish what a fist full of lead couldn't.

"Point being," Baratzi concluded, once more in a calm demeanor, "if we take the Atlas Tear Drop stuff into account, I think the theory checks out."

"Moving on," Romero interjected. "Now, with Mr. Baratzi present, I would like to continue onto our main discussion. For those who have not been fully debriefed on the Florenza-Takeda Exchange, to summarize, they will be meeting at an undisclosed location, which Mr. Baratzi shall inform us on as soon as the information is set. There, they will make an exchange regarding the production and distribution of Compound ZX-78153, aka Atlas Tear Drop, across the Eastern Continent black markets. Our goal is to intercept as soon as the deal is finalized."

"So why don't we target them as soon as the meeting starts?" Den questioned.

"I'm afraid it doesn't work that way," Romero said. "There are steps we have to follow. We need to have full confirmation that the deal relates to Atlas Tear Drop. Otherwise they can contest in court for unlawful espionage."

"All espionage is unlawful," Grill whispered under his breath.

"The Takedas want a live showing," Baratzi explained. "They want to see the immediate effects. That's why they're using Matches as the example."

"Then why not go in as soon as Macchianado shoots up?" Hugo asked.

"Still won't work," Romero said. "Could easily be seen as a placebo effect. Also wouldn't hold up in court. We need to see the results up close."

"And to clarify, Mr. Stats," Baratzi informed Hugo, "Atlas Tear Drop is a pill, not an injection. That kind of stuff straight into your veins? Woo! Make your head explode."

"To clarify," Romero interjected, "what Mr. Baratzi is referring to is the current version Macchianado is suspected of taking. It's been on the market for the past five years. Purer in form and higher in potency. But Mr. Statferd was not wrong in his assumption, as the previous version was originally taken intravenously."

"I'm really confused on this whole thing," Den stated, frustration in his voice. The scarred boy had only just finished his bounty hunting studies and already was given information contradictory to what he had learned. But the government had its own rules and regulations to follow. Things that Den would not normally have to concern himself with, just as the agents could take certain liberties that Den and Grill would not have the right to do. "Why the hell isn't possession enough?"

"We could easily nab them for possession," Romero admitted. "But that wouldn't throw them in long enough. The higher-ups would immediately be bailed out and their sentences would be negligible at best. If we want a full bust, we need absolute proof of this deal going through. Only then can we be sure."

“And this is why I try to avoid these types of jobs,” Grill chided. “Back at the hotel, you spoke about the likes of Jun and Miki Takeda. Is there anyone else of note within their ranks that will be attending?”

“Yes,” Romero answered. “One of very particular note: Kenichi Hirose, the Pale Dragon. I’d like to direct everyone to the file we have on him. I’ll give you all a few minutes to read through the material.”

Kenichi Hirose was an old, yet very skilled member of the Takeda family. One whose reputation dated back to the time of Joey Flowers and the foundations of the Florenzas. A bootlegger in his youth, in the days before the War for Ragnarok erupted, he partnered with Florenza on various occasions. Raking in the profits when possible, but always distancing himself just enough so as to not get caught. He had had his fair share of arrests, but each and every time, he always managed to get off.

Yet as notable as his reputation was, it was his physical appearance that truly caught Den and Hugo off guard. Hirose’s skin and eyes were pure gray. He’d been born with the Silver Flu, a birth defect which caused those affected to have gray skin and gray eyes. They appeared blind, even with perfect vision. There was a time when Den was thought to have had this. But Den’s skin was of a different tone and while his eyes were sunken, he most certainly did not look blind. The differences were comparable to that of a pale man and an albino.

“So why is Hirose coming?” Grill asked. “Sounds like he’s putting himself at risk, especially at his age.”

“Innovation,” Romero responded. “The man has always wanted to be present for the newest technology and medicine. The Takedas will make no deal unless he sees the pinnacle of what Atlas Tear Drop can do.”

“And that ain’t happening without me!” Baratzi spoke up.

“Mr. Baratzi will be the mediator,” Romero informed. “He does not have to say much. Just be present and help find common ground, if the deal starts getting shaky.”

“Scum working with scum,” Grill noted. “Perfect match.”

"Make all the jokes you want, Jackie! 'Cause after this, I'm out! Drinking daiquiris by the beach and all that!"

"You wouldn't last a week outside this city, Baratzi," Grill replied. "It's too nice out there for a rat like you."

"I may be a rat, but at least I won't have to see your face again!"

"Gentlemen!" Romero bellowed. "Any personal grudges will be settled outside of this room and preferably after this assignment has ended."

"Yes, of course, sir," Baratzi apologized in a meek tone.

Grill had no intention of apologizing, not that Romero was expecting him to. Instead, the bounty hunter simply remained silent.

Romero continued his lecture, the rest of it focusing on potential techniques to use and weapons to brandish. He took into account both families' arsenals and how they could work through different strategies, should the situation break down. Grill wondered how much of what Romero was spouting was even applicable to the actual situation and how much Romero was simply extending time just to hear himself talk.

"And with that, we are finished for today," Romero concluded. "Everyone please place all notes you've received today within the disposable unit before you leave. They will be taken to the shredder immediately after this. And a special thank you to Mr. Trent, Mr. Den, Mr. Statferd, and Mr. Baratzi for coming in today. Good luck, everyone. May God guide us through."

"*May God guide us through*," the agents all spoke. It was a common phrase certain sections within Adalia's government would use before a dangerous mission.

"Ugh," Grill winced.

"What's wrong?" Den asked.

"I'm not exactly a fan of that phrase."

"Really? It sounds pretty good to me."

"I doubt you'd still be saying that if you witnessed the things these types of agents can do... Almost blasphemous, really."

"Well, I guess it's time to go," Baratzi said as he placed the towels over his head and hands again. "Have a good one, Jackie! Can't say it's been fun."

"I hear the sewers of Mayline are pretty nice," Grill jested. "You could get a vacation home there. Probably for dirt cheap."

Baratzi walked off with the same agent he had come in with, pretending not to hear Grill's insults, only to start smashing his feet to the ground with each step.

Grill chuckled. Nearby, he could see Romero leaving. The bounty hunter rushed towards him. "Jewels," Grill said before the agent could leave the room. "Let's talk."

"I can't, Jack," the agent replied. "I've got other—"

"Just for a few minutes. I've got some questions for you."

"Anything wrong, Grill?" Den asked.

"You guys can head out," Grill told his companions. "I've got something I need to ask Jewels."

"Sure," Hugo obliged. There was a look in Grill's eyes. A focus that would not stop until he got the answers he was seeking. Answers he might not get if Den and Hugo were with him.

"Thanks, you two," Grill said. "I'll be down in a few minutes." Den and Hugo left. Grill and Romero were now the only ones remaining in their small meeting room. "Now, Jewels... You mind telling me what you've been hiding?"

The agent tried maintaining his composure. But in the presence of a man like Grill, it would be easier said than done.

VIII

Den and Hugo were sitting on a bench just outside Bronco's, still waiting for Grill to join them. It had taken longer than the bounty hunter had anticipated, but still they waited. Evening had already set in. The day had remained cool. A refreshing feeling after the stuffy, needlessly complicated meeting.

The brothers stared at the Lang-Meyer Courthouse nearby. The closer they had gotten to it, the more impressive it looked. The building's finer details came into focus. Stained glass covered certain areas, like a cathedral, making its already towering figure appear absolutely giant up close.

"For what it's worth, I believe your theory," Den said.

"Thanks, Den," Hugo replied. "By the way, congratulations."

"You've told me that a lot the last few days. Not that I'm not grateful."

"I know. But it's not just about you passing the test. You're following through on a goal you set your mind to. You're trying to make a difference."

Den chuckled. "I guess it just feels good having a more direct purpose now. It's like Madame Lake wrote, even if our Journey goes nowhere... at least I've found a field I can be useful in... I hope."

"You'll do great. I know it."

"And you're starting to sound more like Karina every day."

"That's the best compliment I've heard in a long time."

Grill came out from the office and moved towards his companions. He sat down beside them.

"Talk go well?" Hugo asked.

"It took some questioning," Grill started, "but I finally got Jewels to admit something I could tell he was hiding." He turned to Den. "What I'm about to tell you might change your mind on the bust. But you deserve to know, regardless."

Den nodded, appearing more confused than anxious. "Go on..."

"That whole thing about Atlas Tear Drop being more potent in the last five years? Gilligan Hodgson was one of the people responsible for that. The pharmaceutical company he worked for manufactures and distributes Paradicium, one of Atlas Tear Drop's key ingredients. Turns out the man's been sneaking out bits of it for years and had been selling it to Macchianado."

"And how did Romero get this information?" Hugo inquired.

"Baratzi," Grill answered. "Not the most trustworthy source, but an examination of some of Hodgson's clothes proved it. Traces of undistilled Paradicium still lingering in the fabric."

Den let the moment sink in. Hugo said nothing. Knowing whatever came next was Den's choice, and his alone.

"I'm sorry, Den," Grill said. "If you want to turn back now, I understand."

"This changes nothing," Den replied. "I figured that was the case, anyway. Maybe not with the drug itself... But I never thought the man was clean. Doesn't matter... this stopped being about Hodgson a long time ago." The scarred boy cracked his knuckles. "Noland Macchianado's going down... He'll be brought to justice and made to pay for his actions..." Determination flared in his eyes. "I'm gonna kick his ass... I'll make him see God before he meets the Devil."

Chapter 6

Raid at Rubbish Plaza

I

"Rubbish Plaza?" Hugo asked in a confused tone.

"Unofficial name," Grill clarified, "but that's what everyone calls it. A junkyard. Peaks and valleys of unmapped spots. Seems like the most appropriate area for a meeting like this."

"Oh, definitely," Den said. "Take the kids. Walk the dog. Spend a romantic evening with your wife, before promptly delivering the divorce papers. Rubbish Plaza! Fun for all!"

"Any ETA on when you guys might be back?"

"Hard to say. Comes down to if they're peaceful or..."

"In need of a good smacking!"

"Either way," Grill continued, "I'd imagine this will be a long day."

"Understood," Hugo acknowledged. "Then I'll just treat this day like any other."

"If we're not back before closing," Grill said, "please see if Andolini can walk you back."

"I'll be fine, Grill," Hugo assured him. "I can handle myself... Just please be safe. Both of you... That's all I ask."

"We'll be fine," Den said. "We survived a giant plant monster. I think we got this one covered too."

"Won't be the same without the deer, though," Grill quipped.

The trio shared a laugh at Grill's remark. Den was proud to see his newly-appointed master being able to make a joke on his own; Hugo was just happy to see them in high spirits.

They stood in silence for a moment. Letting it pass. Even after their jokes, it was difficult for Hugo not to think of when they were leaving Harten to fight the Maple. All the uncertainties and risks they were taking. Six weeks had felt like a year.

But something still felt amiss. A final bit of unfinished business. One last ritual before they headed off. They all knew it, in some way. Maybe not tangibly, but they knew. Yet no one said a word.

"Well, time to go," Grill stated. "Hugo, we'll see you soon." The bounty hunter gave Hugo a firm handshake.

"See ya, buddy," Den said, giving Hugo the biggest hug he could, at least without breaking Hugo's back in the process. "We'll have another party when we get back!"

"Of course!" Hugo replied. "Though it won't be very big this time."

"Fine by me! A party's a party, whether it's with three people, forty, or a hundred!"

"Absolutely! Later."

"Later..."

Den and Grill made their exit, walking down the road they had chosen. Not taking a single look back.

Hugo went inside the WHS as soon as they left. Not wanting to stand out in the June breeze. Being left out in the cold.

"Did you wish them luck?" Andolini asked.

"Yeah," Hugo replied.

"I gotta say, I wasn't expecting them to look so prepared. But they are professionals! And you're nervous about it, aren't you?"

Hugo had kept the entire mission a secret to Andolini. Even without the NDAs he had signed, it still hadn't seemed right to burden him with the information. Andolini had never pried while Hugo was doing his research on Noland and Tillman. Hadn't asked any questions. Hugo wasn't even sure if Andolini was aware of the research at all. Yet he still remained so very helpful and kind throughout.

"Yes... Who wouldn't be? But I believe they'll make it through. It wasn't that long ago I had a loved one think the same thoughts about me... I made it through then. They'll make it through too. I have faith in them."

"Aye, lad," Andolini agreed with his same, jolly smile. "There's no better faith than that."

II

Rubbish Plaza lived up to its name. Piles upon piles of junk littered miles of land just outside Wayport's primary area. Still within the Terminal City's limits, Rubbish Plaza had become a common dumping ground around the borders of all four connecting states. Less garbage for their own states to sort out. Quick paydays to anyone with enough power to do something about it. Leaving the entire area in a limbo of perpetual dumping.

But there were those who made sport in finding things no one else wanted. For every piece of broken material and half-eaten food, on occasion there could be forgotten utilities and unwanted products that could be taken and sold.

And with as large as the area was, it became a common spot for meetings of all varieties. For both legal and criminal alike. Akin to the golf course diplomacy many business leaders and politicians would partake in. Though far less pretty and with far more abuse on the olfactory senses.

Noland Macchianado and his associates had already arrived at their decided-upon meeting spot. A far more open area, in comparison to the rest of the junk piles. Giving both gangs plenty of space without getting too close to one another. As well as relieving their nostrils from any strong odors.

As planned, Nicky the Grass led the group. Noland stayed close behind, and Baratzi had joined them not long before they'd arrived. A number of lower-ranked men followed along with them, soldiers more than willing to serve if it meant bigger payouts. Some were even vying for the top spot, like Noland. Thugs with ambitions of grandeur, but with minds the size of peanuts. But they were armed and loyal enough. And for those at the top like Nicky, that was all that mattered.

Noland himself was in a trance. His face had gone pale and his lean build had started shriveling up. In the past few days, he had been given an even larger amount of other stimulants to make sure he would not pass out during the deal. But it was the promise of getting his next hit that had truly kept him awake and aware. It would not be much longer.

From the other side of their meeting place came the Takedas. Stern, stoic faces. Sunglasses covering their eyes. Dark hair slicked back by gel and form-fitting coal-black suits which showed they had nothing to hide. Their pistols holstered directly onto their sides. Arms lowered, ready to fire at any given moment. Standard tactics amongst the Eastern gangs, standing in contrast to the Western gangs' concealed-carry preference.

They were men of different faces and different sizes. Yet the way they moved and positioned themselves together, aligned in rows, gave the appearance of discipline and authority. A small army in comparison to the more ragtag bunch of Florenzas on the other side.

At the front was Jun Takeda, the family's primary spokesperson and the one Hodgson had built a rapport with. The one who oversaw the Takedas' interests in Wayport. The late Hodgson had previously regarded him as Nicky's equivalent.

And as with most meetings, Jun's brother Miki stood beside him, maintaining the same stance as the rest of the Takeda soldiers.

But it was the man at the front that caught everyone's eyes: Kenichi Hirose, the Pale Dragon. Translucent was a better word to describe him.

An outline of a man. Shriveled skin so pale it looked as if he could glow in the dark. A clear map of veins running across every bit of exposed skin. Limbs so thin they appeared emaciated. Eyes that were not only faded, but entirely covered in gray, from pupil to sclera. Adorned in a suit so black it was as if his body had disappeared into the shadows. Held up by a cane that seemed to be the only thing keeping his frail body upright.

The rumors Noland had heard and the pictures he had seen still had not prepared him for the sight now in front of him. Hirose's presence gave the mobster a cold chill. Beads of sweat ran down his back. Perhaps it was the withdrawals. Perhaps it was some unseen nervousness regarding the deal. Perhaps he had simply not slept very well. But to Noland Macchianado, the man in front of him was not a pale dragon... he was a living ghost.

No one else reacted to Hirose's apparitional appearance. Each of them remained stoic. No one dared to crack a joke at a man of such high standing and infamous reputation. All that mattered was the deal.

"Welcome, sons of Florenza," the Pale Dragon greeted. It was common vernacular within the underworld to refer to all members as sons of an organization's founder, regardless of actual familial ties. The Takedas had taken it one step further: all members legally changed their names to Takeda at the time of their joining, Jun and Miki included. The Pale Dragon himself was the only exception; he'd been a founding member long before the practice started. "It is a great honor to know Giuseppe's legacy is still alive and well."

"And we are honored to be in the presence of such an illustrious man," Nicky complimented. All at once, Nicky and the other Florenzas gave a small bow. Enough to show their gratitude, though always making sure their eyes were still on the Takedas. "We only hope that we are able to provide you with a product that meets your excellent tastes and standards."

Noland was the last to bow, only realizing the necessity of the gesture once he saw the rest of his crew doing the same. It was an expected flub, given his condition. He had the excuse of not being in top form. No one else had such a luxury.

"If what I've heard is true," Hirose replied, "then it should be more than enough."

"I am of firm belief that it will be," Nicky stated. "And of course, my deepest thanks to Jun, for letting this deal be possible."

Jun bowed. "It is an honor to work with you again, Niccolai," he said. "Just as it was an honor to arrange this meeting with the late Gilligan Hodgson. May he rest in peace."

"It was a terrible loss," Nicky said, putting on a false face of melancholy as he pretended to think of Hodgson. "But rest assured that the work the two of you have done will not go to waste on this day." He turned to Baratzi. "And, of course, special thanks to Baratzi for starting this in the first place. As well as acting as our mediator for today."

Nicky began a small clap, and his subordinates followed suit. The Takedas did not clap, instead bowing to show their gratitude. Baratzi put on a smile, gritting his teeth. This entire charade angered him more with every second of wasted time.

Unbeknownst to all present, a thin wire lined Baratzi's body. A listening device had been strapped onto his left side, covered by several layers of clothing. It broadcasted a signal only a few miles away, to Romero and his crew. They awaited the right time to pounce. But they were still only on the formalities and needed to let the entire deal go through first. This was going to be a long day, Baratzi feared.

"Well, I suppose it's time to start," Nicky stated.

Hirose nodded. "I look forward to it."

From out of his breast pocket, Nicky took out a single blue pill, the eponymous Atlas Tear Drop. "Open up your hand, Noland," Nicky commanded. Noland did so and Nicky placed the pill into his palm. "Don't you *dare* take that until you're ordered to," Nicky whispered into his ear.

Noland said not a word and placed the pill into his pocket. He didn't have to question what might happen should he disobey his order.

"My subordinate here will now move to the center," Nicky said aloud, his tone far more proper and constructed than the warning-turned-threat that had just been whispered. "Noland, if you will."

Noland did as he was told, moving into the gap between the two families. He moved his head around; both families had moved even further apart from one another. His eyebrows rose in confusion, but he was in no place to question.

"As you can see," Nicky stated, "my subordinate, Noland Macchianado, has gone ten days without a single take of Compound ZX-78153, or as it's colloquially called, Atlas Tear Drop. You'll note his lankier build, bloodshot eyes, and paler skin. Signs of withdrawal which he only survived thanks to other stimulants he was given for the duration. Stimulants which were listed and given to you by the late Gilligan Hodgson."

Nicky nodded to his other subordinates. They began moving nearby bricks one by one and placing them in front of Noland.

"These bricks are made of Corridian Ore," Nicky explained, "a standard sediment found throughout the country. It has become the standard for use in the construction of high-security areas, such as bank vaults, due to its ample supply and cheap cost. While seen as a pale imitation of the superior Maizonian Ore, it is still quite powerful, especially in large chunks.

"With the bricks' current dimensions, a person in good shape can lift about five. Mr. Macchianado will now begin lifting these bricks with only his two hands, starting with one and then adding another with each subsequent lift. Before we begin, Mr. Hirose, you and your men are perfectly free to examine these bricks before we begin the test."

Hirose shook his head. "That won't be necessary."

Noland couldn't help but smile. A chance to show off his strength? And in front of a rival family? It was all coming back to him. The challenges of his youth. The applause of the audience. He was practically beaming.

He began lifting one brick, easily moving it up to his chest and then back down again. He did the same thing with two, feeling only a small strain, but quickly chalking it up to not having stretched beforehand... Then came the third, the fourth, and the fifth. With each new lift, the strain grew greater. The sweat had already started dripping down his head. His chest already beat heavily. He continued this lift several more times, but his limbs kept aching more and more. By the time he was eight bricks in, Noland's arms were giving out. The strain was too great.

There was a time when Noland could carry dozens of these together without a thought. When lifting entire piles seemed like nothing. Yet now he couldn't even lift ten. Had he grown this weak already? Had the past ten days of torment broken his body this much? Or had he been like this far longer than he had even realized? Merely a puppet controlled by the Atlas Tear Drop.

"As you can see, Mr. Macchianado is an Enhanced," Nicky continued. "Able to lift more than the average person. However, it was done with great struggle. And an Enchanced at the height of his or her ability has the potential to accomplish far more than these meager results."

Noland couldn't help but grit his teeth at Nicky's comments.

"Mr. Macchianado will now partake in a single dosage of Atlas Tear Drop," Nicky explained. "Once the effects have taken hold, he will restart the test." Nicky snapped his fingers. "You're up, Matches."

With the excitement of a child opening up a birthday present, Noland took the pill out of his pocket and swallow it in one big gulp. Everyone present sat in anticipation, waiting for the drug to take effect. One of the greatest advantages of Hodgson's purer Paradicium was that it allowed Atlas Tear Drop to course through the body at a quicker rate. Its effects took hold far faster.

Noland stood at the center, waiting for everything to come together. His heart pounded in anticipation... and then there it was. The hit. That intoxicating release. This feeling he had been robbed of for what seemed like an eternity. Pure ecstasy.

His pulse quickened. His heart throbbed. He could feel his body bulking up as that sweet, sweet nectar coursed through his veins.

"Notice his immediate muscle expansion," Nicky explained. "It comes as a result of the compound tensing his muscles, as well as his blood flow increasing at a rapid rate. Such strain would kill the average human. But an Enhanced such as Mr. Macchianado can sustain this form for extended periods of time. How long each hit lasts depends on how an Enhanced's body is able to digest the individual elements, as well as how much physical stress is put on the user."

The Takedas and the rest of the Florenzas alike were surprised to see how quickly Noland had grown in size. Noland couldn't help but smile through it all. He had felt the world's applause before. And while these gazes were far fewer, he still felt like he was at the top of the world.

"Now, Noland, if you will restart the test," Nicky ordered.

Noland's sneer returned. "One alone is gonna take too long, Nicky! How about ten at a time?" Noland didn't wait for his superiors' response, instead stacking ten together and lifting them all at once. "How do you like that, huh? Easy pickings!" He could feel all eyes on him.

"Very well," Nicky said. "Double the amount!"

Noland was given twenty and lifted twenty. Noland was given thirty and lifted thirty. Forty came and went as well. Finally, Noland Macchianado managed to lift fifty with his two hands. But it wasn't just the weight which impressed all those seeing it. It was his balance. Noland had no tray to keep the bricks together, like in the past. He only had his hands and his coordination skills. With each new batch, he had managed to both lift and balance all the bricks together without causing them to fall. Noland had reached a new high, as if reuniting with the drug after going cold turkey had only made him stronger.

Noland lowered all fifty bricks back down to the ground, cackling as he did so.

"Mr. Hirose, Jun, and all other Takedas present," Nicky announced. "I present to you the pinnacle of Atlas Tear Drop!"

Applause exploded on both sides, the Florenzas hollering as they did so. The Takedas' claps remained quiet and calm. Kenichi Hirose brimmed with excitement. "What an incredible show!" the Pale Dragon said. "A truly exquisite performance."

"I'm very happy to hear that," Nicky said. "So do we have a deal, Mr. Hirose?"

Hirose chuckled. "Perhaps... Mr. Macchianado has passed your test. But I have a test of my own he must he take."

"Of course, sir," Nicky replied. "Whatever satisfies you."

"Hell yeah, Mr. Pale Dragon!" Noland belted. "I'll take on anything you can dish out."

"*Matches!*" Nicky scolded. "Do not speak to Mr. Hirose in that manner."

The Pale Dragon cackled. "Oh, it's perfectly fine, Mr. Santino. In fact, I like his spunk."

Hirose turned to Miki. "Miki," he said as he snapped his fingers, "you're up."

The silent Takeda brother walked to the center. Miki removed his jacket and sunglasses and gave them to one of his underlings to hold. Just like Hirose, his eyes were pure gray. While he did not sport any of the Pale Dragon's other features, it was still a sight strange enough to wrack Noland's nerves. Miki clutched his fists tighter and tighter. His veins bulged out, face turning red from the strain he was putting himself through. It took several seconds to notice, but it became abundantly clear that Miki's muscles were growing and his height was increasing.

In the span of two minutes, Miki Takeda, who had been the size of an average man, now stood a foot taller than Noland. His face was no longer red, but his veins still bulged. His suit, made of stretchable fabrics, was on the brink of ripping. The Takeda brother took one look at Noland and smiled a large, toothy grin.

There was a time when giants walked the Earth. When their mere footsteps could send ripples through the ground and their stomps could create shock waves. A time when these behemoths of men could conquer whole territories with only a few swipes of their massive clubs. Their origins were unknown, and what became of them in the modern era was shrouded in darkness.

Miki Takeda was no such giant. Yet his current appearance could make grown men fear him, this hulking beast of a man. The time of the giants may have ended long ago, but their legacy lived on in him.

"For as impressive as your feats have been, Mr. Macchianado," Hirose said, "it means very little to me if I already possess men of your ilk. As such, I would like you to engage in a contest of strength with Miki here."

Noland took another look at the man. Miki's smile was one of intimidation. A scathing retort to an opponent he had little care or respect for. Noland couldn't help but make that same smile back. "Yes, sir," Noland replied. "And what might this contest be?"

"We are all busy men here, and I dare not waste any more of your or our time. So I propose a simple test: a contest of strength. Fisticuffs, to be precise. Whoever knocks the other one down to the ground first wins."

"We playing by wrestling terms? Nothing below the belt?"

"I would prefer it so. We are not animals. We are businessmen. Colleagues, at that. If some blood must be spilled, then so be it. But please keep it directed at the face and chest. I expect all of us to go home after this."

"You got it, sir! I'm gonna enjoy—"

Miki punched Noland in the face before the gangster could even finish his sentence. Noland could hear his fellow Florenzas already starting to cheer and jeer. Like they were watching a boxing match on pay-per-view.

Noland maintained his footing. The impact of Miki's punch left less of an impression than Noland had expected. Especially for a blow to the head. He had barely even flinched.

"My turn? Fine then!" Noland landed his first punch straight into Miki's ribs. Like Noland, the Eastern man barely flinched. But underneath the surface, Noland could tell he had made an impact, however small it was. Miki's breathing was already growing heavier, a change so subtle that only someone studying the Takeda's breathing patterns would notice.

"Lay one on me, big guy! Come on."

As Noland requested, Miki's slammed his fist again—this time into Noland's ribs, mirroring the blow he had just been dealt.

Once again, Noland was surprised at how relatively unfazed he was. The blow certainly hurt, but his recovery was quick. Noland did not believe in God, but in this moment, even he thanked the Lord for Atlas Tear Drop's effectiveness.

"Copying my moves, huh? Let's see how *you* like it!" Noland landed a punch straight into the center of Miki's face.

Miki covered his face from the pain. Yet no teeth popped out. His nose only had a slight drip of blood on it. But that smile remained. Miki was enjoying this.

"You some kind of masochist, Mikey?" Noland shouted, intentionally mispronouncing his opponent's name. He didn't expect a response. Not verbally, at least. Only the next fist, this time slamming into his shoulder. "Oh you're trying to weaken my arms, right? Mr. Hirose! Isn't that against the rules?"

The Pale Dragon chuckled. "This may be a contest of strength, but intellect is a necessary tool in all forms of combat. Strike the shoulder, weaken the hit. Weaken the hit, take less damage. Take less damage... win the duel. And of course, you're certainly free to do the same, Mr. Macchianado."

"I like your style, sir!" Noland cracked his fists. "Time to give you another dose of your own medicine, Mikey." Sure enough, Noland struck Miki's shoulder. The Takeda brother flinched from the strike, but stood strong all the same.

"Let's go! Come on, don't be shy. I can do this all day!"

This contest of strength continued for minutes on end. One blow to the next. Each strike causing that much more damage to each fighter. Each punch bringing with it even more cheers from the Florenzas. As the fight continued, the Pale Dragon gave silent permission for his men to cheer. Soon enough, both sides were in an uproar.

For the first few rounds, the two fighters seemed to be at a standstill. But as time passed, Miki's posture grew more crooked. The blood from his nose flowed harder. His skin became bruised and his breathing grew heavier. And while Noland suffered from these conditions as well, it was nowhere to the same extent. Macchianado could have lasted for many more rounds to come. But soon enough it was clear that Miki Takeda was on his last legs.

"You can do this, Mikey!" Noland taunted. "You just have to land that perfect strike on me! It's not so bad."

Miki's smile had grown crooked from the swelling, creating a peculiar half-smile, half-frown. The Takeda brother geared up his fist and swung, only to miss Noland entirely and fall straight to the ground. Exhaustion finally got the better of him.

"Good luck next time, buddy!" Noland screamed as he raised his hands in triumph. The Florenzas cheered on his victory. The Takedas quieted down, but still acknowledged Noland's victory by clapping.

Nicky walked up to Noland, a congratulatory smile painted on his face. "An amazing job, Matches. Hold out your hand." Noland did so. In Nicky's hand was a new bottle of Atlas Tear Drop. He placed it into Noland's open palm. "You've more than earned this. Consider your debt paid off."

"Just doing my job, sir!" Noland replied as he placed the bottle into his pocket. The taunting smile Noland had used on Miki transformed into one of earnest intent.

"As you can see, Mr. Hirose," Nicky spoke, "what we have is top-of-the-line. And we would be most honored to have your partnership."

Hirose laughed at the top of his lungs. "A brilliant contest, if I've ever seen it. Very well, I shall humbly, and happily, accept this partnership."

The two leaders grasped each other's hands. It was a moment of victory for both families, and a truly triumphant one for Noland. This was his next step to rising higher in the ranks and one day becoming Nicky's equal. And perhaps even taking over from the boss, too. No longer would he be a mere loan shark and extra muscle. The future would be his...

And it would all come crashing down with the sound of a single siren.

III

Jewels Romero's team had been watching the entire time. The presentation, the demonstration, the match, and now the deal. All of it came in clear enough, thanks to Baratzi's wire. And while it was certainly not of high-definition quality, it was more than enough to show undeniable proof of the deal. Everything had come together as planned.

Romero's task force had remained several miles away. Positioned just far enough so as to not arouse suspicions. Keeping themselves planted for the long haul, if need be. But they needn't wait much longer. The time was here. The time to strike.

The Florenzas had brought several cases filled with samples to give to the Takedas. Samples the Takedas would then use for their own demonstrations while marketing it in the Eastern underworld. This exchange would take several minutes to conclude, following Hirose and Nicky's agreement. Several precious minutes Romero and his crew would use to their fullest.

Slowly and steadily, the team of agents made their way towards the site. Decked out in armor and weapons. Making sure not to leave anything to chance. Headsets adorned the sides of their faces for instant communication. Smaller than the ones Grill had given Den and Hugo before the Crimson Maple fight, but just as effective.

Den and Grill accompanied them, Grill utilizing his own limb guards and a bulletproof vest. They were far lighter in weight and more practical for maneuvering. A reminder that he was not beholden to the government's command. Not anymore.

Den neglected all such protection, arguing that it would only slow him down and weaken his strikes. The new headset was his only piece of additional clothing—a suicidal gesture for a normal man. But Den was no such man.

"Whatever happens next," Grill whispered to his apprentice, "we stay put unless the action starts." *Action* had been a common word Grill and his fellow soldiers would use in combat. It was a simpler word. A word that allowed them to believe, even for just a moment, that they were going to have fun. An easy distinction that kept their minds less occupied by the horrors they could face at any moment.

"Gotcha," Den whispered back. He wanted nothing more than to punch Noland straight in the jaw, but still held back. Knowing the alternative was a far better, more peaceful solution.

The agents were in place and had already prepared their signal. One of them took out what looked like a handheld boombox and flipped one of its switches. From it came a loud, piercing noise. A siren like the ones used by policemen. It rumbled through the area, catching the attention of everyone around.

"Dammit!" the Pale Dragon swore, knowing full well what was coming next.

"Everyone, stay where you are!" Nicky commanded his people.

"And remain silent!" Jun told his.

Baratzi followed Nicky's orders as if he were a Florenza. Keeping himself calm in the moment. Waiting to see where things would go next. He hadn't had to do a second of mediation. Nor had he barely spoken a word. Everything had gone perfectly well for him up to this point. He just had to be patient for a few minutes longer.

"All my years..." Hirose said under his breathe. "And still they dare to taunt me!"

The agents showed themselves. Guns cocked, but only half pointed at the families. The agent holding the sound box turned off the siren and switched it to a different channel.

"Attention all criminal suspects," came Romero's voice from the box, "this is an arrest! I repeat, this is an arrest! My name is Agent Julius Romero. I am a member of the Narcotics and Distribution Division of the Adalia Safety Department. We expect your full cooperation at this time."

"Yes sir, Officer," Nicky stated. "We will cooperate with you to our fullest abilities and hope this misunderstanding can be dealt with peacefully and efficiently." Each word from his mouth was monotone and vacant. A machine repeating words he had used a hundred times before. Standard capture. Standard procedure.

"I am in agreement with Mr. Santino," Jun spoke. "We have nothing here to hide." This was not Jun Takeda's first bust and it certainly wasn't his first confrontation with law enforcement. These events were merely a misstep in their plans. A hold-up that would be resolved soon enough. Nothing that a game of patience and good representation couldn't fix.

"You are all under arrest for possession and distribution of Compound ZX-78153. Otherwise known as Atlas Tear Drop," Romero continued. "You will be read your rights individually and will be escorted to the Wayport Penitentiary Center for further questioning. Your patience at this time is greatly appreciated."

To their word, neither the Florenzas nor the Takedas made a fuss as the arrests were made, apart from some scoffs and under-breath remarks. Nothing that wasn't protected by Adalia's free speech laws. Everyone stood in line, awaiting their turn. There had been a time when shooting or fleeing would have been the best result. But such actions would only impede, or perhaps ultimately doom, any and all accomplishments the families had made. Better to hold back peacefully than to play a far more dangerous game.

Even the Pale Dragon, as old and tired of such situations as he was, kept himself quiet. Though not without the gritting of teeth and mincing of words. Watching as Miki Takeda was being propped up and handcuffed. Romero had underestimated the number of Florenza and Takeda members who would be present, and so only used handcuffs on the ones he deemed most dangerous.

With the process going smoothly, Den and Grill remained some feet away. Hiding just behind a junk pile. Out of the families' sights. A look of disappointment on Den's face. A look of relief on Grill's.

Then it was time for Noland Macchiando's arrest. Nothing he hadn't dealt with a number of times before. He had practically made friends with some of the inmates during his halfhearted incarcerations. Usually making quips at the tightness of the cuffs or the arresting officer's stench.

But this time was different. Today had been the longest Noland had ever gone without a hit. At least not since he had switched over to Hodgson's purer version. The stronger hit. A hit that his body had grown accustom to over the years. Something that had become a natural part of his daily routine. As common as the brushing of his teeth.

Noland had never taken it after such prolonged starvation—the withdrawals weakening his core, hazing his thoughts. Every second a waking Hell. Until that sweet drop had finally returned... And all the insanity it brought with it.

Chaos factor. Something no party had realized would happen. Nicky had assumed the other stimulants could cover Noland's basic needs. But they merely kept him from dying. Kept him from seething at the precipice. This was something very different. The inner beast in Noland had been satiated with brick-lifting and fisticuffs. While excited, Noland had overall remained in form since the hit. Keeping his anger from erupting. Satisfying his wanton need for violence.

Now he stared at the crowds of federal agents and other gangsters... Dozens of little sheep waiting for the slaughter. Taunting him with guns. Making his blood boil. Interrupting what was supposed to be one of the greatest moments in his entire chaotic life. The day when he could seek ascension. And these little bastards in black suits had ruined it all... It was time for the big, bad wolf to come out and play.

"The cuffs are a little tight," Noland said to the agent. "Care to loosen them a bit?" The agent did not acknowledge Noland's request. "Fine then... I'll do it myself."

In a single movement, Noland stretched out his arms, breaking apart the handcuff's chains. The agent unholstered his gun, only for Noland to land a hook on him, knocking the man down. Another agent tried following suit, only for Noland to punch him down as well.

Through all this, Noland had remained at the center of the area. The perfect spot for everyone to see. Gangsters and agents alike.

"Noland, stop!" Nicky ordered. But just behind him, a roar of cheers came from his underlings, who started following Noland's example.

This was the chaos factor at play. Noland was second only to Nicky amongst the men present. Barrett, Jacob, and Tillman had all stayed hidden, under Nicky's direct orders. The boss's own location was a total mystery. Noland was a fire-starter and talkative. And though many of the gang's higher-ups found his manner of speaking annoying or untrustworthy, such opinions were not shared by many of the Florenza's undermen. At least not in this moment. No, they idolized him. And not out of family loyalty, either. It was simply Noland's charisma. His need to rebel. They had just seen Noland take down a giant of a man. Now it was their turn to do the same...

The brawl began like a firecracker, small bursts that only accelerated in size and damage. It had started with Noland throwing a single punch. Within three minutes, it had evolved into a full-on war zone. Fists bashing into heads. Bullets flying all around. Any hope for peace completely, utterly destroyed.

The Takedas tried to hide from the fight, but in such a moment, any movements could be taken as hostile. And with bullets flying, ricocheting about, it was only inevitable that one would pierce the head of a loyal Takeda soldier. Both Jun and Hirose watched as one of their own fell flat onto the ground. There was no turning back now.

The fighting only intensified. Bodies dropped. Some merely injured. Others not as lucky. And through it all, Noland continued his beatdowns. Even going so far as to start attacking Florenza and Takeda alike. Blinded by bloodlust. Cackling through it all.

"More! More! Won't somebody give me a chall—" From the corner of his eye, Noland saw it. A blur of gray running straight towards him. He had no time to move and was met with a jab into his jaw. The pain was minimal, but the message was clear.

Noland finally got a look at his assailant. Perhaps the one and only person in this forsaken city who could meet his demands. "Weird Boy..." Noland snickered. "Nice to see you again!"

"Den," he screamed. "The name's Den!"

"So you do have a name! Well, suffice it say, this is certainly a surpri—"

Den burst towards him with another jab. "You just gonna stand there and chit-chat all day? Or are you that tired already, Addict? I'm here to kick your ass, not listen to a lecture!"

"Ooh, and he's got a mouth on him, too. Fine then!" Noland swung his right arm in a side hook, only for Den to sidestep the attack by jumping backwards. Not letting the momentum go to waste, Noland used his arched position to deliver a straight kick into Den's chest. The motion of the movements were so smooth that Den didn't have time to block the strike. He took the full hit of the blow.

Den fell to the ground, landing on his hands and one knee. But he did not stay down. The scarred boy used the full strength of his arms to lunge back at Noland. With Den low to the ground, Noland arched his leg back, preparing to kick. Den saw the kick coming and threw his body to the right just as Noland began his attack. He jumped forward and headbutted the gangster in his left ribs. The scarred boy could have sworn he heard a few pops.

Den was now in close proximity to Noland, and the gangster knew this full well. He swung his left arm to his side, putting Den in a chokehold. "Nice try, Denny!" Noland taunted. "But you gotta be more careful than that."

Den struggled to escape the gangster's grip. But without the force or momentum, his attacks could do little damage to a man of Noland's strength.

"Sadly, I'm afraid I'm gonna have to end this. And so soon after our blessed reunion! But I'll give you a little news before you go... Hodgson, that guy you've been trying to avenge, was nothing more than a mule. A selfish fatass who skimmed some off the top for his own desires! You've gone this far just to avenge some egotistical bastard! How does that—"

A bullet flew into the side of Noland's head. Then another, and another. Not enough to kill him. Barely enough to even break his skin. But they kept coming. Each one causing that little bit more damage. Sinking in that little bit deeper. Just enough force to rattle Noland and loosen his grip.

Den did not hesitate. He used what force he could muster and pushed himself back from Noland. Escaping his grip and jumping out of his range.

Noland looked around and saw the one responsible: Jack Trent, the Iron Sniper himself. In the midst of this entire battle, as people on all sides fell to the ground, the bounty hunter placed his full focus on Noland.

Before they had even left the hotel that morning, Grill knew there was nothing he could do to stop Den's attack. He remembered the scarred boy's propensity for thunderous entrances. Both against the Mungo-Boar and the Maple. Grill's training was meant to prepare Den for hand-to-hand combat. He hadn't had the time to alter Den's innate love of battle. Nor did he want to. It would be up to Den to know how to use that animalistic rage to his advantage.

"Thanks, Grill! But I got this," Den shouted over the headset.

"Not from what I saw," Grill replied.

"It's a war zone, Grill! Use your expertise to help out the others."

"I'm your master! I won't just abandon you right now."

"I'll keep my distance! Just please—"

That's when Den noticed the rest of the battlefield in full. More bodies had dropped to the ground. But they were close, very close to the center of the battle, where Den and Noland's fight raged. In the back of his mind, Den had wondered why no one else had interrupted their fight. Then it all came together.

Grill had been targeting and shooting anyone else trying to attack Den. But the scarred boy had been so focused on his brawl that he had only just now noticed it.

"Thank you, Master," Den acknowledged.

"Keep your eyes on Macchianado," Grill stated. "Nothing else matters."

"Aww," Noland said. "How sweet. Could make a grown man cry!"

"Less talking, more fighting, loud mouth!" Den shouted.

Noland spat blood. His fatuous smirk only made Den more charged and ready to strike. "I guess you're right! It doesn't really matter now, does it? Who cares! All I need is this!"

"Bring it on, druggie! I'll smack you down a hundred times over."

The two rushed at one another once more. Their fight had only just begun. And it was anyone's guess who would come out on top.

IV

Romero had been ordered to stay behind. To watch the battle from a close, safe distance. To only leave if his position was compromised. He had everything prepared for just that moment. Pistol in hand. His body calm, yet ready to strike. This was far from Romero's first bust. It wasn't even his most bloody. And through it all, he knew it wouldn't be his last.

From close by, Romero could hear the haggard steps of shoes on pavement, heavy breathing in and out. The sign of someone running away from the action, rather than advancing on it. Romero stayed at the ready as Baratzi came towards him. Weaponless and exhausted, the gangster was clearly stunned by what the bust had wrought. A small sense of relief overtook him as he approached Romero.

"Get me outta here!" he ordered, still catching his breathe. "I did *not* sign up for this."

"I'm afraid we cannot leave at this time, Mr. Baratzi. We'll have to wait until the shots stop."

"What the hell? You can't expect me to stay here! One of those crazy bastards will try to shoot me. I need to get out of here now!"

"Mr. Baratzi, if safety is your concern, please be assured that you are safe from any of your ilk as long as I am with you. If that is not enough, be advised that you will be hunted down to the full extent of Adalian law should you run away from the scene. These are your only options."

"Damn it all!" Baratzi screamed as he threw his arms up and kicked the ground in a rage. Yet for as threatening as he was hoping to come across, his actions seemed like nothing more than a child throwing a tantrum. After a moment, Baratzi calmed down. "Fine. I'll stay. Bad enough I get those blowhards out there shooting like crazy. At least here I got Fed support."

"Thank you for patience, Mr. Baratzi."

For several minutes, the two stayed in place. Eyeing the action going on just outside their reach.

"I have request, Mr. Baratzi," Romero began. "Would you be able to identify several members of both gangs?"

"What? You bastards don't have us all on file?"

"Part of the process, sir. Helps to have a firsthand account."

"Tch. Fine!" Romero handed Baratzi his binoculars.

The gangster placed his entire attention on the battle at hand. Looking over each visible spot and trying to identify those he could find.

"I see Macchianado near the center. He's fighting that weird kid. What was his name? Danny? And man, are they going at it! Like two dogs in a cage fight. Oh, man, I can't wait to see that sonuvabitch get what's coming to—"

With a single bullet to the back of the head, Baratzi was shot dead. The ringing of the shot was drowned out in the chaos of the battle. Baratzi's body slumped over, the binoculars in his hands smashing into the ground as he fell. His blood pooled into a puddle.

Romero gave a light chuckle as he lowered his pistol. A tinge of self-satisfaction came over him. He was still on duty, so he had no time to enjoy this moment. But in his mind, the agent was already planning how to celebrate the occasion. He grabbed the binoculars and stuck them back in his coat. He took out his other pistol and placed it in the still-warm hands of the late Baratzi, positioning his body to make it seem as if the gangster had tried to shoot him. It still didn't explain the exit wound coming from the front of his head. But given the raid's erratic situation, it was not outside the realm of reason that Romero could have managed to move behind Baratzi and shoot him in self-defense. It would have to do. Not that there would be anyone to counter his story.

Baratzi was just scum to be disposed of. Another piece of trash and nothing more. That bullet a final comeuppance. Agent Romero would not weep for him. No one would. He was a seedy man who had been a gateway to far seedier deeds. And now he lay amongst the rats. It wouldn't take long before they started nibbling.

V

Nicky Santino didn't know how many of his men had been captured or how many were dead. Nor did he know the state of the Takedas. As the fighting started, he had managed to get out of dodge. Moving away from the fight and further into Rubbish Plaza. He couldn't concern himself with such thoughts at this moment. He needed to get out. Head back to safety. If the Feds went after him later, he always had his legal crew to smooth things over. Nothing a few tip-offs, bribes, and wise words wouldn't be able to fix... he hoped.

But Nicky the Grass was unfamiliar with Rubbish Plaza. Such a place was far better suited to someone like Jacob and his strange little mind. But Jacob would have been too much of a liability to join today, and Nicky had no real reason to think things would have gotten this out of hand. So he simply moved further into the junkyard, taking his chances.

Soon enough, several figures came closer to him. Nicky didn't know whether they were friend or foe, so he moved a different direction, hoping to lose them.

"Niccolai!" came a familiar voice. It was Jun's. For years, the two had maintained a cordial, professional relationship. Though they rarely saw eye-to-eye. Hodgson had not only been a major part of this deal, he had been an absolute necessity. The primary reason the two were able to work together as well as they had. But he was gone now, and there was no telling what Jun was going to do.

Still, Nicky could not abandon Jun like this. Perhaps there was still some way to salvage the meeting. Nicky moved towards Jun, gun at his side, in case the Takeda tried to make any sudden moves.

"Jun, thank God!" Nicky said. "What's the situation?"

"Terrible!" came Hirose's voice just behind. The Pale Dragon was in no shape to run; a Takeda soldier carried him on his back. His ancient, wrinkled hands clawed into his subordinate's shoulders. "Macchianado doomed this entire deal with a single hit."

"I'm so sorry, sir!" Nicky apologized. "Please let it be known that he was acting on his own in that moment. I tried stopping him. His actions do not reflect the Florenzas'—"

"Don't you give me that crap," Hirose shouted. "I've experienced more busts in my life than you've had hot dinners! I saw how your men reacted once your precious Matches started acting. Savages, all of them!"

"Sir, if there is any way I can pay you back—"

Several bullets flew straight past them. One of them struck the neck of the man carrying Hirose... which in turn meant that Hirose had been struck, too.

The Pale Dragon's holder fell to the ground, bleeding out from his neck, passing on soon after. The position of Hirose's body had made it so that the shot that went through the holder's neck had also pierced the left side of the Dragon's upper chest. Going straight through his grand pectoral. No vitals had been pierced, yet the sheer shock of the hit was already causing great pain in Hirose's body. His clutched at his wounded chest.

"Sir!" Jun shouted. "Please, stay with me!" Jun looked out, immediately seeing where the shot had come from. It was a young Florenza member, probably no older than nineteen, with blond hair and blue eyes. His hands shaking in fear and his gun still smoking.

Nicky didn't recognize the young man. Then again, he hadn't paid enough attention to many of the new recruits. It wasn't his job anymore. Regardless, what that man had just done was arguably even worse than Noland... and he wasn't even going to live long enough to see the consequences of his actions.

Jun, in an absolute rage, grabbed his pistol and shot every bullet out of it. The young man, still in shock, didn't even have the time to react before each bullet made quick work of his head and chest. The young man fell to the ground. He would never know the joys of young love, children, or growing old. Instead his life ended here. A nameless face in a bloody junkyard.

"Jun, please!" Nicky shouted. "The kid didn't mean it! He thought I was being threatened! We can't end it like this! Please, just—"

For the second time, a bullet interrupted Nicky's words. But this one did not shoot past him. It hit him. Or rather, it had grazed him. Straight by his neck. Nicky could already feel the burning of his skin and the trickling of blood. Jun Takeda had shot him in the neck. He still had had one bullet: the one in the chamber. A classic move.

There was no more time for words. Jun may have been out of bullets, but he was also out of patience. He glared at Nicky. A death glare, if Nicky had ever seen one. His anger only broken when Hirose cried out in pain. "Hel... help me!" the Pale Dragon ached.

"You're going to be okay, sir!" Jun pledged. He took his jacket and shirt off, tearing them into pieces and stuffing them into Hirose's wound. With no gauze or other medical equipment, it was the only thing he could do to stop the bleeding.

Nicky stood over the scene, still clutching his pistol. Two shots was all it would take to end this. No other witnesses. Nothing to lose. Yet he still hesitated. What if someone saw from a distance? Witnessing the murder of two high-ranking Takedas at the hands of a high-ranking Florenza? They were already teetering on the brink of something far worse, and

Nicky couldn't risk it. So he fled. Speaking not another word to Jun. He just ran. Ran for his life. Ran to escape the horrors he had just witnessed.

Jun held onto his boss. Keeping him awake. Stopping him from bleeding out. "Please stay awake, boss!" Jun pleaded. "You can't die now!"

"Take... me... closer..." Hirose whispered.

"Closer? Boss, you'll die for sure!"

"That's... an order... Jun..."

Jun gritted his teeth. Even now, in a war zone, he had to follow the orders of his superior. He had no idea how many Takedas had been arrested or how many were dead. He didn't even know where his own brother was in this moment. But he still had a duty to uphold. He grabbed onto Hirose and made the walk back into battle.

VI

"That all you got, Addict?" Den screamed at Noland.

"You wish, Weird Boy!" Noland replied. "You think those scrawny arms can hurt me?"

"Of course not! They're not meant to hurt you—they're meant to kill you!"

"What a coincidence! Mine too! Come on, let's take them out on a date!"

"Oh, you couldn't afford them!"

The two rushed at one another once again. Breaking and weaving. Their fists bashing into one another. Each successful strike only giving the other man the opportunity to lay down another blow as well.

This was a far cry from the alleyway battle, where each successive movement was focused and intentional. These were two wild beasts digging and clawing at each other. Devilish smiles erupting on their faces. Caught in a struggle neither of them imagined, yet yearned to keep going. Even as their limbs weakened and bruised. Their faces swollen and bloody. Legs writhing and buckling. Yet still they flung themselves at each other. Only one would make it out of this fight. And neither had the intention of dying.

Yet fatigue inevitably set in. Their movements slowed. Their reaction times halved. And soon enough, both came down at the same time. A situation which could have allowed one of them to take full advantage over the other instead resulted in a stalemate.

Den and Noland distanced themselves from each other. Catching their breaths, but always watching how the other was processing the moment.

Their physical appearances couldn't have been any different. If their backgrounds had shared any similarities, they'd diverged long ago. Their very souls were the opposite shades of color. Yet in this moment, to these two men, it was like they were staring at a mirror.

"Gotta say, kid," Noland started, heaving with each word, "you're a fun guy to be around... Wish I'd have given you prep time before... Could have made this a regular thing..."

"I'm flattered," Den replied, also heaving. "But I'm just not that kinda guy..."

"My heart aches... But that's fine... Though I gotta warn ya... I'm bad at taking rejection!" Noland made his move straight at Den.

"Don't worry, you'll move on! I'll make sure of it!" Den met Noland's dash with his own. They dodged and weaved once more. Dancing on the blood of enemies and allies. Neither managing to land a single hit.

Noland clenched his teeth. At least one of them had chipped and embedded itself into his gums. He could already feel them bleeding, the taste of iron running through his mouth. The gangster laughed harder than he had laughed the entire day, an intense guffaw resonating on the battlefield. "This is what I needed! Bless you, Weird Boy! Bless you for this wonderful day!"

"You never shut up, do you?"

"What can I say? I got a lotta things on my mind! And the world deserves to hear every single syllable!"

"Then say your last words. 'Cause this about to end!"

Yet before the two fighters could make their final strikes, a sudden screech flooded their ears. It was another piercing wail, similar to the one which had begun this botched bust.

But this siren did not come from a mere machine. It was the work of human vocal cords... The voice of Kenichi Hirose, the Pale Dragon himself. Hirose was an Enhanced. Not the same kind as Den and Noland, whose physical strength and durability rivaled the strongest of men. It was Hirose's voice which ranged beyond human capabilities, able to produce screams that could paralyze friends and foe alike. And at this moment, the old man was screeching louder than he had in decades.

Romero had been aware of this ability, but he was under the impression it was impossible for Hirose to produce such sounds anymore, given the physical state of his body. And under normal circumstances, he would have been correct. But these were far from normal circumstances. The Pale Dragon was dying, shot by people he had thought allies. This was his last, great screech. His final wail against a system he despised. His requiem.

Jun stood beside him, shielded from the screech via a specially-made headset Hirose had given him. Normally, Hirose would have used it on himself, as even the Pale Dragon was not immune to his own screech. But he knew Jun was the future of the family. He could not allow his successor to be broken and deafened. Not when he still had so much to do.

Jun and Hirose were far enough away not to cause permanent damage to most people on the battlefield, but more than enough to stop them from fighting. Many of them collapsed to the ground, Den, Grill, and Noland included.

Until finally, the screeching stopped. The entire junkyard sat still. Not a single word or movement was made. A deathly silence.

Jun took off the headset and sat beside Hirose. "Lead... them..." Hirose spoke.

Jun nodded, tears coming to his eyes. "Yes, sir," he whispered.

"Make... them... all... pay... Don't... stop... until... they... are..." Kenichi Hirose, the Pale Dragon, was dead. He had seen the Old World become the New. He had cofounded one of the greatest crime families Adalia had ever known. And now he was gone. Dying in a junkyard, surrounded by trash. To some, it was a disgraceful end. To others, there was no better place that a monster like him could have ended up. To Jun Takeda, he had lost the greatest man he had ever known.

He wanted nothing more than to shout. To grab his pistol and kill every person in the area that was not a Takeda. But he had much work to do and so little time to do it. He grabbed Hirose's body and moved along, waking up any Takeda soldier he could find along his way. They ran back to their vehicles and left the scene, knowing more agents would inevitably make their appearance. Vengeance could wait another day.

Jun kept hold of Hirose's body, wondering how best to honor the man's legacy. He still did not even know where his brother was.

VII

Den awoke in a daze. His head ached and his limbs were sore. It took a moment for the scarred boy to process everything that had just happened. Grill sat beside him. They were still in Rubbish Plaza, not too far from where their fight had taken place. Federal agents and policemen surrounded the scene, surveying the chaos.

It was only now that Den noticed the bandages around his head and limbs. "How long was I out?"

"About an hour," Grill replied. "Around forty minutes longer than me."

"What the hell was all that?"

"The general term for it is Siren's Requiem, a piercing noise certain Enhanced are able to pull off. It can even deafen people in close proximity. Fortunately, it looks like we were far enough out of range for it to do anything permanent."

Den looked around. "Where's Macchianado? Did they arrest him?"

Grill grimaced. "No. It looks like he managed to escape. He was already gone by the time I woke up. The police and extra agents still hadn't arrived at that point. Would have been easy for him to sneak out."

Den gritted his teeth and gripped his hands. Everything that had just happened. All the bloodshed and death... And the man they had come to stop had gotten away. "Dammit!" Den shouted. "Dammit! Dammit! Dammit!" With his last shout, Den punched the ground below, leaving an impression of his fist. The scarred boy was seething. "Is there anything we can do?"

"Not unless we can get a lead."

"So he's still out there? He caused all this and he's still out there, free to create even more chaos? What the hell was the point of it all if we couldn't even catch one—"

"Den!" Grill yelled, trying to bring his apprentice back in the moment. "We did what we could! It's done! It's not our problem anymore!" He lowered his voice. "Not every case ends in success... We just do what we're able to do. That's all."

Den took in Grill's words, allowing his mentor's advice to calm him down. Yet he still sat with frustration. Wanting to do more, yet knowing full well he couldn't. At least not at this time. At least not now. "I... I did good, didn't I?"

Grill nodded. "Yeah... you did great."

Den looked on at the junkyard. Bodies still littered the area. Some being photographed. Others taken away. And still more remained untouched. All that violence and bloodshed. And within such a short span of time. "All those people..."

"It's the reality of this kind of job," Grill stated. "You just hope you don't have to see it much."

Den unclenched his hands, dipping them down to his sides. The frustrations he had felt melted into a pool of melancholia. The scarred boy sighed. "I don't know if I can do this again... I don't mean bounty hunting... I just mean... this."

Only six weeks ago, when they had fought the Crimson Maple, bodies of deer and other animals littered the grounds of Kelvin Forest. Now, in the Terminal City of Wayport, bodies of men littered Rubbish Plaza. Den had never seen war. But after these two events, he felt like he knew it better than most.

"You don't have to," Grill replied. "There's plenty of ways we can catch bounties without being caught up in messes like this. Small groups, solo catches, petty crimes. Low risk or, at the very least, small-scale risk."

"Grill... how do you... deal with this? I just... I just don't know what I'm supposed to do now..."

"You move on. Simple as that. It happened. We lived. There's plenty of help out there if you need it. But in the end, you just keep living. That's all you can do."

"I'd like that."

"Noted."

The two sat there for some time, waiting until they were given the official go-ahead to head home. Neither was in the mood to talk, exhausted by what had just taken place.

They watched the surviving Florenzas and Takedas being taken away, each one in handcuffs now. And among them was Miki Takeda. He had been knocked out for much of the bust. Exhausted from his fight with Noland. Watched over by Jun, only to get separated from him as everything went haywire. He had only woken up not long before Den had and was still taking in what had just happened. His eyes were empty, but not just because of his gray pupils. That same feeling of melancholy had eroded him as well. The top muscle of the Takedas... now just another broken man being taken away.

"I... kind of feel bad for him. Is that wrong?" Den asked.

"No..." Grill responded. "It just means you're human."

Some miles away, in a safe house built for such an event, a single man stirred in rage.

"That sonuvabitch," Nicky said to himself, neck still pulsating from Jun Takeda's shot. "We had a good thing... And he blew it just like that..." The gangster gritted his teeth, gnashing them back and forth. Clutching his arms, digging his nails into his own skin. He wanted to punch something. Break it. Burst it open. Make whatever living thing he could find suffer.

There was no going back from this. What lay ahead was going to be bloody. But there was one way he could lessen the blow. To dilute the carnage into a mere bloodletting. To take that one last chance before preparing for something far worse. "He's going to pay... That bastard... is going to pay..."

Chapter 7
Wanted

I

The walk back had been Hell. Every bone in Noland's body ached or seized up. But he made it back, all the same. Back to his infested apartment where the roaches lived and the scum floated to the surface. It wasn't much, but he certainly called it home.

Noland flopped onto his mattress as soon as he came in. He didn't care to take a shower or eat from one of his tin cans. Sleep was the only thing on his mind. But his mind was still racing and his head throbbed. He grabbed the bottle of Atlas Tear Drop from his pocket, still fresh from when Nicky had handed it to him, and popped another pill.

While Atlas Tear Drop was classified and generally utilized as a stimulant, allowing its user to get up and go, there were times when it was believed that the pill could also be used as a narcotic. But it required the body to have gone through great strain beforehand. It was theorized, thanks to the drug's quick reaction speed, that it would cause the body to go into overdrive so fast that it made the user completely exhausted, producing more melatonin in the process and inducing sleep.

Due to there being no tests on this, especially given the high amount of regulation put on Paradicium, a theory was all it stayed. It also didn't help that users who claimed to have experienced this reaction, such as Noland, were all long-term users of the drug. Regardless of what current scientific research had said, Noland knew that Atlas Tear Drop woke him up and it put him to sleep. That's all he ever cared about. And sure enough, moments after taking his next dose, the addict finally felt himself drift off.

But Noland Macchianado did not dream. There was only darkness. Every time, regardless of what he had done or where he had been, all he was ever met with was that same black void. No sounds, no smells, and nothing else to see but the dark. Noland wasn't sure if he could call this "nothingness." The color black was certainly something. Even if it had been a white void, that was still something too.

On slow days, when not even Noland could think of something to say, he would ponder if the darkness was what death was like. If at the end of it all, that black void was all there would be. Perhaps that was where he had once been, before his own birth. Perhaps his years on Earth was just a mild respite from the void. Or perhaps Earth was his punishment. Noland rarely waxed philosophical with his colleagues, not even Tillman. These thoughts were his alone. Thoughts that would, one day, drift into the void with him. Utterly forgotten.

Noland wasn't sure how long he had been out when he felt someone pushing his shoulders. "Noland!" came the voice. "Wake up, dammit!" The gruff sound of that particular order was enough for Noland to accurately guess that it was Tillman.

"Wha... what is it?" Noland responded in a drowsy daze.

"Oh, thank God!" Tillman exclaimed, his expression clearly one of relief.

"What? You think I came back here just to die?" Noland chuckled. "Don't worry, Till. I'm alive... I feel like Hell, but I'm alive."

"Good..." Tillman cleared his throat, his usual serious demeanor returning. "If it wasn't obvious enough, the entire deal is already being classified as an utter disaster."

Noland got up and started stretching. "Yeah, I can't imagine Nicky's happy."

"He's furious. Turns out, Baratzi was wearing a wire the whole time."

"That scummy little bastard! I knew not to trust him! Where is he? Think we could round up a couple of guys on him? Maybe give him the ol' torture dance?"

"Baratzi is dead. Shot in the head. We don't know who did it."

"Ha! Well, couldn't have happened to a nicer guy! Still, that's disappointing. Really wouldn't mind biting my teeth into someone else."

"You might get that chance soon... The Pale Dragon is dead too."

"What?"

"Shot in the chest, from what I've heard."

"Oh, crap... I liked that old man..." Noland meant his words. He had enjoyed the back-and-forth he had had with Hirose, however brief their interactions were. Few people had managed to catch the gangster's fancy, but the Pale Dragon had been one of them. It was like he had lost a new friend. "Did the Feds get him?"

"Worse. Allegedly, it was one of our own. Thinking they were going after Nicky. Jun Takeda is... not pleased, to say the least. I'm afraid we're on the cusp of war."

"Damn it all! Wars like that are messy and expensive as all Hell. Our last beef with the Minchesters gave me a headache for months!"

"There may still be one way out of this," Tillman said. From out of his coat pocket, Tillman took out a file of documents. "If we go after the source of this chaos, we might be able to cool things down."

"What, we going after Feds?"

"No, of course not! But federal agents weren't the only ones present at the meeting. As I'm sure you're more than aware."

"You don't mean..." Noland grabbed the documents. They were files on Grill. Much of it was public knowledge and information that had been gathered for some time. Noland looked through the first couple of pages. Sure enough, a picture of Den was among them. Recently labeled as his apprentice. Noland's cackling smile returned once more. "One last time, kid," he spoke to the photo. "One last time..."

Noland was so focused on the photo that he didn't hear the shot coming straight at him. The bullet impacted the back of his skull and several more followed suit, each shot more painful than the last. Noland's legs gave out all at once, nearly crushing one of the roaches as he fell.

"Aaaaaah!" Noland screamed. Turning back, he saw Tillman already trying to reload his pistol. But the old man's hands were shaky, causing him to drop several bullets to the ground. Noland sprang up and rushed him. He grabbed at Tillman's right hand, knocking the gun away and crushing the old man's fingers. Noland could hear the bones crack and shatter. The addict grabbed at Tillman's chest and pushed him to the nearby wall.

"What the hell, Till?! What the actual Hell?" Noland clutched Tillman's chest, making it hard for the old gangster to breathe. But Noland was expecting answers. He softened his grip on Tillman's chest, but still clung hard enough to keep him against the wall.

"It's you!" Tillman shouted as he ached from the assault. "They want you!"

"Me? What did I do?"

"You started it! It was *you*!"

"I was defending myself from the Feds! What else was I supposed to do?" The thought had not truly crossed Noland's mind even once. He hadn't realized just how responsible he truly was. Everything the gangster had done in that moment he had honestly thought was the right thing to do. A victim of his own arrogance. Guilty, above all else, of his own pride.

"It... It doesn't matter!" Tillman screamed in pain. "They want you! They *all* want you! Florenzas, Takedas, everyone else! They're all gunning after you!" With his good hand, Tillman motioned to his coat pockets.

Noland grabbed into them, finding a folded piece of paper inside. Its contents were newly printed. Noland unfolded the paper... and saw a picture of himself staring right back. Underneath were words he had hoped he would never see:

NOLAND MACCHIANADO
ONLY ALIVE

Noland let go of Tillman. The old gangster slumped to the ground. "Nicky and Jun came to an agreement. If you're surrendered... everything calms down."

Noland couldn't believe what he was hearing and seeing. After all these years of impunity, of catch and release, and now he was finally, properly wanted. And by the very people he trusted, no less. "Then why don't..." Noland was shivering, trying to come to terms as fast as he could. "Then why don't the Ta... Takedas just nab me themselves?"

"Bargaining... chip," Tillman stated, huffing his words. "Romero is willing to lower the charges... if they nab you... Maybe even outright drop them."

"So that's it? I'm just meat to be passed around?" Noland gripped his fists. "Screw them," he said. "Screw them... Screw them!" Noland punched his fist into the wall, easily breaking the drywall and leaving a large hole in the room.

"It doesn't activate until tomorrow... They were planning on nabbing you as you slept... I came here... hoping to get you early... Before the bounty hunters and police and agents all came for you."

"And you shot at me?"

"I knew..." Tillman's eyes started watering. His hands shook and his lips quivered. "I knew you wouldn't take it. I thought... maybe I could knock you out with enough shots. A small chance, I know... But I didn't want to see you like... like..."

Something broke in Tommy Tillman at that moment. Something innate. Something that had defined his entire life. He was not a man who cried, always taking his frustrations and worries out on someone or something else. A snide remark. An overly-critical joke. Even his own fists. Yet now here he was. Slumped over in a roach-infested apartment complex with dim, broken lights. Fingers shattered. Chest pulsating... And all at once, Tillman finally cried. Tears streamed down his face. Try as he might to cover the sight with his hands, it did nothing to hide what he was feeling in this moment. "I'm sorry, Mac... I'm so..."

Noland Macchianado had been an inmate, a powerlifter, a loan shark, and a gangster. Different hats across different lives. Different people. Different places. Yet Tillman had been his one constant. The closest thing to a father he had ever known. He barely remembered his mother. He never knew who his actual father was. But Tillman had been there. For both good and ill alike.

Noland grabbed Tillman's pistol, put the safety on, and placed it in his pants. He threw what few things he had in his apartment in a single bag. It wouldn't be long before his life was on the line. He had no time for pleasantries. No time for goodbyes.

Noland gave Tillman one last look. Not in disgust nor in love. He simply looked at the crying, old man bleeding on his floor. They locked eyes one final time. Tillman asking forgiveness. Noland rejecting it. He turned away from his mentor and ran out the door.

Tillman sat there for minutes on end, his own blood staining his crème suit. Eventually, his tears subsided and he calmed himself down. He took out his cell phone and dialed a number. "Nicky? It's Tillman," he said in his usual gruff voice. "Noland wasn't here. I don't know where he is. I'd suggest checking his usual spots first. Probably went out thinking it was a victory... Yeah, I'll call you if I hear anything else."

Tillman hung up the phone and got up from his puddle. He closed the opened front door before slumping onto Noland's mattress. He lay there for some time, taking in the ruckus and screams of the complex. So different from the luxuries of his own abode. It was almost relaxing. The old man would lie there until sleep got the better of him. Even he wasn't sure if it was exhaustion from the stress or his body going into some kind of delayed shock from Noland's attack. It didn't matter. Tommy Tillman wasn't sure if he would wake up from his nap. And not too long after, he wished he hadn't.

II

Noland Macchianado had no money on him. Or rather, not much. Merely a few ones and fives. But nothing that could get him out of Wayport and into a new life. He needed something more substantial. It didn't have to be liquid cash, just something he could sell. And the first place that came to mind was a place he hated going to, but knew there might be something he could nab: Brockson's Grotto.

Like gasoline to a fire, news of Baratzi's death had spread fast. The man had been so connected that almost everyone in Wayport's criminal underworld had spoken to him at least once. Now they all wanted a piece of what he had left behind.

But Baratzi had kept his finances secret. And with the revelation that he had recently been working with the government, it was almost certain that most of his assets had been seized. But there were still things out in the open that were rife for the taking.

Yet by the time Noland had arrived on the scene, the Grotto had already been pillaged. The tables had been turned over and the food and drink in the back already taken. Even the silverware, whose designs Baratzi had personally approved of, had been stolen.

Noland made his way to Baratzi's office, only to find that it too had been ravaged. The furs were stripped and the diamonds ripped out from the desk. The couch cushions and pillows were nowhere to be found. The red-and-gold painting was stained in black and white. A clear message from his many detractors. Noland wondered if even the bare desk and couch would still be here in a few hours.

Brockson's Grotto, once considered the finest restaurant in all of Wayport, had been laid to waste mere hours after its owner had died. No honor nor remembrance for his passing. No thought about the lives of the employees who worked there. Everything just stripped away. Jerry Baratzi was not a good man. Everyone who knew him knew his deeds all too well. There was nothing more appropriate to his legacy than this. Everything gone, as if he had never existed.

Noland did not care about the wreckage around him. Instead, he tried sifting through the ruins, hoping to find something that had been lost in the chaos. Perhaps a single diamond that had been caught between the rubble or some silverware that had been thrown down without anyone noticing. Instead, all Noland could find was a bottle of cheap wine. Barely anything of value, but he was desperate for something, anything to barter with. At the very least, the bottle would fetch a few more Rias than he already had.

Noland stopped his search when he heard the clicking of a gun just behind him. "Well, well, well, if it isn't Macchianado." Noland turned to see his potential assailant. Chuck Brisken was staring him down with a double-barreled shotgun.

"Brisket, my man!" Noland greeted, putting on his usual, talkative façade. "How's it going? Eating well? Of course you are!"

"Oh, you know me, Matches. I get what I want. And word through the grapevine is that you're about to get on the wanted posters in just a few short hours. Be a shame if someone grabbed you early and just waited for the bounty to activate."

"Me? Wanted? Naaaah! Probably just some pissed-off street urchin spreading rumors because he's jealous of my wild success."

"I'm afraid my sources are very formal, Matches. Now, be a good boy and let's just do this calmly. You don't wanna die and I don't wanna kill you. It'd be a waste for both of us."

"Look, Brisket, I really like you and all, but would there be any way we could forgo this dance? Because like you said, I *really* don't want to kill you right now. Think of all the laughs we've had!"

"Cheap laughs and cheaper booze ain't got nothing on all the Rias on your head! Now come with me quietly or I'm gonna have to—"

Noland threw the wine bottle straight at Brisket's face. Shards embedded into his eyes. The booze soaked and burnt his exposed skin. Noland gulped down another pill and punched Brisket in the stomach. The bounty hunter's fat folds saved him from direct harm, but still caused him to bend down in pain, dropping his shotgun in the process.

Noland grabbed the gun and wasted no time aiming it straight at Brisket's head. "Sorry, Brisket, nothing personal!" Noland fired off the gun, blasting Brisket's head open. His large body bashed onto the booze-soaked floor.

The blast caught the attention of other people just outside, giving off the idea that more loot had been found. People started racing back in, only to find nothing more than the corpse of a very large man, his left hand wrapped in a cast.

Noland ran out of the Grotto before the people had arrived. Dashing out as fast as he could. Staying in the shadows and out of public view. If Brisket was aware of his bounty, then who else was? How many potential hunters were already getting their weapons ready and just waiting for the dawn to arrive?

The wanted gangster stopped near an alley and sifted through his bag, hoping no one would see him. A needle, superglue, a half-eaten bag of potato chips, leftover stimulants for his withdrawals, some narcotics to help him sleep, a small bag of saline in case he got too dehydrated, a remote control from an old television he didn't even have anymore, and other pieces and bits of knickknacks. Nothing but junk, really. All except for that stuffed bear. Wrinkled and broken. Crushed between the refuse and the rubbish. Yet he clung to it all the same. Something so innocent drenched in the blood of his darkest deeds.

He had no pictures of loved ones. No memories of a better past. His awards and accolades all hidden away in Tillman's mansion. They weren't even his now, anyway. As Neil McKorkendale, he had officially left all his assets to Tillman. He truly had nothing. There was only the now. The uncertain, dangerous now. The now that he had chosen.

But within this pile of garbage was the file Tillman had brought with him. No doubt used as nothing more than a distraction, Noland thought. A tool to catch him off guard before Tillman had started shooting. But the information was correct and clearly up to date, given Den's new position as Grill's apprentice.

Noland looked through the notes more thoroughly. He had only sifted through the first few pages before. Perhaps something within these files could point the gangster to something more substantial. Anything was worth getting out of Wayport.

For the next few minutes, Noland Macchianado learned information on Grill he hadn't known before. Yet his story as the Iron Sniper, the Silent Death, and the Kataloosa Ranger meant little to the gangster in his current dilemma. The same applied to what little there was recorded of Den. Noland knew he had heard the name "Madame Lake" at some point in the past, but that too was useless.

The gangster had nearly given up until he reached the last page of the file. It was an entry on the third member of their trio: Hugo Statferd. Complete with a picture from Hugo's official Historian license.

A memory stirred within Noland. A memory from nearly a month ago. The last night he and Tillman had gone to see Old Man Andolini. He had planned to go back there soon, but the withdrawals he had to endure prior to the Takeda meeting had kept him preoccupied. Not that Andolini had much to give... Or did he?

At the front entrance of the WHS were stacks and piles of books, but they were cumbersome and it was doubtful he could fetch much money from them. He had no way of knowing priceless first editions from cheap, one-Rias trash novels.

No, it was the backroom where the treasure truly lay. All those old trinkets and antiques from long, long ago. Things Noland never cared for. Seeing them as nothing but useless junk... How wrong he was. There were things in this world treasure hunters would kill for. All Noland needed was just one of those pieces in Andolini's collection to be worth something, and he would be on easy street.

But there was something more to Hugo's picture that Noland couldn't quite grasp. The young Historian looked so very familiar. He tried remembering when he had seen his face before, but his recent bout of withdrawals had done damage to his short-term memory. Until a name came through his head. A different name than what was on file: Dominic Sullivan. The young man who was helping Andolini clean up his pigsty of an office.

And here this young man also was, the friend of two men he had come to hate so very much. This entire time, there had been another linchpin. Another person against him. The time he had met the young Historian had been cordial. But if this man knew Den, knew what had occurred between them... It all finally clicked together...

Noland gazed out at the moonlit night. Even in this alley, the Lang-Meyer Courthouse still towered over all. A thought rang through his head. A thought that made the gangster giggle in excitement. A plan was unfolding, and now he knew where to go and what to do next.

"Sullivan..." Noland whispered to himself. "Hugo..." he whispered again. "Statferd."

III

It had been a very long day for Hugo Statferd. Hours of waiting to hear from his companions as they embarked on a dangerous mission to capture an enemy who had nearly killed Den. Hugo could still remember the face of Noland Macchianado. Those killer eyes and that callous smile. He wondered how many people had died looking at that face. The last sight they'd ever see in this mortal coil.

But after some time, the call had finally come. Den and Grill had made it out safe and sound and were heading back to the hotel. Not without some wear and tear in their voices, especially Den's, but they had made it out safe enough. Grill had offered to stop by. Check to make sure Hugo and Andolini were safe. But the Historians declined, even with the concerning revelation that Noland Macchianado had escaped.

There was still plenty of work to be done and they were not about to stop because of unsubstantiated fear. Noland was not aware of Hugo's connection to Den and Grill. He didn't even know Hugo's real name. And while it was possible Macchianado could still stop by, given his connection to Andolini, Wayport was a big place and Macchianado had many connections. The chances were sadly not zero, but they were far from high.

Grill relented to Hugo's logic, but had no intention of letting the young Historian walk alone in the dark. He promised to come pick up Hugo at closing time. A time which would soon be here.

The day itself had been simple, all things considered. Just a normal day of categorizing what remained of Andolini's books. June had been a very productive month, thanks to Hugo's help. The young Historian wasn't sure how much longer they would be in Wayport. With Macchianado's inevitable capture and the WHS's refurbishment, it was almost certain they would be departing soon. Just a simple matter of when.

Then Hugo thought of Andolini. He would be all alone once more. And even with Macchianado out of the picture, who was to say another associate wouldn't simply take over his debt? Perhaps Tommy Tillman himself or one of the various gangsters Agent Romero had talked about. It made Hugo nervous leaving his friend like this. But Andolini had lived a long life before Hugo had ever stepped foot in it. The old Historian would be able to carry on somehow.

"Think it's time to turn in for the night, lad," Andolini said. "A little earlier than planned, but I think we've earned it. Good work as always, Hugo!"

"Thank you, sir," Hugo replied. "You too." Hugo logged off from the computer and helped Andolini turn off all nonessential components. Everything that was not involved in the preservation of artifacts or part of Andolini's living conditions.

"You going to be okay here tonight, sir?" Hugo asked as they moved into the backroom.

"After hearing what I've heard... I admit it does give me goosebumps. But at the same time, as you said to Mr. Trent, I cannot live in fear like that. I may not have built this building with my own two hands, but I certainly crafted and shaped its interiors. This place is my home."

"If you need anything, just call us. Okay? We'll be here in a flash."

Andolini smiled once more. "I know you will, boyo. You're a trustworthy sort."

A knock came at the door. "That's Grill," Hugo stated. "Must have thought we would be closing up early too. I'll come back to finish up after I've let him in."

"No need, Hugo! You can head out. I can finish the rest just fine."

"No, no. I insist! I'll be right back." Hugo went back to the front entrance to greet his companion. He hadn't seen Grill nor Den since they had left for the bust. After such a long day, it would be nice to see them again. He felt like he hadn't seen them in days.

Hugo unlocked the door and opened it up. To Hugo's horror, Noland Macchianado stood right in front of him. "Dominic! Didn't think you'd still be here at this late hour! How's life treating you? You miss Castella at all?"

Hugo froze on sight. He had no idea what Noland was playing at or what he was hoping to accomplish, but here he was. And all the young Historian could do was play it cool.

"Noland, wasn't it?" Hugo replied. "Yes, things are going quite well around here. It took some time, but I'd say we've made this place spotless!"

"Oh wow!" Noland replied, faking a surprised look. "From pigsty to wonder house! You and Andi must have been slaving away all this time to get this place shipshape! You know, I've known Andi for years and years, and it's never looked as good as it does right now! I'm telling ya, Dominic, ever thought of taking a side hustle as an interior decorator?"

"Well, I wouldn't know anything about interior decorating. I just know what looks good."

"Speaking of looking good, I was wondering, you think you could show me around the backroom again? I haven't seen it a while and I was curious if Andi has got anything new."

"New? I don't think so. It's basically been the same stuff day in and day out. I doubt it's anything you haven't already seen before."

"Maybe. But I know you weren't here last time I saw it. So I figured it wouldn't hurt to, ya know, check it out again. For old time's sake, if nothing else."

"Sure. Sure, I get you." Hugo turned around. "Mr. Andolini!" he shouted. "*Mr. Macchianado* is here. He wants to look at the backrooms!" Hugo made sure to place an emphasis on Noland's name. Trying his best to inform Andolini of the danger.

There was a pause in Andolini's response. "Oh, aye!" he finally said. "Come on in! Plenty of wonderful things to see!"

Hugo breathed in and out. Light enough that Noland wouldn't notice, but deep enough to keep the young Historian calm. "Right this way, Noland!" Hugo said.

It was only a few short steps into the backroom. Hugo wasn't sure what Andolini was planning, if anything. But he tried to give his colleague enough time to do something about the situation. Taking smaller steps. Extending their walk into the room by however many precious seconds he could muster.

They entered the room. And everything was quiet. Andolini simply stood nearby one of the glass cases. "Hello, Noland," Andolini greeted. "Glad to hear you've taken interest in my collection. Many wonderful pieces of Wayport history around here."

"Yeah, I know I haven't been one for all your old mumbo-jumbo stuff, but lately I've been feeling kind of nostalgic and all. Figured it was time I learned a little more about my dear old city." Noland started looking around, eyeing every piece as he walked by it.

The two Historians kept quiet. They knew Noland had no interest in their commentaries and contexts. At this point, it wasn't difficult for Hugo and Andolini to notice Noland was spending more time with the most valuable-looking items. Even moving his hands about, pretending to hold them. As if figuring out what their weight was.

As this went on, Hugo slowly started moving away from the backroom. Trying to get to the front desk without Noland being any the wiser. Where the phone was sitting. Where all it would take was a few buttons to call the right people.

"Beautiful collection, Andi," Noland said.

"Thank you, Noland," Andolini replied. "I try my best."

"It is really is beautiful... What do you think this stuff could fetch?"

"Excuse me?"

"I'm just curious, is all. Antiques of this caliber are sure to fetch a pretty Rias. Some of these have gotta be worth five figures, at least."

"I... I hadn't truly thought of it like that. As I've said before, these were all donations. I couldn't possibly factor in their price."

"Ah, come on! I'm sure you can think of something! Dominic, what do you think?" Noland turned his head to where Hugo was. The young Historian had made it to the front desk, his hand right next to the telephone. "What ya doing there, Dominic?" All focus Noland had placed on the antiques was now centered once more on Hugo.

"Oh, just checking in on a friend," Hugo replied. Sweat dripped from his back. He could feel his heart racing. "He's sick and I just needed to make sure he was okay before I went home."

"That's too bad!" Noland replied as he started making his way towards Hugo. "I didn't mean to interrupt your time with him and all!"

"No, it's fine. You were talking to Mr. Andolini, so it seemed like the best time to do it."

"Oh, by all means, call him! What's his name? I'd like to give my condolences to him over the phone, if you don't mind." As Noland moved closer to Hugo, so too did Andolini move closer to Noland. Hugo could see Andolini tremble.

"Um... I mean, that's very kind and all, but I'm afraid he's not good with strangers."

"That's perfectly fine! It's just that I love meeting new people is all. It'll only take a second. And then you can get right back to it."

By this point, Noland was right next to Hugo. Eyeing the phone. Looking to see what numbers Hugo would type. The young Historian could feel the faint hint of Noland's breath down his neck.

"Okay, Noland... Sure. I'll just... make the call..." Hugo hesitated. He didn't know what numbers to press. He started moving to the digits closest to him, unsure where he would go from there. But he still pressed it.

He was a few numbers in when Noland moved even closer to him. "Let me guess..." Noland softly spoke, coming in almost like a whisper. "Your friend's name is... Den, right?"

Hugo could feel his heart stop.

Without another second wasted, Noland swooped around Hugo and placed his arms around the young Historian's neck, planting him in a choke hold. It was strong enough to keep Hugo in place, but loose enough to allow him to breathe normally.

Andolini watched on, completely frozen in terror. The white noise of the unfinished phone call echoed around them.

"Dominic, Dominic, Dominic..." Noland said straight into Hugo's ear. "Or should I say... Hugo? Hugo Statferd? Why oh why would you try to hide that wonderful name, Hugo? It's so nice! Dominic Sullivan's really nice too. But it's just... it's just not Hugo Statferd, you know? It doesn't pack as much of a punch, at least in my opinion!"

Hugo said nothing, trying his best to remain calm and collected. Now was not the time to show weakness. He couldn't afford a panic attack at this moment.

"Playing the quiet game now, huh? It figures. Your good buddy Den did the same thing when we first met. But the next time? Oh, he wouldn't shut up! Always had to find some smarmy comeback to my remarks! So I guess in that way, you two are the exact opposite! Well, you know what they say, opposites attract and all!"

Noland turned his eyes to Andolini. "Now, Andi, if you know what's good for both yourself and Mr. Statferd here, you're gonna waltz back to your little collection, take every piece out of their cases, and put them in my bag. You do that and we're all good... okay?"

Andolini stood in silence. He watched as Noland gave his commands. Seeing Hugo now caught in the struggle. And yet the young Historian remained calm. Not for a second had Hugo broken under the pressure. Not back when he had first met Noland and not now. Sure, Hugo was nervous. Who wouldn't be? But Hugo hadn't given up. Andolini had noticed that. Hadn't let himself be taken over by the fear. Even now, with his life on the line...

For many years, Andolini had put up with so much. When a superior insulted him, Andolini grinned and bore it. If a colleague stepped on his shoes, he would be the one to apologize. Even when someone lashed out physically, punching his stomach or sweeping his feet, the old Historian would smile and ask if he had done anything wrong.

Noland Macchianado had been the worst of all. He did all those things. At different times and in different moods. Some days he was merely joking around. Others, he had no qualms forcing Andolini to quiver in fear. And each and every time, he had made that laugh. That same, echoing cackle. The spawn of a hyena laughing at his misery.

Now Noland was cackling again. Already believing he had taken control of the situation. Believing wholeheartedly that Andolini would just grin and take it. But there was something Noland never truly understood about the old Historian. Something he never cared to even realize: Andolini was a patient man, but even he had his limits. Limits that would reset between each visit. But this time, the walls were crumbling all around him... and he had finally had enough.

There was no warning. No sign of what was to come. There was only the charge. Andolini ran straight at Noland with a speed the gangster had never expected. Eyes aflame and teeth gritted. Hugo had seen Andolini jolly and he had seen him depressed. But never angry. Never the ferocity that had just come out. And it was all pointed towards Noland.

And that ferocity made its impact. As soon as Andolini started his charge, Hugo could feel Noland's grip slipping. The gangster was in fear. Fear of whatever retribution was about come his way. Hugo relaxed his body, anticipating the impact that was to come.

And come it did. Andolini smashed his fist straight into Noland's forehead. The blow was so hard it caused Noland to let go of Hugo, allowing the young Historian the chance to get away. Weaving past Andolini as the two began their fight.

Hugo moved as fast as he could to the backroom, making it to the emergency switch and turning it on. He had hoped to avoid using it, not wanting to cause unnecessary chaos. But Noland had played his hand and escalation was now the only course of action.

By the time Hugo turned back around to see what was going on, the fight had already ended. Andolini was lying on the floor, his head beaten and swollen.

Their clash had been brief. Andolini was not an Enhanced. And despite his large frame, he was not in good shape either. As a result, Andolini's punch had not caused any real damage to Noland. In fact, the punch had broken the old Historian's hand on impact. It was Noland's own fear that had been his temporary undoing. Terrified of a rage he had never seen before. Yet as soon as he was struck, the gangster knew he had nothing more to fear. But Andolini didn't stop. He threw another punch, only for Noland to easily dodge it. The gangster gave a one-two strike to Andolini's face. Downing the old Historian in seconds.

The emergency bell rang through both Hugo and Noland's ears. Hugo could bear it. Noland could not. Noland had dealt with loud noises ruining his plans twice already. He was not about to let this third time be the same.

"Oh, Hugo!" Noland called out. "How about we play a game! Let's see how long you can last before the cops show up! It's gonna be fun! But remember, *I play for keeps*."

Noland rushed at Hugo. The young Historian tried to move around the backroom, but he did not possess Den's speed nor Grill's agility. He was just a normal young man with not much athletic prowess. He tried moving back to the front entrance, but Noland would block the way, causing Hugo to rush back into the backroom. It was like a sick game of tag Noland was playing. And he loved every second of it.

Noland matched Hugo's speed easily and ran straight for him, placing the young Historian in another choke hold. Only this time, Hugo tried fighting back. Pushing his nails into Noland's arm and biting into his flesh. But the gangster didn't react. Instead, he continued to laugh. "So sorry, Hugo! You lose! But hey, don't worry, this isn't the end. Not at all. We've still got another round to play! We just need to switch venues."

Hugo felt a sting at the back of his neck, piercing into his skin. It was a needle. A needle injecting who-knows-what straight into his veins. The young Historian continued to struggle, only for his body to feel weaker and weaker, until eventually going limp. The last thing Hugo saw was the face of Andolini sprawled out on the floor. Beaten and bloody, but he was breathing. Hugo felt a small sense of joy seeing him. At least Andolini was alive. Hugo had no idea if *he* was going to be.

It is in the luxury of comfort, when man has time to consider his own mortality, that he feels his own fear. But it is only when staring into the eyes of death, when bravado is null and there is nowhere to go except through, that a man shows himself for who he is. Is he coward or warrior? Only through his actions does a man truly know. A warrior may turn coward. Just as a coward may turn warrior. History is only a guide, not an absolute. It is that singular moment in time that determines the victors from the victims. And where their path shall take them next.

—Pierre Ornakoff, *The Warrior in Men*, 468 AU

CHAPTER 8

HOSTAGE

I

There was nothing. Only a black void. It was all Hugo Statferd could comprehend. For a moment, he wondered if he had died. If the nightmare he had experienced had finally come true. Yet within that nothing came a something. And that something was a heartbeat. His very own. Neither fast nor slow. Just the same rhythm he'd always known. The same, steady beats that dictated the very flow of his life. Hugo Statferd was not dead. Merely passed out. And something within his mind was still going. Still ticking on.

Noland Macchianado had drugged him. To what end, the young Historian did not know. But he was aware now. In that void, he tried desperately to push himself awake. Concentrating within the nothing to comprehend his reality once more. He thought of Den and Grill. Karina and Rindi. His parents. His teachers. His friends. His colleagues. His achievements. His sins. Each person, each interaction, each memory was a part of him. He was not nothing in the void. He was Hugo Statferd. All those memories circled together, pushing through. And all at once, the void broke apart. Hugo Statferd had woken up.

Pure white, windowless walls. Stained plastic chairs which sat to the side. There was no other furniture, paintings, or shelves. For a moment, it seemed as if Hugo had exited a black void, only to awaken in a white one. But this was most certainly not the case. He was simply in a white room.

His new surroundings were not what one would call hospitable. But they were certainly not boorish either. They simply lacked the right accommodations. There was a single door in and out. The room seemed large enough to fit a long table. The perfect size for a meeting room. At least he wasn't in a dungeon.

Hugo tried to find his bearings. He was sitting down, his back to one of the walls. He could not see nor feel any bruises or additional scars on him. No signs of abuse while he was out. His neck felt slightly stiff from the injection, but nothing more. His arms had been tied together with rope. His legs were stretched out, but also tied together. Another rope connected his arms and legs, making it difficult for him to get up on his own.

At one of the corners sat a light-gray bag, looking as if it had been stuffed to the brim with trinkets and novelties. A light sparkle came from the top item. On further inspection, Hugo realized that the bag was Noland's. The very same one he had brought with him to the WHS. And the trinkets and novelties? Some of it consisted of random items, such a bag of saline that appeared half-full, but the rest of it were the very antiques Andolini had kept preserved. The sparkling item was the dagger from Adalia's expansionist period. The items' cases had presumably been broken in and taken with Noland's bare hands. Hugo couldn't begin to think of the degradation the items were already suffering, crumpled and stuffed into a bag with no thought or care. All the work Andolini had put into preserving them now all for naught.

Yet of all the oddities of his current situation, what struck Hugo the most was what was on his right wrist: a watch. A simple watch that seemed like nothing special. It was only on further examination that Hugo realized what it actually was. It was the watch Andolini had gotten from Gretchen the day before. One of the watches of President Josiah. For some reason, Noland Macchianado had put this watch on Hugo's wrist. And the young Historian hadn't the faintest idea why.

Hugo heard a flushing sound from nearby. The whiteness of the walls had made it difficult for Hugo to notice the second door in the room. The one to the bathroom. From out of it came Noland Macchianado. His body looked fatigued and thinner. Eyes more bloodshot and strained. His entire expression was one of exhaustion. Yet as soon as he saw Hugo, awake and aware, Noland's fatigue made way for vitality. He smiled once again.

"Well good morning, sunshine!" Noland said. "Or should I say, middle of the night. But it's definitely past midnight now. So welcome to the new day! Sleep well? Have any good dreams? Kiss a princess? Fight a dragon? Do both of those things at once? But really, how ya feeling?"

Hugo simply looked at his restraints.

"Oh, don't mind those, Hugo! They're just precautions. Nothing more. I just can't have you leaving."

"Where are we?" Hugo asked.

"Good question. Unfortunately, I can't tell you that. Not yet, anyway. It would ruin the surprise. But don't worry, all will be clear soon enough."

"Why are you doing this?"

"You know, I figured you'd ask that. And despite our previous interactions, I knew you'd deserve to know that much." From out of his bag, Noland took out a folded piece of paper. He unfolded it and showed it to Hugo. It was Noland's very own wanted poster. "Yep. That's me. The big star at the center! I'm sure you've seen plenty of these wanted posters. Your buddies sure have."

Hugo looked at the poster, but did not say a word.

"Long story short," Noland explained, "I pissed off my bosses, another gang's bosses, and the Feds all at once. Now here I am! Noland Macchianado: fugitive! Could probably write a book about it. Maybe even a movie! But alas, there is no starring role for this wayward businessman. Instead I am doomed to run from friend and foe alike... Unless I can get some cash on hand and get outta this joint. And that's where you come in, Mr. Statferd."

"I'm your hostage."

"'*Hostage*' is such a negative word. Let's just say you're helping me out. And pals help each other out, don't they? So really, we're pals. And from the bottom of my heart, I say thank you, pal!"

Noland sat back, expecting a response from Hugo. For seconds on end, he waited for the young Historian to say something. Even after the appropriate amount of time had passed, Noland still sat there waiting for some kind of response. An entire, long minute passed with absolutely nothing. The longest minute of Hugo Statferd's life. The silence had become comical. So Hugo finally said something. "You're... welcome?"

"Oh, it's no trouble at all!" Noland replied immediately. As if the past silent minute hadn't even happened. "I'm just glad to have a pal willing to help me out of a jam!"

"Okay..."

"Now, I'm sure you're wondering how this whole 'hostage situation' is going to go down." Noland raised both of his index and middle fingers and moved them up and down as he said the words "hostage situation." The kind of gesture a person would make when trying to mock a word or phrase.

Noland took out his cell phone to show Hugo. It was circular in shape and folded in half. With minor adjustments, it could pass for a woman's makeup mirror. Yet once unfolded, revealed the usual screen and numbers that all of its mobile ilk possessed.

Cell phones were still a relatively new commodity. It had only been a decade since they had become commonplace. But even then, they were still quite expensive. Den and Hugo had never needed one. The headsets they had used back in Harten had been more than enough. Even Grill, who could certainly afford one, had generally avoided using them, not liking the idea of someone being able to call him at any moment. This was Hugo's first real interaction with these new phones, and it wasn't a particularly positive one.

"It's pretty simple," Noland continued. "While you were in dreamland, I called Inspector Walton and told him everything I wanted him to know. The ransom, the stakes, blah, blah, blah. And of course, I made sure he informed your two best buddies. I told him I'd call him back in a bit, at my earliest convenience. So that being said, would you please be so kind as to give me the phone number to your hotel room?"

"Why?"

"Oh, did I forget to mention that? Sorry, my bad! I just thought it would be funny to give your ol' buddies a little ring-ring! Don't worry, Walton knows. In fact, he's probably already got his people swarming the place as we speak!"

"And if I don't tell you?" Hugo asked.

Noland laughed. "I think you know."

Hugo simply nodded and gave the number.

Hugo Statferd had faced danger before... but not like this. The Crimson Maple had been a different story. In that time, at least Hugo knew he was dealing with a force of nature. Man-made, yes. But it was still a creature that followed its natural instincts. However abhorrent they may have been. For as much destruction as the Maple left in its wake, there was always a method to its madness. A desire to consume. To live.

The young Historian was not dealing with such a beast. He was dealing with a man. A broken addict of a man, but a man nonetheless. A man who could lie and manipulate the situation to his own ends. His scope far smaller than what the Maple had wrought. But the wounds he could inflict would be far more damaging to the relatively few people he would leave in his wake. Noland Macchianado was not the Crimson Maple. He never could be. Yet to his victims, he was something far worse.

"All that being said," Noland continued, "it ain't time to call back just yet. So, to pass the time, I was wondering if we could do what good pals do and have a little chat!"

"Okay... Can I ask you a question?"

"Sure, pal, fire away!"

"What are you gonna do after this? Where are you going to go?"

"Hmm.... That's a good question. But for obvious personal reasons, I think it's best to keep that one confidential. Again, good question though!" Noland took out his bottle of Atlas Tear Drop and popped another pill in his mouth.

"Can I ask another question?"

"Ask as many as you'd like!"

"Think you'll be able to get more Atlas Tear Drop where you're going?"

"You kidding?" Noland huffed. "Adalia's full of this stuff! Doubt it'll be as potent as ol' Hoagie's batches, but we all have to make do in trying times!"

"And who's gonna pay for it? You? From what I've read, it's pretty expensive. You're not gonna have Tillman's money to save you this time."

"You really think Wayport is the only game around these parts? Hell, around Adalia? Listen here, Statferd, there's enough guys that would kill to have someone like me on their team."

"Or enough guys that would kill you for the money. What makes you think they'll be loyal? All it takes is someone with a connection to the Florenzas or the Takedas to rat you out. And it won't be pretty either."

"Oh, you sweet, little man... then I'll just have to smash them like I did Hoagie!"

Delusional. Absolutely delusional. In his stupor, Noland had become awash in his own visions of grandeur. Again. A puppet to his own dreams. And Hugo knew that. There was no point in arguing against his logic anymore. The fact that Noland had remained calm was a blessing in itself. To poke the bear any further would be to face his claws. Hugo knew that danger all too well.

"You know..." Noland spoke up. "Den was a lot more fun to talk to. Always had some comeback to my comments. Tit for tat, punch for punch, and all that."

"Sorry," Hugo said as unapologetically as he could. "I'm not Den. I'm just his best friend."

"Nah, I get it. I'm the same with Tillman... *Was*... the same way..." Noland moved his head down as he thought of Tillman. Their last moments together still cycling through his mind. While Hugo did not know the context for Noland's current sorrowful gaze, the look itself was enough for the young Historian to grasp the inner turmoil his captor was facing. A small light in the dark.

"You don't have to do this," Hugo suggested. His voice calm, as if speaking to a crying child. "If you turn yourself in, I'm sure we could get you protection. Maybe even a good defense lawyer—"

"I ain't going!" Noland screeched. "Not to that. Not to them!"

Hugo felt his heart stop yet again. And even after it continued to beat, the stunned silence remained. That outburst was enough. There was truly no reasoning with him now. Neither by challenging his thoughts nor sympathizing with his plight, however artificial that sympathy actually was. Hugo was dealing with a child. A child with immense strength. A child who could not be controlled.

"Okay..." Hugo replied in a low whisper.

They sat in stark silence. And in the corner of the room, where the bathroom was, a noise all too familiar to Noland echoed on.

Hum, tick, drip. Hum, tick, drip. Hum, tick, drip.

Noland may have escaped his captors. May have fled from his apartment. Yet those same sounds followed him. Ever encroaching. All-consuming. A past he could never ignore. A future entirely unknown.

II

When Grill had first reserved his and the boys' rooms at Merryville Suites, the bounty hunter had requested that they be connected. While not a deal-breaker, it was something he preferred. Allowing them to quickly contact one another, should the need arise. Now, nearly a month since their arrival in Wayport, Grill's preference had paid off.

Noland had made a direct request to Inspector Walton to only call through Den and Hugo's room number. Perhaps the addict took some sick pleasure in it, or maybe he just found it funny and nothing more.

Either way, federal agents and police officers alike now crowded both rooms. Den and Hugo's living room had been made the primary space, while the entirety of Grill's room was being used for equipment and other personnel.

"For the last time, Romero," Inspector Walton shouted, "you do not have jurisdiction in this case!"

"Mr. Statferd is only in this position because of the actions of my team," Romero countered. "It is required that I follow through on this assignment."

"You want me to call the governors?"

"You want me to call the President?"

"Would you both shut up?!" Grill shouted. Not caring who he offended or how it was done. "Don't act like either of you can assert that kind of authority! Especially not in a case like this! Either one of you leaves or you *both* get along! Is that understood?"

Both men huffed, but nodded in agreement.

Grill couldn't help but smirk. Even in a situation as dire as this, he took a small amount of pride in bringing Romero down a peg.

"Now," Grill began, "do we have everything prepared?"

One of Romero's men came towards them. A briefcase in hand. "One hundred thousand Rias, as requested," Romero stated.

"I'm impressed you got it so fast, Romero," Walton said.

"I assure you, Inspector Walton, we have enough emergency funds for such situations," Romero said.

Grill looked over the briefcase, yet something seemed off. He took it from the agent. Holding it in hands. He placed the briefcase on the ground, opened it, and started counting. It only took a few seconds for him to realize what was wrong.

"What the hell is this, Jewels?" Grill asked. In his hands were piles of five-Rias and ten-Rias bills. Nowhere near the amount that would cover Noland's ransom.

"We did not see it in our best interests to potentially lose that kind of investment on a case we believe will be solved very soon." Every word from Romero's mouth was cold. Not an ounce of humanity lurked within. He might as well have been a robot with the way he explained his reasoning.

"Investment?" Inspector Walton shouted. "And you dare call yourself a protector of the people?"

"No," Grill denied. "No, we're not gonna do that, Jewels... We are not risking Hugo's life just so your boys at the top don't have to stretch their Rias a little further this month!"

"As I said, we believe this situation will be solved very soon," Romero repeated. "My team is ready to go as soon as we can ascertain Mr. Statferd's whereabouts."

"And what makes you think I'll let you do that?" Grill stared at Romero in the eyes. Challenging his authority.

"We only have one man to take out this time, Jack. Even if he's fueled by Atlas Tear Drop, I assure you that Macchianado will be dealt with."

Something in Romero's words caught Grill off guard. But it wasn't the inhuman tone. It was something more sinister. "'Take out?'" Grill questioned. "What do you mean 'take out?'"

"A turn of phrase, Jack. Nothing more. I, of course, meant that we have only one man to subdue. But as you know, if push comes to shove, we will utilize lethal force."

"No..." Grill shook his head. "That's not what that means... I know enough of that lingo to know you never use that phrase unless lethal force is an absolute necessity."

"Phrases change, Jack. I don't understand why you're putting so much focus into my specific choice of words."

"Oh my God..." Grill whispered. Romero's plans. His dismissals. The way in which the raid had gone down. Every question the bounty hunter had wondered about over the past ten days had finally made sense.

"You son of a bitch..." Grill said under his breath. "You son of a bitch!" He screamed. "This whole thing! This whole mess! It was never about Macchianado or any of the Florenzas or even the Takedas, was it? It was Baratzi. It was *always* Baratzi!"

"Jack, I don't know what—"

"Baratzi was the one with the connections! The one who basically had the blueprints of every bastard in this city! How many talks did you have with that gold-toothed rat, Jewels? How much information did you get out of him? Well it must have been enough to justify blasting his brain into the pavement!"

"My God..." Walton said. A witness to a revelation he did not expect.

Romero stayed quiet. A common tactic for a man of his profession, especially when exposed.

"Now you're silent..." Grill said. "Of course. Then can you at least answer this question? Did you have any real intention of 'subduing' anyone else? Or did you just happen pull a raid out of your hat and figured that was the best way of executing Baratzi? It could have been any deal, couldn't it? But no, you wanted it to be convincing. Figured it would look great to have someone like me involved too!"

"I did what needed to be done," Romero finally said. "I realized that your expertise and Mr. Den's abilities would be beneficial—"

"That's all I needed to hear. Not. Another. Word." Grill growled, staring down the man he had once thought a friend. "Hugo could be dead right now... I don't give a damn about your statistics or theories... I just needed to know whether you still had your soul or not."

"What has occurred with Mr. Statferd is certainly unfortunate, and we will do everything within our power to—"

Romero didn't expect the blunt force of Grill's fist to his face—a right hook straight to his jaw. The agent stumbled back, but kept his footing. He did not cry out in pain nor did he look Grill in the eyes. He already knew what he was going to see.

Grill too possessed the eyes of a killer. But these were not the eyes of someone like Noland Macchiando. Macchianado killed for fun and for the sake of his own pride. Grill killed with purpose. Whether it was to end a conflict, acquire a bounty, or to enact his own sense of justice. Those were the eyes Romero knew he would see. Ones he never wanted to see again.

"If something happens to Hugo..." Grill said, prematurely stopping his words. "Don't make me do something I won't regret..."

Romero had hoped those eyes were not for him. Yet he had known Grill long enough to know the score. Whether it was a threat or a warning, connections or not, Romero knew where he now stood with the bounty hunter.

"Get out," Grill demanded.

Without saying another word, without making another excuse, Romero simply walked out of the room.

"Inspector Walton," Grill said. "You're in charge. If need be, I will happily write you a check for the ransom."

"Thank you, Mr. Trent," Walton replied. "I need an update on the ransom!" Walton spoke to his people. "Repeat: update on the ransom!"

For a single moment, Grill thought of his days with Romero. Those days in training, on leave, and in battle. Those small moments the two had shared. The brotherhood they had crafted with so many other men. When Jewels still had a soul. When he still knew what he was fighting for. Grill mourned that loss for but a second and then moved on.

III

Den and Hugo's bedroom had been the one area across both rooms which had remained untouched in the investigation. Den sat on his bed. His sights set on Hugo's empty mattress.Some hours ago, the scarred boy had returned to his room, somewhat relieved to have finished his task. Over the next few hours, he took a shower and ordered room service. Trying to enjoy the rest of his day. Waiting for Hugo to come back. He had managed to nap for a short time. He dreamt of Fairchild again. His kind words and simple joys. Those precious moments he had spent with him. Now a whole decade had gone by. Light teardrops stained his pillow as he woke up.

A sudden knock on the door would soon bring his whole world down. Hugo had been kidnapped. And by the very bastard Den had been unable to stop. Twice, at that. The investigation ramped up, but Den was in no mood to do anything else. He had retreated to his room and remained there.

Hugo's life was on the line... and Den blamed no one but himself.

Grill slowly creaked the door open and came in, quickly closing it behind him. He sat right beside Den. "Romero's out," Grill stated. "He and his men will still be helping with backup, but it's in Walton's hands now. I know we don't know him well, but I certainly trust him more."

"Gotcha..." Den quietly acknowledged.

"We're gonna get him back, Den," Grill said. "No matter what."

"Yeah..."

The moment sank in. That solid, quiet moment. It was one thing for Den to sit alone. Where he could be with his thoughts. Tell himself what he wanted to hear. But now Grill sat beside him. A reminder of the world just outside his room.

Tears came rushing from Den's eyes. The scarred boy wept.

Grill placed his hand on Den's shoulder, as he had done before. The only way he could silently express that he was here for Den.

"*I did this*," Den whispered.

"No," Grill replied. "No, you didn't."

"But I did... I was so set on beating Macchianado that I didn't even think about the consequences. The thought of him escaping hadn't even crossed my mind. I should've just listened to Inspector Walton from the start. But no, I had to be the strong man! I had make sure I wasn't the victim... And now Hugo's the victim again. First a bear and now this! I did this! I did all this!"

Den was in hysterics. He saw no one but himself as the villain. The one to be despised. Every second of self-loathing all coming down on him at once. In this moment, he wanted nothing more than to crawl up in a ball and escape from everything. Den was most certainly not suicidal, but for a brief moment, he wondered what it would have been like if he hadn't been born.

"Den, I need you right now," Grill responded, his voice tense, yet still commanding. "I can't have you falling apart!"

"*I did this! I did this! I did this!*" Den kept repeating. Anxiety and fear had fully taken over. There was no thought on what to do next. No focus on how to save Hugo and stop Noland. There was only the fear and the blame. Nothing more.

"Den!" Grill raised his voice. Yet it did nothing. Den merely sat there in his trance. An unwavering slave of guilt. The bounty hunter thought back to their battle with the Crimson Maple. In that very moment when Den and Hugo were at their breaking point. Those two young men were not soldiers. They were not even militia. They were simply good souls trying to do what they thought was right. Yet they still lacked the discipline to deal with such situations.

But Grill was no therapist. No expert in human psychology. He hadn't the words to calm Den down. So the bounty hunter did the only thing that came to his mind.

In a single motion, Grill slapped Den across the face.

Not once had Den been slapped in his life. Madame Lake had been too distant, Fairchild too loving, and the Statferds, in the few times they ever had to discipline Den, used their words and words alone.

Even when he would roughhouse with Hugo, Barton, or Ox, it only ever consisted of tackles and grappling. And tame roughhousing at that, given how careful Den had to be with his strength, even in those playful moments.

But a slap was something that had never crossed his mind. In the past two weeks, he had been punched and kicked, battered and bruised, but never slapped. The sheer force of impact, the quick strike of pain, and the lingering feeling that such an act created. Den was not injured by it. It had left no mark upon his cheek. Yet that tangible feeling remained.

And all at once, Den's thoughts disappeared. Those broken, self-flagellations that did nothing but drain his body and weaken his spirit. Thoughts that had placed him in the darkest crevasses of his mind. A belief that he was truly nothing but both an abuser and a victim. Everything that Fairchild had taught him not to believe. Everything that Den wasn't.

Den had not fallen asleep, but it felt as if he had awoken in a cold sweat. He panted, trying to get a breath of air. Now he was back in the present. Grill still by his side.

"I'm sorry for that, Den," Grill said. "It was the only thing that seemed right."

"No," Den responded, still catching his breath. "I should apologize. Those thoughts... they're not me. They never should have been... But they were. And I thank you for taking me out of that."

"Victim and victor," Grill repeated.

Den nodded.

"Den, let me show you something I've been keeping quiet about." While law enforcement was using his room, Grill had moved his things temporarily into Den and Hugo's bedroom. From his bag, the bounty hunter took out a familiar item: a small wooden cross with the letters J-A-C-K carved into it.

"Is that... Bloodless Jack's cross?"

"The very same," Grill confirmed. "I've had this since I... put Jack Riviello out of his misery. It's been with me ever since. Not always on me, but always nearby."

"Why did you keep it?"

Grill looked at the cross. The bounty hunter realized he hadn't even thought of the words to describe it. Yet all at once they flowed out anyway. "I carry this cross as a reminder to myself. A reminder to stay grounded. To not be pulled in by guilt. Nor to become complacent in my goals. Jack did. He did a long time ago. And look where it got him. I refuse to go down that path. Not anymore."

"I... I understand," Den said. "But... I don't know if I have something like that."

"You do. You always have... When was the last time you prayed?"

It was a simple question. Something Den would have quickly and easily answered not two weeks ago. But since then? Since his first fight with Macchianado in the alleyway? He had spoken that silent prayer for Hodgson's soul... and nothing since.

That was what had felt so off that morning. Den had been so focused on their mission, on his revenge against Noland, that he had forgotten to pray. He had prayed for victory before they left to fight the Crimson Maple. He had prayed for the souls of those lost. For humans and animals alike. He had prayed for that young boy named Vito he had met the first day they arrived in Wayport.

Den was not suffering a crisis of faith. Merely a loss of focus. Placing too much attention in the here and now. Not on the beauty of something so much greater.

"Longer than I ever should have," Den answered.

Grill got up from the bed. "I'll give the time you need." Grill walked out of the room, shutting the door behind him.

Den sat on his bed, alone once more. He took deep breaths. Calmed his pulse. Let the silent echoes of the universe take hold of him.

Den had no position of prayer. No specific messages or phrases he used. God was all around and he believed it with his entire being. So why take some kind of stance or utter some mantra? To be attuned to God meant that all places were churches. All places the Lord's dominion.

Yet it was on a day like this he needed something more. Something to calm his anxious mind. He knelt down on his knees and clasped his hands. The very same ritualistic gesture that had been repeated for so many generations. It gave him that little extra ounce of comfort. A momentary respite. He did not practice what he was about to say. He did not need to. All at once, Den let out his very soul and prayed.

Dear Heavenly Father, I don't where Hugo is. I don't if he's safe... or if he's even still alive. He's the one who showed me the world. The one who guided me forward after Fairchild was

blessed into your kingdom. I don't know if I have the strength to find him or save him... So please, in your eternal power, help me and Grill find him. Help bring him back to us.
—Amen

Den's eyes flooded once more. He hadn't realized just how much he had already cried. A single bead dripped into his mouth, its salty taste stinging his tongue ever so slightly. For several minutes, Den remained in silence. He looked towards Hugo's bed again. His journal still sat in place. Today's page untouched. Just a blank space and nothing more.

The scarred boy got up, grabbed the journal, and turned it to the page of the day. He held onto Hugo's personal pen and placed it just above the page. His hand quivered. Asking himself whether he had the right to touch the very journal Hugo had committed himself to.

His concentration was broken when a loud noise rang through his ears. "Den!" Grill shouted from the living room. "It's Macchianado!"

Den dropped the pen and journal and rushed into the living room. The time was here. Whatever happened next, Den would face it. He finally remembered where he stood.

IV

Hugo had maintained his silence in the hours since Noland's outburst. Since then, at irregular intervals, the gangster would start spouting off useless information. Some fact about the weather or an anecdote about when he had beaten a guy up with a broken lamp. He didn't try to ask Hugo his opinion. Sometimes he didn't even acknowledge the young Historian's existence. He was entertaining an audience of one. And in between these rants, Noland would take out his bottle and swallow another pill of Atlas Tear Drop.

By this point, at least on the surface, the full effects of the drug seemed to have stagnated. Noland was no longer feeling highly stimulated, nor was the drug knocking him out. He didn't even seem to be popping pills out of a craving for it. He would take a pill and nothing would happen. He treated them as if they were potato chips.

Hugo did not know the full extent of Atlas Tear Drop. But he knew the dangers of Noland's constant popping. Even if he appeared fine on the outside, it was reasonable to believe that his body was ravaging itself on the inside. Still, Hugo could do nothing in this situation and it was doubtful Noland's strength had diminished. All he could do was wait for the addict to make the call. Whatever came next was not for him to decide.

Without warning, Noland clapped his hands together. The sudden noise startled Hugo, though he had managed to contain it to a simple flinch. "Game time, Hugo!" Noland announced. "Let's see how the opposing team is doing!" Noland opened his phone and dialed the number to Den and Hugo's hotel room.

Back at the Merryville Suites, Walton, Grill, Den, and Walton's subordinates gathered around the phone. Inspector Walton himself answered it, turning on the speaker phone, allowing everyone in the room to hear. "Hello?"

"Wally! Glad to hear ya! How's the wife?"

"She's good, Noland... Now, may I ask about Mr. Statferd?"

"Hugo? Oh, he's fine! Hugo, why don't you introduce yourself to Inspector Walton!" Noland walked up to Hugo and placed the phone by Hugo's face.

"Inspector?" Hugo spoke, his voice quiet and timid. Den felt just a little calmer as soon as he heard Hugo's voice. But the tone in which his brother spoke only fueled Den's rage even more.

"Yes, this is Inspector Walton of the Wayport Police Department. How are you doing, Mr. Statferd?"

"I'm fine, sir," Hugo responded. "Nothing bad to report... What happened to Mr. Andolini? Is he okay?"

"He's fine, Mr. Statferd," Walton confirmed. "Bruised and beaten, but he's expected to make a full recovery."

"Tch! Figures!" Noland spouted. "Guy didn't have the decency to live well, so of course he didn't have the decency to die well either!"

Hugo couldn't help but turn his eyes to Noland. The addict was now sitting right beside him, his breathing even heavier than it had been before. This close, the perspiration on Noland's skin was noticeable. He was sweating buckets.

"Thank God..." Hugo exhaled in relief. "What about Den and Grill? Are they with you? Can I speak to them?"

Noland quickly moved the phone away from Hugo and back to himself. "Yeah, let's do that. I'd love to hear their sweet, sweet voices!" Noland pressed a button on his phone, enabling his own speaker phone to function. "Alright, boys, we can hear you loud and clear!"

"Hugo?" Den spoke. "Hugo, are you okay?"

"I am, Den," Hugo answered, still weak in voice. "And I mean it... He hasn't harmed me... He knocked me out with something earlier, but that's was it."

"What the hell did you do to him, Macchianado?" Den said.

"Relax, Denny!" Noland replied. "Just a little sleepy-time shot to help with the move. Nothing too offensive to his system. He's fiiiiine!"

"We have the money, Macchianado," Grill informed. "We're ready for the exchange."

"That's great, Mr. Iron Sniper! Or should I say, Silent Death? Maybe even Kataloosa Ranger? Seriously, who the hell goes to Kataloosa? Big empty desert of nothing!"

"What are your demands, Macchianado?" Grill asked, ignoring Noland's comments.

"Nothing too showy. Just the hundred thousand at the spot of my choice... But! I expect you to follow my directions to a T! I think you know as well as I do what it will mean if you don't."

"I swear, Macchianado," Den howled, "if you do anything to—"

"We understand," Grill interrupted. "We'll follow your orders."

"Well, well, well! Sounds like someone's a bit agitated," Noland chided. "Tell me, Den, what would you do to me if something... happened to

Hugo?" Noland grabbed Hugo's shoulder. The young Historian started shaking from the touch. "Anything at all. Use your imagination! I'm listening."

Den was angry. He almost started to scream at Noland, only for Grill to grab his apprentice's mouth and silence him. Without saying a word, Grill shook his head at Den.

"To repeat, we'll follow your demands, Macchianado," Grill spoke. "Please give them to us."

"Now, wait just a minute! I asked for Mr. Den's answer. And I'm not hearing it! We can get back on track once that happens."

Grill looked at Den and took a breath in and out. The scarred boy understood his master's order and did the same. Grill let go of Den's mouth and nodded, giving him the go-ahead to speak.

"If something happens to Hugo," Den said in a calmer tone, "then I'll make sure to win next time."

"Good answer!" Noland yelled. Hugo's shivering had only grown more noticeable. "Oh what's the matter, Hugo? Cold? You know, Den, I think your buddy here could use a jacket!"

"Just..." Hugo spoke, tears starting to well up in his eyes. "Just give me them your demands, Noland... Please..."

Noland laughed. "How could I say no to a face like that? I know you can't see, Denny Boy, but your pal seems to have sprouted a little leak!"

Den kept his mouth shut, knowing any more words would only be playing into Noland's sick game.

"We're ready to hear you out, Macchianado," Grill said.

"Very well! At present, we are currently in a vacant room near the top of the Lang-Meyer Courthouse. It seemed like a great place to really take in the scenery!"

The Lang-Meyer Courthouse had been going through a new round of refurbishments. Particularly to the upper levels. Nothing which affected its primary operations, but one which temporarily postponed many of its social gatherings. Current construction had been halted due to a minor supply chain issue, but was expected to start back up within the next week. At this time of night, with barely anyone at the facility, Noland Macchianado had managed to sneak into one of the unfinished rooms without anyone noticing.

"Now, this is the most important part," Noland continued. "One hour from now, a *single* person will meet us at the top veranda, ransom in hand. And I mean *one*! No accompaniment. No hidden gunmen. Just me, Mr. Statferd... and Mr. Den. There's a score I'd like to settle with him before I make like a bandit outta this city."

By this point, Hugo was crying. His sobs were audible through the other end, echoing across the hotel room. The eyes of all the policemen turned to Den at once. As did Grill. Den took another deep breath, trying his hardest to ignore Hugo's suffering. "Understood," Den acknowledged. "I'll be there."

"Great! Fantastic! Wonderful! I'm looking forward to seeing your shining smile once again, Denny Boy! You know what they say, third time's the charm! Until then—"

"Wait!" Hugo shouted, tears still flowing down his face. "Please, Noland! Let me speak to Den."

Den gripped his fists, controlling his anger, but wanting nothing more than to punch Noland once again.

"Geez, Hugo," Noland replied, "didn't think you for the passionate type! But I am nothing if not humble!" Noland positioned his phone to Hugo's face once more.

"*Den...*" Hugo began. Again, his voice dropped to a whisper. There were words he needed to say and he was trying to get them out as best as he could. "*I know you blame yourself... Please don't... What's happening is not your fault...*" Hugo paused. He closed his eyes and let out a few deep breathes. He let the seconds pass before opening his eyes once again. "*But if there's something you can do... All I ask...* is for you to kick his ass to next Tuesday."

The crying stopped on cue. All the shaking, mumbling, and hesitation in his voice was gone. "Save me, Den!" Hugo bellowed. "Blow this stupid bastard away!" These were not the pleas of a hostage. This was an order.

An order to a friend he trusted more than anyone else in the world. "You can do it, Den! Kick. His. Ass!" Hugo's scream was defiant. Resolute in his rebellion. He stared Noland down. A wry smile growing on his face.

"Hit me! Kill me, if you want," Hugo yelled at Noland. "It won't stop the rampage that's coming for you!"

Noland stood in profound shock. Not even sure how to react.

On the other end of the line, Den smiled too. Every muscle in his body pumping with excitement. "We're coming to save you, buddy," Den said. "And Noland, we're gonna finish this. Me and you. Just! You! Wait!"

"Hahahahaha!" A fit of laughter engulfed Noland all at once. "You guys got guts! Alright, then. I promise not to harm even a single hair on Mr. Hugo's head! But, oh, you better believe that's only gonna get me even more pumped. Until then, Den!" Noland hung up his phone.

At the hotel, Den looked at his hands, trembling after his great proclamation. He took in several more breaths. Calming his nerves. Thinking a short, silent prayer between each one.

Inspector Walton's team scrambled. "You heard him, everyone," the inspector ordered. "Start assembling a team to surround the courthouse! But you will by no means enter it under any circumstances! Is that clear?"

"Sir, yes, sir!" Walton's team acknowledged.

Den listened to Walton's order. He couldn't help but smile. Regardless of how they had first met, he was proud to be working with the inspector at a time like this.

Grill stood by his side. "Do you want me to sneak in? I'm sure I could find some way to take him out."

Den shook his head. "No. This is his challenge and I'm his only player. It's something I have to face alone. Besides, we're already risking enough with Hugo as it is."

"Understood. Then I'll join the task force and get as close as I possibly can," the bounty hunter said. He moved closer to Den, making sure to look him straight in the eyes. "But remember. You're not facing this alone. Not really."

Grill was Den's master and his friend. A man he had known for a little under two months. Yet the bonds they had already shared meant the world to him. And in this moment, Grill was even more than that. He was a big brother. One he knew would look out for him.

"I know," Den agreed, determination swelling inside him.

V

"Quite a performance," Noland said to Hugo. "Though I shouldn't be so surprised. Should I, Mr. Sullivan?"

Hugo continued his staredown, his trail of false tears already starting to dry. "I meant what I said," the young Historian stated. "I won't back down."

"Oh, don't worry! Defiance like what you're doing is boring. You're clearly not afraid anymore. Where's the fun now if I can't rile you up? So I guess I'll just kick back and—" Noland slammed his fist straight into the wall. Just barely missing Hugo's face. Yet the young Historian's look didn't change. Not a single second of surprise. Not a tinge of fear. Determination and undying courage flamed in his eyes.

"And let the next hour pass by," Noland finished. Most men Macchianado had met usually fell under two categories: those below him who feared him and those above him who loathed him. He had no true friends. Only acquaintances and underlings he could boss around. Even Tillman, the closest person in his life, had no qualms asserting his dominance whenever he pleased. But even they were all gone now.

Hugo was a rarity among them. A young man much weaker than Noland himself, at least in terms of strength, who nonetheless showed no fear of him. Defying his authority and spitting in his face. Any nerves and dread the young Historian may have previously felt had all but evaporated.

Yet Noland felt no frustration in his defiance. No need for anymore lashing out. Rather, what he felt for Hugo in this moment was respect.

Not the kind he was forced to give his superiors, motivated by fear and ambition. It was true, honest respect. A rarity in his world, where power and vying for power was above all else.

But even respect could only get one so far. And Noland was at his wit's end. He was not done with Hugo Statferd, the false Dominic Sullivan. He had one more task to accomplish. But not yet. Not until the time was near.

So Noland Macchianado sat back on one of the chairs and relaxed his body. Knowing full well Hugo would be watching him for the rest of their short-lived cohabitation. But he didn't mind. The clock would soon run out. The final phase was about to begin.

We're gonna save you, Hugo! I promise! Just leave everything to us!

—Den, June 26, 840 AU

CHAPTER 9

CITY OF THE END

I

11 years ago...
August 13, 829 AU

There was not a single skyscraper which touched the clouds of Wayport. None except the Lang-Meyer Courthouse. Old laws on the books had made it so that no other buildings could surpass its height. A relic from its outpost days. The initial rulings had only allowed three-story buildings to be put in place. And though that number had increased over time, none among them had even come close to capturing the courthouse's size and majesty. A beacon of light in a city of dark.

The building housed several verandas for various gatherings and exhibitions. The view alone was always reason enough to attend whatever function was being held next. A truly stunning sight. The view from atop the world.

Yet shadows still formed even in this supposed house of justice. Connections deep within the rot of Wayport. The newly-christened Noland Macchianado stood at the highest veranda. The sights of the

city washed over him. The wind caressed his bangs. The cold chill was a refreshing surprise on his healing scars.

"Great view, right?" Tillman asked.

"Oh yeah," Noland responded. "Just didn't expect it to be so..."

"Breathtaking?"

"Big! But why bring me here, Till? Why this place specifically?"

"One word, kid: Perspective." Tillman waved his hand about, as if presenting the entirety of Wayport to Noland for the very first time. "This whole city can be ours."

"No offense, Till, but I already saw the top of the world once. And it all literally fell down on me."

"Kid, what you experienced was the top of a very small world. Power lifting? So what? But this? This is the gateway to actual power. Power you can't even wrap your head around. The connections. The influence. To control Wayport is to control Central Adalia. The very heartbeat of the country. Sure, it doesn't have the glamour of the coastal cities, but it's got more than that. This is where the real magic happens."

"I don't know, Till. You're asking me to be, what? A loan shark? A drug peddler?"

"I'm asking you to be a businessman."

Noland looked down on the city, its glowing lights shining like a star-lit field. People of all types and from all places living their lives. He didn't know what to say.

"You want to start from the bottom again?" Tillman asked. "With the rats? With all those little dregs? Well I got something to tell you, Matches. You ain't got the talent of that Baratzi kid. And you can't exactly make money off your name, either!" The old gangster took out a pill bottle. One Noland was quite familiar with. "And there's no way in Hell you could afford these!"

"I'll wean off them," Noland finally responded. "Or at least find something cheaper."

"And what about the scalpers? What about those very dregs taking all your money and leaving you with nothing?"

"I'll figure it out somehow."

"But you don't have to." Tillman's voice calmed. "Remember that one time in Dorado? When that rival of yours, what was his name?"

"Gordon Gapher."

"Yeah, Gapher. Egotistical little redheaded prick, wasn't he? Always flaunting his records. Looking good for the press. Loved people licking his boots. Until he had the gall to insult you! To push you around! Everyone else would just take it. Not wanting to cause a ruckus. But not you! Not Mac McKorkendale. No, sir!"

Noland started cracking a smile.

"And what was it you did?" Tillman tried remembering. "Two jabs and a hook?"

"Three jabs, a hook, and an elbow straight into his eye! Last I heard that bastard still had to take his meals through a straw!" The two men cackled at the memory.

"And remember how it felt? To rip his power away and assert your own? That sweet release? No one dared to insult you again. Gapher didn't even sue because you scared him that much! You grabbed power... And in time, you'll have so much more!" He rattled the bottle. "Just these babies, me, and..." He tapped Noland's biceps. "That's all you need."

Noland's smile grew sharper. Teeth gnashing. That very moment flowing through his mind. Gapher's mangled jaw and pierced eye. Someone who had towered over him for so long reduced to a pile of bone and muscle.

He looked out at the city one last time. All those little lives scattered about. Ants, worms, and rats in a pile. All those flashing lights across all those buildings. None standing so tall as where he was at this moment.

"All right," Noland agreed. "You got yourself a deal."

They shook hands. "Here's to the future!" Tillman declared. A match made at the top. With nowhere to go but downhill.

II

The Lang-Meyer Courthouse was not the most well-guarded spot in Wayport. There was always a door just barely propped open or a handle slightly turned. An easy way for security to get around without the risk of alarms going off. The irony of their convenience only partially lost on them.

Noland had seen the building's insides and outs enough times to understand its basic structure. He knew the layout of the security cameras to know where to move and dodge. Knew enough of the guards' patterns and predilections to sneak inside with them being none the wiser. The extra strain of carrying Hugo's unconscious body had meant almost nothing to Macchianado.

The room they had sat in had been a testing ground of sorts. A room intentionally left white so as to try out new paints and other design choices. To see how new furniture could be arranged for both efficiency and style. Eventually, it would become a normal room like all the rest, but at a time like this, with construction stalled, the white void had become a safe haven for the gangster.

"Party time!" Noland yelled. With the force of his own two arms, Noland ripped apart the ropes restraining Hugo's legs, as well as the ones connecting his arms and legs together. But the arm restraints stayed. Hugo didn't have to guess why.

"Up you go, Statferd!" Noland said as he helped the young Historian onto his feet. "It's probably obvious enough, but please don't try to run. Would be a bad time for all of us, if you did."

"Don't worry. I have no intention to," Hugo replied. "You think I'd miss out on the beating you're about to get? Wouldn't miss it for the world!"

"A few minutes before our sad farewell and *now* you finally make a comeback like that? I swear, in a different life, I probably could have been best friends with you two freaks!"

There was something deep inside Hugo that had changed. A cog in his machine that had finally been broken. Or, perhaps, one that had finally started moving for the first time in a long time. The young Historian's body was calm, his heart pumping as it did every day. His back stood up straight. His breathing relaxed. The scars upon his chest feeling as smooth as the day he was born. Hugo Statferd was not afraid.

III

Den had not expected the stairs to be so long and winding. The spiral staircase, located at the centermost point of the courthouse, had been standing since the building's outpost days. Back then, it had been surrounded by iron bars, allowing for sturdier protection from attacks. While the bars had long since been removed, the spirit of their structure lived on in the rail guards which had taken their place.

Den clutched the briefcase as he walked up. Thanks to Grill's generous donation, the case was indeed filled with exactly 100,000 Rias. He was careful in his steps. Not wanting to accidentally trip and spill the contents all the way back down. He couldn't afford to mess this up. Each second was another step upwards. Each step meant getting that much closer to Hugo. No matter what came next, Den would not stop until his best friend was safe. Even if it meant losing his own life.

The walk up felt so very short and yet like an eternity all the same. Soon enough, Den had made his way to the top veranda. He had seen pictures of it. It was a ravishing place when fully supplied. Chairs and tables of the finest design and comfort. A piano on the side. Perfectly positioned for the best outdoor acoustics. This area could stand several hundred people and still allow wiggle room for guests to come in and out.

Den walked outside. None of those exquisite features graced this area now. Every piece of furniture had been moved to avoid the elements. It was a blank canvas ready to take shape.

And on the other side of the veranda stood Noland and Hugo. Noland's bag of treasures sat just to his side. "Den!" Noland greeted. "Glad you could make it! I'm sorry to say that the other guests had to cancel last minute. So it's just the three of us. But whatever! Guys' night out! Good times!"

The structure of Noland's eyes was something Den had never seen before. Still round in appearance, but shriveled and red. Looking similar to the crow's feet now blemishing his temples. His frame was more gaunt, yet his muscles still rippled. His veins were even more swollen than they had been before. And that same smile Noland loved to give was now stained with yellow teeth. Just like the newly emerging color of his skin. It hadn't even been half a day since Den had last fought him, yet the damage from his excessive use of Atlas Tear Drop was already taking its toll. Noland Macchianado, whether he knew it or not, was dying. And it didn't take a medical expert to figure that out.

"Hugo!" Den shouted. "You okay, buddy?"

In stark contrast to Noland's moribund appearance, Hugo was nearly unchanged. His hands had remained tied up, his clothes were slightly tattered, and his face was a shade of red. But this was not from physical abuse, merely aftereffects of the forced crying the young Historian had done in order to fool Macchianado.

"I am, Den!" Hugo replied. Den was surprised to see the determination in Hugo's eyes. No sign of weakness. No loss of will. His posture was upright. His voice loud. It hadn't been long ago that Den had consoled him in Kelvin Forest. Yet now he was standing tall in the face of uncertainty. The scarred boy felt a swelling sense of pride in his brother. "He hasn't done anything else since the call, I can assure you of that!"

"Alright then, Noland," Den hollered, "let's start the trade!"

"Fine by me!" the gangster replied. "Let's get this party rolling!"

Den walked up to Noland and handed him the briefcase. "For little old me?" Noland smirked. "I'm flattered! Now, if you don't mind, please move back. I'd like to count my earnings before I let Mr. Statferd go!"

Den started walking back to where he had been standing. For only a second, the scarred boy exchanged glances with Hugo. Since the young Historian was restrained, the two could not do their signature head taps. Instead, the brothers simply nodded towards one another.

Noland ran through every bill, each one of 100-Rias value. Fortunately, the gangster was a fast counter and only needed to see the corners of each bill to confirm their validity. The counting ended quickly.

"Thanks for the patience, boys. Now my turn!" Noland grabbed at Hugo's hand restraints and ripped them off. "It's been fun, Statferd. We should do this again some time!"

Hugo said nothing in response. Not even looking at Macchianado as he ran straight towards Den.

"You're welcome!" Noland yelled. "Tch. Some people! You show them a good time and they run out before you can even make them breakfast!"

Hugo greeted Den with a hug, but kept his stoic distance. This was not the time to let his emotions out. It would be soon, but these next few moments were paramount.

"Easy on the family reunion, boys! We're not done just yet," Noland reminded. "You hear that, Denny Boy?"

The young Historian clenched his brother tighter. "You can do this," Hugo whispered. "Like I said... Kick his ass."

Den cracked a small smile. "You can count on it."

Hugo let go of Den and watched as the scarred boy moved closer to Noland. The two foes met one another at the center of the veranda. Just as they had met at the center of the junkyard.

They stood in silence for a moment. The boy with gray skin and the jaundiced man. The night wind blowing against their cheeks. Eyes locked for one last time.

"Let's be honest here," Noland began, "I don't think either of us is in the mood for a full-on, knuckle-dragging brawl. It was fun the first two times, but I believe this is one of those occasions where the third time is most certainly not the charm!"

"Then what do you have in mind?" Den questioned. Fists already clenched. Just waiting for the fight to begin.

"Well, I assume you happened to see me fight that mute Takeda guy earlier, right? Something like that. A nice, wholesome round of fisticuffs! Whoever goes down first is the loser! And you know what? I'm such a nice guy that I'll let you go first! So come on, let's go! One more show for the road, before I hit that dusty trail!"

Den hesitated. Fisticuffs? That was it? With as sickly as Noland appeared, it seemed too convenient that the gangster would suggest something so simple. But Den assumed the drugs were affecting far more than just his body. Perhaps, in his own sick way, this methodology was Noland's way of evening out the playing field. Though whether it was for himself or Den was anyone's guess. Perhaps Macchianado didn't even know. All Den knew for certain was that he now had the perfect opportunity to strike. Deal as much damage as his fists would allow. And he was not about to pass up that chance.

Den squeezed his clenched fists harder and tightened his muscles. There was no smart remark to make. There was only this moment. Den railed his right arm back and flung it straight into Noland's jaws. He could feel the breaking of teeth and the warm splatter of blood on his knuckles.

Noland was pushed back as Den's fist separated from the gangster's flesh. The addict remained standing. "Hahahahahaha!" That same, piercing laugh still came out of his broken mouth. "What a punch!" Noland said as several of his teeth fell to the floor. "Good stuff! Looks like you still had some left in the tanker there, Den!" He spit out a chunk of blood. "My turn!"

Den stood in place and kept his muscles clenched. He remembered his standoff with Pork Roast. The sheer force of the boar's tusk ramming into him. Whatever Noland was about to throw, Den had no doubt in his mind he could take it.

"But first," Noland added, "there's something I've been wanting to get off my chest! Or should I say, out of my pocket!" Noland took out what appeared to be a remote control for a television. "Now you may be asking,

'Noland, is that a clicker in your pants or are you just happy to see me?' Well, my scarred rival, what I actually have in my hands is a simple control switch. Doesn't do much, but, oh boy, what it *can* do is a sight to behold!"

"What are you getting at, Noland?" Den questioned.

"I'm not getting at anything. It's what the remote can get *in*, that's the real question!" Noland pressed the power button.

Just then, Hugo could feel a small prick at his wrist. The Historian eyed the spot. It seemed to be coming from underneath the bottom of his watch.

"Feel that, Statferd?" Noland asked. "It's something I was able to cook up while you were sleeping! That prick? It's a needle! A needle I was able to rig in there just right!"

"What the hell are you doing, Noland?!" Den screamed.

"Let's call it evening the playing field. You see, in that needle is a nice sample of Atlas Tear Drop. Broken down and turned into a fine powder. All I gotta do is press the power button again... and it will be injected directly into Statferd's bloodstream! A nice boost for you and me, Denny Boy! But fatal to a bookworm like him."

For the first time since the phone call, Hugo's stoic expression morphed into one of fear. His heart raced and his eyes twitched. He looked at Den. Unsure of what to say or do.

Den was furious. His urge to bash the man's skull was more powerful than it had ever been.

"I wouldn't do anything drastic, Weird Boy!" Noland spoke. "You strike me now and I might accidentally press the button through no fault of my own! Why, it wouldn't even be me, really! The true culprit would be the force of gravity descending upon my person from your very fist! So really... it would be like you were doing it! So before you hit me again, please ask yourself... 'Do I *really* want to kill my friend right now?' Hahahahaha!"

Den was at a stalemate. Unable to do anything in his power. He looked at Hugo again. The young Historian was frozen in fear. There was only one thing the scarred boy could do now. He had vowed to make sure Hugo was safe… no matter what.

"Fine…" Den agreed. He calmed himself down. Relaxing his muscles and letting his hands go limp. "Go ahead."

"Glad you see it my way!" Noland threw a left jab into Den's face, the force of the blow hitting Den far harder now that his body had gone slack. Still, the scarred boy kept his footing.

"Your turn, Den!" Noland said. "Although, I doubt the option sounds very attractive right now. Tell you what, let's add a little rule. We can choose to pass each turn. How does that sound?"

"I… I pass," Den responded.

"Den, no!" Hugo shouted. The shock of Noland's attack broke the Historian from his fear-induced trance. "Don't worry about me! I said kick his ass, so kick his ass!"

Den said nothing to Hugo. Not even turning back to acknowledge his friend's plea.

"So this is what they call brotherly love!" Noland taunted. "Not that I'm familiar, but I gotta say, you two make it look *very* good! So in appreciation, let me give you a good show!"

Noland threw an uppercut at Den's jaw. Pushing the scarred boy back, but once more keeping his footing. Den wiggled his chin. Nothing broken, but the pain was real. He had no idea how many hits he could take, but he was going to take them regardless.

IV

Grill wanted nothing more than to kill Noland Macchianado. The bounty hunter had heard every word of their exchange thanks to the wire Den was wearing under his shirt. The very same type of wire Baratzi had worn during the raid. Noland had made it clear that no one else could enter the courthouse, but he had said nothing about letting them listen in. Given the gangster's narcissistic tendencies, he probably would have enjoyed it.

Every part of Grill seethed in anger. He had dealt with many corrupt beings in the past, whether as a soldier on duty or when taking on a bounty. Utter scum who threatened the lives of innocents. But in the past, Grill could compartmentalize the actions of his targets and move on once the mission was done, treating it as just an assignment and nothing more. But Macchianado was different. He had hit where it hurt the most, targeting the young men he had sworn a brotherhood to. Going after the very people who, in some way, Grill now saw as his family.

Grill and other members of both Inspector Walton's and Agent Romero's task forces sat on the roof of a shopping center near the courthouse, generally acknowledged as the second-highest spot in Wayport. Yet the difference was still stark. The courthouse stood at least five stories above. With the scope of his rifle, Grill could just barely see the fight.

No shot he could fire would do any good. There was too much distance between their locations. Too much wind resistance as well. And even if he somehow could, there was no telling what Noland would do if Grill could manage a clean shot. For all intents and purpose, to shoot Macchianado would be to activate his kill switch and take Hugo with him.

Grill cursed under his breath. "Everything I've done... and I can't even manage to save my friends?" He had no choice but to hold steady and wait. Because no matter what came next, Grill knew one thing was certain. Noland Macchianado was going to die tonight. And if it had to be by his own hands, then so be it.

V

Den had taken punch after punch. Never resisting. Always passing. Noland would give the scarred boy a moment to stabilize himself again to catch his breath and prepare for the next attack. Only to land another blow even harder than the last.

Noland's entire setup would be meaningless if it meant killing Den in only a few blows. He wanted to work for it. Feel the tension rising as the scarred boy suffered more and more. Waiting for just the right moment when the final burst of ecstasy could be unleashed. But it wasn't the time yet. There was still more of him to break.

Noland's shots had varied. In the jaw. In the forehead. On the temples. In the chest. On the shoulders. In the stomach. Still, Den's bones remained unbroken, but the pain was taking its toll. His head pulsated. Welts formed at his temples. His nose ran with blood. And while his eyes remained unswollen, they still teared up from all the hits. A natural defense mechanism to try and counter the abuse.

Hugo couldn't turn away from the sight, wanting nothing more than to run to Den's side and take the hits for him. But he knew his brother too well to know that wouldn't work. If anything, it would only lay even more abuse onto Den as he would struggle to make sure Hugo remained unscathed. So the young Historian stood there. Watching every second of the slaughter.

He had tried to remove the watch, but it had been wrapped tight, the bottom pasted to his skin. With every movement Hugo would make, the needle would only sink in further. There was no telling how much deeper it needed to push in before the drug was properly injected. How many precious millimeters remained between the Historian and a fatal overdose. Hugo gritted his teeth, eyes watering. A scream ran just beneath his throat, yet was afraid to come out.

The beatings continued for minutes on end. Yet still Den took every lashing, punch, and kick. Standing tall through it all. The scarred boy didn't have a plan. Couldn't think of a way out. Nothing that wouldn't kill Hugo in the process. Den had vowed to save his brother, even at the cost of his own life. And he meant every single bit of it.

Yet with each subsequent strike, Noland's smile grew thinner. And after a few more rounds, it had all but vanished. "Hmm..." Noland pondered. "I'm think I'm bored..." He tapped his head, pondering to himself the very statement he had just made. "Yeah, I'm bored... So what are we to do now..."

Den and Hugo remained silent. Waiting to see what Macchianado would say next.

"I guess I hadn't thought how I would feel when I got to this point. I had built up this whole spectacle in my head. Thinking it was gonna be a lot more grandiose than it's really ended up being. What's that saying? 'Expectation is the harshest mistress?' Something like that... I don't know, I guess this whole thing's lost its luster... You know what? Screw the game!"

Noland sat down on the ground. "I give up. You win!"

"Wha... what?" Den was unsure if he had heard the right thing or if his beatings had left him with some kind of concussive hallucination. The scarred boy had never suffered from such a symptom, but there was always a first time for everything.

"Yeah, I'm done. Think I'm gonna go now. I've had my fun and I'm sure you're ready to get back home. And from the looks of things, you're gonna need a huge helping of ice packs. Probably gonna clunk out the hotel's ice machine!"

"So... that's it?"

"Yep. That's it... Just one more thing." Noland got back and held out his right hand. "I'd like a handshake."

"Handshake?" Den questioned.

"A handshake," Noland confirmed. "It's not normal I fight a guy three times. Especially not like this. And since it's really doubtful we'll ever see each other again, I figured we might as well end it on a high note."

"... Fine."

"Den!" Hugo shouted. "Don't listen to him! He's trying to bring your guard down! He's not done yet!"

"Hugo," Den spoke softly, "please..." The scarred boy smiled at his brother. "If this saves you... whatever he has planned... it's worth it."

Hugo wanted to shout at Den and tell him he was wrong. Scream at his brother to fight back. But he knew nothing would change his mind. He was stuck on the sidelines and already knew the results of the game.

"Alright, Noland," Den said. "A shake it is."

Den moved to Noland and extended his hand. He met the gangster in the middle. Their handshake was firm, but cordial. As if they were old acquaintances reuniting at a dinner party. As if all the blood they spilled had meant nothing. There was a quiet ambiance to it all. Here they were, standing at the top of Wayport, the moonlit night casting a shadow upon them both.

"Yep..." Noland said. "A high note... for me."

Noland slammed his right leg straight into Den's ribs. The impact knocked the wind out of the scarred boy. The gangster then punched his left fist into Den's cheek. Followed by a right fist into Den's chest. Each strike the hardest Noland had delivered since their fight began.

Den tried keeping his stance, but his legs wobbled and he finally fell to the ground.

"*Den!*" Hugo shouted. Even knowing what was coming, the young Historian still did not want to see it become real.

Noland kneeled and started striking Den with his fists. Just as he had done to Hodgson. "You think I was just gonna quit? Just like that? Oh no, Mr. Den, I'm not leaving this spot until I can't hear a single beat coming from your heart! Until I can be absolutely sure I'll *never* see you again! Die! Die! *Die!*"

Hugo couldn't watch anymore. He couldn't witness his brother suffer like this. He stared at the watch. The damnable watch that had made him a hostage. Such a fragile thing, and yet it had caused him so much pain. To think Noland would sacrifice one of his own precious pills just to make sure he and Den suffered... Or was that really the case?

Sacrifice, Hugo thought. *Sacrifice... one of his...* His mind cleared. And all at once, the young Historian knew what needed to be done.

"And just think, the last thing you'll see is me! Smiling away as I send you off to the great beyond!" Noland screamed. "No more dreams, Dennny Boy! Only night—!"

A striking sound came through Noland's ears. But it was not the shrieking, piercing noise that had interrupted his day so many times already. It was a shattering note. The shattering of glass.

Hugo screamed.

Noland paused his punches and looked up.

Hugo was sitting on his knees. Blood trickling down his wrist. The glass of the watch shattered on the ground. The needle embedded into the young Historian's wrist. His hand twitching from the pain as he gritted his teeth.

"Den!" Hugo screamed. "Kick. His. Ass!"

Den had lain stagnant on the ground. Accepting the reality of his fate. Thinking this was his last day. But the sounds of Hugo's yell, the strength in his voice... The scarred boy didn't need to see what had just happened. He already knew. It was enough to wake him up.

Den rushed back up, delivering a punch straight into Noland's crotch. The gangster cried out in pain, lowering his arms.

Den sent a one-two punch into Noland's jaw. More teeth fell out from the strike. The scarred boy wasted no time. He didn't give Macchianado a chance to breathe. He was on the offensive and was ready to make his comeback.

Den slammed his fists into every part of Noland. Bashing him down the same way the gangster had just done to him. There was a sweet release to it all. A catharsis Den had never felt before. At least not since the Grizzly Back he had fought so long ago.

Noland's body broke down. Bones shattered and muscles tore. Every ounce of abuse the gangster had inflicted on someone else was finally coming back to him tenfold. This was everything Den had wanted since he had witnessed Hodgson's murder. He was finally, truly, kicking Noland's ass, and he didn't want to stop.

Only for the image of Hugo to flash in his head. Hugo had just poisoned himself. Den had no time for the frivolities of revenge. Not anymore.

The scarred boy stopped his mad rush of fists, leaving Noland to lie in a puddle of his own blood. Beaten, battered, and broken. His small whimpering of pain just barely coming out of his swollen mouth.

Den ran back to Hugo, not giving another second's attention to the gangster. The young Historian was still on his knees.

"Hugo!" Den screamed. "Please be okay!"

"I'm... I'm okay," Hugo assured, winded but still aware, conscious, and smiling.

"Hugo... What the hell did you do?"

"I called his bluff... and it paid off. I should already be convulsing right now... but I'm not... In fact, going by the droplets that are coming out, I'm pretty sure this is saline."

Den tapped his finger onto one of the droplets and lightly touched it to his tongue. "Holy crap. You're right!"

Hugo took another breath, easing himself. "The man's been popping Atlas Tear Drop like candy over the past few hours... Something in the back of my mind figured he couldn't stand to lose even a single dose... It all clicked into place once I remembered that he had a bag of saline in his possession. A bag that looked half empty... Truth be told though, I had no way of knowing if any of my deductions were correct. I just had to take the plunge. And whaddaya know? I guess he ended up the Old Maid."

"You crazy bastard," Den said, a smile coming across his face as well. "You did it! But for the love of God, don't do it again!"

"Wasn't... planning on it..."

Den clutched Hugo, tears falling from his face. Hugo patted Den's back with his good arm. No tears came from Hugo, only relief.

"Ha..." came Noland's voice. "Ha... Ha... Ha..." The gangster tried so hard to laugh, but all he could do was make painful grunts.

"I think," Hugo said, "it's over... Let's get out of here... The police can do the rest."

Den and Hugo huddled together, holding each other's weight. Slowly walking away from the scene. They passed by Noland's broken body, keeping a clear distance as they moved away.

"He's got Andolini's stuff in his bag," Hugo explained. "We should take it with us."

"Gotcha," Den replied.

They reached the bag, just outside the opposite exit. An elevator sat close from where Hugo and Noland had come from. The brothers smiled at its sight. Happy to know they wouldn't have to make their way downstairs in their current state.

Den looked at the bag for just a moment. Sure enough, many of Andolini's antiques were inside. Tarnished, some even broken, but they were all still here.

Just near the bottom, Den saw something out of the ordinary. A stuffed bear was lumped between the relics. The same one he had seen Tillman carry in the alleyway. Den had no way of knowing that it had come from Hodgson. Though given the context, it wasn't difficult to assume it had been used to hide Atlas Tear Drop. Still, the scarred boy kept some comfort in its sight. Perhaps Noland, deep down, still had his soul. However buried it now was.

Hugo grabbed at the bag with his good arm and flung it over his shoulder. "Let's go," Hugo said. The brothers only made it a few steps before they heard another noise.

"Where the hell... do you think... you're going?" Noland said from behind.

Den and Hugo turned around. Noland Macchianado was standing once more. His face still bruised. His legs still shaking. His teeth torn asunder. His bleeding had stopped and his muscles were expanding. But it was his eyes that were the most disturbing... Cold and black. The very same soulless eyes Den had once gazed into when he fought the Crimson Maple. What little remained of Noland Macchianado was now lost in the abyss of pure addiction. Unrelenting and unceasing in his anger. Someone was about to die.

"Ha.... Ha... Ha..."

VI

Neil McKorkendale had undergone many reconstructive surgeries. Almost every part of him had required some form of repair. And among these were his teeth. Tillman had spared no expense in making them feel lifelike. Yet at one time, when McKorkendale was awake and aware of his situation, he had requested to have one of his caps hollowed out. The athlete had thought it could be a good way of sneaking things around, in case he ever needed to.

Later, as Noland Macchianado, he would use this false molar for many different tasks. It had been easy for him to hide small amounts of contraband within the hollowed-out shell of his false tooth.

A few hours earlier, as Hugo slept from the concoction of narcotics Noland had injected him with, the gangster had slipped one final pill of Atlas Tear Drop into his cap. He wasn't sure if he would need it, but kept it anyway, knowing full well the strength Den possessed.

Now, at the top of the Lang-Meyer Courthouse, Noland's final usage of the tooth had paid off. As he had writhed in pain from Den's barrage, he broke off the cap—one of the few teeth that had stayed in his mouth—and swallowed it whole.

At death's door, and with nowhere else to go, Noland could feel the burst of energy flowing through him once more. This final moment of pure bliss as his body was rupturing and breaking. Every part of him in pleasure and pain at once. Even in his broken state, Noland knew he only had a few minutes left... But it was all he needed to fulfill his last wish. Noland Macchianado was about to die. And he was going to take Den with him.

"Hugo, run!" Den screamed as he rushed straight towards Noland.

The scarred boy sent another flurry of punches at Macchianado. Each making an impact. Each as strong as Den could muster. But none seemed to affect the gangster. On the contrary, Noland smiled even more as Den's punches connected.

But there were barely any teeth in Macchianado's smile now. Merely a gaping, bloody maw that greeted Den. A black void at the back of his throat. The same void as his eyes. Noland Macchianado didn't seem human anymore. There was now a monster where he had once stood.

Noland flung his arms at Den. The scarred boy dodged the strikes several times, but the strain of Noland's previous abuse was starting to take its toll on Den. He could feel himself growing punch drunk, his vision blurring and his movements getting sloppy.

It was only inevitable that Noland was finally able to grab Den's throat. He could feel the weight of Noland's hands digging in. Every second made it harder to breathe. His limbs began flailing. Eyes bulging. The veins on his gray head pumping.

Den's arms were already weakened from the fight, but as his oxygen was being cut off, he could barely even move them now. He had no way of getting out of this attack.

Hugo couldn't believe what he was seeing. Once again, Den was at Noland's mercy. Once again, Hugo was watching his brother die. A rage built in the young Historian. A rage he had never felt before. He was not about to sit there and watch the inevitable unfold again. Not after everything they had gone through.

Hugo stared into the bag. The dagger still poked out. It was dulled and rusty. Just barely holding on. But it was a weapon. And that's all it needed to be.

The young Historian grabbed the dagger and ran straight for Macchianado. The gangster was so focused on his revenge that he paid no attention to Hugo's charge, giving the young Historian the opportunity to stab the dagger straight into Noland's chest.

Hugo wasn't aiming for his heart or his arteries. He just attacked whatever open spot he could find. He pushed the dulled blade in as deep as it could go.

The shock was enough to cause Macchianado to let go of Den. The scarred boy fell to the ground, just barely able to catch his breath.

Noland wailed in pain. But these were not the screams of a man. They were not even the cries of a human. Hugo did not believe in demons, thinking the stories of old to be merely legends from peoples who did not recognize certain animals. Equating them to the devilish creatures they had heard in stories for generations. But staring at the face of the creature once known as Noland Macchianado, toothless and voided, made Hugo Statferd believe, if only for a second, that perhaps the legends were not so far off.

Noland screeched into Hugo's ears. His hands moved towards him, trying for Hugo's throat as well. The young Historian stepped back, but knew he was not fast enough to avoid what was coming. Macchianado moved so close to him that, once again, he could feel his bloody, stinking breath on him. Hugo closed his eyes, waiting for the pain... only to hear the impact of a bullet to flesh.

Hugo opened his eyes once more. Noland Macchianado was standing in place. Unmoving and unfeeling. Burrowed into the side of his skull was a bullet. A Buster Bullet, large and round, that had just embedded itself into his head. Hugo backed away from the beast and watched as Macchianado collapsed to the ground. He made no sound. No noise. No gesture. Whether the shot had actually killed him or not, Noland Macchianado was no more.

VII

It had been the most difficult shot Jack "Grill" Trent had ever made. A shot that had taken his entire being to manifest into this one, single moment. It had been impossible before. Noland Macchianado's movements had been too erratic. But in that final moment, as Hugo stood up and saved Den, Grill knew he could take the shot.

But the distance was still too great. The wind too strong. And the angle too high. He only had one shot at this and only one Buster Bullet at that, a compliment from Inspector Walton's team. So Grill positioned himself as far back on the shopping center's roof as he could and placed his full concentration on his one, clean shot. His head pulsated and his nose bled. His veins popped and even his ears went deaf. All he could see was the side of Macchianado's head.

And as the wind blew in just the right direction, as Grill positioned his gun at just the right angle, he made the shot. The Buster Bullet flew through the air. Pushing against the winds, careening upwards until it finally found its mark and drove straight into Macchianado's skull.

Grill would have cheered in that moment, if his entire body hadn't given out at once. Walton's men caught him before he hit the ground. Grill felt dizzy and weak. Yet in that moment, he knew he had just saved his friends. He didn't know what he had just done to his body, but he already knew it was worth it.

VIII

Den took in several deep, painful breaths. Hugo sat by his side. The brothers were exhausted, sitting just near the exit. They had chosen to forgo even the elevator, instead waiting on a dispatch crew to arrive and get them.

Noland's body remained slumped on the ground, still lying in the same spot he had fallen when Grill shot him. The dagger still embedded into his chest.

"Is he dead?" Hugo asked.

"No," Den replied in a soft voice. "It's faint... but he's breathing."

"How?"

"Maybe the drug made his body that hard?"

"Yeah... I guess that makes sense."

Even with all the wounds he had endured and all the pain he had suffered, Noland Macchianado was alive, at least physically. Yet there was not a hint of awareness in his body. Not a tinge of soul. Just the broken, mangled flesh that remained.

The brothers kept watch over the gangster. Hoping and praying that he would not somehow spring back to life once more. But such a time never came. The police and emergency medical team arrived shortly after, inspecting the crime scene and checking on Den, Hugo, and even Noland.

Den would get sent to Hearts & Minds Medical Center, Wayport's premier hospital, to check on his physical condition. As would Grill. Hugo would be tested to make sure whatever narcotics Noland had put into his body had not caused any serious or lasting harm. Their hotel rooms, as crowded as they had been, would remain vacant for the next few nights to come.

Noland Macchianado, for all his crimes, was taken straight into Hearts & Minds' ICU, where he would be watched over. Both by the doctors and by Romero's own men. Not a single member of the Florenzas or the Takedas dared step foot on hospital grounds.

It had been a night of suffering and pain. A night that had nearly cost the trio of travelers so very much. But it was also a night of triumph and renewal. A night that had tested them to their very limits. And they had survived.

The city had lived under the watchful eye of the pale-lit night. Now the dawn had finally arrived.

IX

28 years ago...
November 17, 812 AU

It was the last insane asylum on Adalia's Eastern coast, four slabs of concrete and steel housing the mentally deranged and the societally sick. For 138 years, the Rockvale Sanatorium for the Mentally Unwell had opened its doors to patients of every kind. Male and female. Fit and fat. Young and old. Now it was entering its final days. A mix of new legislation, health concerns, and a deepening recession meant that the lights could no longer be kept on. Meaning it was ripe pickings for those with more than enough influence and power to take what they wanted. However they felt like.

Tommy Tillman had found himself in the pediatric wing of the establishment. His person adorned in the finest suit and coat that money could buy. His eyes set on a singular goal.

There had been a boy that had caught his eye. A problem child from a broken home. His mother died when he was so very young and his father was a complete unknown. He had been raised in a nearby orphanage until a string of bizarre animal deaths pointed to the culprit being the boy in question.

He had a temper. One that was unwieldy when fully unleashed. He had caused grievous injuries to his fellow inmates. And not just to the children, either. Full-grown men had been sent to the medical ward after allegedly being beaten by the boy. One of whom was said to have died from the injuries.

So many strange occurrences, and yet it only fascinated Tillman even more. So much so that he had arranged a meeting with the boy.

From across a thick, plastic divider, Tillman sat. A moment later, the boy entered from the other side in small handcuffs. He was bruised on his left cheek and hobbling slightly. A large orderly stood nearby.

The divider had several small holes, allowing Tillman and the boy to communicate thoroughly. Tillman greeted the boy with a smile. The boy simply stared back.

"Hello there, young man. My name is Thomas Tillman. You can call me Tom or Till if you'd like. And what's your name?"

"Mac."

"Good to meet you, Mac. Or would you rather be called by your family name?"

"Ain't got one. Just Mac."

"I see... So, why did you do it, Mac?"

"He tried to kill me."

"Who?"

"Big Bongo."

"Is Big Bongo the dead man?"

"Yes."

"And who is Big Bongo?"

"Boss. What Big Bongo says, everyone does."

"And what did you not want to do?"

"Bad things."

Tillman sat for a moment, expecting elaboration from the worn and torn child. Yet nothing came. The boy's stare was stern and focused. As if ready to pounce, should another attack come.

"Would you like to get out of here, Mac?"

"And go where?"

"With me."

"And do bad things?"

"Of course not."

"Then what?"

"What's your favorite sport, Mac?"

"Ain't got one."

"Then what do you like to do outside, just for fun?"

For the first time since their conversation began, Mac started to ponder. It was a question he had never been asked, requiring an answer he had never said. "He told me I'm good at lifting."

"Big Bongo?"

"Yeah. He said I could lift more than a man four times my size."

"What if I told you that you could lift as much as you wanted? And even get paid to do it?"

"Construction?"

"Oh no, no, dear boy. Something far more... glamorous."

From out of his breast pocket, Tillman took out several photographs and held them so that Mac could see. Athletes of every kind adorned them. Baseball, basketball, track, and swimming. An assortment of the most physically fit people in the world vying to mold their bodies to their utmost peak and prove to both themselves and the world that they were the greatest of all.

Mac stared intently at the pictures. Examining each photo with as much care as he had the time to take in. "And these people are rich too?" the boy asked.

"Of course," Tillman responded. "If they spend their money right."

"They live in mansions?"

"A few. Others don't, but that's because they're not spending their money wisely."

"Can I live in a mansion?"

"One day, perhaps. If you play your cards right."

"Don't know how to play no card games."

"A figure of speech, dear boy."

Mac did not respond. He merely gave Tillman a quizzical look. It was enough to make the man chuckle.

"Tell you what. You lift enough weights and make enough money, then I'll buy you a mansion myself."

Mac let Tillman's words sink in. It was more information than the boy was ever used to. He didn't know how to weigh his options or think about second opinions. It was a deal better than he had ever known. So why not? “Okay, Mister. I’ll lift weights for you.”

Chapter 10

PROMISE

I

The bullet had not killed Noland Macchianado. But it had certainly damaged him. Yet somehow, his body still functioned, however feebly. His mind had utterly collapsed. Organs had scattered and mixed. He'd been stabilized only by the immediate care of medical workers who quickly came onto the scene. The fact that he could breathe, even with support, was a miracle in and of itself.

Noland had known many people, yet at this moment, as his body lay in a hospital bed, only a single soul sat near him. A chaplain by the name of Morrison. Someone Noland did not, nor ever would, know. Morrison was not a native of Wayport, nor was he very familiar with it at all. He had only moved to the Terminal City the previous year. It was not uncommon for him to deal with cases like this. A criminal at death's door, in need of praying for his eternal soul, whose sins could have very well outweighed his conscious deeds. But still a child of God. Someone who, in the end, deserved that last chance at salvation.

Morrison prayed his usual prayers. Read aloud from Bible scriptures he already knew from heart. But there was a staleness to his words. A hanging sense of stagnation. In a place like Wayport, Noland

Macchianado was certainly not the first criminal he prayed for, nor would he be his last. Just another parasite blighting a rotten city. Fifteen months in and the chaplain had already witnessed the horrors the underworld could wrought. The aftermaths of too many lost souls taking a plunge they would always regret. Guilty and innocent alike.

Yet he persisted because that's what he knew. It was all he could do to stay in the faith. To remind himself that everyone could be saved, whether or not they deserved it. Following God's word for as long as he could.

But maybe he could just stop the prayers for today. Tell his superiors that he had done his duties already. At least he would be done with this case. At least he could move on to someone more deserving. Morrison paused his readings. Letting the moment sink in. The silence broken only by the clock still ticking along.

Morrison heard the room door creak open. From just outside, the chaplain could see a government agent standing on the other side of the wall. A bodyguard on standby in case Noland woke up and went loose. Not that there was any sign of that happening.

But it was not the agent coming in. Instead it was a strange-looking boy with white hair and scars all over him, bandage wraps covering his head and arms. A boy the chaplain would later learn was named Den.

"Excuse me," Den said. "May I come in?"

"Of course," Morrison replied.

Den closed the door behind him and moved close to Noland.

"I take it you are familiar with Mr. Macchianado?" Morrison asked, his demeanor calm and inviting. Standing in contrast to the questions that persisted in his mind.

"Yes," Den replied. "We weren't... weren't exactly friendly."

Morrison had only been told briefly about Macchianado. That he was a drug pusher and loan shark, finally paying for his actions. He didn't know Den's affiliation, though the chaplain guessed it was more than likely antagonistic in nature. Still, the boy remained calm and composed, eyes set on Noland's unmoving body. He stared at his face. Much of it had been completely wrapped and sewn up. A tube went down his throat. Yet Den knew it was him.

"Has anyone else come in?" Den asked.

"No," Morrison replied. "Apart from a few agents and myself, I'm afraid you're the first one."

"Oh... okay."

For the next few minutes, Den stood at Noland's side. Morrison watched Den's behavior. The scarred boy showed no anger toward the dying man. Nor did he show sympathy. Den merely stood by Noland, watching as his vitals slowly dropped lower and lower.

Morrison had thought of asking another question. Perhaps seeing if this boy was a person of faith as well. Yet he couldn't muster up the words to say so. He just watched Den looking on, pretending to sift through his Bible every minute or so.

"May I pray for him?" Den finally asked, catching Morrison off guard.

"Of course, dear boy," the chaplain responded. "Everyone is deserving of prayer."

Den did not know the true weight of Noland's sins. He did not know how many crimes he had committed. How many lives he had taken. How many innocents he had hurt. Yet he remembered that stuffed bear. That single, innocent bear. On the run and nearly dead, yet he still clung to that bear. His saving grace in a life of sin.

Den cupped his hands together. Morrison followed suit. The chaplain did not know what words the scarred boy would speak. He merely listened. Taking in the prayers of this strange-looking boy.

> *Dear Heavenly Father, please guide this helpless soul. His sins are too great to comprehend, yet I believe that in your light there may still be some salvation for him. For he was once but a child left out in the cold. Torn asunder by this broken world. If salvation be not your will, then at least let his punishment be swift. For we are all but puppets to our sins.*

To all his victims, may they be at peace. To all his loved ones, may they go without worry. I know not what you will deem him, Father. But I know that it shall be good and just. As are all things in your light.

—Amen

Morrison could feel a single tear roll down in his face. He wiped it off as quickly as he could, hoping the scarred boy did not see it.

But Den had not moved away from Noland. He simply watched on once more. Seeing his vitals dropping to their lowest point.

Morrison felt a sting in his heart. He was a chaplain, a man who had sworn himself to God, and yet he had been so brazen as to ignore his duties. Yet this boy, this strange-looking boy from parts unknown, had prayed for a man who had hurt him. Letting go of all earthly reservations in these final moments.

Morrison believed in Divine Providence. He believed all things happened for a reason. To see Den do what he had done was a true act of God. A moment in time the chaplain would never forget for as long as he lived.

He joined Den in his watch. Together they stood and waited for the inevitable. It would only take a few more minutes for everything to finally come to its end.

At 6:25 p.m., on the evening of June 26, 840 AU, Noland Macchiando passed away from systemic heart failure. His wanted poster had been rescinded prior to its official activation. There would be no funeral service. Merely a small, private gathering. His few possessions left in the care of his superior, Thomas Tillman. The only father he had ever known.

II

"I never thought I would be this bored," Hugo said.

"Ah, come on, buddy! It ain't so bad," Den replied. "They got all-you-can-eat gelatin today! That's *definitely* worth something."

"If I derived as much pleasure from a hospital stay as you do from gelatinous desserts, I would be a very happy and fulfilled individual."

"See? Now you got something to strive for!"

The past two days for Hugo Statferd had been tedious at best. Despite being the least injured of the trio, the young Historian had been kept the longest. Though this had primarily come from an insistence on Grill's part to make sure nothing of Noland's concoction had caused any lasting damage. Thankfully, every test had shown that the dosage was nothing more than basic sleeping meds. Something that could easily be bought over the counter. Presumably purchased by Macchianado in order get some sleep during his withdrawals.

Den's injuries had healed far faster than expected, allowing the scarred boy to be released within twenty-four hours of his check-in, in spite of the beating he had taken from Noland twice in a row. At the same time, his hunger had increased several fold. Implying that the rapid healing of his body, relatively speaking, had been possible thanks to a far larger caloric and nutritional intake. But these were merely theories that would require more testing to be certain. Testing Den was not interested in undergoing.

Grill was the next to check out. It was already a rarity for the bounty hunter to suffer side effects from his Enhanced abilities—a result of many years training himself across a multitude of dangerous areas and stressful situations. But Grill had never made a shot like the one he made on Macchianado. Especially with as much as he had on the line. Ultimately, the bounty hunter had avoided suffering long-term damage to his body, simply needing an extra day of recovery before he was ready to go. But he had been rendered unconscious for some hours after the fight, making it clear that pushing his body to such a limit should only be used as a last resort.

Hugo did not possess his friends' Enhanced abilities. And so had been stuck making sure everything within his normal human body was functioning well. His only salvation from the tedium came from books he had borrowed from the hospital's small library. But it was almost time for the young Historian to check out as well. He just needed to wait for the final confirmation.

"All-you-can-eat gelatin? Now that's a feast for both the eyes and the mouth!" came a voice entering the room.

"Mr. Andolini!" Hugo exclaimed.

Andolini had pulled through. The abuse he had suffered from Noland had been quick, though the damage had been palpable. For several hours Andolini had also been unconscious, even feared to have been rendered fully comatose. But soon enough, the old Historian had managed to pull out of it. And like Hugo, he was not an Enhanced. But unlike Hugo, he was not a young man either.

His broken hand was in a cast and his head injuries had required several stitches. While his legs had not suffered any physical damage, it had been difficult for him to walk, requiring the old Historian to move around in a wheelchair, pushed by a nurse. Still, Andolini was expected to make a full recovery. But it would take time and patience. Time and patience that Andolini had in spades.

"Want some, sir?" Den offered. "Lime is my favorite!"

"I'm actually partial to banana, myself," Andolini replied. "Odd choice, I know. But I've loved it since I was a wee lad. But lime is good too!" The old Historian grabbed one of the many gelatin cups Den had ordered, under Hugo's name, and happily devoured it. "Best meal I've had all week!"

"Have the doctors given any updates?" Hugo asked.

"Oh, yes," Andolini answered. "They said I can go home in a few days. I never knew how much I missed my cot!"

"But what about..." Hugo tried to find the right words to inquire about Andolini's current predicament.

"What about your legs?" Den asked. Once more, Hugo found himself appreciating the bluntness of his brother's words.

"That's the crux of it. I can move them," Andolini explained, shaking his feet as he did so. "I just need to get my balance back in order."

"You're gonna need some assistance, then," Hugo stated.

"It'll be fine, lad. I can just move a bit slower while I get my strength back up."

"With one hand, and head trauma? With all due respect, sir, I've seen your routine for about a month now. I don't think it's wise for you to be moving like that. At least not so soon."

"Oh, this is nothing, Hugo. I'm doing perfectly well!" Andolini made his same, sweet smile. Yet just under the surface, Hugo could see his true thoughts. The shaking of his hands. His unsteady breathing. The downplaying of his condition. Gino Andolini was in no position to continue his work for the WHS, at least not alone. And everyone, especially Andolini himself, knew it.

"I'll do it," Hugo stated. "Please, Mr. Andolini. Let me help you!"

"No need, Hugo. Besides, you're on your Journey! Plenty of places to see and people to meet. I don't want to hold you back from all that."

"I'm only just a month in. I've still got two whole years to explore. In the grand scheme of things, what's another few month—" Hugo stopped. He turned to Den, remembering the whole point of their Journey in the first place.

But Den simply nodded with Hugo. "I know what you're thinking, buddy," Den said. "But don't worry about me. Fact is, Madame Lake's already been gone for a while now. Who knows where she might be? If helping Mr. Andolini means postponing our search for a bit? Then it's totally worth it!"

Hugo couldn't help but smile. "Thanks, Den." He turned his focus back to Andolini. "Mr. Andolini, you don't have to face this alone. We're not gonna leave you out in the cold."

“Hugo… Den…” He had faced so many hardships alone his life. Had taken so much grief. Reaped the results of his past sins and poor choices. Yet now, these two young men, still so early in their lives, had brought with them salvation for this old, wounded Historian. Andolini could feel the tears roll down his face. “Thank you both! Thank you!”

“I know! It melts your heart, doesn’t it?” asked another familiar voice entering the room. A voice Den, Hugo, and Andolini knew all too well and one they were quite happy to hear. Blond hair, loose clothing, and a permanent five o’clock shadow adorned the face of the lean man coming in. Nash Ortega had arrived.

“Nash?” Hugo exclaimed. “When did you get here?”

“Just now,” Nash replied. “Just got straight off the Righton Train. Man, I forgot how slow that thing moves! Seriously, my butt is aching.”

“Absolutely,” Den agreed. “I knew someone else would understand my plight!”

“Nash…” Andolini said, wiping his tears. “I didn’t think you’d come.”

“Of course! You think I’d just leave a fallen brother down on his luck like that?” Nash gave a firm pat on Andolini’s back.

“Okay! I’m definitely out of the loop on this,” Den exclaimed.

“I had called Nash to discuss the damages Macchianado had done to the WHS,” Hugo explained. “I just thought you were gonna hire a repair crew or something.”

“And what?” Nash replied. “Go on blind faith and assume they’d do it the right way? Not my style. Besides, I had been meaning to see Gino again. Been too long, as far as I’m concerned.”

“That’s sounds wonderful, Nash,” Andolini said. “How long are you planning to stay?”

“Hmm…” Nash pondered. “That depends… How long will it take you to recover?”

“Nash… You don’t mean…”

“Absolutely! You need help. And frankly, I’ve been meaning to stretch my legs a bit more lately.”

Andolini had not expected to cry as much as he did. But he couldn't help it. In this moment, he knew he was truly blessed. "God bless you, Nash. Thank you so very much!"

"Nash... thank you," Hugo said. "But what about Harten?"

"Clark's in charge. Weldon hasn't shown his face even once since Victor's verbal beat down. So things have been pretty chill. Plus, Rindi's really been taking charge lately too. Seriously, I think you'd be proud of your wife!"

"She's not my..." Hugo couldn't even finish his sentence. His face blushed red.

"Oh, aye?" Andolini spoke. "You know, I've heard you mention that name a few times, but I didn't think it was so serious!"

"Even more than that," Den added. "They made smoochy-smoochy right before he left!"

"Ah, young love!" Andolini shouted.

Den, Nash, and Andolini laughed in unison. And for even as embarrassed as he felt, Hugo started laughing too.

Each of these men laughed their hearts out. Laughed their frustrations and fears away. They had faced struggles and hardships in such a short amount of time. Yet they had survived. However damaged they were. They had lived another day and would hopefully live for many more days to come.

"By the way," Nash spoke as their laughter died down. "Where's Grill? Thought he'd be here with you guys."

"He said he had some errands to run," Hugo said.

"I wanted to go along," Den added, "but he insisted I stay to watch over Hugo."

"Which is probably his nicest way of saying he needed to go some place quiet," Hugo interjected.

"Hey! I can't help it if I happen to bring the mood up everywhere I go!"

The room filled with laughter once more. Yet in the back of his mind, Hugo pondered where Grill had gone off to. He did not worry for his friend, even in a place like Wayport. Yet once more his curiosity was piqued. There was still so much he wanted to know about Grill. So many unspoken words he was desperate to hear. But that would be for another time.

Their mission was complete. Their next destination unknown. The next step in their Journey now so close at hand.

III

Contrary to what the obituaries had written, there had been no "small, private gathering" for the late Noland Macchianado. No service. No remembrance. Not even a toast. He had no friends. And the only man he had ever considered family was in no position to honor his memory. Not after the chaos he had created for everyone involved. Not with the carnage that was still to come.

The higher-ups of the Florenza family had indeed come together regarding Macchianado. But it was to analyze and strategize what to do next. Once again situated in a vacant motel room in another part of Wayport's slums, Nicky, Jacob, Barrett, and Tillman all discussed what the future had in store.

"Geez, would ya look at that nick?" Barrett said, eyeing Santino's injury. "A nick on Nicky. Ha!"

"Shut the hell up, Barry!" Nicky screamed. "Jodie nagged me enough last night. Nearly woke up the kids."

"To be fair, a mark like that doesn't exactly make for the most attractive feature. Not unless you're a total freak!"

Nicky gave his colleague his most intense glare. The kind of look he rarely gave to anyone outside of his worst enemies. Much less one of his most trusted allies. This was no time to be making petty jokes.

"All due respect, sir," Barrett added, softening his tone and lowering his eyes. "So... what are we supposed to do now?"

"The Takedas will lay low for a while..." Tillman explained. "The Pale Dragon's passing will not just be ignored... There are ceremonies to do. Wills to sort out. Respects to pay."

Tillman's words were low and hushed, his usual gruff voice just barely audible to his colleagues. Even after everything, they dared not say a word of ridicule to the man who had just lost a son.

"But once that's done," Nicky explained, "after that initial shock has calmed down... prepare for war, boys."

"It's that bad?" Barrett uttered.

"You don't shoot the Pale Dragon and expect things to just blow over," Nicky said. "Matches' cadaver—" He stopped for a moment. Rethinking his words. "Macchianado's passing won't mean much in the grand scheme of things. The boss says to be ready for anything."

"Burn the Takedas! Rip their flesh! Roast their fields!" Jacob screeched.

"Might just be what we're gonna have do, Jacob." Nicky nodded.

"What if we captured the Iron Sniper?" Barrett suggested. "He's a big name!"

"And he's connected with the Feds," Tillman noted. "Not happening."

Barrett started shaking. Desperately thinking of ways to try and avoid an all-out war. The thought alone was terrifying enough.

"We could offer up Tommy!" Barrett blurted. "If Matches would've worked, Till's gotta mean something to them."

Tillman looked at Barrett in both shock and disgust. He didn't even have the words to say.

"We do *not* sell out our own like that," Nicky screamed. "And don't you dare make a suggestion like that again!"

"But we just did it with Matches," Barrett defended himself. "I was only trying to calm things down!"

"Matches was different. That junky bastard caused this whole mess! Till is a Florenza! A true one! He was making this family a fortune while your mother rocked you to sleep. He stays! Apologize! Now!"

The large man bowed to Tillman, his hands shaking even more. Barrett's fear only grew as Nicky screamed. "I'm so sorry, Till. It was just a moment of weakness."

Tillman huffed and averted his eyes from Barrett.

"My sincerest apologies as well, Till," Nicky said. Santino had been so wrapped up in his anger that he hadn't noticed what he had said until it was too late. He meant every word of it, but even he knew when it was appropriate to say certain things and when it was not.

"No, you're right," Tillman replied. "Mac... Matches... Noland... was a bastard... You did what was right... He got what was always coming to him... What's done is done."

A knock came from the door.

"We don't want your damn housekeeping!" Nicky shouted. "Go away!"

Another came from the door.

"Oh for the love of God! We're good! Thank you! Leave!"

A third knock came from the door.

Nicky Santino was not having any of this. He rushed to the door. Intending to scream his heart out at whatever lowly maid was simply trying to do her job. Letting out all of his frustrations into a single mad burst. He opened the door.

Grill stood on the other side.

IV

All four gangsters stood in silence. It took each of them a moment to realize that the visage of the Iron Sniper was not some mass hallucination. Grill was real and he was here.

The bounty hunter maintained a lax stance. Arms to his side and back straight. He stared at Nicky. Waiting for the gangster to respond. Yet for second after painful second, the silence lingered. Grill was in the lion's den and the lions were petrified.

"What the hell are you doing here, Sniper?" Nicky finally asked after a beat.

"I have a blank check and a pen full of ink," Grill stated. "Name the price and I will happily pay for Gino Andolini's debt right here and right now... Although, I supposed I should be asking Mr. Tillman." The bounty hunter turned his attention to the old man. Maintaining his stance, even with Nicky right in front of him.

"What's his price, Tillman?" Grilled asked.

"It's..." Tillman paused. "It's not for sale. We wrote a contract. He's mine."

Slowly, Grill entered the room and walked towards Tillman. The bounty hunter made no move towards his holstered gun. Showed no sign of fear in front of the men who could technically be classified as his enemies. And still Grill walked until he was right next to the old man.

"Name... your... price," Grill spoke again, slowly and meticulously.

Tillman stood in shock. He had no words to say. No remarks to make. The Silent Death was staring him in the face. The man who had just killed Noland. And he showed not a single hint of regret. "Two hundred thousand Rias," Tillman finally said.

"Done," Grill replied. The bounty hunter moved to the room's table, took out his checkbook, and wrote all the necessary information down. He ripped the check out and handed it to Tillman. All the while, Nicky, Jacob, and Barrett stood and watched. There was no telling what Grill was capable of doing in this moment. And there was no need to find out.

"Tha... Thank you," Tillman said in his same low tone.

"You will mail me the contract immediately upon depositing this check. You know where I'm staying," Grill commanded. "You will not see Andolini again. If you happen to bump into him on the street, you will immediately walk away. You will not make small talk. You will not try to redeem yourself. You. Are. Done."

Silently, Grill walked back towards the door. Not even acknowledging Jacob and Barrett. Barely even acknowledging Nicky. Until the bounty hunter reached the front door once more and turned around to face them all.

"And if any of you pursue us to seek some kind of revenge, I will only give you this one warning: Don't. You all know who I am and you all know what I'm capable of. Deal with your petty squabbles yourself." Grill slammed the door as he left.

Still, the four gangsters stood in silence. Grill's warning echoing in their minds.

"Silent Death makes you sleep!" Jacob yelled, fear in his eyes. "Silent Death makes you sleep!"

Barrett fell to the floor. He could feel himself starting to hyperventilate.

"Dammit!" Nicky said, punching at the nearby wall. "Damn it all!"

Tillman looked at his check. The name "Jack Trent" was written in cursive. He placed his gloved fingers on the name, the ink just barely smudging the tips. He placed the check in his jacket pocket. "I... I think I'm going to go to the bank."

Tillman walked out of the room. The sounds of his colleagues' anger, frustration, and anxiety echoed out across the motel.

For a time, the old man walked alone, his last moments with Noland still playing in his mind. The last time he ever saw his face and heard his voice. All the times they had spent together and the moment that had brought it all to an end.

After passing a certain alley, a young boy walked up to Tillman, his speed faster than that of a normal boy his age. "Did you need me for anything, Mr. Tillman?" the boy asked.

"Nothing in particular, Vito," Tillman replied. "I was just about to go to the bank and was wondering if you would like to come along."

"For what? I don't have any money."

"Maybe not now, but you will when you're older. And it's good to understand money when you're young. Keeps you from making poor financial decisions down the line."

"No offense, Mr. Tillman, but that sounds kinda boring."

"I thought the same thing too, when I was your age. Just a bunch of grownups rattling on and on about boring stuff... But then I started making money. And now, I live in a mansion."

Vito's face lit up with Tillman's words. "A mansion?"

"Let me show you something." Tillman took out Grill's check. "Two hundred thousand Rias. Would you like to know how I spend it?"

"Yeah!" Vito replied ecstatically.

Tillman chuckled. "Alright, then. Let's head to the bank!"

Tillman and Vito walked side by side, Vito skipping along as he did. Free from Baratzi's control, yet still so very vulnerable.

"Hey, Mr. Tillman, I was wondering," Vito said, "what's with your hand?"

"What's that, Vito?"

"Your hand. It's shaped kinda funny."

The two stopped for a moment so Tillman could remove his gloves. His left hand looked the same as it always had. His right hand was bandaged up... and missing two fingers. The damage Noland had caused to Tillman's fingers was far more serious than the old man had first thought. Had he immediately gone to the hospital, they could have been salvaged. Yet in the hours he sat alone, weeping in the dark, the damage only accrued. Infection spread. And by the time he went to have it checked, it was already too late. Amputation was the only possible solution. His middle and ring fingers were now gone. The small nubs just above his knuckles were the only reminder they were once even there.

"What happened?" Vito asked in a concerned tone.

"An accident, dear boy," Tillman responded. "An accident... and nothing more."

V

He had promised to protect them. Promised to make sure that nothing bad would happen to them. Grill had said as much to Karina. And to

Voltaire, Rasmus, and Nash. Yet everything had fallen apart. And even now, with everyone safe and recovering, it still didn't erase what had happened. How the actions of one psychotic killer nearly cost them everything. But Grill blamed himself more than anyone else. He had broken his promise. His vow to his newly-forged brotherhood. How could he possibly face them again, knowing all this?

Grill slowly walked back to the hospital. Taking his time, letting the June breeze waft through his hair. July was just about to start, so he was enjoying what might be the last cool day he would experience for a while. He wasn't sure when Hugo was being checked out, but knew the young Historian was safe with Den by his side.

Grill had rarely made time for himself since their Journey had begun. He was always focused on their mission or spending time with Den and Hugo. Times he enjoyed more than anything else. Still, it was nice to take this small stroll.

But there always seemed to be something else around the corner. And in this case, he spotted a man he wished he would never see again.

"Jack," Romero said as he walked up to him. "We need to talk."

Grill tried paying his former colleague no attention. Blatantly walking past him. Ignoring his very existence.

"It's about your pay," Romero explained as he started walking beside Grill. "It took a few days to come through, but I believe you'll find it quite satisfactory." The agent started taking out the checks from his pocket. "And, of course, they are addressed to both you and Mr. Den. I also requested a bonus for you both, considering how things went. Please accept these with our deepest apologizes."

Romero held the checks out to Grill. Slowly, the bounty hunter and the agent stopped walking. Grill eyed the checks, paid to the order of "Jack Trent" and "Den of Faradin." He took them both and placed Den's check in his pocket, but kept holding onto his own. Placing both hands on it.

Grill looked Romero straight in the eyes as he ripped his own check in half. He ripped it several more times after that and gave the torn pieces of paper back to Romero. Grill had still said not a word. He simply walked away.

"Kataloosa," Romero said. The name was enough for Grill to stop once again. Though he did not turn around. "They're old reports, but we know Madame Lake has had some connections in Kataloosa. Thought you should know."

Grill made no remark nor confirmation. He simply walked on once more. Leaving Romero to stand alone.

Grill continued his walk for some time to come. He had barely registered what Romero had said. Kataloosa had felt like such a long time ago. A different place in a different time. When his priorities were strained and his life had little meaning. When he had no idea where he was going and what he would do.

His thoughts were broken as he heard a ring come from his pocket. Grill had finally purchased a cell phone. The past few days had given him a new perspective on the importance of keeping in touch with the ones he cared about. He answered it.

"Hello?"

"Grill?" came a voice the bounty hunter had recently become all too familiar with.

"Ms. Karina?"

"Hello, Grill," she responded. "I think you know why I'm calling."

"Yes. And I just want to say how sorry—"

"I'm not asking for an apology." Karina's interruption was stern, yet calm.

Grill remained quiet. Knowing it best to let Karina say what she needed to say.

"Just give me an explanation," she continued. "That's all I'm asking."

"It was a miscalculation based on bad evidence. If we had—"

"Oh for the love of God! Don't give me that kind of talk."

Once more Grill went silent.

"Den's told me how much you hate that kind of political speak. I'm not some colonel asking about deviations in the plan. I'm asking *you*. Why in the hell did it get to this?"

Grill remain silent for another moment longer. Even he was stunned at his own explanation. Eight years out and yet here he was trying to walk around the issue. Had Romero tainted his mind that much? Or had he just returned to the bad old days of his previous life? He didn't need to come up with pretty words. All Karina was asking from him was to speak through his heart.

"I underestimated our opponent," Grill explained. "I didn't think he'd try to target Hugo. He had given a fake name and for all I knew Hugo was safe where he was. I didn't think Macchianado had the wherewithal to do what he did... And for that, I'm sorry."

"Remember our talk at the party?"

"Of course." It was a talk he wasn't about to forget. The silent, peering eyes of Nash, Rasmus, and Voltaire staring down on him as Karina spoke. The sharpness of her tongue only making her warnings all the more potent. "If you believe I have violated my promise, then I will leave as soon as possible."

Karina let Grill's word sink in. "Can I ask you something?"

"Of course. Anything."

"Can you promise me that the boys won't be in danger going forward? That this time you really *will* keep them safe?"

For the first time in quite a while, Grill had the urge to lie. To tell her how much she needn't worry. That he'd maintain a closer eye on them and better his sharpshooting capabilities to make sure of it. That he was someone Karina could trust with her brothers. All it would take was a few, simple words.

"No," he responded. "The fact of the matter is that I have no idea what we may be facing in the future. I barely know who Madame Lake is. I don't who she's connected to, nor if she's one to hold grudges with people. And that's not even including where exactly we may end up next. It could all be smooth sailing or it could end up being more dangerous than even I could imagine... So, no. I cannot promise you that. I cannot lie to you like that. All I can say is that I will protect them to the best of my abilities. Because that's all I can ever do. All I can ever vow."

"Thank you," Karina said. "You have no idea how relieved that makes me feel."

"Ma'am?"

"'A *warrior who lies can boast about the heavens. A warrior who is true can only say what he knows.*' It's a line I heard Hugo recite once. Trying to memorize it for one of his classes. It stuck with me. They were words I wished I had heard when I was traveling. Would have saved me a lot pain and a lot heartache. I can't help but think of them again.

"I just got done talking with Hugo and Den. I was concerned and scared beyond belief. But the moment the two of them spoke, I knew they were okay. I can happily say that the confidence Hugo displayed during the Crimson Maple stuff wasn't just a fluke. It's in him. Just as I always knew it was."

"He's strong," Grill stated. "I once told him about what separates the victims from the victors. And he is no victim... Not anymore."

"And Den hasn't lost his inner self. He could one day lift a mountain, and it wouldn't change how strong he is on the inside."

"He's got more potential in him than anyone I've ever seen. I am proud to be his master. Proud he is my apprentice."

"Grill... those boys are going to change the world. I don't know when and I don't know how. But they're on a path that will make them so much stronger. And I am honored to know that you are on their side."

"Thank you, Ms. Karina."

"You're welcome, Mr. Grill."

They sat in silence together. Letting the moment sink in. Weaving another silent vow.

"Okay," Karina spoke. "I said what I needed to say. I'll check up on you guys in a bit. Have a good one, Grill."

"You too, Ms. Karina." Grill hung up the phone.

The bounty hunter hadn't realized how close he was to the hospital now. In a few minutes he would reunite with Den and Hugo. His regrets left by the wayside. His promises renewed.Wherever they would go next. Whatever would happen, he would face it with them. Their bonds stronger than words, thicker than blood, and harder than steel.

VI

"Once again, Mr. Den, I am honored to be at your service," Lance Decker said, still adorned in his immaculate suit. "Without further ado, I present you with Madame Lake's second letter."

The trio had finally made their way back to the First National Bank of Wayport. Den held the letter in his hands—the same normal design as the previous one. Den, Hugo, and Grill huddled together, all eyes on Madame Lake's next message.

Den,

By now, you have found your calling. Or at the very least, a job you can be proud of. Even if you're not, please know that I am so very proud of you. You have taken your next step to independence. A far more important step than you may ever know.

I know I was barely a mother to you, but I hope that these letters can at least compensate in some form. However little it may truly mean.

But I must stress again. I have no singular answer for you. I can only give you possibilities. Three of which I believe may point you in the right direction.

The possible locations are Mayline City, Kataloosa, and Miracle Land. I have had a vested interest in each of these locations at different points of my life. There may be something in these places that could point you in the right direction. Though I cannot say for certain they will still be there by the time you travel to them. I have no control over such things.

I understand that these are very disparate locations. But suffice it to say, my interest and focus over the years has been eclectic. I just hope that, even if you find nothing, you can at least learn and understand more about yourself on these travels. That you may grow into the man I know you can be. Good luck and never give up on that spark that is in you.

—Till our lines entwine again,
Madame Lake

"So our options are Mayline, Miracle Land... or Kataloosa," Grill stated.

"Miracle Land? The theme park?!" Hugo asked, exacerbated.

"Miracle Land it is!" Den shouted.

"That wasn't a suggestion, Den," Hugo clarified. "I just wasn't expecting Madame Lake of all people to have an interest in Miracle Land, of all places."

"She has some interest in architecture," Den noted. "Maybe she built one of the rides! Ooh, maybe it's one of the roller coasters! I'm already giddy with excitement!"

"*Kataloosa*," Grill read again, it kept repeating in his mind. Once more that name had returned. Was Romero somehow aware of Madame Lake's letter? Or was this yet another bit of Divine Providence? If Madame Lake indeed had some interest there, it only made sense Romero would potentially know. Regardless, it was a place Grill knew he couldn't ignore. Not anymore.

"Kataloosa," Grill stated. "I think we should go to Kataloosa."

"Aw, come one, Grill! It's Miracle Land!" Den objected. "I've never been. It'll be so much fun!"

"I understand, Grill," Hugo nodded.

"Not you too, buddy!"

"Den, please tell me you remember one of your teacher's nicknames."

Den rubbed his temples. "Iron Sniper, of course. Silent Death, pretty scary... The Kataloosa Ranger..." In an instant, the scarred boy saw his master in a whole new light. "Holy crap, Grill! Were you a cowboy?"

"Sheriff, actually," Grill responded. "But it's... a little more complicated than that," Grill responded.

"Complicated, my foot! Forget Miracle Land, at least for now. I wanna know more about the Kataloosa Ranger!"

"There will be time for all that later," Grill said. "If we're going to Kataloosa, I'm gonna need to start making arrangements immediately."

"Alright, then!" Den shouted. "Are we all in agreement?"

Hugo and Grill nodded.

"Then it's settled! Our next stop: Kataloosa!"

VII

Night had fallen on Wayport once more. The Lang-Meyer Courthouse, in spite of all the commotion, had finally resumed its refurbishments. The trio stayed in their hotel rooms, enjoying their last night in Wayport. The travelers had no interest in going out on the town. They had already seen enough of the city as it was. A quiet night in had seemed the best respite. One where they could kick back and enjoy some easy, leisurely activities.

In Grill's room, the trio had ordered room service and pay-per-view movies. They spent the next few hours enjoying the finest food Merryville Suites' restaurant had to offer, regardless of how expensive it was. All while enjoying the latest shlock action films. Light on story, big on explosives. Not the highest form of cinema, but it was certainly to their liking. After everything they had gone through, this was a night Den, Hugo, and Grill had craved for a long time. And it had been even better than they expected.

The credits rolled on their last film as they finished their massive bowls of ice cream, their bellies full and their minds entertained. Satisfaction to the fullest.

"Well, I can honestly say now that the skyscraper stuff you see in movies is total garbage!" Den proclaimed.

"I know what you mean," Hugo agreed. "It's like they never take wind resistance into account."

"Or the actual impact of a bullet," Grill added.

The trio laughed at their comments. Knowing they'd forget the movie soon enough, but happy they had made the time to watch it. To keep their minds off the world and just enjoy it for what it was. There would be time for higher cinema later. Tonight, they had some fun.

Hugo yawned. "Think I'm gonna turn in now. Long day tomorrow and all that."

"What?" Den exclaimed. "I thought we were gonna play a few rounds of Old Maid again!"

"Sorry, Den. Guess this whole thing's come full circle."

"Before you go to bed, Hugo, there's one last thing I'd like to say," Grill stated.

"Sure, Grill," Hugo replied. "What's on your mind?"

"This is something I know I'll regret if I don't say it now." Grill paused. "I can't promise that the rest of our travels will be safe. Far from it. This could very well be the norm. If not even worse. Neither of you are soldiers. You're both too kind for that. And I don't mean that as an insult, neither to you nor to my fellow veterans. But if at any point either of you want to go back to Harten, I will not judge you. I will understand."

"No," Hugo said, almost instinctively. "I'm staying. Here for the long haul." Hugo's words were straightforward. His tone confident and strong. These were not the hollow vows of a boy too naive to admit to his own weaknesses. This was the conviction of a man now ready to face those weaknesses head-on. Hugo moved his head to face Den. Looking at him straight in the eyes. "No matter what."

Den didn't know whether to feel invigorated or overwhelmed. His buddy, his brother, standing taller than he had ever stood before. The scarred boy cracked a smile and nodded his head. "No matter what," Den repeated. "We'll face it head-on!"

The brothers clasped their right hands together in a strong shake and tapped their heads. "And if we run into some no-good bastard," Den continued, "I'll kick his ass, for good measure!" Den and Hugo laughed at the remark. Grill smiled.

"You're right, Grill," Hugo said. "We're not soldiers. That's not our place. A soldier follows rigorous commands. Unwavering in his duties. But us? We're just travelers... Travelers who can change in the moment. Adapting to whatever we're facing. Not having to ask permissions from higher-ups. Just doing what we think is right."

"And that's how we'll survive," Den added. "No... Actually, that's how we'll thrive!"

Grill's smile turned into a chuckle. "It's innovative thinking, I'll give you that," he said. "Alright then." From the mini-bar in his fridge, Grill pulled out a small bottle of bourbon and promptly opened it. "Forgoing chocolate this time, I propose a *real* toast." The bounty hunter took three plastic water cups, compliments of the room, and poured small shots into each of them.

"You serious, Grill?" Den asked, a little more excitedly than either Hugo or Grill was expecting.

"Of course," Grill replied. "The drinking age in Corridia is eighteen, correct? Same applies in Wayport."

"Den hates alcohol," Hugo replied. "It's why he didn't take a sip of Giorgio's wine at the party. Even though Dr. Voltaire said it was fine."

"Well, yeah," Den confirmed. "But being *offered* a drink? That's the sign of being either a beautiful woman or a *real* man! For obvious reasons, I will assume the latter!"

Hugo chuckled. "I can't argue with that logic!"

The trio grabbed their plastic cups and raised them.

"To the next steps of our Journey!" Grill said.

"To the discoveries we shall make!" Hugo added.

"And to all the awesome things we're gonna do!" Den finished.

"Cheers!" they shouted together. A brotherhood forged in chocolate. A promise vowed in bourbon. A trio ready to face the world.

VIII

Hugo Statferd was tired. Yet he could not sleep. The excitement of what was to come kept him awake and aware. In Grill's room, Den and Grill were still playing Old Maid, probably longer than they had planned. Hugo couldn't stand lying in bed any longer and got up, turning the nearby lamp back on as he did.

He opened his journal to peer through his notes. Much of it had been fairly similar entries. Mostly just cataloging the changes that had been made to the WHS. Nothing of real interest to read.

Hugo peered at Den's entry. Short and straight to the point. There was a melodramatic flair within his three sentences. An honesty only someone like Den could convey. An honesty which soothed Hugo's heart. It didn't matter what blood or documents said, Den was, and always would be, his brother. No matter what.

The young Historian was startled as he heard the phone ring. Possibly a reminder from the front desk about their checkout time the next day. It was annoying, but Hugo picked it up anyway, just in case it was something important.

"Hello?" Hugo answered.

"Hugo?" came Rindi's voice on the other end.

"Rindi, hi! I'm sorry. I didn't expect you to call at this hour."

"To be honest, I didn't expect to make the call at this hour."

That beautiful voice. That soft tone. Her sweet words coming through with every syllable...

This was not the first time Hugo and Rindi had spoken since his departure. He had made a promise to call her at least once a week. Their chats usually consisted of how their personal lives were going, Harten's current state of affairs, how Karina and the others were doing, and, of course, Hugo telling Rindi about what he had experienced. Knowing that, just on the other end, she was listening intently.

Hugo knew her voice well enough that he could picture each expression she was making. The most beautiful face he had ever known. He had missed seeing her every day. Missed talking to her the way he did. But these phone calls had been a respite from the daily grind. And now, after everything that had just occurred, it was an oasis.

"What, you just wanted to hear my soothing voice?" Hugo joked.

"Well... yes," Rindi flirted.

Hugo didn't need to look in the mirror to know he was blushing. "To tell you the truth, I'm glad to hear your voice too."

For the next few minutes, the two chatted as they normally would. Hearing the updates from home and the local stories to tell. Until Rindi's voice grew slightly melancholic.

"What's the matter?" Hugo asked. "Getting tired?"

"No... I mean, yes... It's just... I wanted to make sure you were okay. Wanted to know that, after everything I heard, that you were still... you... Does that makes sense?"

"Absolutely. And to be honest... I think the answer is a little bit of 'yes' and 'no.' I managed to stay strong while I was being held hostage. Never had a panic attack. But then after everything cleared... I had expected some kind of delayed reaction. A pressure release after it all ended... But nothing came. Not a single sharp breath or chest pound. I just felt, for lack of a better term... good. I don't know if this is an improvement... or if something in me broke."

"Can I ask you a question?"

"Of course."

"Do you still feel like you? Like Hugo Statferd?"

"Yes. Every part of me."

"Then that's your answer."

"Rindi... Thank you. I miss you."

"You're welcome, Hugo. I miss you too."

Not fully together, yet certainly not apart. The words they spoke to one another laying the foundation for the rest of their lives. A promise to the future. One these young souls would keep with them in all the hardships to come.

IX

In a quiet apartment, nestled within the downtown district of Wayport, Jewels Romero sat by himself. His first bit of true rest in days. The fallout from the Florenza-Takeda Exchange still haunted his memory. He was already on his third glass of whiskey. Watering it down with a can of Fritz Cola, his favorite soda brand. Along with several slices of a small pizza he had ordered from a nearby pizzeria.

Trying to forget every bad decision he had made. Trying to ignore everything he had done to Grill, Den, and Hugo. Trying to think back to better times when Jack Trent was his brother-in-arms and the world didn't seem so gray. When there were just enemies to take out and missions to accomplish. When he actually felt proud of his job.

Romero had set his phone to silent, only to go off if certain numbers called. Numbers he absolutely could not ignore. Whether on the phone, in the bathroom, eating a meal, or with a woman, his obligation to answer these numbers was air-tight.

So it went without saying that one such number would call at a time like this. Ever the dutiful agent, Romero answered.

"Agent Romero speaking," he said.

"Are you certain they're traveling to Kataloosa?" the voice on the other end asked.

"Absolutely positive. Trent has already purchased train tickets to Rain Way and the rest of their trip will be done through Durango Brothers Desert Bus. No other places to go when following that route."

"And their estimated time of arrival?"

"Depends on the desert itself. Though I'd say around late afternoon on July 1st. If you you need to prepare for anything, I'd suggest doing it now."

"No, I should be fine... Other than the information you sent, is there anything else you'd recommend?"

Romero chuckled. "Those three are a helluva lot more resourceful than I gave them credit for. But if you really want my advice? I'd say just go with the flow. Resisting them will only cause more problems. Play their game with them."

"Alright. Thank you for your time, Agent Romero."

"One last thing, Agent McIntee."

"Yes, sir?"

"Are the reports of Dusk Caravan's activities in Dorado true?"

"... It's... difficult to ascertain at this time. Information is too sparse and inconsistent to be truly certain of anything right now. But rest assured, sir, I will keep a vigilant eye for whatever may or may not be happening."

"Understood. That's all that can be said of any of us."

"Enjoy your day off, sir."

"Thank you, Agent McIntee. Will do."

Agent McIntee hung up, leaving Romero once more alone in his one-room apartment. Left with no one but himself for company. Perhaps tomorrow he would go out and mingle. Meet another lady to spend some time with. Or strike up a friendly conversation with a few guys. The world was his oyster... and he felt so lonely.

He thought once more of Grill and their old platoon. Thought of the moments when they felt like they could face the world, no matter what came their way. But those days were long gone. Dead, buried, and rotting. Romero had made his choice. Now he was lying in it. Never sure if he was lying in his bed or in his coffin.

X

It had taken several days for the backroom of the WHS to be fully repaired. And even then, each of the glass cases had only been set back to their default settings. Andolini had made specific adjustments to each item stored within. Exact temperatures and air quality. Something that he had fine-tuned over the years. Fortunately, the old Historian had kept records of his exact settings. Allowing Hugo and Nash to set them back to the exact degrees.

The newly-repaired collection was still a sight to behold. Noland Macchianado hadn't had the time to sell any of the antiques prior to his death, so every one of them had been returned home. Yet it was obvious that their quality had suffered. Precious pieces of history chipped away. Documents crumpled and ripped. Dirtied by the contents of Macchianado's unsanitary wears.

And then there was the dagger. The stain of Macchianado's own blood was now dried black upon it. Hugo peered at its new coat, both proud and ashamed of what he had done.

"You did good, lad," Andolini said.

"I know," Hugo replied. "Truth be told, I don't even regret it. Den's life was on the line. I just wish none of it had happened to begin with."

"Well, think of it this way. What happened to us happened in Wayport. And this collection exhibits Wayport's history. The new markings on that dagger are just the latest addition to this collection. The latest part of Wayport's history."

"Yeah... I guess you're right."

"Plus, let's be honest here," Nash interjected. "You stabbed a guy. That's pretty cool."

"I don't know if 'cool' is the right word here, Nash," Hugo replied. "But I can definitely see where you're coming from."

"Hey, I certainly can't say I've blown up a giant plant monster *and* stabbed a wanted criminal in the chest. And all in the span of, what, six weeks?"

"Well, when you say it like that, it does certainly put things into perspective."

Andolini laughed. "You'll be going far, Hugo, my boy! I think Victor Rasmus would be proud."

"I'd like to think so," Hugo replied.

"He is, Hugo," Nash affirmed. "Trust me... even if I have no idea where he is right now... again."

Hugo chuckled. "Yeah, that's Master for you."

"Before you go, lad, there's one last thing I wanted to give you," Andolini said.

"Oh, sir, you don't have to!" Hugo replied. "Just being here has been an amazing experience on its own."

From the front desk drawer, the old Historian took out a watch. One Hugo had recently come to know intimately. President Josiah's watch had been fully restored.

"Gretchen knows a restorationist and he was kind enough to fast-track its repair," Andolini explained. "I would be honored to give you this, but I understand if you can't accept it, given the mess that came with it."

The watch's glass had been fully replaced. Its hands had been smoothed and a new coat of paint covered everything that had been chipped away. And of course, the bottom had been fully redone. Completely cleaned and free of any needles or other sharp objects. A century-old watch now made brand new.

Hugo grabbed the watch from Andolini's hand and held it in his palms. The source of one of the most horrific nights of his life... and he held it with pride.

"I'll take it," Hugo said, strapping the watch to his wrist. The young Historian was surprised how comfortably snug it fit.

"It suits you perfectly, dear boy," Andolini said. "Perfectly."

"Hugo!" Den shouted from the front room. "You ready?"

"Yeah, coming!" Hugo replied.

The young Historian took one last look at the backroom. Its collection as pristine as they could make it. Each precious treasure once more in its rightful place.

Hugo, Nash, and Andolini made their way to the front room. Den and Grill were standing near the entrance, bags fully packed and ready to go.

Hugo grabbed his bag and saddled it on himself once more. And even though it was carrying the exact same amount of weight as it had been when he had arrived, it felt so much lighter.

"There's one last thing that needs to be done," Grill said. From out of his bag, the bounty hunter took out a single sheet of paper. Thick and laminated, it was clearly a document of some notable worth. "Gino Andolini, I hold in my hand the contract you had previously signed with Noland Macchianado, regarding your debt to him."

The sight of the document alone was enough to shock Andolini. "Where did you get that from, Mr. Grill?"

"Simple. I bought it."

"Bought it? But that must have been a hundred and fifty thousand Rias!"

"I knew Tillman was extorting me. Part of the business, I suppose."

"Mr. Grill... Mr. Trent, thank you! I promise to pay you back. No matter how long it takes. I will make sure every Rias is counted!"

"Oh, I wouldn't worry about it. Because as you can see"—Grill ripped the contract in half—"it doesn't exist anymore. What a strange turn of events."

Gino Andolini had already cried enough times in the past few days. Now he found himself doing it one last time. "Thank you, Mr. Grill! Thank you! Thank you! Thank you!"

Andolini grabbed Grill and gave him the biggest hug his old body could muster.

"No—*oof!*—problem!" Grill could feel his spine pop. "But, Mr. Andolini, don't mistake my generosity for mere kindness. You once said it yourself. Debts are sins made to weigh you down. Sins that drag you as deep as they can until you suffocate. I never want to see you in this financial state again. Do you understand me?"

"More than you can comprehend, Mr. Grill!"

"Don't worry, Grill," Nash said. "With me around, I'll make sure he knows where every Rias is going."

"You know I never thought about it," Hugo said, "but you've always maintained a steady budget."

"You can't live a chill life without knowing where the money's going," Nash said.

"Yeah," Den agreed. "But it also helps to bum as much gelatin off a patient as possible!"

"Den, that was you who did that," Hugo stated.

"Yeah, and I'm proud of it too!"

The five men gave a hearty laugh, letting their last bit of comedy naturally die down, allowing the silence to come in.

"You know what they say," Nash said, "'Parting is such sweet sorrow.' Still, what's a good handshake or hug between friends?"

"Aye," Andolini agreed. "'Tis the only way for men to truly give their fondest farewells!"

The five men exchanged handshakes and hugs. Short, quick words that still meant the world to each and every one of them. A remembrance of what had been. A promise of more to come.

"See you later!" Hugo shouted as he, Den, and Grill set off.

Nash and Andolini waved their goodbyes from just outside. Hugo looked on as their figures slowly disappeared into the background. Two Historians he had come to care for so much, shaping their futures in their own way, just as Hugo was shaping his.

"Kataloosa can't be accessed by train," Grill explained as the trio made their way to the station. "The closest we can get is a place called Rain Way. A hole in the wall that's basically just one big gas station. We'll stock up on supplies there and then make our way to Kataloosa."

"So what? Are we supposed to walk the desert?" Den asked. "Wait! Can we rent camels? *Please* tell me we can rent camels!"

"No need," Grill replied. "We'll be traveling on a desert bus. Basically an all-terrain vehicle that will take us the rest of the way there."

"With air conditioning?" Hugo asked. "Please tell me it'll have air conditioning!"

"That's just the start!" Grill replied. "The latest models can survive sand storms, bullets, and there's even rumors that some can withstand a ballistic missile!"

"I see someone's excited for the newest toy!" Den smirked. "Though I still think camels would be better."

"All due respect, Den, but I'm not sweating like that if I don't have to," Hugo stated.

"I guess a camel ride will just have to stay in my dreams... for now! Mark my words, buddy, the moment the opportunity presents itself, I'm riding a camel and naming him Geordi! I'll take it back to Harten and give Buckley a new friend!"

"And I'm sure Buckley and Blakely will love it."

"Of course they will! They'll even adopt him! A camel in Kelvin!"

"Your imagination never ceases to amaze me. Will you write a storybook about it?"

"Hell yeah! And it'll be a bestseller, too!"

"Looking forward to reading it," Grill joked.

The trio made their way to the train station. The sins of Wayport behind them. But for just a moment, Den, Hugo, and Grill all took one last look at the Lang-Meyer Courthouse. Still encompassing everything around it. Its grand size always a reminder of where the people of this Terminal City stood. And at the same time, the trio turned their backs on it. Not bound by the tower or what it stood for.

Den, Hugo, and Grill were not puppets to be controlled. Never bound by the whims of someone else. They were travelers. Always looking towards the next destination. Free to chart their own paths. Free to explore wherever they wished. Free to be the men they were always meant to be.

The future was waiting for them. One step at a time.

Today we say our goodbyes to Wayport. A fond farewell to the struggles of the last month. And yet I will never regret my time here. All the hardships and pain. All the fears and tears.

Everyone breaks in due time, but with strength, luck, and determination, we rebuild. And with Den and Grill by my side, I will not fear.

Because I know that whatever comes next, we'll be ready. No matter *what it may be.*

—Hugo Statferd, June 30th, 840 AU

Made in the USA
Coppell, TX
09 July 2025

51640413R00173